THE SECRET READER

SMALL TOWN ROMANCE

BARRINGTON SERIES

SUSAN MACKIE

small town publishing

Original watercolour painting for the cover by Fiona Hayes Art @fionahayesart

Cover Design by Small Town Publishing

❋ Created with Vellum

THE SECRET READER

When a comment at book club sets a project in motion, more than one secret is revealed.

The Barrington girl-posse continue their monthly book club meetings, and somehow it becomes an incubator for new business ideas. And relationships.

Rachael struggles daily with her grief and attends to share memories of her daughter. But book club gives her much more.

Judith arrives, believing she's ready for retirement. Or is she?

Harry Stewart is home from up north, and on the first night he bumps into little Freddie Campbell at the local pub. Except she's not little any more.

Millie is happy in the café and with Finn, but her estranged daughter Hanna says she's coming to visit. Can they mend their relationship?

And Hanna would rather read than take a chance on a player.

Over six months, catch up with old characters and new, as secrets are revealed and lives changed.

For Diane,
who wrote the first review for the first book.
Forever grateful.

Susan Mackie

WHO'S WHO IN BARRINGTON

This is the ninth story in the series but it's the fifth full-size book. There are also three novellas and a short story.

While it's best to read the other stories first - in case you haven't, or you've forgotten who's who - here is a cheat sheet for you.

Rose Gordon Hamilton (writer and Councillor) married to
Angus Hamilton (Vet) – we met them in **Charlie's Will.**
Own Barrington Homestead and farm & the Vet practice.
Son **Charlie** (pre-school).
Daughter **Harper** (infant)

Steve Webb, Mayor of Barrington and wife **Rachael Webb**
parents of Debbie (deceased) and father-in-law to **Jamie Tait**
(grazier) – we met them in **Coffee is my Calling.**
Grandson **Warwick** (nickname **Woz**, day care).

Harriet Russell Murray married to ***Drum Murray*** (grazier, Councillor) – we met them in ***A Place to Start Over.***
Own Montrose Homestead and property.
Harriet's office is within Evans Real Estate.
Billie – Drum's daughter (primary school).
Hamish - their son (infant)

Meggie Hamilton (Angus's sister, in business with Harriet) engaged to ***Max Masters*** (Vet, Angus's partner) – we met them in ***Meggie & Max.***
Meggie's office is within Evans Real Estate.
Indiana – Max's daughter, lives away.
Tommy – Max's son (primary school).
Debbie-Anne (nickname ***Dee*** - their infant daughter)

Melanie Mitchell Evans (Vet nurse) married to ***Ben Evans Jnr*** (nickname ***Little Ben***, Evans Real Estate) – ***all books.***
Tiffany – Melanie's daughter (primary school)
Bronte - their infant daughter

Laura Harrison (farmer, bull breeder) dating ***Ben Evans Snr*** (nickname ***Big Ben***, Evans Real Estate) – we met them in ***A Place to Start Over.***

Nicole Reid Stewart (accountant, BnB owner) married to ***Robbie Stewart*** (builder) – we met them in ***Ragged Mountain Ranges.***
Harry Stewart – Robbie's son
Lucy Reid – Nicole's daughter (high school)

Millie Tucker owns cafe and is in a relationship with ***Finn Anderson*** (Barrington Ridge Estate) - we met them in ***The Barrington Book Club.***
Millie's children - ***Hannelore & Matthias.***
Finn's son - ***Lucas.***

Frederica Campbell (***Freddie***) – 3rd year Vet Science at Uni, daughter of local grazier, works at Vet Clinic in Uni holidays – we met her in ***Charlie's Will.***

Cathy Laing – retired from the cafe.
Kristen – Cathy's daughter – works at cafe.

1

FREDDIE

FREDDIE STOOD AT THE BAR, TAPPING HER CREDIT CARD
impatiently on the counter. Friday nights at the Top Pub used to
be quiet affairs. Locals perched around the bar, sharing yarns,
families heading to the bistro for a meal, and country music
playing softly in the background. Not tonight.

The bar was packed. A younger crowd than normal, possibly
due to the late fall of snow in the Tops. Snow always brings the
punters to town.

Catching the barman's eye, she leaned across, shouting above
the music and noisy buzz of voices. 'Light beer please, in a stubby.'

The barman nodded and Freddie looked over her shoulder to
the front door. She was waiting for someone, and if he didn't
show up soon, her older brothers would be in for their Friday
night drink and dinner. She didn't want them to know she was in
town. Her family thought she was studying for next week's exams
in Newcastle.

Reaching up, she tugged her baseball cap a bit lower. Her

distinctive long red hair was tucked up underneath. A couple of older locals had nodded to her when she walked in, but although they knew her and her family, they weren't close friends. And they wouldn't know she wasn't supposed to be here.

Beer in hand, she cruised to a small table in the corner. It had three high chairs around it and she slid onto one of them, crossing her long denim-clad legs as she took a tentative sip of beer.

Freddie checked her watch. He was late. *Damn! Should have met somewhere else.*

More people arrived, and she half stood, trying to see across the heaving mass of talking-laughing-drinking patrons. A movement on the other side of the room caught her eye. A well-built stockman looked right at her momentarily, before shifting his gaze to new arrivals.

Freddie took a breath and pulled her cap lower, partially hiding her face. *Bloody Harry Stewart! I thought he was working on a cattle station in North Queensland!* She chanced another peek, but he was now in conversation with Little Ben Evans. *Phew, he didn't recognise me. Last time he saw me I was in high school, wearing my hair in pigtails.* She grinned to herself. Harry Stewart definitely wouldn't recognise her these days. She'd grown taller, developed womanly curves and was no longer a rambunctious tomboy, competing with six older brothers on the farm.

Still distracted, she hadn't noticed a tall, lean young man enter through the front door. Strong arms wrapped around her waist from behind as he whispered in her ear, 'You look good enough to eat.'

Freddie grinned, half-turned on her seat and kissed him quickly on the mouth. 'I hope you're not dying for a beer. It will take fifteen minutes just to get to the bar.' She picked up her drink, took a swig, and passed the bottle to him. He raised it to his lips, sipped, then threw his head back, draining the bottle. He leaned closer. 'Two of your brothers were parking when I walked in. We need to leave. Now.'

Freddie froze, then chuckled. 'They've got no idea I'm in town. You go out the front, I'll slip out the back. I'll meet you at the usual place.'

2

———

HARRY

Harry focussed on Little Ben's question, nodding as he answered. Despite his nonchalance, he was hyper-aware of Freddie Campbell on the other side of the crowded room. 'Drove into Barrington just now, been on the road for several days. Thought I'd have a cold one and something to eat before heading out to Dad's.' He grinned at Ben. 'They're not expecting me until tomorrow, so I don't want to arrive right on dinner time.'

'Not that they'd mind when you arrive, Harry. Saw Robbie at the saleyards last week. He seemed more than keen you were coming home.' The larger man paused. 'How long have you been up north?'

'Fourteen months. It's been a great experience and I've learned some new skills. But mate, I'm happy to be home. Dad says he has a lot of work lined up, enough for both of us.' He nodded towards the bar. 'Can I get you a beer, Ben?'

'Nah, thanks Harry. I'm picking up a couple of wood-fired pizzas from the bistro to take home to my girls.' Ben began to move away, but turned back when Harry clapped him on the shoulder.

'And I hear congratulations are in order, Ben. A little girl?' Harry raised an eyebrow.

'Yeah, Bronte. She's almost eight months.' Little Ben shook his head, face alight with pride. 'She's a rascal too, crawling already.'

'Off with you, mate, don't let those pizzas get cold.' As Ben moved into the next room, Harry made his way to the bar, peering again at young Freddie, still settled at the table in the corner. Her hat was pulled low. *Is she hiding? From whom?* He wondered then if she was old enough to be in a pub, but when he did the maths he realised she had to be twenty, at least. He shook his head at that. He was almost twenty-four himself.

Harry ordered the beer and paid, then looked across to Freddie again. He was mates with her brothers. He and Callum had been in the same year at school, and they had all played footy and cricket together.

Drink in hand, he moved through the crowd in her direction, but before he reached her a younger man put his arms around her from behind. Freddie turned and kissed his mouth.

Harry frowned. He didn't know the young bloke. He thought he'd amble on over and introduce himself. Before he took another step, they moved quickly from their table. The bloke left through the front door and Freddie through the back. *Going to the bathroom perhaps?* He continued to the table she'd been at, set himself down on the bar chair and placed his beer down. He'd just ask her who the young bloke was, when she came back.

A minute passed, then two. Suddenly, a huge hand wrapped around his shoulder, and he was looking into the grinning faces of

Callum and Douggie Campbell, two of Freddie's older brothers. 'Harry! Mate! When did you get back?'

'Today, Callum.'

'Another beer?' Callum pointed to Harry's half-empty glass. 'Douggie, grab a jug of beer and fresh glasses.' Callum sat down while his brother pushed through the crowd to the bar.

'I can only have one more Cal. I'm driving out to Dad's straight after. I'm keen on a feed though. Want to grab a pizza?'

'Good idea. We can go through to the bistro when Douggie gets here with the beer. They do wood-fired pizzas now. They're not bad.'

Harry nodded, then looked towards the back exit, where he'd last seen Freddie. She'd be back by now if she was returning. Or perhaps she was meeting her brothers in the bistro.

'What's young Freddie up to these days Callum?'

'Freddie?' Callum frowned. 'She's doing Vet Science at Uni. Mum spoke to her this afternoon. She's studying. She has exams next week.' He made room at the table for Douggie, who had returned with beer and glasses. 'We're going to order pizza and eat with Harry.' Callum had to shout to be heard.

'Pizza. Good.' Douggie swallowed half the contents of his glass, then stood, picked up the beer jug and holding it aloft he cut a swathe through the crowd with Callum and Harry behind him.

As he moved into the next room, Harry took one last look around the bar. Freddie hadn't returned. She was definitely hiding her presence. And she didn't want her brothers to know. *So just who is the bloke she kissed?* He shook his head. She wasn't *his* sister, but it still niggled at him. He was mates with her brothers.

AN HOUR LATER HARRY HESITATED IN THE DOORWAY OF the kitchen, trying to mask the surprise he felt at his step-mother's words when he asked where his father was.

'He's gone to the café to pick Lucy up. She works there after school a couple of afternoons a week, and on Saturday. She's late tonight, the tennis ladies had their AGM at the café, and Millie asked Lucy to stay a bit longer.' Nicole flipped the switch to turn the jug on. 'Coffee Harry? Or a beer? Or dinner?' She glanced at her watch.

He sauntered further into the room, leaned down and wrapped his arms around her in a quick hug. 'Thanks Nik, but I've eaten. I didn't want to get here right on dinner time with no warning.' He glanced around the kitchen. It seemed smaller than he remembered. Or perhaps he was larger.

'I should have told you I'd be home today.' He gave her a lopsided grin. 'I thought I'd surprise you. And Dad and Lucy.' If he were honest with himself, he'd hoped they'd be overjoyed to have him home after more than a year in northern Queensland, working on one of the largest cattle stations in the state.

'You could arrive in the middle of the night, Harry, and be welcomed. And fed.' Nik patted his shoulder, then nodded towards the window. 'That will be Robbie and Lucy now.'

Stepping across to the window, Harry looked down to the driveway. A light flicked on at the front of the house, illuminating Robbie as he stepped out of his work truck. Harry chuckled as Lucy bounced on her toes in apparent excitement as she pointed to Harry's Ute, parked to one side. Lucy looked up and saw him at the window and waved, grinning broadly. She ran into the house and Harry laughed, striding to meet her at the top of the stairs.

She flew into the room and almost winded him with the force of her hug.

'Harry! Harry! You're home! Why didn't you tell us you were coming today?' He wrapped his arms around his step-sister, more than a little pleased at her enthusiasm.

'I wasn't sure I'd get here today, Luce. But I had a good run from the Darling Downs.' He kissed the top of her head. 'Are you taller? You're certainly stronger than I remember.' Harry looked over her head to his father, Robbie. He'd kissed Nik quickly and was waiting to greet Harry. A lump caught in Harry's throat. He'd missed them all. But his dad. Well. He missed him the most.

Lucy stepped away, and Harry walked to his father, holding his hand out to shake. They were the same height and build. Tall, broad-shouldered men. Lucy always referred to them as cowboys. Robbie met him and gripped his hand, hard. Then pulled him closer for a man-hug, his other hand on Harry's back.

'Harry. Son. Good to see you. Really good to see you.' Harry watched Robbie swallow a couple of times as he spoke. His father's response matched his own. Just as he hoped it would.

Later, after he'd brought his swag in from the car, Harry caught up on their news.

'We told you about Debbie Tait. And little Scarlett.' Nicole breathed in through her nose. Yes, they'd told him about the accident. It was five months ago, but he wasn't likely to forget the shock he'd felt when Robbie called. 'Lucy had started working at the café for Debbie. Then for Millie, who was the manager there while Debbie...' Nicole couldn't finish the sentence and Harry nodded his understanding.

He spoke gently. 'I know Nik. Very sad news. I was so sorry to hear that.'

Trying to lift the mood he turned to Lucy. 'So you're the head chef at the café now Luce?'

Lucy giggled, shaking her head. 'Don't be silly Harry. But I've been working there for six months and I love it. You have to come and meet Millie. She's super nice.'

'Good for you Luce. I'm proud of you and I'm keen to meet Millie.' He meant it. Lucy was such a shy girl when she arrived in the area with her mum just a few years ago and he was happy to see her confidence in herself and her job. Nik had told him she was doing well at school too. Lucy flushed, her pleasure obvious.

'Go and shower, Lucy and get ready for bed, please.' Nik ushered Lucy from the room.

Harry turned to his father, looking sheepish. 'I bumped into Callum and Douggie Campbell tonight. I didn't want to arrive right at dinnertime, so I had a beer and pizza at the pub first. They mentioned they have work available, if I need it.'

'Campbells?' He heard the hesitation in Robbie's voice. 'Of course. For cattle and horse work. That would be the best place.' Robbie leaned forward. 'But son, as I mentioned last week on the phone, I can use you if you want fencing and building work. I've got a lot of projects lined up.'

Harry grinned, letting out the breath he didn't realise he was holding. 'Really Dad? I left you with no notice. I heard what you said last week but ...'

'Robbie Stewart and Son, it says on the side of my truck. If you're keen, I have the work.' Robbie stood up, and Harry found himself on his feet, too. Standing eye to eye with his father, he swallowed once, before pulling him into another man-hug. They stood like that for a moment, the strength of their relationship restored, when Lucy returned.

'Harry! I want to talk to you about the horses and show you how I've been looking after them.'

Grinning at his father, Harry turned to his step-sister. 'I want to hear about the horses Luce. How about we do that in the morning before you go to school?'

3

—————

MILLIE

MILLIE CHECKED HER WATCH FOR ABOUT THE TENTH time in as many minutes. Hannelore would be here soon. She swallowed, then ran her hands down her side and over her hips, unconsciously sucking her tummy in.

The café had only just opened, and Kristen was making coffee for the early regulars. *I shouldn't be nervous. She's my daughter. And we've been speaking on the phone a bit recently.* But before that, they'd had no contact for close to a year. The last time she'd seen her, they'd argued. Well. Not exactly argued. Hanna had been angry. At Millie. For the marriage ending. She'd taken her father's side and had slung cruel barbs at Millie. Words Millie would never forget. She sighed then. *Hanna is my daughter and I will always forgive, even if I can't forget.* But she hoped Hanna had matured enough for them to spend a few days together without fighting.

Movement at the counter caught Millie's attention. 'Mr Mayor. Hello.' Millie greeted Steve Webb warmly as she moved to the coffee machine. 'Your usual?' Kristen dashed back into the kitchen to prepare the breakfast orders.

'Yes. Thanks Millie.' Steve moved to a table just inside the door and snapped open his copy of the local paper. He was reading an article on the Council budget as Millie delivered his coffee.

'I read it online early this morning. The media is focussing on the rate increase, despite it being almost the lowest in the State.' Millie put her hands on her hips. 'While we'd all like lower rates, Council has to deliver services. I don't envy your role, Steve.'

'Thanks Millie. I wish everyone saw it your way.' He set the paper down and sighed. 'Rachael was verbally abused in the supermarket yesterday. She was furious. She's my wife, not the Mayor, but locals expect her to be across every decision Council makes.'

'That's awful. Rachael doesn't deserve that.' Millie shook her head.

'While I have you here Millie, I've been approached by a law firm to take over the space upstairs, now that Douglas has retired. I'm meeting with them at eleven and then we'll drop in here for a light lunch. Can we grab that quiet table right at the back, please? Say, from twelve?' Steve sipped his coffee, looking over the rim at Millie.

'Of course. Would you like a platter of wraps and sandwiches made up? For how many?' Millie took an order pad from her pocket, then paused. 'Did Douglas mention Frances? I haven't seen her for three weeks.'

'Yes please. Lunch for five people.' Steve added more softly, 'Douglas says Frances isn't doing well at all. She's having more bad days than good. But he's determined to keep her at home, with help from nursing and home care. Steve shook his head sadly. 'She was such a vibrant woman. It's hard seeing her like this. It's a terrible disease.'

'I asked Douglas if he'd bring her to book club next week, but he said it may make her anxious, so best not to.' Millie shook her head, then turned back to the counter when her name was called. 'Have to dash Steve, but I'll see you at lunchtime.'

Smiling, Millie walked briskly towards her daughter. Hannelore smiled back and Millie felt a small amount of tension leave her shoulders. *She looks tired. And nervous?*

Millie threw her arms around Hannelore and hugged her tightly. Tears came to her eyes when her hug was returned, with even more gusto than hers. 'Hanna! You're here!' She wiped a tear from the corner of one eye, surprised to see her daughter's eyes were moist with unshed tears too. Millie suspected there'd been a romance in the west, and Hannelore's call last month to ask if she could visit had Millie thinking the romance, if there was one, was over.

'Mum! You look wonderful!' Hannelore took a step back and looked her mother up and down. 'You've changed your hair too.' She leaned in again. 'I can see you've lost weight Mum, but it's more than that. You look younger. Happier.'

Nodding happily, Millie touched her daughter's face. 'And you're just gorgeous, as always.' She glanced around with a frown. 'Do you have more luggage?' She could only see a backpack and one small suitcase. *Not enough luggage for a long stay then.*

'Don't look like that Mum. I travel light.' Hannelore's gaze swept around the café, before returning to look Millie in the eye. More quietly, she said, 'It's lovely, Mum. It's a gorgeous set-up. And it's yours?'

'It is. Or it will be.' Millie saw Steve get up, his paper under his arm. He'd be heading to Council. But she called out, hoping he wouldn't mind a slight delay. 'Steve, excuse me. Have you got a moment?'

'Of course.' Steve walked over and held his hand out to Hannelore. 'No introduction needed. You're a lot like your mum.' He was relaxed and friendly.

Hannelore shook his hand. 'Hannelore Tucker, but I prefer Hanna.'

Tucker? Not Schmidt? Since when? Something she'd need to discuss with Hanna. Later. 'Steve is our Mayor, and also the land-lord here.'

Hannelore looked quickly from Millie to Steve, then said quietly. 'I heard about your daughter, Steve. I'm very sorry.' She smiled gently, and Millie saw that Steve was instantly drawn to her warmth and sincerity. 'I was just saying to Mum how gorgeous the café is. What I've seen so far.'

'Thank you Hannelore. Yes, Debbie left a legacy in this town, but Millie has put her stamp on it too. We're lucky she came to Barrington when she did.' Steve touched Millie's shoulder lightly as he spoke, and Millie flushed at the warmth of his words. She wanted to say *she was the lucky one*, but Steve was already moving towards the door.

Turning back to Hannelore, Millie hugged her again quickly. There was a queue at the counter, and Kristen had popped out of the kitchen to serve. 'It's getting busy in here. I need to get back to work. I can give you the key to the apartment. It's just down the street.' Millie pointed. 'Above the post office. The second room is all set up for you. Relax, unpack. Wander back down when you're hungry. I have a few bookings for lunch, and Steve has a business meeting here at twelve, so if you can wait, we can grab a late lunch together, around one-thirty. Okay?' She pulled the keys from her pocket and handed them across. She hesitated, then placed her hands on Hannelore's shoulders and looked at her intently. 'I'm so happy you're here, and I can't wait to catch up on your news.'

'Thanks Mum. Me too.' Hannelore blinked, took the keys, and with a quick smile over her shoulder, wheeled her suitcase out behind her.

———

MILLIE SAW THE GROUP HEAD UPSTAIRS JUST BEFORE eleven. A young couple in their early thirties and an older man. All very well-dressed. Very lawyer-ly. Steve and Rachael had gone up a few minutes before. Millie hoped they had small-town experience, or were prepared for it, at least. The city lawyers she had experienced had been very different from her dealings with Douglas.

Plating up the sandwiches and wraps for Steve's group at eleven-forty-five, Millie was dismayed when a large coach pulled in. She watched as dozens of senior citizens poured out. She wasn't expecting the bus. The café was already busy and Kristen was flat out in the kitchen. But a snowfall in the Tops over the last week may have re-routed an outing for the tour operators. She straightened, then smiled as the first customers came through the door. Mainly older women, they arrived in groups and took over every available table.

Kristen poked her head out of the kitchen. 'Mum's away today Millie, or I'd call her. Do you think Melanie can pop down and help?'

Millie finished the platter, straightened her shoulders and took her notepad out. 'We'll be okay. I'll tell them there'll be a slight wait, but I'll start taking orders now.' She paused. 'It'll be scones, cakes and sandwiches. Just start prepping what you can, Kristen.'

4

HANNELORE

'Wow!' Speaking quietly to herself once she closed the door to the street, Hannelore looked up the staircase. *What a grand old building. No wonder Mum loves it.*

She carried her suitcase up the stairs and unlocked the door to the apartment. The main room was filled with light and Hannelore turned around in delight. Big rooms, high ceilings. Gorgeous. 'What a stately old girl you are,' she murmured as she found the second bedroom. Large, with a generous wardrobe.

Placing her suitcase and backpack on the bed, she walked across the hall to the bathroom. Enormous, with an old-fashioned clawfoot tub, but the shower recess was modern and sported an oversized shower head. Her mum had always liked a strong hot shower, and Hannelore was sure this one would be exactly that.

Taking her coat off, she arranged it over a chair in the corner of the room, then walked back to the living area. It was nicely set up. She didn't recognise the furniture. Her mother must have started again after the divorce. It suited the apartment. Hannelore found the kitchen, filled the jug and put it on. There were several glass jars of herb tea and a small teapot. *Nice. You're all class, Mum.* Making a pot of chamomile and lemongrass tea, Hannelore walked back into the main living area while it steeped.

Standing at the big front window, she looked up and down the street, noting cars moving in and out of parking spots and people making their way quickly along the pavement. It was cold, there'd been snow in the Barrington Tops overnight, but she noticed some people stopping to chat in the street, waving to each other and two young women coming out of the real estate agency were laughing together.

The apartment was chilly, but not cold enough to turn the heat on, so Hannelore curled up in a chair by the window and people-watched while she sipped her tea. The tension in her shoulders relaxed and a feeling of optimism began to bubble away inside her chest.

It had taken several days to get here. The bus from Margaret River to Perth, then an overnight flight to Sydney. She'd stayed with her brother Matthias in Sydney for two nights, before heading to Barrington by train. He was in his last year of university and already had a town-planning internship with North Sydney Council. Matty had only been to Barrington a couple of times since their mother moved here. He said he liked it and it suited her, but it wasn't for him.

Hannelore didn't mind small towns, and she'd loved Margaret River. For a while, she thought she might stay there, but her relationship with Anthony-the-two-timer had come to an unpleasant end. *They say girls often choose someone like their father.* That's exactly what she did. Anthony was selfish and narcissistic, just like her father, Rudy.

And now she felt bad. When her parents were struggling in their business and marriage and fighting all the time, Hannelore had often taken her father's side. She remembered yelling at her mother two years ago, saying *no wonder Dad had a girlfriend because you're fat and ugly.* She hung her head in shame. She was only nineteen at the time, but that was no excuse! She couldn't believe she'd said those words to her mother. Couldn't believe she'd hurt her like that. But she had. And then she'd left, angry at both her parents, for she'd finally seen her father for what he was, and how he treated her mum. But she hadn't been emotionally mature enough to deal with it, and she'd struck out for Western Australia, having heard there were good jobs there. When she left, she'd just finished her pastry chef apprenticeship with her father. She'd found work in a bakery, and it had been, mostly, a good two years.

After her break-up with Anthony-the-liar, she had a small glimmer of what her mother must have gone through with her father. She shook her head again. Her mother had forgiven her, she knew. More than that, she'd never mentioned the argument and the harsh words thrown at her. But Hannelore hadn't forgotten. She wanted to make amends. Build a new relationship with her mother. She cried for a moment, shivering briefly when she relived that terrible scene in her mind. *The pain her words had caused had been clearly visible on her mother's face.*

Hannelore took her cup to the kitchen and washed it and the teapot. Then she stood under the shower for the longest time. It was strong and hot, and she let it wash over her, imagining it was washing away the last of her childish selfishness. She was determined to be a better person and was hoping Millie would give her a chance here in Barrington, even though, in her heart, she knew she didn't deserve it.

Towel-drying her dark blonde, wavy hair, she walked back to the big window overlooking the street. Her tummy rumbled. It was just after eleven-thirty, and Millie wouldn't be free for a couple of hours. Maybe she could rustle up a snack here in the meantime. Turning away from the window, a large bus caught her eye, and she turned back. Not a bus, a coach and it stopped right in front of the cafe. Women began to pour out of it, heading into the café in small groups, smiling and chatting. Hannelore frowned. Millie had mentioned regulars and a business lunch for the Mayor this morning but nothing about a coach.

Without thinking it through, Hannelore raced back to her room and pulled out black jeans and a white shirt, slipped her black boots back on then grabbed her coat and the keys and raced out the door. She tied her hair into a high pony as she ran down the stairs two at a time before darting across the road to the café.

The place was packed when she ran in. Millie was taking orders from the largest group by the window. Hannelore ducked into the kitchen.

'Hi, I'm Hanna, Millie's daughter. You must be Kristen?' She could see Kristen was flat out, preparing sandwiches and plating up scones.

'Hi Hanna. Nice to meet you.' Despite being busy, she grinned, and Hannelore smiled back. She relaxed slightly.

'I'm here to help. Apron?'

Kristen pointed to a shelf beside the door. 'Good timing. The bus is a surprise. I'm okay in here, but Millie is swamped.' She looked past Hannelore out the door. 'And here's Mayor Steve with his group. Can you take that platter out to them, then plates and cutlery, and get their drink orders, please?'

Hannelore had removed her coat while Kristen spoke and tied the cute little apron with the café logo on it around her waist. She picked up the platter of sandwiches in one hand and the five plates and sets of cutlery in the other and backed out through the door. The Mayor had led his group to a table at the back, the only empty one. It had a reserved sign on it, luckily for them.

Arriving at the table just as the group sat down, Hannelore smiled at Steve as she placed the platter in the centre of the table and set the plates and cutlery down for each of them.

'Hanna! Lovely to see you again.' Steve turned to the woman beside him. 'This is my wife, Rachael. Rachael, this is Millie's daughter, Hannelore.'

'Well, I could see who she was straight away. Welcome.' Rachael laughed and Hannelore felt a tremor of pleasure at the sound.

'Hello.' She smiled at Rachael, then looked around the group. 'May I take drink orders? Coffee or tea?'

The smartly dressed younger woman at the end of the table nodded. 'Double shot latte please.' The rest of them named their drinks, and Hannelore memorised the order. It was one of her special skills. The woman narrowed her eyes at her. 'You haven't written that down.'

'I've got it.' Hannelore almost winked at Steve, who was leaning forward. 'Double shot latte, two flat whites, one on almond milk, one cappuccino, and a skinny mocha for you, Rachael.' The young woman looked momentarily perplexed, then began speaking to Steve, effectively dismissing Hannelore. She sped back to the counter to find Millie at the coffee machine.

'Mum.' Suddenly tongue-tied, Hannelore fiddled with a cup and murmured, 'I saw the bus pull up. Thought I'd come over and help.' She looked up then to find Millie looking at her, her face flushed but her delight obvious.

Hannelore grinned back, relieved. 'I have the coffee order for the Mayor's group. I can use this machine if you want me to make them?'

Millie added milk foam to the two cappuccinos she'd made, then placed them on a tray. 'Brilliant, do that. Once you've delivered them, you can start on the drinks for this group, and I'll check on Kristen.' She paused, her eyes laughing. 'My girl. Thank you.'

5

HARRY

HARRY STRETCHED, THEN SAT UP. HE'D SLEPT SOUNDLY in his old room. It was early, just on dawn and the temperature lower than he was used to. There'd been snow in the Barrington Tops a few days ago. He shivered, then stood, pulling his jeans on. Certain Lucy would be awake soon, he wanted to be ready to check the horses with her.

Robbie appeared as he padded into the kitchen and turned the kettle on.

'Morning Dad. Tea?' Harry grinned. His father always woke up with the sun. it was something they had in common.

'Yes, thanks. Sleep okay?' Robbie took two large mugs from the cupboard and rummaged around for tea bags, his shoulder brushing Harry's. Harry leaned into him for a moment and they shared a look.

'Slept well, thanks. A bit cold this morning, though. I couldn't find my heavy jacket in the back of the wardrobe. Didn't need it up north.' Harry poured boiling water over the teabags and watched Robbie add a generous tipple of milk to each mug.

Robbie grinned. 'Nik pulled it out last week when you said you were on your way home. She wanted to air it. It's hanging in the laundry.' Turning back to Harry he nodded towards the window. 'There was a frost overnight, but I'd say we've had the last snowfall. Days should begin to warm now.'

Harry leaned against the kitchen counter. 'What do we have on today Dad? I know it's Saturday, but I'm happy to start work.'

'No real work until Monday. But Nik has some ideas about the old carriage shed. Wants to convert it to more accommodation.' Robbie raised his eyebrows, but Harry could see he was as keen on the project as Nicole.

'Sounds good. Does she have plans?' Harry sipped his tea.

Robbie snorted. 'Plans? Do you not know Nik at all? Of course she has plans!' Laughing, he rinsed his cup and turned it upside down on the draining board. Harry followed suit, smiling.

Voices could be heard from the other end of the house. Robbie leaned in. 'The girls are awake, and Lucy will be keen to take you to the horses. I'd show you the plans for the carriage shed, but I know Nik will want to talk you through them herself.' Harry barely had time to acknowledge Robbie's words with a smile and nod, when Lucy burst into the room, a jumper over her pyjamas.

'Harry! Let's check the horses, our coats are in the laundry.' As she trotted from the room, she called out, 'Harry! Come on! I have to get ready for school. And I want to make pancakes for breakfast.'

Straightening, Harry elbowed his dad briefly, jerking his head in the direction Lucy had gone. 'Horses. And pancakes. I'm off.' He slid in his socks to the top of the stairs and waved to Nicole as she stepped out of the master bedroom in a dressing gown, her hair messy.

'Run Harry!' Her laughter followed him down the stairs, and he felt warmed by the knowledge that he was home *with his family*. For a long time, it had been just him and his Dad, but Nicole and Lucy had added a whole new dimension to his life, and he freely admitted that he loved it.

———

LATER, AFTER PANCAKES AND LUCY'S DEPARTURE FOR school, he pored over the plans Nicole laid out on the kitchen table, listening carefully as she explained her concept.

'We've finally cleared everything out and we've been using it to park the cars. But Robbie has added a carport to the side of The Stables accommodation and we can extend that a bit further for our vehicles. The footprint is about the size of a two-car garage, but the roof is high, so I'm thinking a loft bedroom will work. That gives us room inside for another bedroom, a bathroom and an open-plan living area with a functional kitchen.' She looked at Harry expectantly. He could see how keen she was.

'It's good Nik. And you're keeping the timber-clad exterior and iron roof?' He glanced at Robbie. 'Is all the timber okay Dad? And the roof? It's old.'

'The cladding is mostly rough-hewn vertical split timber, but it's hardwood and has lasted the years. Around one hundred and forty years, I'd say. There's no sign of termites or wood rot, but some of the planks have water damage around the bottom, so we need to replace those. The roofing iron is newer, it must have been redone at some time. A small section needs replacing and we will add proper guttering.' Robbie pointed at sketches on a second plan.

'Inside cladding? Vee-jay panels like the stables conversion?' Harry was getting excited, he liked working on a building he could be proud of.

'Yes, that's exactly it.' Nik moved closer, her enthusiasm evident. 'We can put the loft at one end, see here,' she tapped the plan, 'over the kitchen, bathroom and small laundry. Then the main bedroom and living area will have vaulted ceilings. I've asked Robbie if we can keep the beams visible. They're basically just small tree trunks with the branches cut off.' Her eyes shone as she looked at Harry and then Robbie. 'So much character in them. But we'll add ceiling cladding above that, and insulation in the walls and ceiling too.'

'Heating?' Harry peered down at the floor plan, visualising how it would look when finished.

'We thought about putting in a firebox, but they can be problematic with small children. So we'll put in ducted air. It costs more than reverse cycle units but will be less intrusive.' Nik looked up. 'What do you think Harry?'

'It's great Nik! I love the way you've renovated and repurposed all the buildings here. Your ideas are beautiful. And with the building structure already in place, the cost to renovate isn't prohibitive.' Harry wished more people in the area had Nicole's vision. Renovate and repurpose rather than tear down and rebuild. 'And lots of character, in keeping with the main house, the courthouse,' he chuckled, 'and the stables conversion.'

'But the massive doors on the front will have to come off. They're way too big and heavy. We'll do a new front façade, in keeping with the style. The timber in the doors can be re-used too.

We'll do a small porch at the front and another on the northern side, off the living area.' Robbie pointed to a sketch of the proposed front entrance. 'The roofing iron has already arrived, only six sheets. So I want to do that today while the weather is fine. When we get that finished, we can start on the internal cladding. But the electrician won't be here until mid-week so we can't close it up completely, they will need to run conduit in there before we add insulation.'

Harry nodded. It all sounded good. 'And Monday? Where will we be then?'

'We're working on some short-term accommodation out on the Barrington East Road. The original old schoolmaster's cottage. It needs a new veranda and we're shifting some internal walls to make a bigger bedroom with ensuite.'

'That's on the old Forbes farm. Are they still dairying?' Harry frowned, trying to picture the cottage. He thought it had been used as accommodation for farm workers for many years.

'That's the one. They're out of dairying now. Moving into beef, I think. The income from the cottage will be handy for them.' Robbie pushed his chair back as he spoke.

'Tourism has become a solid economic driver in the area Harry. And we're working together to market the region. There will be more cottages like this one, to do up in the future.' Nik reached for the plans strewn across the table, gathering them into a neat pile.

'Great. More work for us, eh Dad?' Harry nudged Robbie and grinned.

6

FREDDIE

Friday night and she's back in Barrington, waiting. Freddie checked her watch. Again. *He's always late. Why?* She sipped her drink, a vodka and orange, and with her cap pulled low she watched the door. Not as busy as last week. If her brothers arrive they'll spot her straight away. As it was, she'd parked her old Suzuki Jimny behind the Vet clinic and walked around. *Just in case.*

Her phone vibrated, and she reached into her pocket.

> Sorry! Can't get away. Family thing.
> Meet u later? Usual place? 10pm? XX

Freddie frowned. *He could have told me sooner. I would have stayed at Uni. Studied.* She took another sip of her drink, tapping her fingers against the table, while she decided if she wanted to hang around. Her brothers would be here soon, maybe she would head back to Newcastle. She decided not to text him back straight away, make him stew.

'Freddie? Freddie Campbell?' Startled, Freddie looked up. Bloody Harry Stewart, standing right beside her. She blinked. *Bloody Harry Stewart is hot.* She'd had a crush on him when she was younger, but *oh gosh*!

Decision made, she frowned. 'Harry Stewart?'

He laughed heartily. 'I deserved that. Yes, Freddie. Hello.' He gestured to the bar chair beside her. 'May I? Or are you waiting for someone?'

Freddie narrowed her eyes for a moment. *He was in the bar last week. Had he seen her, ah, friend? Maybe.* 'Only my big brothers. Thought I'd surprise them. They usually come in on Friday night for beer and pizza.' She reached up, tugging her hat off. Her long, curly, auburn hair tumbled over her shoulders. Wide-eyed now, she added, 'No need to hide now; they'll see *you* straight away. You're ah, quite a big bloke, Harry.'

His look told her what she needed to know. Yes, he'd seen her last week but he hadn't told her brothers. And he was looking at her differently. Not like the annoying younger sister of his mates. She chuckled inwardly. *She was flirting with Harry Stewart.* And he looked uncomfortable about it. Awkward, but interested. She leaned forward slightly, allowing her shirt to gape slightly, revealing a hint of cleavage. *Take that, Harry Stewart!*

'Harry!' Freddie heard the familiar voice and peered around Harry's large frame. She grinned and waved to Callum and Douggie as they strode across the room. 'And Freddie!' Callum was only two years older than her, and they had always been close. He threw his arms around Freddie, then kissed the top of her head. Douggie reached over and tousled her hair. 'Does Mum know you're in town? She didn't say anything.'

'It's a surprise. Thought I'd meet you for dinner, then follow you home.' Freddie drew in a breath at the pleased looks her brothers gave her. *I really should come home more often.* She grinned and leaned back. 'Get yourselves a drink brothers, then buy me some dinner!' Freddie stood, 'but first, I'll slip out to the bathroom.'

Once she'd left the room, Freddie looked at the message on her phone again. Tapping quickly, she replied.

> Not tonight. Dinner with my brothers then home to the farm. Maybe tomorrow before I head off.

7

———

HARRY

Freddie Campbell. All grown up. Harry felt his pulse go up a notch when she took off her cap and shook out that magnificent mane of hair. The hair he used to tease her about and tug on the school bus. *Not just all grown up. Stunning.* He concentrated his gaze on her face as they chatted, but when she sipped her drink his eyes skittered lower, to her chest. He quickly looked away, towards the door of the pub, hoping she hadn't noticed. Hoping her brothers would arrive. *This is uncomfortable. I'm attracted to Freddie Campbell.*

He saw the way she looked at him, too. And in normal circumstances he would do something about it. Flirt a bit and see where it leads. For about the tenth time, he reminded himself that this was Freddie, the younger sister of his best mates. He noticed something else. She was flirting with him. She leaned forward, showing a glimpse of her cleavage. *Where and when did she learn to do that? It was deliberate and she was aware he was uncomfortable.*

31

Wanting to take control of the situation, he leaned in, about to ask her just who the young bloke was she'd kissed last week. Before he could get the words out, Callum and Douggie arrived. Freddie seemed genuinely pleased to see them, told them she was here to surprise them. But Harry couldn't help wondering if she'd had plans with her friend from last week? He shook his head as he followed the three of them through to the bistro. *All was not as it seemed with young Freddie. Beautiful Freddie. Freddie-with-a-secret.*

8

HANNELORE

Working all week at the café with her Mum had gone well. Millie seemed delighted she was here and had offered her ongoing work. Kristen was great, about her own age, and Hannelore felt a friendship beginning.

Millie said on that first night, that she was paying the café off. Keeping the wages down, working as much as she could herself, was part of the strategy. But she could offer Hannelore the same pay rate as Kristen, at least to start with. It was less than Hannelore could get as a pastry chef, especially if she went to a restaurant or hotel on the coast, but she was living rent-free with Millie, so it would be okay for a few months. She'd give Barrington a chance. Time to see how she liked it and to help her mum take full owner-ship of the café. It felt good helping Millie.

They hadn't talked about *that day*. The day she'd hurled abuse at her mother and Hannelore knew Millie wasn't keen to bring it up. But it was playing on her mind and she wanted to talk about it. More than that, she needed to apologise. She hoped it might lead to more conversations about what happened between her parents. And she wanted to share her own experience, with Anthony-the-cheater. But she didn't want it to have the opposite effect and open old wounds. So she said nothing about the past and they had a happy week, working together and sharing an evening meal.

Millie had a schoolgirl working most afternoons at the cafe. Lucy was a keen baker and Hannelore was drawn to the younger girl. On Friday after closing time, Hanna had shown her how to make Choux pastry for profiteroles and eclairs. They'd had a great time for a couple of hours until Lucy's older brother messaged that he was waiting outside to take her home.

Hanna cleaned up and closed up, then walked down to the pub. Her mum was at a friend's place for dinner. She hadn't admitted it outright, but Hanna thought that Finn, the friend, was more than that. If he was, Hanna was happy. She hoped he treated Millie well. She looked better. Happier. Yes, she'd lost a bit of weight and changed her hair, but Hanna thought the real change was the confidence her mum had in her work, in the business and her general happiness.

Stepping into the pub, she said hello to the bloke behind the bar and requested a glass of red wine. Then she moved through to the bistro. She ordered a small eye fillet steak and settled at a table. There were families at two tables and several couples of varying ages, at others. She watched as three tall men, two with bright red hair and a young woman about her own age, walked in. They looked like siblings, but the third man, with the dark hair, didn't have the same hair or features. He was tall and broad-shouldered and laughed with his friends as they studied the pizza menu. From her position to one side, she noticed how the dark-haired man looked at the woman in the group from time to time. *Chemistry? Something.*

Country music played in the background, giving off a nice vibe. Hannelore opened her Kindle and read while she ate her meal. She sometimes found eating alone in a restaurant or cafe uncomfortable, and reading made her feel less conspicuous. Less alone. And she was reading *Down the Track* by *Stella Quinn*. At one point she laughed out loud as she turned a page, then glanced around to see if anyone had noticed. *Stella Quinn was so darn funny!* The dark-haired man in the other group gave her a curious look and Hannelore quickly returned to her book.

Her meal finished, Hannelore sipped on the last of her wine as she finished the chapter. A shadow fell across the screen and Hannelore looked up to see an attractive woman with dark auburn hair smiling at her. She was holding an infant in her arms. Hannelore smiled back.

'Hello. I'm sorry to interrupt your book, but you have to be Hannelore, Millie's daughter?' The woman smiled again and Hannelore grinned and nodded.

'I'm Rose. I'm a friend of Millie's.' The woman patted the little one in her arms. 'And this is Harper.'

Hannelore stood up. 'Hi Rose.' She peeked at the face of the baby, almost asleep on her mother's shoulder. 'Hello Harper,' she said more quietly, then straightened, meeting Rose's eyes. 'I was just about to head off, but I had to finish the chapter.' She chuckled, pointing to her Kindle.

'I totally get that. What are you reading?' Rose moved the baby to her other shoulder.

'Down the Track by...,' Hannelore laughed as Rose finished the sentence.

'Stella Quinn. I Love Stella's books. She's clever.'

Hannelore was impressed. She loved meeting fellow readers. Just then, a tall nice-looking man joined them, a little boy holding his hand.

'This is my husband, Angus. And wee Charlie.' Rose turned to her husband. 'This is Hannelore, Millie's girl.'

Angus grinned at his wife, his smile including Hannelore. 'Hello Hannelore. Welcome to Barrington. I heard you arrived in the nick of time on Monday.'

Warmed by his words, she nodded. 'Please. Call me Hanna.' She looked down at Charlie. 'Hello Charlie. Oh! What's that in your hand?' Reaching down, Hannelore grabbed the small boy by the wrist, shaking it gently. A slightly squashed chip fell out. She grimaced, then looked up at Rose. 'Sorry, I think he picked it up off the floor just there ...' She stopped, wondering if she had over-stepped. But Rose and Angus laughed.

'Not unusual. He's eaten worse.' Angus took the tissue Rose handed him and wiped the small boy's hand. 'No harm.' He picked Charlie up and turned to his wife. 'I'll wrangle Charlie into the car.' And to Hannelore, he said, 'Nice to meet you, Hanna.'

'Nice to meetcha Hanna,' Charlie echoed and they all laughed.

'I'd better go too.' Rose moved the baby a bit higher on her shoulder. 'You should come to book club on Monday night. We're reading *The Grazier's Son* by Cathryn Hein. We meet at the café.' Rose trailed off.

Nodding enthusiastically Hanna reached out, touching Rose's arm. 'I'd love that. Mum has been talking about book club.' Eyes shining, she added, 'You're *that* Rose. Rose Gordon. I've read *Controlling Interest, and* loved it.' Rose blushed and Hannelore liked her even more. A fabulous Australian author, right here in Barrington, and modest.

'I'm finished. I'll walk out with you.' Hannelore packed her Kindle away and walked to the door holding it open for Rose to navigate through with baby Harper still in her arms. Hannelore glanced back into the room. A nice pub. No, a *good* pub.

Roving around the room, her eyes fell on the young group, then stopped as the dark-haired man looked right at her. He raised an eyebrow and Hannelore blushed. *He thought she was checking him out! Arrogant. And probably in a relationship with the girl there because the other two would be her brothers. Huh!* She lifted her chin in a you-can-look-but-you-have-no chance gesture, turned on her heel and followed Rose out, closing the door firmly behind her.

9

———

MILLIE

Pulling up at the vineyard, Millie hadn't felt this nervous about seeing Finn since the first few days of their romance. But that was many months ago. Finn appeared at the downstairs door, the light from inside illuminating him in silhouette.

Millie stepped out of her car and began to walk across. Before she was close enough to see his features, she already knew he'd be smiling. Even from here, he gave off a sense of welcome and warmth.

Finn stepped forward as she approached and wrapped strong arms around her. 'Millie'. The way he said it, so simply, conveyed a whole lot of feelings and she almost cried as she melted against him, breathing, 'Finn. Hello,' into his shoulder.

They stayed like that for a moment, until Lucas called out from upstairs. 'Dad. Dad! The pasta is bubbling over. I'm taking it off the heat!'

Leaning back, now with his hands on Millie's shoulders, Finn raised an eyebrow. 'No Hannelore?'

'No. Finn, I'm sorry.' Millie felt the tears she'd been holding back trickle down her cheeks. Finn looked at her for a moment, his confusion obvious, but he drew her against him and held her until her sobs subsided. Somehow, this gave her strength, and she sniffled once before fumbling in her jacket pocket for a tissue.

Wiping her eyes, Millie shook her head sadly. 'I couldn't just *bring* her. I need to talk to you first. I'm sorry Finn, I've avoided telling you the whole story about my relationship with Hanna.'

'You never have to say sorry to me, Millie. I can wait until you're ready.' He took her hand, leading her to the bottom of the stairs. He made a noise in his throat and Millie looked at him sharply. 'But I asked Luke to stay home tonight, to meet Hanna for family dinner. He's more than a little bit pissed with me. I think he had to cancel a date in town.' He chuckled quietly. 'Although who he's seeing appears to be a secret he wants to keep.'

Millie felt terrible as she walked upstairs. Her relationship with Lucas was friendly, but not close. And now he'd most likely be cranky with her too. *I should have told Finn. And why did I agree to dinner tonight, bringing Hannelore? I haven't talked to her about Finn. And I haven't talked to Finn about her, in any real sense. I'm such a coward.*

Stepping into Finn's apartment, she smelt a delicious combination of tomato, garlic and mushroom. And she already knew there was pasta. An Ed Sheeran song was playing in the background and walking further into the room, she saw the polished timber table set for four.

Lucas was stirring a pot at the stove, and turned around, a broad smile on his face. 'The ravioli has been saved.' He gave a little bow and Millie giggled. 'And the sauce is nearly ready but the garlic bread needs another five. Enough time to get the ladies a glass of wine, Dad.' As the words left his mouth he looked more closely at Millie, then behind her.

'Um, no Hannelore?'

'No son. Last minute change of plans.' Finn strode into the kitchen and opened the oven slightly, letting more delicious aromas into the room. But Millie hadn't moved, and as she met Lucas's gaze, she felt tears welling in her eyes again. Embarrassed, she stepped over to the table and slung her handbag over the arm of a chair, her back to the men.

She felt a hand on her shoulder and turned, expecting Finn. But it was Lucas, his expression concerned. 'Millie? Is your daughter okay? Has something happened?'

Millie could only shake her head, but the tears came anyway, and she retrieved her bag, thinking she'd just leave; this had been a mistake. But Lucas surprised her. He placed his arms around her and hugged her tightly. 'I don't know what's happened Millie, but you can't leave now. You're upset and shouldn't drive.' Removing one arm, but the other still around her shoulders, he passed her a napkin from the table. 'And you need to eat. So sit down, Millie, I'll pour you a drink, and you can tell the Anderson Men all about it.' His words brought a smile to her face, and she wiped her eyes again.

Leaning into Lucas for a brief moment, Millie murmured, 'You have no idea how much you've helped, Luke. Thank you.' Smiling across at Finn, then back to his son, she added, 'Yes, we need to eat. But first I might just go and fix my face. I'm sure I have mascara everywhere.'

As she walked to the bathroom, she heard the men speaking

in low tones. She tried to ascertain if there was any anger in their voices, if Luke was still mad at his father. But she couldn't detect any. Feeling more settled, she stepped into the small room, washed her hands and removed the last vestiges of mascara.

Returning to the dining area, she saw the garlic bread on the table, three bowls of pasta and glasses of red wine. 'Thank you. Both of you. I am so sorry to arrive like this, without Hanna and with no explanation.'

'All good Millie. Let's enjoy dinner, and we can chat while we eat. But no pressure.' Finn raised his glass. 'To friendship. And family.'

Lucas passed the garlic bread to Millie, saying quietly, 'I can eat, then go downstairs if you need to talk with Dad. But Millie?'

His expression was sincere. *He really is a younger version of Finn.* 'Yes?'

'I, uh, just want to tell you that, ah, you're the best thing to happen to Dad. In a long time. And, ah, I'm kinda used to you being around. Please don't change that.' Lucas shifted his gaze to his father, then back to Millie.

'Oh Luke. Thank you!' Millie felt tears coming again and wiped them away with her serviette. 'Now I'm crying again. But Luke, they're happy tears. Really.'

'Excellent!' Luke grinned and took a sip of wine. 'Let's eat.'

Finn grinned too, and she saw pride in the look he gave Lucas. Millie took a bite of garlic bread and realised how hungry she was.

———

LATER, WHILE LUCAS ATE HIS SECOND HELPING OF

pasta, Millie decided she would talk to Finn and Lucas about Hannelore.

'She was always closer to her father, then became an apprentice pastry chef under him. As our marriage began to fall apart, and the business, she took Rudy's side. Always. But to be fair, Hannelore didn't *know* my side. I hid the worst of it from the kids, as much as I could. As everything imploded, she finished her apprenticeship and announced she was leaving. Heading to Western Australia.' Millie gave a wry smile. 'I think it was to be as far away from us, *from me*, as possible. She blamed *me* for the marriage break-up. She knew her father was having an affair, but in her mind I hadn't, um.' Millie stopped, unsure if she could repeat the scathing words Hannelore had said. 'She just blamed me. I think she always tried so hard to get her father's attention that blaming me was easier. And she had no real knowledge of the financial stuff going on.' Millie didn't want to elaborate on Rudy's gambling and poor investments. She felt partly responsible that she hadn't been aware in time.

Finn nodded and Lucas gave a small smile. Millie continued. 'The thing is, Hanna and I haven't been in touch much, until recently. The first year or so, she barely responded to my texts and emails, and for a while, I thought I'd lost her altogether. So when things began to improve, just in the last few months, I didn't want to do anything to change that.' Millie inhaled deeply. 'We began to communicate more easily. I shared stories of my life in Barrington; how much I love it here and about the café, and especially the opportunity to make it my own. But I'm ashamed to admit that I didn't talk about you Finn, and how close we've become. If I mentioned you at all, it was in passing, as another new friend like Rose, Angus and Steve and Rachael. I'm sorry. And when you invited us to dinner tonight, both of us, I knew it would be obvious that we are more to each other than friends. And I honestly didn't want to blindside Hanna, have her find out that way.' Millie hung her head then, almost mumbling the last words. 'And I've not had the courage to tell her.'

Lucas blinked a couple of times but didn't comment. Finn looked surprised, but not upset. His voice was gentle. 'Tell her what, exactly, Millie?'

Millie flushed, then glanced at Lucas. But she lifted her chin and spoke directly to Finn. 'That I love you, Finn Anderson. I need to tell Hannelore that I love you.'

'Yes!' Lucas pounded the table with one hand and laughed out loud. 'I knew it! Dad loves you too Millie, in case he hasn't actually said it!'

'Oh, I've said it. Many times.' Finn winked as he reached over, the wine bottle in his hand. 'More wine Millie?'

Millie felt lighter. *Unburdening oneself is a good thing, right?* She placed her hand over her glass. 'No thank you, Finn. I want to drive home soon. Hanna should still be up, and I'll sit with her and have this conversation. I also need to ask about her life in recent months. I sense something happened to change her perspective. This is a conversation I want to have with my girl, and I'm hoping it will go well, and she may choose to stay a while in Barrington.'

Millie pushed her chair back, then reached across the table, gathering their dirty plates. Finn put his hand on her arm. 'We can clean up, Millie.' He stood then and wrapped his arms around her.

Lucas scrambled up from the table. 'I'll clear. You two, ah, say your goodbyes.' He gathered several dishes and retreated to the kitchen.

Millie stood on tiptoe and kissed Finn gently on the lips. 'That's quite a boy you have there. To be honest, I wasn't sure what he thought of me. Of us. Until tonight. I can't tell you how happy I am right now.'

'To be honest Millie, I wasn't sure either. Oh, I knew he liked you, he'd have said otherwise. But I didn't realise how much. It's a man-thing. We don't always have these conversations. And seeing his response to you tonight, I think we should.' Finn kissed her back. 'Come on, I'll walk you down to your car.'

'Just a moment.' Millie stepped into the kitchen. Lucas was at the sink, rinsing the dishes. 'Luke.' He turned. Millie opened her arms. 'I just want to thank you. For tonight.'

Lucas grinned. 'You're okay Millie Tucker.' He hugged her quickly, then turned back to the sink, his face flushed.

Note to self, Millie Tucker. It's okay to show your feelings.

10

RACHAEL

Barrington Book Club – Rachael, Rose, Millie, Hannelore,
Kristen, Melanie, Harriet, Meggie, Nicole
Apologies - Laura
Book – ***The Grazier's Son*** by Cathryn Hein

RACHAEL WAS PLEASED TO SEE HANNELORE BEHIND THE
coffee machine when she arrived for book club. Something about
her reminded her of Debbie at that age. Rose and Melanie stepped
through the door soon after and Meggie and Harriet walked in
together. Nicole popped out of the kitchen behind Millie,
carrying a tray of assorted sandwiches and slices.

They chatted together happily, laughing and calling to each
other as they moved towards their usual table. Rachael followed as
if pulled by invisible strings. She adored these young women,

Debbie's friends. Spending time with them reminded her of her daughter. But Debbie should be here too, chatting about her children and placing the food on the table with her usual warmth and generosity. *Not lying beneath the ground, her baby girl in her cold lifeless arms.* Rachael blinked, consciously trying to smile and hoping she wasn't grimacing instead.

'Here Rachael, sit by me.' Rose gestured, her face glowing with health. And something else, her expression enigmatic. *Understanding.* Of course. She was Debbie's best friend. *She knows.* Rachael took a deep breath and slid into the seat Rose offered. She leaned down to retrieve the paperback she'd brought, taking a moment to collect her emotions.

Rachael had only recently joined book club. She'd never been a big reader. But out at the farm a few months after the accident, helping Jamie sort through Debbie's clothes and personal belongings, she'd been drawn to a huge stack of paperbacks. Debbie had always had a pile of books on her bedside table. Rachael had intended to take them to the second-hand shop but picked one up and opened it. Seeing Debbie's name and the date written on the flyleaf in her lovely, rounded handwriting, Rachael had held it to her chest.

She'd brought the books home, several boxes of them, and began reading. As she did she recalled snippets of conversations about some of them. She heard Debbie telling her *I read until midnight, couldn't put it down* and how she and Rose would discuss comments made about certain books at book club.

Debbie was gone, but reading the books she'd read and loved, comforted Rachael. She had been thinking about book club but made no moves to attend until Rose dropped by one day and over a cup of tea, invited her. Rachael was almost positive Steve had been behind the invitation, but she didn't care how it happened, she loved it. Now she couldn't understand how she had lived without reading all those years. Her only regret was that she had missed an opportunity to share her love of books with Debbie.

Rachael looked around the table. Everyone had settled into chairs. Some had a particular spot they preferred, and she loved the way they joked and laughed together, sharing their news and hopes. She also liked the easy way they mentioned Debbie from time to time. Whether it was about something she'd said or done, or about the food, the café or even a book they'd read. At book club, Rachael was not alone in her loss, and talking about Debbie, knowing she was alive in the hearts and minds of these women, helped.

'Sandwich, Rachael?' Millie pushed the plate of snacks closer and Rachael grinned and reached for one.

'Egg and lettuce, cut into triangles, no crusts. Delicious.' Rachael smiled at Millie and raised an eyebrow. 'And very Country Women's Association Millie. Is there something we should know?'

'Ha! No Rachael. And there's corn beef and pickles too. Very CWA!' Millie picked one up and took a bite. 'If you don't mind me asking, Rachael, how did you go with the Solicitors last week? Are they keen to move into the rooms upstairs?'

'Sadly, no.' Rachael considered her words for a moment. 'Barrington is too small for them, apparently. *Provincial* was the term the young woman used.'

Rachael turned to Harriet, who had cleared her throat. 'Honestly Rachael, we may have dodged a bullet there. They looked at some houses too, but nothing seemed to be quite *up to scratch*. We need a law firm that understands small towns and communities. Like Douglas. And Frances.' She paused. 'And that's not all. Douglas did a lot of conveyancing and estate work, and it seems likely that one of the franchise firms may set up here. But I think they're looking at shop-fronts at street level. The stairs in this building may be problematic.'

Nodding, Rachael conceded that Steve had said something similar. 'We've looked at putting an elevator in, but we'd have to take space away from Greta's Gifts and Flowers to do it. And if a conveyancing firm does set up down the street, we may have to consider repurposing the rooms upstairs.'

Meggie chimed in. 'Really? You know it was an apartment before Douglas bought the building. Back when it was still a bank?' She clapped her hand to her forehead. 'Sorry Rachael, of course you know that! Steve was the bank manager here for years.' She shook her head and Rachael laughed.

'You're right though Meggie. It was a residence. Gerald Allman, the loans manager, lived there for quite a few years until the bank closed the branch.' She shut her eyes for a moment, trying to recall how it looked before Douglas Barlow turned it into a law office.

'The office that Douglas used was the master bedroom, and the file room was a second, smaller bedroom and there still is a rather large bathroom and separate toilet facing the rear. The main reception area was previously the lounge and living area, with the kitchen and laundry overlooking the rear yard. There are back stairs and a two-car garage, separate to the carport and entrance you use Millie, to get into the café.'

Turning back to Meggie and Harriet, Rachael asked the question she felt they were all waiting for. 'Do you think it could be, or should be, turned back into accommodation?'

Meggie nodded vigorously. 'I do Rachael. I'd love to come up and have a look if you and Steve are interested. Short-term accommodation would be perfect. We have so many small weddings and events in the area now that I know we could fill it at weekends for you, at the very least, which would equal what you'd get per week as long-term accommodation. Any mid-week stays would be a bonus.'

Rachael turned to Nicole. 'Robbie did the renovations at your place Nik. You have the old courthouse and outbuildings beautifully restored on the outside, yet with every convenience on the inside.' She watched Nicole nod. 'But I also know the interior design was your project Nik.' She saw Nicole flush, with pleasure she hoped.

Looking around the table, Rachael smiled and pushed her copy of *The Grazier's Son* forward. 'We've taken enough book club time talking about what we could do with the rooms upstairs, let's talk about Cathryn Hein's fabulous story, shall we?' She gazed at Meggie and then Nicole and added, 'But I intend to talk to Steve about your suggestions. If he's interested, I'll get back to you.'

Sitting back, Rachael was happy to listen to comments about the book, occasionally making an observation of her own. But her mind was racing. She needed a project and perhaps repurposing upstairs was it. A little flutter of enthusiasm tickled her chest.

'I adored Darcy! I wish there were pictures of some of her outfits.' Meggie waved her arms about as she described her favourites from the book.

'And Stirling, but I was kept guessing about the bad guy until close to the end.' Melanie sighed. 'I could see him though, in my mind's eye.' She giggled and Rose nudged her.

'The romance made me tingle ….' Hannelore blushed. Rachael saw Millie raise an eyebrow, but she didn't comment.

'The food got me. Cathryn Hein writes such great food!' Kristen licked her lips and Millie and Hannelore laughed out loud while the rest chuckled. Almost a mirror image of her mother, Rachael saw Hannelore's expression change from laughter, to wishfulness, then back to laughter. Rachael wondered about that.

Another half hour passed and the group began to gather their things to depart. As Millie and the younger women began clearing the table, Meggie asked what their next read should be.

'Is anyone keen to try an Aussie mystery?' Rachael spoke quietly, she'd never recommended a book. 'There's a mystery series by Phillipa Nefri Clark – she wrote *The Stationmaster's Cottage,* which I think you read, um, earlier.' *When Debbie was at book club.*

'Um, the first one is called *Lest We Forgive,* and it's the first of about four, I think. *Detective Liz Moreland* stories.' Rachael looked at Rose, who nodded encouragement. 'I have the paperback. It was… It was in Debbie's bedside table stack.' She finished hurriedly. 'I'd like to read it as a group unless you're not keen.'

'I'm keen.' Rose spoke quietly.

'I have it on my iPad, but I haven't started it. I'd love to read it for book club.' Nicole smiled warmly and Rachael quietly released the breath she hadn't realised she was holding.

They all spoke at once then, some saying they'd order the eBook, and Meggie said she'd pick up paperbacks from the bookshop in Taree that week for anyone who wanted one. Millie said yes to that, but Hannelore touched her arm. 'I read it in Sydney, I left it at Matty's. I'll get him to send it up for you, Mum.'

Rose offered Rachael a lift home, but she said she'd walk, it was only one block. The ten minutes it took to reach home were precious. Rachael could almost feel Debbie beside her on the way. The feeling dissipated as she pushed open the front gate, but the loss was gentle on her soul.

11

HARRY

'The old bank building? Above the café?' Harry frowned, trying to picture the upstairs. 'I don't think I've ever been upstairs.' He grinned at his father. 'I've never needed legal advice.'

Robbie snorted. 'Of course not. You were still at school when we did the conversion for Douglas. I remember exactly how it was before.' He turned to Nicole, 'but I'm sure Rachael will want to modernise it too. When can we have a look?'

Harry watched Nicole's face as she placed her phone on the table. They'd just come inside for morning tea after finishing the interior walls of the garage conversion. There was something she hadn't told them, he was sure.

'That was Rachael.' She took a breath, her face radiant. 'Yes, she wants you to come and have a look. Tomorrow if you can. But she wants me to come too.' She placed her hands on the back of her chair and leaned forward, her excitement palpable. 'Rachael wants *me* to come because she's asked me to do the interior design, right down to fixtures, fittings and furnishings.'

Almost in slow motion, Harry saw surprise, then pleasure, cross his father's face. Robbie walked to Nicole and wrapped her in his arms. 'Of course she asked you Nik. Your vision for this place, the stables and now the old garage, is beautiful and absolutely spot-on.'

Harry walked to the kitchen sink, reached for the jug and filled it. He turned and leaned back against the bench with his legs crossed at the ankles and his arms folded. He was trying to look casual, but he knew his face would reflect his father's. Grinning, he simply said, 'Proud of you Nik.'

———

RACHAEL AND STEVE WERE WAITING BY THE FRONT doors downstairs. Meggie joined them as Robbie, Harry and Nicole walked across the road.

Harry waited with Robbie for the others to go up the stairs first. Robbie pointed to the stair treads and raised his eyebrows, murmuring, 'Original rosewood, they just need to be sanded and oiled.'

There was a small landing at the top of the stairs, with ornate double doors that opened inward. They were painted, but Harry looked at them closely as he walked in. *Hardwood too, nice.*

Rachael, Nicole and Meggie walked from room to room, talking loudly and throwing ideas around. Harry followed Robbie and Steve into the kitchen area, where Steve placed a wad of plans on the counter. One was an old floorplan of the building, possibly the original. The other was the building plans of the renovations Douglas had made after buying the building, including the café and gift shop downstairs. Harry knew his father had worked on the upstairs area but a city contractor had done the shops downstairs.

The women joined them and Steve spoke first, looking from Nicole to Meggie. 'What do you think?'

'There's room to turn it back into a two-bedroom, but I think it would make a gorgeous, spacious one-bedroom apartment.' Meggie spoke confidently. 'Short-term accommodation in the centre of town will appeal more to couples than families. Two bedrooms would be fine if we could squeeze in two bathrooms, but a second bedroom offers no real return on investment without an ensuite.'

'I agree, Meggie. We generally book The Stables out with one couple, effectively getting very little return for the second bedroom.' Nicole drew the original plan closer. 'The main office is in the footprint of the original bedroom, and the file room, here, was a second bedroom. We could turn that into a walk-in wardrobe, although it has a big window facing west, looking over the Bucketts Mountain.' Nicole pointed to the rooms on both plans, before walking out into the main reception area.

'The living area is light-filled and runs right along the front of the building, facing east. Without adding walls back in, I'd leave it open plan and use furniture to create a cosy dining, lounge and perhaps a sitting room over there.' Trying to keep up with Nicole, Robbie drew out a tape measure and Harry hurried to hold one end as he measured the length of the room, jotting figures in a small notebook he pulled from his top pocket.

'What about the kitchen Nik? It was always quite small, and Douglas turned it into a kitchenette. Do you think we should put in a larger one, with a butler's pantry?' Rachael frowned slightly and glanced at Steve. 'We don't want to over-capitalise.'

Nicole shook her head. 'The kitchen is fine. A new countertop and drawers with compact equipment. Cosmetic changes. Visitors don't want to cook. They have the café downstairs and pub meals too. They just want to be able to store snacks and drinks and be able to heat meals up if they choose to stay in.' Nicole looked at Meggie for confirmation, Harry thought, and she also nodded.

'The original laundry was down in the garage. There's still a tub there.' Steve looked at the kitchen again. 'Do we need a laundry?' He turned to Nicole, who seemed firm on that idea too.

'Yes, some people might stay more than a few days. I think we could steal a metre or so from the dining area and add a washer, dryer and washtub in a cupboard here, with doors that hide it away.' Nicole gestured to the area and Robbie and Harry quickly measured the space.

Nicole continued, 'The only item that needs more than cosmetic work is the bathroom. Douglas removed the old bathtub, leaving the shower, basin and toilet but the space is quite large.' She threw open the bathroom door. 'Put in a double shower and double sinks and move the toilet to the side, with its own door. Remove the blind from the window and replace it with frosted glass. It will be light-filled and beautiful.'

'I love it. I love the whole idea.' Rachael was beaming, and Steve looked chuffed, too.

'Okay Robbie, Harry.' Steve put his arm around Rachael's shoulders, drawing her close. 'Can you quote up the building work please.' He turned to Nicole. 'Nik, can you work with Rachael on colours and styles, choose the bathroom fixtures and fittings and so on? Can you provide a quote for consulting and design?'

'I have wholesale suppliers for most of that. And for the furnishings.' Nicole grinned at Rachael. 'We'll have so much fun shopping!'

Harry saw a change in Rachael then like a cloud had lifted. She smiled broadly then walked back to the front window with Nicole, talking about styles and colours.

Meggie saw his look and grinned, then nodded. She turned to Steve, 'This is a good project, Steve. For the town, for tourism.' She lowered her voice slightly, 'And for Rachael.'

And for us. Harry knew it was a project he'd be proud of.

12

HANNELORE

Book club had been brilliant. Hannelore hadn't been entirely sure, as most of the women were a bit older than her until Kristen said she was keen to come too. She liked Kristen, they were the same age and they were having fun at work. They planned to go to the pub together on Friday night, for a drink and a meal.

Chuckling to herself, Hannelore thought about book club again. It hadn't been very structured. Just a bunch of friends having drinks and snacks and sharing their news, before they all had a quick chat about their chosen book.

At first, she'd felt a bit impatient, wanting to get to the book stuff. She'd always loved books and once wanted to be a librarian, but her father had encouraged her into an apprenticeship, and she wasn't sorry, she loved being a pastry chef. *But she would have loved being a librarian too.* She pushed that thought from her mind. But sitting back, listening to the book club members chat with each other, she sensed a connection. A strong thread of support that somehow tied them all together. And her mum was now a big part of that.

In the moment she'd felt a twinge of jealousy at the easy way the other women included Millie. Then Rose Gordon had drawn *her* into the conversation, asking her thoughts on the book and what her other recent reads were. And then Hannelore *got it.* It wasn't just a book club, it was a private support network. And she knew she could become part of it, if she wanted.

The other big thing that had happened during the week, was the lovely dinner and conversation she'd shared with her mum in their little apartment on Wednesday night.

Millie had finally come clean about her friendship with Finn and confessed it was a *thing*. More than a thing, Hannelore thought, but she'd make her own mind up on Saturday night when they went to Finn's for dinner.

Hannelore had been a bit embarrassed about some of her mum's revelations. That she *stayed over* at Finn's sometimes, and he stayed here in the apartment with her sometimes too. Millie didn't use the word *sex*, but of course, that's what *staying over* meant. Without meaning to, Hannelore had screwed her face up a bit, then quickly tried to hide her shock.

Millie had looked at her, one eyebrow raised, and said drily, 'I'm forty-three Hanna, not dead.' Hannelore had snort-laughed then, she'd just taken a sip of wine, and Millie had joined in. They'd laughed until they cried and when Millie passed her a tissue, she looked slightly concerned.

'You don't mind, do you Hanna? That I've found someone?' She wiped her eyes as she spoke.

Hannelore thought about it, wanting to find the right words.

'I don't mind Mum. You deserve to be happy and treated well.' She'd looked away for a moment, then turned back. 'I'm sorry Mum. I'm sorry for the way Dad treated you. But I'm even more sorry for the way I treated you.' She began to cry. 'I always took Dad's side. But I *knew*. In my heart, I knew he was doing the wrong thing. By you. By us. By the business and even by the women he was with.' She hiccupped, crying harder. 'Oh Mum, you should have left him years ago. Did you stay for us? Is that why?'

Millie passed the tissues to Hannelore. She'd been crying too, but now she seemed calm. And a bit sad. Hannelore didn't want to make her sad.

'I have to take responsibility too Hanna. I've been digging deep, wanting to understand my actions and responses to your father and what happened in our marriage, and in our business.'

Millie leaned forward, placing her hand on Hannelore's arm. 'Yes, I stayed for you, but not in the way you think. Early in the marriage, you won't remember, I used to stick up for myself and stand up to your father. But there was a day when we were shouting at each other that I saw your little face, you'd come into the room, and I realised how distressing that was for you. How confusing. So I stopped. Stopped shouting, stopped being so combative. And by doing that I gave my power away.'

'Gave your power away?' Hannelore wasn't sure what Millie meant.

'Yes. By not objecting and by agreeing to do things Rudy's way, I gave him any power I had in the relationship. And the more I did that, the worse it got.' Millie straightened and looked directly at Hannelore. 'I'm ashamed of myself, now. I could have handled it so much better. I could have pushed back and disagreed without all the shouting. But the upshot was, that as the years passed, I came to believe what he told me.'

'What do you mean?' Hannelore was invested, she needed to understand the dynamic that was her parents' marriage.

'I'm not sure how much to tell you, darling girl. He'll always be your father. But what I'm saying now, is my problem.' Millie sighed. 'The way I'd allowed myself to never be equal in the relationship. At home and at work. So when he told me our business success was all due to him, his cooking ability, his way with people. I believed him. When he said we'd do better if I pulled my weight more, I worked harder. When he told me he didn't like the way I looked, I'd go on a crash diet. I thought about leaving, many times, but I'd become convinced that he was right. That I'd never be able to support you and Matty without him. So I stayed. And my unhappiness led to over-eating. In secret. And this, in turn, seemed to push him to treat me more poorly than ever. So in a way, Hannelore, I brought this on myself.'

Hannelore stood, shocked and also indignant. 'No! No Mum. It was him. It was deliberate. I can see it now. He wanted a hard-working wife and gorgeous kids in public, but at home, he really didn't do much with us. He never came to school for meetings with teachers, speech days or sports days. *You* came. *You* always came! But I remember him telling a customer when I was in the café one day when I was about twelve, how proud he was of my school results. He never told *me* that, but overhearing it made me want to hear it again. So I worked like crazy through school.'

She sat down and leaned into Millie, speaking more quietly. 'I just wanted him to give me some attention. Mum, did you know that I wanted to be a librarian? I loved books so much. I even thought I might write one day.'

'I did ask you once, Hanna. You were always reading. I wondered why you chose to be a pastry chef. When I asked you though, you seemed excited to be starting an apprenticeship with your father.' Millie looked down.

'When he asked me to come and work with him and become his apprentice, I was so thrilled to have his attention, that I said yes. The thought of being with him every day was a gift. But Mum, now I see that it merely served his own ends and he treated me no better than any other staff, and sometimes worse.' Hannelore shook her head.

'There were times I hated it and hated him, but I couldn't articulate it.' She looked up, 'and I didn't want to admit it to you. So, I planned to leave and go interstate to find work the moment I was qualified.'

She didn't speak for a moment, and Millie waited. 'Once I was away from Dad, I began to see him more clearly. That's why I dropped Schmidt. I don't want to carry his name. But I'm proud to use yours. I'm Hanna Tucker now.'

'Oh, Hanna!' Millie opened her arms, and Hannelore fell into them, hugging her tightly. 'I wondered about your name change. Now I understand.'

They stayed like that for a minute, until Hannelore leaned back. She smiled at Millie. 'But Mum, I'm not unhappy about my profession. I love it. I love cooking and I especially love working with you.' She giggled and was pleased to see Millie's expression lighten. 'And as to the librarian thing, we have book club. I'm loving book club.'

Millie laughed out loud. 'I love it too. But you do know it's about more than just books?'

Hannelore grinned. 'Oh, I know that. It's just another reason to love it.'

13

FREDDIE

ANOTHER WEEK, ANOTHER FRIDAY NIGHT AT THE TOP Pub. She'd suggested Saturday night this time, but he had a *family thing* on again. Freddie peered around the bar, it was starting to fill up. She wondered if she'd see Harry Stewart again. Not that she was interested, but she liked the way she made him uncomfortable.

Freddie giggled. *Being a woman is a powerful thing.* She'd only discovered it when she went to university. Before that she'd been a tomboy, trying to keep up with – *and compete with* – her six older brothers.

Yet here she was, in her hometown, secretly meeting her lover. She was hiding him from her family. From her brothers in particular. They'd always told her they'd *rough up* any boy who fancied her. They'd meant it when she was in her teens, and it had thrilled her that they cared so much. She wasn't sure they'd do it now, and she could probably come clean about seeing someone.

She rolled her shoulders and peeked at the door again. *He was always late.* Freddie had him convinced her brothers would hurt him if they knew – but she really loved the secrecy, the creeping around. It made their relationship way more exciting. She wondered if she'd like him with the same intensity if everyone knew.

The door opened and Kristen Laing appeared. Freddie turned her head, hoping she wouldn't see her and come over. Kristen had been a couple of years ahead of her at school and she'd always been friendly. All good, though; another girl was with her, and they were talking as they walked in. Someone Freddie didn't know. Long hair, pretty. She watched them pause at the bar, chat for a minute, then move through to the bistro. She breathed out.

Her phone beeped. She glanced down.

> I'm outside. Your brothers just pulled in. XX

Freddie stood, finished her beer, and walked swiftly to the back exit, tapping her phone as she went.

> Meet you at the usual spot.

> I'm happy to come in. It's time we told them. XX

Freddie frowned, looking at the screen. *Where was the fun in that?*

> Too dangerous. See you in 5.

14

HARRY

Pushing through the door ahead of Callum and Douggie, Harry scanned the room. He caught a glimpse of Freddie disappearing through the back exit. *What the heck is she playing at?* He was beginning to worry about her. He was sure she was meeting someone. Someone her brothers wouldn't like. Callum and Douggie were good blokes and adored their little sister. *Who wouldn't they like?* He frowned. *Someone married?* Surely not. The fellow he'd seen her with was young.

Part of him wanted to follow her, but Callum caught his attention and pointed to the bistro. 'Did you see who just walked in there, mate?'

'Nah. Who?' Harry peered over Callum's head through the half-glass doors to the bistro area.

'Kristen. Laing.' Callum's face flushed, almost as red as his hair.

'Kristen huh?' Harry remembered Kristen, she was a year behind them at school. She'd been away at university but was back, working at the café. Lucy had mentioned her. He recalled her as friendly and somewhat shy. Nice girl.

Callum looked at Harry, then to the bar and back to the bistro. Douggie had already lined up at the bar and Harry began moving that way. 'She's with someone, but, uh, mate, we were planning to get pizza anyway. Wanna grab our beers and go in straight away?'

Harry laughed. *Callum had it bad.* 'Sure. The beer will taste the same in any room. You grab a table in there, and I'll help Douggie with the drinks.' He tried to peer through the doors but couldn't see Kristen. He turned back to Callum. 'Who is she with? A bloke?'

'Nup. A sheila.' Callum headed into the other room, calling back over his shoulder. 'Hurry up with those drinks.'

Harry reached the bar and Douggie handed him two beers. He was chatting to blokes from their footy club. 'Callum's gone to the bistro and wants us to … er … have our drinks there.'

Douggie looked at Harry for a moment. 'Mate. I saw Kristen come in. Callum's got it bad for her.' One of the others laughed and nudged Douggie. 'Harry, you go in. Cal needs a wingman.' Douggie raised his glass, taking a giant swig. 'I plan to stay in the bar and chat with the fellas for a bit. Order your meals, I'll get something later.' Douggie turned his back and continued his conversation. Harry sighed and, with a beer in each hand, walked through to the dining area.

Callum was leaning against the side of a booth, chatting to Kristen. His body blocked Harry's view of the other girl, but he did notice a set of shapely denim-clad legs as he walked across the room.

Harry was right behind Callum and about to pass him a beer,

when Callum suddenly threw his arms out, waving them about as he spoke. Harry caught a glimpse of Kristen's smiling face before both glasses of beer were unceremoniously knocked from his hands, spilling down the front of his shirt and jeans.

'Fuck it!' He thought he swore under his breath, but Callum turned at the same moment, apologising profusely, his face redder than ever, before mumbling about serviettes and shooting across to the bistro bar. Harry held his shirt away from his skin. *The beer was bloody cold.*

Kristen offered him a tissue from her purse, 'You always were a bit clumsy, Harry Stewart.'

He grinned and raised an eyebrow. 'Clumsy or not, I don't think this,' he waved a hand in front of his wet shirt and jeans. 'Is my fault.' And that's when he saw her. The gorgeous blonde he'd spied in the pub a couple of weeks ago eating dinner by herself. She was looking where he was waving his hand. Right in front of his very wet groin area.

She looked up at him, unsmiling. 'I beg to differ. *You* startled Callum.' She smiled at Kristen then and Harry wished she'd turn that smile on him. 'Callum was very ... um ... focussed on his conversation with Kristen. He had no idea you were *right* behind him.'

Kristen looked past him and waved, and Harry turned to see Callum almost running towards him with a small towel in his hand. Harry put out his hand to slow Callum down, then took the towel he offered. Harry began swabbing at his chest, then he raised the cloth to his nose. He handed it back to Callum. 'This stinks mate. Of beer.'

'Bruce behind the bar gave it to me.' Callum fidgeted for a

moment. 'It can't smell any worse than you, now. It's just beer. Your shirt is starting to dry already.' His tone was hopeful.

Looking down, Harry sighed. His shirt was damp, his jeans were more wet. He'd tell Callum he'd go home and not worry about pizza tonight.

Before he could, Callum spoke quickly, almost urgently. 'Kristen and uh ... Hanna ... just asked if we'd like to join them for dinner. You know, share a couple of pizzas.' He peered past Harry. 'Where's Douggie?'

'He's abandoned us, mate. He's catching up with the footy club blokes at the bar. He said he'd get something later.' Harry looked down at his wet clothes again. 'I should go and have a shower and clean myself up.'

'Oh. Really?' Callum had turned to Harry, his back to the girls. He wiggled his eyebrows up and down, trying to communicate something. Harry got it. Callum wanted time with Kristen and he needed Harry to keep the other girl, Hanna, company.

Harry sighed, then looked around Callum, speaking directly to Hanna. 'I can stay if you don't mind the smell of beer?'

Kristen spoke quickly, 'Stay Harry. We don't mind, do we, Hanna?'

Hanna replied, quite drily, Harry thought. 'It is a pub. Some beer aroma is to be expected.' She slid over in the booth as she spoke and Harry sat down. His damp jeans made a squeaking noise on the seat and the girl sniggered. Callum was already next to Kristen with a menu in front of them, discussing their favourite pizzas.

After the longest moment, Harry sighed. 'I'll get two more beers shall I?' He turned to Hanna. 'I'm Harry, by the way. Harry Stewart.' He held out his hand. 'What would you like to drink?'

'Hannelore Tucker. Hanna to my friends.' She shook his hand. It felt small in his, but strong. 'I'll have a glass of merlot, please.'

'Hannelore?' He'd never heard the name before.

She rolled her eyes. 'German-born father. It's pronounced Hanna-lore-ay.'

He tried saying it again, then raised his eyebrows. 'May I call you Hanna?' He glanced across at Kristen and Callum, he was sure their hands were touching under the table. 'We have, uh, friends in common. Does that help?'

Hannelore smiled then and her whole face lit up. *Gorgeous, and smart too, he'd wager.*

'Okay. Call me Hanna. But the jury's still out about the friends bit.' But he sensed she was playing with him, and he grinned.

'What's Kristen drinking? I'll get her another.' They looked at the other two.

Hanna giggled quietly. 'Vodka, lime and soda for Kristen.'

His shirt dried, but he knew he reeked of beer. Despite the discomfort of his still-damp jeans, he enjoyed himself. Hanna hadn't been long in Barrington, she'd travelled from Western Australia. It seemed she was working with Kristen at the café for a while. It sounded like she was back-packing around, and he wasn't sure if she was just over from Germany or if she'd been here longer. She didn't have an accent, but he'd met other travellers and knew many of them studied English at school. She didn't tell him much else, but now he remembered Lucy talking with great enthusiasm about cooking something with Hanna just the other night. *He needed to pay more attention.*

He had two beers but refused a third. He couldn't drive if he had any more, and he and Robbie were starting Rachael's project in the morning, pulling up the floor coverings, and taking the cupboard doors off the small kitchen. He needed to be on his game for that. He asked Hanna if she needed a lift home, but she said she could walk.

Callum made the same offer to Kristen. Harry thought Kristen lived in town near the golf course. She accepted Callum's offer, and within moments, Harry and Hanna were standing on the pavement outside the pub together.

Harry held his hand out, 'Goodnight Hanna, it's been lovely to meet you.'

Placing her hand in his, she grinned. His hand almost tingled when he grasped hers and he couldn't take his eyes off her smiling mouth. *He wanted to kiss her.* But he wouldn't. He barely knew her. *But he wanted to.*

As if she could read his thoughts, she pulled her hand from his. 'Goodnight cowboy.' *Did she just wink?* And she was gone, walking along the street. He wanted to watch where she went. *Don't be a creep Harry.* He turned down the side lane and walked to the car park behind the pub.

15

MILLIE

Millie had spent the night at Finn's. Now that Hannelore knew about their relationship, she could be more open. Finn said he was looking forward to meeting Hannelore properly, although he'd said a quick hello earlier in the week when he dropped into the café. Millie sensed he was a bit nervous. She couldn't blame him, she'd been wary of Lucas at first, wondering what he thought of her spending so much time with his father.

Millie unlocked the cafe door. It was early and the girls weren't in yet. They had dinner together at the pub last night and Millie had told them she'd open up. After turning the light and coffee machine on, she heard a tap at the door. She'd been about to unlock it and turn the sign to 'open'.

Walking across, she saw Hannelore, smiling through the glass and dressed for work.

'I must cut you a key to the front door Hanna.' Millie gazed into Hannelore's face as she breezed in. She seemed fresh and happy. No sign of a hangover. 'Good night?'

'Great night, thanks, Mum. Not a late one, though.' Hannelore walked into the kitchen area, returning with a clean apron over her work pants, her hands behind her doing up the ties. 'I was in bed by ten and started the second book in the Phillipa Clark series. You know, Detective Liz.'

'I've almost finished the first one myself.' Millie started making coffee for them. She expected customers to begin arriving any minute. 'Did you have a nice time with Kristen?'

Hannelore laughed out loud. 'I didn't have a lot of time with Kristen before ... er ... the blokes joined us.'

'The blokes?' Millie was amused.

'Yes. Callum Campbell and his wingman. He's a local farmer and has a huge crush on Kristen. The funny thing is, she's always liked him too.' Hannelore shook her head. 'It didn't matter, we had a lively chat, the four of us. But it wasn't late.'

Millie was about to ask about the wingman, but Kristen breezed in through the back entrance. She looked at them and blushed. 'Sorry, I meant to be here a bit earlier. Um, I had to get a lift, I left my car here last night.'

'No problem Kristen.' Millie didn't want to make her uncomfortable. 'If you two can start baking, I'll set up the front counter.' Millie handed the girls a coffee each and returned to the counter. She heard snippets of their conversation. 'No. He didn't stay. But I had to ask Mum to drive me in today.' Hannelore murmured something and they both laughed. Then she heard Hannelore say, 'I don't think so. He's a bit too confident for my taste.' She'd definitely have to ask who the other *bloke* was.

Lucy flew in through the back door. 'Hi Kristen, Hi Hanna! Hello Millie.'

Millie nodded at her bright young face. 'You're right on time, Lucy. How did you get in here today?'

'My brother drove me in, he's working on the apartment upstairs with Robbie today. Mum's coming in later this morning.' Lucy tied an apron around her waist.

Millie smiled, then turned as Melanie arrived, wee Bronte in her arms and Tiffany beside her wearing a little backpack. 'Hi Melanie. You're early.' She leaned down, 'Hello Tiffany.'

'Hello Millie.' Tiffany moved to one side, where Hannelore had just set out a tray of assorted slices she'd baked the day before.

'We've got a special clinic this morning. Free de-sexing and micro-chipping cats. Council is keen to reduce feral cat numbers in the region, so they've sponsored it. I'm expecting it to be busy and I'm hoping Bronte will have a bottle and then a nap in the flat out the back until Mum comes to get them in a couple of hours. Ben has appointments today too, so we're a bit stuck, but Tiffany will play with her if she wakes up.' Melanie moved Bronte to her other hip. 'I'll have my usual latte, and two cappuccinos, please. Angus and Max are both on duty for this. And Tiffany will have a chocolate milkshake.' Melanie glanced at the slice on display. 'And four pieces of slice too, please, Millie.'

'It's a good program. I read about it in the local paper.' Millie began making the drinks.

'Yes it is. Mayor Steve and his team are doing great work.' Melanie glanced towards the kitchen, then back to Millie. 'Hanna seemed to enjoy book club last month. Do you think she'll come again next week?'

'Yes! She loves reading. And chatting about books. And I think she's got a girl-crush on Rose. She told me this week that she's thought about writing too, one day.' Millie knew she was grinning but couldn't contain how happy she was to have Hannelore here.

'Excellent. We'll see her then.' Melanie reached for the cardboard box holding the drinks. Tiffany took the bag filled with caramel slices.

'Wait Mel. I'll walk these down for you.' Millie called into the kitchen, 'Hanna, can you cover the counter for a minute, please?' Hannelore appeared and said a cheery good morning to Melanie and Tiffany, then exclaimed over Bronte, who chose that moment to clap her hands.

Millie returned just as their regular Saturday morning customers began arriving. By mid-morning, they'd had their usual breakfast rush, and it settled into a less frantic coffee and cake service. There had been a bit of noise from upstairs, some banging and then a noisy power tool. Millie knew it would only be for a short period, but it was a bit disconcerting for their customers.

Hannelore asked Lucy about it. 'What are they doing up there, Lucy? I saw your mum go upstairs about half an hour ago with Rachael.'

'Renovating the office back into an apartment. I helped Mum choose the colours for the new kitchen.' Lucy sounded excited.

'Wow! They spoke about that at the last book club. They've cracked on with it quickly. Sounds exciting. Do you think we can go up and take a peek later?' Hannelore looked keen. Millie was surprised, she'd never shown interest in the renovation shows on television. But she had made some insightful comments about their rented apartment above the old post office when she arrived.

'Will it be a bit like our place over the post office Lucy?' Millie knew the buildings were a similar age.

'Um,' Lucy hesitated. 'I think it's not as big as yours, Millie.

And only one bedroom. I can ask if you can have a look, but it might be best to wait a couple of weeks. They're just pulling out old stuff today. The kitchen and floor coverings, I think.'

———

LUCY WENT HOME JUST AFTER LUNCH WITH HER MUM AS the café was quiet on Saturday afternoons. Kristen left shortly after, but Millie noted a whispered exchange with Hannelore before she left.

'Everything alright with Kristen?' Millie placed a whole apple strudel that Hannelore had cooked that morning into a container, putting the lid on firmly. 'We'll take this out to Finn's for dessert.' She grinned. 'The Anderson men like their sweets.'

'Yep. Kristen's good. Callum asked her out tonight. He wanted to take her to the movies in Tuncurry. She asked if I'd go too, but I don't want to be the third wheel. But now I think she's going to say no and we'll have a meal together during the week.' Hannelore sighed. 'Honestly, Mum, she's a year older than me, and she's liked Callum for ages. But they're both a bit shy. I think they just need a nudge.'

'That may be true. I've never heard Kristen talk about anyone special or going on dates. I don't think she's a big drinker or pub-goer either. She's a bit of a family girl. Close to her Mum. And she has an accounting qualification but seems happy to work here. Something's keeping her in town.' Millie raised her eyebrows.

'Yeah, she's close to her mum. And talks about her family a bit. But honestly, I think it's Callum. She said he and his brothers were a bit *rough and ready* when they were younger. Her words. And she's been waiting for him to grow up.' Hannelore leaned against the counter. 'But I really like her, and I think we're going to be good friends. And I like Callum too.'

Hannelore chuckled. 'Kristen wants to introduce me to Callum's brother Douggie. He was there last night but stayed in the bar.' She leaned towards Millie, saying in a loud whisper, 'I don't think Douggie's my type, but a girl has to look after her pals.'

Millie laughed, then asked, 'Who else was there last night? You said Callum had a wingman.' Her phone buzzed as she spoke. She whispered 'sorry' to Hannelore and answered cheerfully. 'Finn! Hello.'

Finn asked her to pick up some parmesan cheese. Millie smiled to herself. His pasta dish was his 'go-to', and he'd want to impress Hanna.

She turned to Hannelore after ending the call, untying her apron as she spoke. 'Finn needs a couple of things from the supermarket. I'll go and pick them up, then go home to have a shower and change. Do you mind waiting until three and then closing up? I doubt you'll have more than a coffee or two to make.'

'You go Mum. I've got a banana bread baking, it only needs another thirty minutes. I'll close up and come over to get ready after that.' Hannelore brushed her away, and Millie walked out, looking forward to the evening at Finn's.

———

MILLIE BUMPED INTO MELANIE AT THE SUPERMARKET. She was alone, her mum must still have the kids. 'How did the clinic go, Mel?' Millie placed a knob of parmesan in her shopping basket.

'Great. Busy. We only finished an hour ago.' Melanie leaned against the ice cream freezer. 'I think we'll run it a couple of times a year if we continue to get Council support.'

'Are you picking the girls up now?' Millie picked up a basil cashew dip.

'No. Ben has them, he finished earlier and took them home for lunch.' Melanie looked over her shoulder, then said quietly, 'I'm taking my time. If I wait another half hour, he'll have them bathed.'

Millie laughed. 'Good strategy.' Looking at Melanie again, she saw a slight frown on her face. 'Would you like to come up to my flat and have a glass of wine with me? Hannelore is just finishing some baking at the café, she'll be a little while.'

Melanie seemed to hesitate, and then she nodded. 'Why not? Can I put the ice cream in your freezer while I'm there?'

'Of course.'

Up in the apartment, Millie poured two glasses of white wine and opened the basil dip, putting a few crackers and some olives on a plate. They sat by the window and chatted about the apartment and what the renovations upstairs from the café might look like. But Millie sensed Melanie had something on her mind.

Their wine was almost finished, and Millie didn't want to push. And she thought Hannelore would be home soon.

But Melanie seemed to have decided. She spoke quietly. 'I've got a problem, Millie. I haven't mentioned it to Ben, and I can't talk to Meggie or Rose about it. Harriet's in Sydney and I will speak to her next week. But,' she nibbled her bottom lip, 'I'm freaking out a bit.'

Millie set her glass down. 'What is it Melanie? I'm not sure I can help, but you can talk to me. Safely.'

Melanie's eyes filled up with tears, and the words burst from her mouth. 'I think one of them is having an affair. Cheating.' She wiped a tear from her cheek as she shook her head sadly.

'Cheating?' Millie was shocked. 'Who? How?'

'I know, the thought shocks me too.' Melanie nodded. 'I wasn't sure, but it's been a few times now and I need to say something.'

'I still don't understand Mel. Tell me what you know.' Millie waited.

'There's a flat, at the clinic. Angus lived there before he met Rose and Max lived there too, with Tommy, when they first came. It's just a motel room, really.' Melanie seemed to dig deep to find her words.

'Go on.'

'We only use the flat if one of the men, Angus or Max, need to stay over to be close to a sick animal. And since Bronte was born, I've been using the room as a sort of nap-area-come-play-room.' She took a deep shuddering breath. 'A few weeks ago, on a Saturday, I went in to do some bookwork. Sometimes it's easier when the clinic is closed. I had Bronte with me, Tif was with Ben. I took her into the flat, intending to put her on the bed for a nap. And I smelt it.' She wrinkled her nose.

'Smelt what?' Millie was mystified.

'Sex.' Melanie whispered the word.

'Sex?'

'Millie, the bed smelt like sex. I pulled the sheets back. And. Well. The bed has been used. For sex.' Melanie sniffled and Millie handed her a tissue. 'Rose and Meggie are two of my closest friends and one of their husbands is *having sex* at the clinic.'

'It does sound bad. But let's think this through. Is it possible one of them, Angus and Rose or Max and Meggie, are just having a little away-from-the-house-and-kids romp together? Who else has access?'

'Oh. I didn't think of that. Maybe. We all have a key. The staff.' Melanie's face seemed to lighten. 'Perhaps that's all it is.' Then she frowned. 'But Rose and Meggie know I use the bed for Bronte. I think they'd change the sheets.' She shook her head sadly. 'But the men mightn't do that. Change the sheets. Oh Millie, what should I do? Confront Angus and Max? Tell the girls?'

Millie leaned forward. 'It still doesn't seem right. Wait another week Melanie. You say you've noticed on a Saturday. Maybe someone else has found a way in and is using it as their own private love nest. It's possible.'

Slowly nodding, Melanie agreed. 'Okay. I'll wait. I've changed the sheets.' She looked up then. 'What if we all had dinner on Friday night at the pub? The gang? And I'll check next morning.'

'Good plan. Let's keep it between us for now. You don't know enough to confront anyone. And Melanie, whatever is going on is not your fault.' Millie spoke firmly but kindly.

'I know. But they're my best friends.' She looked across at Millie. 'Thank you. I feel better, having shared it. And we have a plan too. I can wait a week.'

'Good.'

16

HANNELORE

No one came in at all, and at exactly three she took the banana bread out of the oven, setting it on a tray to cool. Her tummy rumbled and she peeked out at the front counter. Empty. She opened the fridge and took out a chocolate brownie. She wasn't sure what time they'd have dinner, and she'd only had a coffee since breakfast. Taking a huge bite, she walked out the front to turn the sign to closed. She just needed another half hour for the banana bread to cool, before she could put it away.

Stepping to the door, she was almost knocked over as someone opened it from the outside at the same moment. The chocolate brownie slipped from her hand, landing on the front of her shirt. She looked up, to find Harry Stewart from last night standing there. He grinned. Then tried to straighten his face into a 'sorry' expression.

Hannelore tried to speak, but her mouth was full of brownie. *Why did she have to take such a huge, greedy bite?* And she knew her teeth would be covered in chocolate. Holding her hand in

80

front of her face, she mumbled, 'What are you doing here?' His eyes were dancing as they moved from her face to her chest and back. *What? Cheeky brute.*

She looked down. Her white shirt was covered in chocolate crumbs, and some had managed to wedge themselves in her cleavage, she could feel them there.

'Perhaps this is karma, Hanna. You know, me with my beer-sodden shirt and jeans last night. Now you with your, ah, shirt.' He laughed when she opened her mouth to speak. 'And your teeth Hanna. Chocolate brownie. Everywhere.'

She stepped back, letting him in, then closed the door and turned the open sign around. On the way to the counter with Harry trailing behind her, she frantically ran her tongue over her teeth to remove as much of the brownie as possible. Once behind the counter, she turned to him. 'I was just about to close up. But the coffee machine is still on if you'd like one?'

'Coffee would be great but only if you have one with me.' Harry gazed at her. *He really does have lovely eyes.* Shaking her head at her thoughts, she paused when he spoke again.

'Oh sorry. If you don't have time ...'

'I have time.' Laughing she reached for a cup. 'Let me guess. You're a double-shot cappuccino?'

'Sure. Why not.' He folded his arms over his broad chest and leaned back. His tone was light, as he squinted at her for a moment. 'And you're a chai latte because it's afternoon and you've had too many coffees already.'

Hannelore laughed then. *Damn him.* That's exactly what she was going to make for herself. 'You've got me there. A logical assumption, however. But you've scored a brownie point. Well, not a point, but a *piece* of brownie, if you'd like some?'

His eyes roved again to the front of her shirt. 'Do I, ah, need to excavate it myself?' He waggled an eyebrow. 'Not that I'd mind. But Hanna, we hardly know each other.'

'Stop it!' She had to stop making the latte, she was laughing so much. She relaxed. Sure, he was charming, like Anthony-the-narcissist had been. But somehow Harry Stewart was more wholesome. She wondered if she could trust him, get to know him. He seemed interested in her.

They drank their coffee and shared a brownie. Chatting quietly, Harry asked her if she was staying long in the area.

Hannelore looked at him for a moment. 'Maybe. Mum's here. I'm thinking about it.'

'Mum?' Harry looked confused.

Giggling, Hannelore said, 'I can't believe you don't know. Millie is my mum.'

'Oh!' He looked at her strangely for a moment. 'I've been away. I've only just met Millie, she's lovely. I can see the resemblance now. Lucy should have told me.'

'Lucy? How do you know Lucy?' It was her turn to look confused.

'She's my step-sister.' He grinned. 'I pick her up here at night after she cooks with you. If I had known, I might have come in, instead of waiting in the car.'

Hannelore stood and picked up their cups and plates. Turning away from him, she spoke over her shoulder, 'If you had known what?' *She was flirting. She knew it. He knew it.*

He walked to the front door. 'If I had known how gorgeous you are. And fun.' He opened the door. 'I'll see you very soon, Hanna Tucker; thank you for the coffee.'

———

Hannelore tried to relax on the way out to Finn's place. She held the container of strudel on her lap while Millie drove, pointing out a few landmarks before stopping at the entrance of Finn's driveway to show where his property started and ended. The lower ground was all vineyards, but the back seemed to go higher. It was tree-covered and pretty.

Pointing at the low hills, she turned to Millie. 'Horses? Are those horses way over?'

'Yes. Rescue animals mostly.' Millie slowed as they drove past a large shed with pretty gardens at the front, and outdoor seating. 'That's the cellar door. The other shed you can see behind is plant and equipment.' She stopped in front of a second two-level building, a bit like the cellar door on the outside. 'And this is Finn's. He lives upstairs. Luke has an apartment downstairs. And there's another apartment for seasonal workers.' Millie stepped out of the car, looking over the roof at Hannelore. 'When they're picking they have extra help.'

'Of course.' Hannelore nodded. 'Same at Margaret River over in the west.' She fidgeted with her dress for a moment. She was nervous. She'd met Finn a couple of times, but this was a family dinner. She wondered if Millie had told him the horrible things she'd said to her. She really wanted him to like her.

Walking behind Millie to the open front door, Finn met them with an expansive smile. He kissed Millie and hugged Hannelore, saying 'welcome to Barrington Ridge Wines.' She was surprised by the hug but pleased too. Her father had never been openly affectionate.

Upstairs she met Lucas. He asked her to call him Luke. He was a couple of years younger than Hannelore, and seemed a bit nervous too, although he was warm to Millie. The conversation flowed and Hannelore relaxed. Finn and Luke adored her strudel, with Luke having a second huge helping. He was very lean and Hannelore wondered exactly what he did in the business. A bit of everything, she supposed. She helped him clear the table and wash up, leaving Millie and Finn to chat quietly in the living area.

'Are you staying tonight Hanna?' Luke passed her the last pasta pot to dry up.

'No. Well, I don't think so.' She frowned, looking into the other room. Finn had his arm around her mum. 'Mum didn't mention it. I, um, didn't bring my stuff ...' She trailed off.

'All good. She doesn't always stay.' Lucas shrugged. 'But I can run you home if she wants to and you're uncomfortable. Although we have room.'

Back in the lounge, Hanna wanted to have a word with Millie, but there wasn't an opportunity. They chatted, and she liked the music playing in the background. Vintage stuff, but good. By nine she was tired, it had been a long day. She stifled a yawn, but Millie saw it.

Millie leaned into Finn beside her on the sofa for a moment. Hannelore marvelled at the way they were with each other. No tension and they liked teasing each other and making jokes. Very different to her memories of her parents together. Millie made the first move. 'We must go Finn, it's been a long day. Thank you very much for dinner.'

Hannelore stood up, feeling a bit awkward and not sure if Millie would rather stay. 'Yes, thank you very much, Finn.' She hugged him quickly, then turned to Lucas. 'And thank you too Luke, it's been great to meet you.'

'You too Hanna. But just so you know, I only like you because you make great strudel.' He grinned and Hanna laughed with him. He was a lot like Finn, and more mature than most younger men she'd met.

Finn walked downstairs with them and Hannelore hurried to the car, leaving her mum at the front door to say goodbye. Millie was in the car a minute or two later and they waved to Finn as they drove out.

'You could have stayed Mum, if you'd wanted. I would have driven home and picked you up in the morning.' Hannelore hoped her mum knew she wouldn't mind. Although she wouldn't have stayed herself.

'I know I could have. But coming home with you is just as nice.' Millie giggled then. 'Can I ask what you think? Now that you've met Luke too.'

'Oh, you want to have the girl-chat after the hot date?' Hannelore laughed. This was a side of her mum she'd never seen. *So funny.*

'I guess so. Do you mind?' Millie glanced at her and Hannelore chuckled. 'I don't want any gory details, Mum, but no, I don't mind. I like Finn. I like the way he treats you. It's different. And Luke is lovely. More mature than I expected.'

'Different?' Millie frowned.

'Watching you and Finn teasing each other, joking around...' Hannelore looked out her window, but all she could see were fences and paddocks as they drove by. She turned back to Millie. 'You and Dad *never* had that sort of relationship. It was always so. *Intense.* And not in a good way.'

Millie sighed then. 'I know. It's *easy* with Finn. I didn't know a relationship could be easy.'

'Easy. Yes, that's what it looks like. Easy.' Hannelore thought about it for a moment. 'My relationship with Anthony-the-pig was never easy Mum. It was hard. I'd like to try easy too, one day.' They could see the town lights, and Millie slowed down. Hannelore turned in her seat as Millie pulled into the car park behind their building. 'It's good for me to see you happy like this, Mum. It makes me realise I could be happy with the right person too.'

Millie locked the car and took Hannelore's hand as they walked to the back door. 'Good.' She spoke quietly. 'I want you to see a happy relationship first-hand.' Millie seemed to hesitate. 'You haven't said much about your relationship with Anthony, but I'm beginning to understand why you came here.'

Hannelore squeezed Millie's hand and simply nodded.

17

———

RACHAEL

Barrington Book Club – Rachael, Rose, Millie, Hannelore, Kristen, Melanie, Harriet, Meggie, Nicole
Apologies - Laura
Book – ***Lest We Forgive*** by Phillipa Nefri Clark

WALKING DOWN THE STAIRS, RACHAEL MARVELLED AT how much Robbie and Harry had done in a couple of weeks. The carpet had been pulled up, and the linoleum on the kitchen and bathroom floors. The kitchen cupboard doors had been taken off and the whole place seemed bigger. The main bedroom and living area faced east and were light filled, while the kitchen, bathroom and the small second bedroom were on the other side of the building. She was going to Taree with Nicole this week to choose fixtures and fittings for the bathroom and kitchen and choose appliances. She was really excited about the project.

Rachael locked the door after stepping into the street, then smiled hello at Rose, Meggie and Harriet. They'd arrived together and she could see a bottle of wine poking out of the top of Harriet's tote bag. She grinned. *Wine, good. She felt like celebrating.*

'Hi Rachael.' Meggie looked behind her. 'Oh, you've locked up. I wondered if we'd have time to take a peek?'

'There's not much to see yet Meggie. The floor coverings are out, and the kitchen is pulled apart. To be honest, Robbie's cracked on with it so quickly, I think it will be almost ready to let by next book club.' Rachael acknowledged their congratulations, as they walked through to the café.

Millie waved from the table at the back. She was setting down wine glasses and chatting with Melanie and Nicole. Rachael settled into her usual chair, facing the counter and front door. From the kitchen, Hannelore carried a charcuterie board in one hand, and Kristen followed with plates and napkins. 'Hi Rachael, how are you?' Kristen set a plate in front of her.

'Great, thank you Kristen.' She pointed to the beautifully laid-out board. 'This looks very tasty. Almost too good to eat.'

'Hanna's idea. She talked Millie into getting a few boards, to experiment with shared platters. I'm not sure I could lay it out this nicely though.' Kristen nudged Hannelore, and Rachael was amused to notice how she blushed at the praise.

Shrugging her shoulders, Hannelore waved away the kind words. 'It's getting warmer, so we were looking for ideas that don't require cooking, as such. Sometimes people just want a snack. A share platter for two, four or even six can offer up a variety that generally pleases everyone in the group.'

Millie had nipped back to the kitchen area, returning with a wine bucket for the bottle Harriet had produced. She laughed.

'Actually, we're experimenting on you. This is a platter for six. There's nine of us tonight, Laura's still away. I have a plate of sandwiches too, and a platter of sweet snacks. But I want to gauge how this is for a group, see if it's enough.'

'It's a lot of food Millie.' Rose leaned across, placing a selection of cold meats and cheese on her plate. 'But I'm sure we can demolish it. Lovely with a glass of wine.' She grinned. 'So happy we've all weaned our babies.' She looked at Meggie. 'It's just you Meggie, with little Dee.'

'Dee is brilliant, she's almost three months.' Meggie poked her tongue out at Rose. 'And I'm allowing myself a small glass of wine from time to time. I've expressed enough milk for the next twelve hours.'

Rachael clapped her hands. 'Well done Meggie. A small glass won't hurt.' She looked at Millie then. 'But one bottle between all of us won't go far. I can nip down to the bottle shop and pick up another.' She began to stand.

'Stop Rachael!' Millie held her hand up, laughing, and Rachael sat down. 'I have a case of Finn's wine in the cool room. We can grab one when we need it.'

They ate and chatted for half an hour. Rachael asked Nicole to describe the colours and style they'd selected for the apartment. Nicole simply picked up her iPad, flicking through until she found the mood boards they'd created together for the look. She shared them with the others and they all seemed impressed. Hannelore asked a few questions, as did Harriet. But they loved the concept and Rachael felt sure it would be a success. Worst case scenario, they could leave it as long-term accommodation, if short-term didn't work.

'And the book? *Lest we Forgive*?' Hannelore spoke up. 'I'd

already read it, so Mum has my copy.' She lifted the book in front of her, turning it so they could see the cover. 'This is the second one and I'm almost finished. It's called *Lest Bridges Burn*.'

Rose leaned forward. 'Phillipa Nefri Clark has written in a few genres and I especially love her small-town stuff, although the Rivers End series also has a mystery in each one. But this one, this series,' she looked at Hannelore, 'yes, I've read all three, and I'm waiting on the next one. These are as good as any crime fiction I've read. She writes so well...' Rose seemed to trail off, and Rachael leaned forward.

'What Rose?'

Rose shook her head. 'Sometimes I doubt myself. There are so many good books around. So many Aussie authors creating original, compelling fiction.' Looking sheepish, she added. 'I don't know.'

'You're right Rose. There is a huge pool of talent and a great number of books to choose from.' Harriet spoke firmly and Rachael found herself nodding in agreement. 'And yours are right up there. Don't doubt yourself. *Your* words are compelling. I can't get enough of your stories. And I want more.'

'Oh me too!' This was Hannelore. Rachael looked at her with interest, the younger woman was leaning towards Rose, one hand across the table, touching Rose's arm. 'Your books are brilliant Rose. Really they are. When Mum told me she *knew* you, I almost wet myself with excitement. You're one of my favourite writers. Ever!'

Rachael laughed and turned to Rose. 'Couldn't have said it better myself, darling Rose.' And was pleased to see everyone echoing Hannelore's sentiments.

Rose picked up her glass and took a sip. Rachael saw she was close to tears. 'Stop it. All of you. You'll make me cry.' Rose turned to Hannelore. 'And you've just made my week. Month. Year. Thank you.'

'Uh-huh. That's all good.' Melanie made a funny face. 'Love you, Rose.' She tapped her phone and Rachael wondered what she'd say next. 'But did anyone else *listen* to this book?' They shook their heads and she continued. 'It's narrated by. Wait for it. John Woods.'

'John Woods? The actor?' Rachael was surprised. He was Australian acting royalty.

'Yes. John Woods. Oh my gosh. He's sooo good. His voice....' Melanie rolled her eyes and they all laughed.

'I really need to try audiobooks.' Rachael said it aloud and Melanie looked across. 'Yes, you do, Rach. Yes you do.'

They chatted about the book a little more and Rachael drank her wine and relaxed. She loved this group of women. And having the young ones join them now, Hannelore and Kristen, was refreshing.

They chose *The Accident* by Fiona Lowe as their next read. Rachael was looking forward to it. But then, she'd read anything these women recommended.

The second bottle of wine finished, the book discussed and the platter almost empty, they began to say their goodnights and drift away. Rachael found herself outside with Rose, Meggie and Harriet, watching Hannelore and Millie walk up the street.

'It's been lovely. Thank you girls.' Rachael leaned forward and gave Rose a hug.

'Rachael?' Harriet was peering in the window of the little gift shop on the opposite side of the front door to the café. 'Is Greta getting out of the business?'

'No.' Rachael joined her at the window. 'Not that I'm aware of.' She looked through the window. There was very little stock on display. 'She's been away quite a lot. Her mum lives in Victoria and has been unwell.' Rachael frowned. She needed to check if Greta was up to date with the rent. Steve would know. Losing a tenant right now would be poor timing, as they were expending quite a lot on the renovation upstairs.

'It's a good position, Rachael, although smallish.' Harriet placed a hand on her shoulder. 'If Greta does want to get out, we'll find someone to go in, don't worry.'

Walking home, Rachael worried despite Harriet's comment. Buying the building had been a decision of the heart for Rachael, rather than a well-thought-out plan. But Steve was strategic, and at the time, he said they'd be fine. But he had budgeted for rent from the professional rooms upstairs. Rachael knew they had sunk their superannuation money into the building and didn't have a loan, but losing the rent from the gift shop was problematic with the apartment renovation expenses. Standing in front of her house Rachael paused. *What's the worst that can happen?* Sighing, she pushed open the garden gate. If Debbie were here, she'd tell her to keep the faith. Rachael put her hand to her chest and hurried inside. *It will be okay.*

18

HARRY

Harry worked at Nicole's carriage shed project at the start of the week, supervising the plumber and electrician and installing the kitchenette, while Robbie sanded the timber floors at Rachael's project. Harry had wanted to do the work in town, to see Hanna at the coffee shop again. But Robbie had more experience with floor sanding. Robbie had asked why he was so keen to be in town, but Harry wasn't prepared to admit anything. Not yet, anyway.

But on Friday he was back upstairs in the old bank building, painting the interior. They'd sanded back all the architraves and skirting boards to the original cedar, and he was now painting the timber vee-jay walls a light colour called *clotted cream* up to the picture rail and *dove grey* above.

The pressed metal ceilings were twelve feet high and painted white. The main bedroom was large, with white ceilings and very pale sage-green walls.

Rachael and Nicole had said the floors would remain bare

except in the kitchen and bathroom, which would be tiled. They were buying large rugs for the living area and bedroom. The whole apartment already had ducted air conditioning from its time as Douglas Barlow's office.

Harry straightened and rolled his shoulders back before looking at his watch. It was morning tea time, so it wouldn't hurt to wander down to the café to get a cold drink. He'd take a fifteen-minute break. Robbie should be in then, and maybe Nicole. They wanted to measure up the small bedroom for walk-in-robe cupboards. A bit of a waste, Harry thought. It could be a second bedroom or maybe a study. But what did he know? Short-term guests probably didn't need that. But they wouldn't need a massive wardrobe either.

He saw Hannelore as he stepped inside the café. She was chatting to a group to one side, taking orders.

Millie was at the counter. 'Hi Harry. Have you been working upstairs?'

'Yep. I came in early before you opened. Painting today.' Harry pointed to the banana bread in the display. 'Can I get an iced coffee and a slice of that please Millie?'

'Sure. Takeaway?' Millie took his money.

'No, I'm taking a break. I'll just sit over by the window.' He pointed to a spot where he could people-watch. *Hannelore-watch you mean.* He chuckled to himself.

'Take a seat; it will be right out, Harry.' Millie bustled around and he sat down, pulling his phone from his pocket. From the corner of his eye he could see Hannelore heading back to the kitchen. He'd hoped she'd come over and say hello. But she was working. He got that.

Turning his attention to his phone, he lost track of time and was startled when Hannelore placed his drink and snack in front of him.

'Hello Harry Stewart.' She had her hands on her hips.

Flicking his phone off, he grinned at her. 'Hanna. Thank you.' She didn't move but raised an eyebrow. *What?* 'Just taking a break from painting. Upstairs.' Now he was rambling, but the look in her eye made him nervous.

'It's Friday, Harry. I get it. Just swiping, hey? A little bit left. A little bit right?' Her tone was light, but Harry caught an under-tone of *something*. And now she thinks he was checking the phone for a Friday-night-hook-up. *Damn.*

'Yeah. Sure.' He pointed to the phone. 'Do you, er, ever?'

'No Harry, you won't find my profile there.' She turned on her heel. 'Enjoy your morning tea.'

And now he *felt* like a heel. What if he was? Swiping. But he knew it made him look like a player, and now he was sorry he'd looked at his phone at all. And then it vibrated, jiggling across the table. Harry picked it up quickly, glancing across the room to see where Hannelore was. At the counter and looking right at him. *Damn.*

'Hello mate.' He spoke quietly. It was Callum.

'Want to catch up at the pub tonight Harry?' Callum sounded keen.

'Well, I can mate. But I thought you were going to ask Kristen. Maybe you should go stag tonight.' Harry wanted to give Callum a nudge towards Kristen.

'No. Mate. I *need* you.' Now he sounded desperate. 'Kristen will only come if Hanna comes too. She wanted you to come.'

'Hanna wants me to come?' He searched for Hannelore. She was clearing a table up the back. He could feel himself grinning.

'No mate. *Kristen* wants you to come.' Harry deflated. And Callum sounded exasperated.

'Um. I'm at the café now. I'll check with Hanna and call you back.' Harry finished the banana bread. He knew Hannelore had baked it. It was so good he wanted to lick his fingers. But he didn't. He used the serviette she'd set down with the plate. Downing the last of his drink, he stood up. Picking up the glass and the plate, intending to take them to the kitchen, Hannelore was beside him again. *Stealthy.*

'Thanks Harry, but I'll take those.' Hannelore laughed at his expression. 'I've seen you drop stuff, remember?'

That was more like it. He didn't mind a bit of teasing if it meant she wasn't looking at him with suspicion. Holding his phone up, he said, 'That was Callum. It seems he and Kristen are meeting at the pub. They've requested my company.'

'Oh yeah, I know.' She rolled her eyes. 'Kristen's so shy, she won't go alone.' She shook her head. 'Honestly, what is it with those two?'

Harry defended his mate. 'Callum's a good bloke. And he's liked Kristen for a long time. He doesn't want to rush her or screw it up. Unless it *bothers* you, I'll come along.'

'You don't bother me, Harry. But what happened to your hot date?' She jerked her chin at the phone in his hand.

'Mates code of honour. Callum needs me.' He wasn't going down that particular rabbit hole, standing in the middle of a busy café. 'I'd better get going.' He jerked his chin to the ceiling. 'I'm painting today.'

He was amazed to see her expression change completely, interest lighting up her face. She stepped closer. 'Do you think I could sneak up? Have a peek?' She was so close he could smell her hair. A citrus fragrance, fresh. He'd agree to just about anything.

'Um, sure. If you can be spared for a few minutes.' Millie was at the counter. She waved and Hannelore shot over, speaking quickly to her.

Harry couldn't catch what Millie said, but Hannelore bounced back to him, saying, 'I've got ten minutes. Come on.'

Harry opened the door and she ran lightly up the stairs in front of him. He told himself not to stare at her bum. But he stared anyway.

She was jiggling on the spot outside the apartment door. He opened it slowly, liking the way she lit up when he did. 'Enjoy a bit of renovation, do you Hanna?'

'Yes. No.' She shook her head as she stepped inside, gazing around the main room. 'I have no experience, but I love our rooms over the post office, and I'm really curious about this place.'

Harry walked her through the apartment, describing Nicole's idea of creating 'rooms' using furnishings in the large main room.

'Oh, that's clever. Keep it open plan but make cosy areas. I love the light that comes in here.' She followed him into the kitchen, and he told her they were putting on new cupboard doors and a new benchtop, but keeping it as a kitchenette rather than a full kitchen. She asked about the colour scheme, and he admitted he wasn't sure about the kitchen.

In the main bedroom, she turned around. 'I love the colour in here. So pretty.' She touched the floor. 'Lovely, but it will need rugs.' He nodded and led her to the small second bedroom that he hadn't painted. As he did, Robbie arrived with Rachael and Nicole.

Harry popped out of the room, Hannelore behind him. He

didn't have to explain her presence but did anyway. 'I went down for morning tea, and, uh, Hanna was keen to have a peek.'

'I love it.' Hannelore walked across to Rachael. 'I can picture it already. The paint you've chosen is perfect. Subtle, but pretty. I can't wait to see it furnished.'

Rachael looked pleased. 'Thank you Hanna. It's mostly Nicole's ideas.'

'Not really Rach.' Nicole dropped some fabric samples on the floor. 'You chose the bedroom colour.'

Robbie had his tape measure out and a brochure on modular wardrobes in his hand. 'I'm going to measure up in the small room.' He moved off.

Hannelore had begun to move to the door, but she spun around. 'What? You're making the small room into a wardrobe?' she wrinkled her nose, then looked at Rachael and Nicole. 'It will be huge, and overkill for short-term visitors.'

Rachael nodded. 'I know. But what else do we do with it? Make it into a small bedroom, that will rarely be used?' Nicole nodded in agreement.

Hannelore looked disappointed and mumbled 'okay' as she waved and moved towards the door again.

'Wait Hanna.' Nicole spoke firmly. 'What would *you* do with it? The small room?'

'Really? You want me to tell you?' Spinning around, Hannelore almost ran back to the room in question. They followed her. 'The window is large, with a lovely view. I'd build in a big window seat right here, with lots of cushions. It would make the best reading nook. And on each side of the window, some built-in bookshelves. There's not a lot of room, but they will frame the window seat beautifully. And it faces west, so white shutters over the window, that can open right up for light and warmth, especially in winter.'

Harry was leaning on the door jamb just inside the door. He could picture it. It would be a really inviting spot, for a reader. But Hannelore hadn't finished.

'One big soft armchair, a side table and a little desk and chair against that wall on the side.' She turned back to Rachael, waving her hands around. 'I can see it already.' Then she stopped. 'I'm sorry. It's just an idea. It's a room I'd spend time in.' Her voice faltered.

Rachael stepped forward, putting an arm around Hannelore's shoulders. 'I can see it too, Hanna. You've described it so well and it's beautiful and provides a separate space for someone to read, or work, and would be really cosy in winter.' She turned to Nicole. 'What do you think, Nik? Why didn't we come up with this idea?'

Nicole laughed and clapped her hands. 'Honestly, I think it's going to be the room that sells the place to visitors. I'm so glad you came up for a look, Hanna.' She turned to Robbie. 'Can you measure up a window seat and the bookshelves Robbie? I'm picturing timber painted white with white shutters. And navy on the walls behind the bookshelves.'

'And a lighter blue on the other walls? Duck egg blue?' Rachael had a hand to her chin as she questioned Nicole.

'Yes.' Nicole clapped her hands.

Hannelore looked at her watch and jumped. 'Holy guacamole! I've been gone nearly thirty minutes. Mum will be swamped.' She ran from the room, waving and saying, 'bye everyone, bye Harry, see you tonight.'

Harry felt his face fill with colour and turned away, taking the end of the tape measure from Robbie. Rachael and Nicole wandered back into the other room.

'Tonight, hey son?' Robbie nudged him with his shoulder.

'It's nothing. We're keeping Callum and Kristen company at the pub. That's all.' Harry tried to make his tone casual. But Robbie knew him well.

'I'll see you there tonight too.'

Now Harry was surprised. 'You will?'

'We're catching up with a few people. A lot of people actually, including Millie and Finn. Lucy is going to babysit for Melanie and Ben.'

'Oh. Good.' But Harry didn't really mean it.

19

———

FREDDIE

FREDDIE WAS AT THE PUB AGAIN, BUT NOT HIDING THIS time. She was meeting her brothers and Kristen Laing for dinner. Douggie told her it was a date. Callum and Kristen. Freddie hadn't wanted to go then, but Douggie said Harry Stewart would be there too, which suddenly made it interesting.

Her lover was meeting her at their usual spot, after dinner. Freddie had tossed up whether to invite him, then she remembered how she'd made Harry Stewart squirm when she'd flirted, just a bit. *This should be fun.*

The night was warm, so she wore a maxi-dress - low cut, sleeveless and fitted to the waist, before dropping to her ankles, her feet encased in flat leather sandals. The dark green gingham set off her flame-red hair, which flowed over her shoulders in loose waves. Discarding the jeans and boots she usually wore, Freddie felt feminine in the dress and knew it suited her fair complexion.

Running a few minutes late, Freddie parked behind the pub and walked through from the back. Once inside the bistro area, she gazed around. There was a large table with a big group already seated, including Rose Gordon. Freddie waved and would have walked over, but she heard Callum call her name.

Turning, she saw them in a booth. Callum and Kristen, Harry and Douggie and a blonde girl she didn't know. She was sitting beside Harry, with Douggie, Kristen and Callum on the other side of the table.

'Hello big brothers.' Freddie grinned. Callum slid out of the booth and hugged her, whispering 'thanks for coming' in her ear.

'Hey, Sis.' Douggie grinned at her, a glass of beer in his hand.

'Hi Freddie.' Kristen smiled, then pointed to the other girl. 'This is Hanna.'

'Hello Hanna, nice to meet you.' Then she nudged Harry. 'Slide over Harry Stewart.'

Harry slid closer to Hanna, and Freddie sat next to him, letting her thigh touch his as she did. He moved his leg. Freddie chuckled to herself. *This was going to be so much fun.*

'Wine Freddie? Or a beer?' Kristen nodded at the open wine bottle in the ice bucket near Hanna. The other girls were drinking wine, and Freddie preferred beer. *But when in Rome.*

'Wine is great, thank you.' Freddie watched Harry reach for the bottle, filling the empty glass in front of her. Looking at Harry through her lashes, she murmured, 'Thank you, Harry.'

'Has your year almost finished Freddie?' Kristen was lovely, including her in the conversation. Freddie decided she was a good match for Callum.

'Yes, just a couple of weeks to go, then I'm home and working at the practice here for the next couple of months.' Freddie sipped her wine. It was a bit dry for her; she hadn't learned to appreciate wine yet.

'Freddie's doing Vet Science. She's been working at the local clinic since High School. Angus, and Max, too, have been very encouraging.' Hearing the pride in Douggie's voice as he explained this to Hanna, warmed Freddie's heart. She was lucky with her brothers. The older four were married, but they all lived in the area.

'Oh, well done Freddie, that's a lot of study. Do you have a particular interest, like a specialty, or will you be a country Vet?' Hanna smiled warmly, but Freddie was cautious. She took a while to warm to strangers.

'Equine, horses, will always be my first love, but I think I'll be a country Vet. I'm hoping the practice here might be big enough for me when I'm ready.' Freddie smiled at her brothers. 'Then I can be close to home, keep a horse of my own at the farm.' She waved her arms at the larger group on the other side of the room, where Vet Angus Hamilton and his partner Max Masters sat with their wives. 'I ride Rose's horses when I'm home.'

'Oh really? Rose has horses?' Freddie watched the other girl's face light up. *Interesting.* She also saw Harry looking at Hanna with interest, after she mentioned horses. *Are they together?*

'Yes. She's an excellent stock woman herself. But with the children now, has trouble finding time.' Freddie responded, then asked a question of her own. 'Do you ride, Hanna?' She saw the other girl swallow, before answering.

'Not really. I mean, I have a few times. But I've never owned a horse. But if I stay here, in Barrington, it's something I'd be keen to do.' Hanna changed the subject then, picking up a menu. 'Pizzas? Are we sharing?'

They all began speaking at once, and Freddie leaned into Harry, who held a menu for the three of them to look at. She pressed her breast against his bicep, and he was stuck unless he slid closer to Hanna. He looked at her, a small frown between his eyes, but she just smiled sweetly and pointed to the menu. 'Margarita for me. And maybe a garlic pizza to start, if you're all keen.'

Douggie, always a big eater, answered straight away. 'Garlic pizza, and I'm for a meat lovers.' They chose two more, and Douggie and Harry went to order. As Freddie stood up to let Harry out, she offered him some cash, but he shook his head. Douggie spoke up. 'Put your money away Sis, I've got this.'

Callum and Kristen were speaking quietly together, so Freddie turned to Hanna. 'What brings you to Barrington, Hanna?'

'Mum is here. Millie Tucker. At the café.' Hanna smiled, and Freddie saw just how pretty the slightly older girl was.

'Oh, of course. I know Millie. Not well, but the café is my favourite coffee place when I'm at home and working at the Clinic.' Freddie grinned. *So she's not here for Harry.* Hasn't followed him from up north or wherever he was.

The rest of the night was fun as they all chatted and laughed together. Freddie felt sorry for Hanna a few times, when they talked about their high school days and some of the antics her brothers, and Harry, had gotten up to. She might have felt left-out but she seemed happy to listen and take it all in and laughed along with them. Freddie thought she could quite like Hanna. And she'd always liked Kristen. Liked her whole family. It was obvious to her that Callum and Kristen were at the start of something. *Good. Callum deserves to be happy.* She wondered if Douggie fancied Hanna, but he didn't pay her any more attention than he did anyone else, so she thought not.

So that left Harry. He was attentive to Hanna, but not overly.

And they seemed to know each other a little bit. But Freddie could sense they weren't together. *Unless they were really good at hiding it like she was.* That made Harry fair game. Freddie chatted with Harry more than the others and sat close enough that part of her body was always lightly touching part of his. No one else noticed, but he shifted a few times, just a little, in his seat and she knew he was trying to signal her to stop. *Stop what? Talking? Flirting surreptitiously?* She also knew that he was having a physical response to her, otherwise he wouldn't be uncomfortable and move away.

Sitting quietly for a moment as the others chatted together, she studied Harry. Tall. Broad shouldered. Dark hair and suntanned skin. His biceps were almost too large for the shirt he wore, with the sleeves rolled above the elbow. *Harry Stewart was hot.* She wondered if he would be interested in a little dalliance with her. She thought he'd have some experience. *Could be fun.* Then her phone vibrated and she remembered where she was, and who she was going to meet.

Checking her watch, she saw it was almost nine. She had to go. Finishing the wine in front of her, she looked across at Callum. 'I'm off Cal. Thanks for dinner, Douggie. Goodnight.' She stood, making sure her goodnight took in all of them.

'Are you heading home now Hanna?' Douggie looked towards the bar. 'I might catch up with a couple of mates for a beer, but I'll be home soon.'

'Yeah. I'll go home now.' She leaned around Harry, pressing her chest against his arm again. 'See ya soon, Hanna, in the café. I'll be home over the summer.'

The other girl smiled. 'Lovely to meet you, Freddie. Yes, I look forward to it.'

He was waiting. She walked into his arms. 'Ssh. Can't be long. I told the boys I was heading home.'

'When are we going to stop sneaking around Freddie?' He sounded exasperated.

'Soon. Now kiss me.'

20

MILLIE

With seven couples at their table, it was noisy. Millie and Finn were at one end, with Melanie and Ben closest to them. Robbie and Nicole were on one side of the table, with Rachael and Steve facing them. The three younger couples were at the other end, but Millie loved how they all interacted. Sometimes there were several conversations going at once and at other times, like when Steve talked about the changes to the regional planning scheme, everyone listened, then asked questions.

Finn knew Ben well, and Robbie had worked on the buildings out at the winery. Finn was good with people. Relaxed, and sometimes really funny. While the men were talking, she leaned closer to Melanie. 'Any signs of, uh, visitors, at the clinic flat this week Mel?'

'No. It is strange. Always the weekend. I still haven't said anything to Ben, but when we leave tonight I'm going to tell him I need to get something from the clinic. So I'll check.' She looked around the table and then back at Millie. 'Angus and Max are here.

So if there's any activity I'll know it's not them.' She drew in a sharp breath. 'Oh gosh Millie. I hope it's not them.'

'Me too Mel. But watching them tonight, the way they look at their girls, I just can't believe it would be either of them. There has to be another explanation.' Millie gestured towards the other end of the table where Angus had his arm resting along the back of Rose's seat, his hand gently rubbing her upper arm. Meggie had left her chair, and was perched on Max's knee, speaking animatedly with Harriet.

The group ordered a la carte, rather than sharing pizzas, and Millie was pleased. The grilled barramundi steak and salad were delicious. She'd cut a bit off to give to Finn, exclaiming over the lemon myrtle sauce. In return, he placed a couple of garlic prawns from his pasta onto her plate. She giggled and he looked at her, eyebrows raised.

'What?'

'This.' Millie waved her fork at their meals. 'Meal sharing. I thought only old married couples do that.' She laughed again, not realising Melanie had been listening.

'Oh, we do it all the time. And Ben will finish off anything I can't eat.' She looked fondly at her husband, definitely the tallest man at the table. 'My man likes his food.'

After their meals were cleared, some of them moved around the table. Somehow the women ended up together at Millie's end. Rachael looked at the men at the other end, now talking about the saleyards development. 'It's a typical Australian night. A few beers, or wines, and they gravitate to their mates.'

Harriet nudged Rachael. 'It's not so bad Rach. Sometimes we like to have a chat away from their man-ears.' Millie topped up their wine glasses, except for Meggie who was drinking soda.

'A sip or two at book club is one thing, but I'm driving the six of us home tonight. We're in Drum's car. I'm not taking any risks.' Meggie sipped her soda.

Harriet turned to Rachael. 'By the way, did you find out what's going on with Greta? Her shop hasn't been open at all this week.'

Rachael sighed. 'Yes. She's closing down. She's moving in with her mum in Victoria, who is quite sick as I understand it. She has continued to pay rent, right up to the end of this month, but she's not renewing her lease. It's quite a small shop, not suited to much other than a gift shop or florist, or possibly a babywear shop. I can't think of anything else we need in town at the moment. The garden centre is hiring a florist, and they're going to do a bit more giftware once Greta finishes.'

'That's good, though. At least we'll still have a florist and giftware.' Millie glanced across to where Hannelore was sitting with the young ones. They were laughing and chatting and she saw they were sharing pizzas. She'd made some friends already and was talking about staying. Millie was pleased. It had crossed her mind that the shop next door could be a good little bakery, specialising in pastries and fancy fare. For Hannelore. But as soon as it crossed her mind, she dismissed it. If Hannelore wanted to start a small business in specialty baked goods, perhaps wedding cakes too, she could run it from the café without the overheads, or risk. It was something she'd like to offer her, once she was a bit more settled.

'There's something we don't have in Barrington, that I'd love. But I'm not sure the town is large enough to support it.' Rose lifted her glass, her expression sombre.

'Really? What Rose?' Rachael tuned in straight away. 'What business *wouldn't* work in Barrington?'

'A bookshop. There hasn't been one here for years. People buy online now or pick up books from the chain stores in Taree and Forster.' Rose smiled at Meggie. 'That's what we do for book club.'

'A bookshop.' Rachael seemed surprised but interested. She looked across at Nicole. 'What are your thoughts Nik?'

'I'd love a bookshop.'

Melanie quickly chimed in. 'Me too.'

Millie nodded. 'And me. I still prefer paperbacks. And Hanna is a huge reader. Sometimes she has a book in eBook, audio and paperback because she loves it so much.'

Harriet had looked thoughtful through this exchange. She set her glass down. 'A bookshop. You're right, the town probably isn't big enough on its own. It needs to be niche.'

Rose cleared her throat. 'I'm not sure if this is niche Harriet. But you know I'm an Indie author? So I self-publish, which I love. But the biggest problem for Indie authors, the hardest thing, is to get our books into bookstores. That's the domain of traditional publishers. Yes, I have my books in a few small independent stores and, of course, all the online retailers, but there's nowhere here for readers to buy my paperbacks unless they come to me directly. I'm a local author without a local book store.' She shook her head sadly. 'I get it. Margins are small so it's about volume, and this town hasn't got the population. But we do get a lot of visitors. It's a thriving tourist town.'

'I've thought about it Rose. Selling your books in the café. But I don't have any other gift lines, so I haven't followed through.' Millie looked at Rachael. 'But I have thought about it.'

'I love the idea. A bookshop. But finding someone willing to take it on. I don't know Rose. I'll talk to Steve about it.' Rachael glanced at her watch. 'It's almost nine; Steve has to be in Taree first thing tomorrow; he'll be wanting to head off.'

Steve and Rachael left, then the six young ones. Millie noticed young Freddie Campbell had left, and Callum's brother had gone to the bar. Hanna was over there with Harry, Kristen and Callum. They were having dessert and she heard Hanna laugh. *Good. That's a nice friendship group, right there.*

Half an hour later Millie and Finn were still at the table with Ben and Melanie. Robbie and Nicole had left shortly after the others. Hannelore and her group had left. Harry had gone out the back, most likely to his car, and Hannelore walked out through the front door with Callum and Kristen.

'We might head off.' Melanie looked pointedly at Millie.

'Oh, us too.' Millie blushed. 'I'm going home with Finn tonight. His car is out the back near yours.'

Finn chuckled. 'We're old enough to stay at each other's place without embarrassment Millie.' He leaned in. 'But I don't mind when you blush like that.' He winked. 'I have plans.'

Millie gave him a little push, laughing. 'Stop it. I know it's okay. I'm just not used to it.'

Ben threw back his head and laughed. 'She's not saying no, Finn.'

21

———

HARRY

BLOODY FREDDIE CAMPBELL. SHE'D FLIRTED WITH HIM all night. It was so obvious. And if it was obvious to him, it would have been to Callum and Douggie. *He'd never go there.* She was playing with fire. *He'd* never follow through, but another man might. She knew she'd been pushing his buttons and he was pretty sure she's done it before. Little Freddie Campbell was no angel, of that he was very sure. But the thing that bothered him most was Hannelore's reaction. She'd raised her eyebrows a couple of times and he'd grimaced, trying to let her know the flirting was one-sided. She'd been pleasant all night, but Harry suspected she'd been hurt before. Maybe her last boyfriend was a player. And now she thought he was too. At this rate, he'd end up in her *friend zone*, and that's the last place he wanted to be.

He'd offered to walk her home, but Callum was parked on the main street, and Kristen said they'd see her to her door. Quietly seething, he'd walked through the back of the pub to his car. He backed out of the car park and headed down the laneway that ran behind the commercial buildings. He stopped when he saw Freddie's little Suzuki Jimny parked behind the Vet clinic. *What are you doing here, minx? You said you were going home to the farm half an hour ago.*

Harry was going to drive on, but curiosity and a little bit of anger over her earlier behaviour got to him. He needed to have a talk to her and tell her to stop messing around with him. It was never going to happen.

He parked his Ute and walked quietly to the back door of the clinic. It was unlocked. *Of course, Freddie would have a key, she works here in the holidays.* Harry opened the door quietly. He suspected she was meeting someone. Someone she couldn't tell her brothers about.

Stepping into the back entrance, he looked at the door of what he assumed was the flat. The light was on in there, he could see it under the door. The rest of the building was in darkness. Taking a deep breath, preparing himself for possible conflict, Harry opened the door. Freddie was lying on her side on the bed, her back to him, naked. 'Freddie.' His voice was stern. 'Get dressed!'

She jumped up, not even trying to hide her nakedness, just as the young bloke, the one he'd seen at the pub with her weeks ago, stepped out of the bathroom. He had jeans on and was doing his shirt up. He looked startled, then scared, then determined. *Bloody hell!*

The young bloke looked at Harry belligerently. 'Who are you?'

Freddie was dressing now with her back to him. She snarled. 'You can't be here Harry Stewart. Are you spying on me?'

Harry leaned on the wall, ignoring Freddie and looked at the other man. 'More to the point. Who are you?'

Freddie turned around, her dress on and her hair messed up.

CHAPTER 21

She was angry, her eyes filled with tears. She yelled at her lover. 'Get out! Go! Quickly!' He looked like he wanted to say something, but she pointed at the door and screamed, 'Get out! Now!' He left.

Freddie turned to Harry, her face almost as red as her hair. 'You've ruined it. You've ruined everything! Why couldn't you mind your own business?'

'Freddie. Stop.' He stepped over and held her shoulders. 'What you're doing is wrong. You know it, or you wouldn't be sneaking around like this.' She began to cry and he drew her to him, patting her back. He never knew what to do when a woman cried. 'Come on Freddie. You need to go home.' He looked at the bed. It was messed up. It was obvious the lad was her lover. Harry didn't know what to do or say.

At that moment, the door opened, framing Ben and Melanie Evans.

'Harry!' Ben roared. 'What the fuck?'

Harry released Freddie who fell into Melanie's arms, crying profusely. 'Freddie. You? I can't believe it. And Harry. She's a bit young isn't she?' Melanie looked shocked.

Freddie looked at Melanie, speaking between sobs. 'We. Cant. Tell. My brothers. They'll. Kill him.'

Harry began to speak, but Ben held his hand up. 'Go home, Harry.' Ben turned to Freddie. 'I can see this is consensual Freddie. But if you can't tell your family who you're seeing, then you shouldn't be seeing him.'

Freddie suddenly looked terrified. She turned to Melanie. 'Please don't tell Angus and Max. Please. I don't want to lose my job.'

Melanie looked uncertain. 'I'm not sure about that Freddie.

I'll think about it. I'm very disappointed in you.' She looked at Harry. 'But even more in you.'

There was no point explaining. And he still didn't know the name of Freddie's boyfriend. Harry left. But he hated the cloud of suspicion that left with him.

22

HANNELORE

AT FIRST, SHE'D BEEN AMUSED BY THE YOUNGER woman's antics. Her flirting was obvious. Kristen saw it too. But Freddie's brothers seemed oblivious. Harry was uncomfortable, and Hannelore thought he wasn't enjoying the younger woman's attentions. But she had to admit, the girl was gorgeous. And very bold.

But as the night wore on it became a bit tedious. And Harry didn't do much to stop Freddie. When he offered to walk her to her door at the end of the night, Hannelore might have, but then she remembered him messing with his phone. Maybe Freddie was his hot date, his booty-call. She didn't know him well enough to be sure. So she left with Kristen and Callum.

Callum said good night, then walked to his car. Kristen stayed at the door with Hannelore for a moment. 'There's something I'd like to talk to you about at work tomorrow.' Then she ran to the car, getting in quickly. Callum pulled away from the kerb slowly and they both waved.

Hannelore let herself into the apartment. Millie had gone to Finn's. She didn't mind, she liked having the flat to herself. But she was kinda glad Finn hadn't come here after the pub. *That would be awkward.* Out of sight out of mind worked for her.

Slipping into boxers and a tee, Hannelore curled up on the sofa with her book.

23

FREDDIE

Freddie was out of sorts as she parked at the stables at Barrington Homestead the next day. She'd waved to Angus as she drove in and he was heading out. Briefly, she wondered if Rose was home. *And if she knew.*

The horses trotted into the yard when she called them. Freddie threw some hay into the feeder. Walking among them as they ate, she calmed down. Freddie stroked Cotton, rubbing her shoulder and neck. The buckskin mare lifted her head from the hay and nudged Freddie, drawing her lips back to nibble at her hand. Freddie laughed and produced a small apple from her pocket, which the horse took with her teeth, nodding her head up and down as she chewed.

Tying Cotton's lead rope to the fence, Freddie brushed her gently, then nipped into the stables to retrieve a saddle and bridle. Most of the other horses wandered out of the yard once the hay had been eaten. The routine of saddling Cotton further soothed

Freddie's wounded soul. 'Wounded pride, really.' The mare nodded as she spoke as if she agreed.

Opening the gate to the laneway, Freddie led Cotton through, closed the gate and mounted in one quick movement. With a gentle nudge of her heels, the mare broke into a trot before cantering past the home paddock full of young stock to the track that led to the creek.

Freddie relaxed, enjoying the warm breeze against her face and the gentle rocking movement beneath her. But she thought back to the night before. To her humiliation. First Harry walked in on them, then Melanie and Ben appeared. The worst part was the conversation this morning with Melanie at her house. She had demanded Freddie drop in and speak with her, so she could decide whether to tell Angus and Max.

'What on earth were you thinking Freddie?' Melanie placed a cup of tea in front of her, but her tone was exasperated. And slightly angry.

Shaking her head, Freddie had replied. 'I wasn't thinking Melanie. I'm sorry. It will never happen again.'

'Do you have your key to the clinic with you Freddie?' Melanie was stern. Freddie had never heard her speak like this to anyone.

'Yes.' Freddie took her keys from her pocket, removed one, and placed it gently on Melanie's kitchen table. 'Are you going to tell Angus? And Max?' This was her biggest fear; that she would lose her holiday job and the opportunity to join the firm full-time once she was a qualified Vet.

'I haven't decided.' Melanie pressed her lips together in disapproval, before taking a sip of her own tea. 'I need more information. How long have you been using the flat as.' She stopped, sighing loudly. 'As a place to have sex. I was going to say as a love-nest, but Freddie,' she narrowed her eyes this time, 'I have the feeling it's more about the sneaking around, isn't it?'

That had surprised Freddie. She hadn't expected Melanie to be so blunt. Looking Melanie in the eye, Freddie decided to tell the truth. Or most of the truth, anyway. 'It's not easy having six older brothers Melanie. They'd always told me they'd beat up any boy who showed interest in me. I believed them for a long time. And if their intention was to make me too nervous to date, it probably worked. And their threats, whether serious or not, also stopped local boys from asking me out. My brothers had them bluffed.'

'Until you went away to university. Right?' Melanie's expression had softened, but only slightly.

'Yeah. It wasn't until I went off to uni. That's when my brothers weren't around to keep an eye on me. I ... ah ... realised that boys ... er ... men, found me attractive.' Freddie set her cup down on the table. 'I'm not proud of it, Melanie, but it felt a bit like power, having boys asking me out, competing for my attention. I'd never experienced that. Before.'

'Alright. I understand. You're an adult now, and you have every right to date and, um, explore your sexuality. But why here, Freddie? And why use the clinic flat? Surely you knew you'd leave, um, evidence of your, uh, adventures. Why take the risk?'

Freddie didn't want to answer that. She wasn't sure how to tell Melanie that the most exciting part *was* the sneaking around. Almost being caught by her brothers, week after week, had heightened her excitement.

Melanie continued. 'Is it because of Harry? He's a bit older than you. Not too much, but I know he's friends with your brothers. Was it to protect Harry?'

Freddie grasped this with both hands. 'Yes. Yes, it was to protect Harry. We're not ready to tell everyone, you know, it's early days. He lives at home still, and apart from our cars, there's nowhere to be together, in private.'

'So what now Freddie? If I tell Angus and Max, you may not lose your job, but you would lose some of their trust.' Melanie shook her head. 'I'm not sure whether I should keep your secret. If they find out and learn that I knew, *I'd* lose their trust.'

'I'm sorry Melanie. It will never happen again.' Freddie shook her head sadly, hoping Melanie would be convinced to remain silent.

'It won't happen again because I will be checking. I don't know whether you deserve to have a key, but they're expecting you to start work next week.' Melanie seemed to decide as she spoke, and she pushed the key over until it rested by Freddie's hand. 'I'll keep your secret for now, Freddie. But one suspicious move, and I *will* tell Angus. Do we understand each other?'

'Yes Melanie.' Freddie took the key, keeping her head down as she returned it to her key ring. Looking up, she widened her eyes, hoping she looked contrite and genuine. 'You can trust me, Melanie. I'm truly sorry.'

Stopping by the creek that ran through the back of Rose's place, where it bordered the State Forest, Freddie dismounted. She tied Cotton to a tree and stepped through the undergrowth to the edge of the water. She looked around, standing silently on the creek bank. A flock of pink and white galahs rose from a tree on the other side of the creek. Freddie removed her hat and drew her tee shirt over her head. She kicked her boots off, then undid her jeans and shimmied out of them. Standing tall in her black undies and bra, she peered across the rushing stream, her eyes roving along the edge of the forest for several metres each way.

Movement caught her eye. He stepped out of the tree cover and waved. He dropped a small backpack in the grass on his side, then waded into the water wearing only shorts. He stopped halfway, his smile broadening to a huge grin, as she undid her bra, dropping it on the ground. In one fluid motion, she stepped out of her undies and entered the water. He held out his arms.

24

MILLIE

TRADE WAS STEADY, AND BY LATE MORNING MILLIE thought she'd take a quick break. Hannelore, Kristen and Lucy had the café covered. Melanie had arrived by herself, ordered a latte and walked to the back table. Millie joined Melanie, carrying two lattes.

'By yourself this morning Mel?' Millie settled in a chair with a view of the front counter.

'Yes. Ben has taken the girls to visit his dad and Laura, they got home from Tasmania last night.' She sipped her coffee, making an 'aah' sound as she did. 'I'm going to meet them there for lunch.'

Millie smiled, then asked quietly, 'Did you go to the clinic after the pub last night? We saw a little jeep parked there when we left.'

'Yes. It was Freddie.' Melanie rolled her eyes.

'Freddie?' Millie frowned, trying to picture him.

'Frederica Campbell, our Vet intern. She works at the clinic during her university breaks.'

'Oh! That Freddie! Yes, she's Callum's younger sister.' Millie paused. 'Um, Callum and Kristen are seeing each other, I think.'

'Yes. You're right. I saw them last night with Freddie, Harry and Hanna.' Melanie paused. 'I thought Hanna and Harry may be an item?'

'No. I don't think so.' Millie shook her head. 'Although it's possible he's interested. Or just friends. He drops into the café and chats to her when he's working upstairs.' She frowned then. 'Why do you ask?'

Melanie grimaced, then sighed. 'This is to go no further. But we found Freddie with Harry at the clinic. It didn't look good.'

'Really? Harry?' Millie thought about it. 'He's a nice lad. Honestly, I wouldn't have thought it of him. The sneaking around.'

Melanie finished her latte. 'I've had Freddie at our place this morning. She says it's because he's mates with her brothers and she thinks they'll hurt him.' Sighing, Melanie pushed her chair back. 'I'm not going to tell Angus and Max. But I've given her a warning.'

'Hmmm. Keep your eye on her anyway, Melanie; my gut says there's more to this.' Millie walked to the door with Melanie. 'Bye Melanie. See you at book club next week.' She watched Melanie leave, then glanced into the kitchen. Hannelore and Kristen were chatting happily. *Should she warn Hannelore about Harry? Or let her work it out?*

25

RACHAEL

Barrington Book Club – Rachael, Rose, Millie, Hannelore,
Kristen, Melanie, Harriet, Meggie
Apologies – Laura, Nicole
Book – ***The Accident*** by Fiona Lowe

Running slightly late, Rachael was the last one to arrive at the café for book club. She'd been caught up at the farm with Jamie Tait, visiting her grandson Warwick. He was a sturdy little chap and Jamie was doing a great job raising him, without Debbie. He had help from his parents, and Rachael and Steve had him for a sleepover once a week. But seeing Warwick emphasised the loss of their daughter. Rachael felt a light cloak of sadness settle on her as she drove away. It lifted, however, when she entered the café to a chorus of cheerful greetings from the book club girls.

Returning their greetings, she joined them at the table, accepting the glass of wine Millie placed in front of her.

'Gosh, I'm keen to discuss this one. I've never read a Fiona Lowe book before.' Rachael placed her paperback on the table with a smile. 'I don't think I've ever stayed up late to finish a book. I really couldn't put it down.'

'Oh me too!' Harriet chimed in. 'It was very twisty, I kept reading because I had to know the truth. And it didn't turn out at all the way I imagined.'

'This right here is why I question my own writing.' Rose laid her hand on the book in front of her. 'There is so much talent in Australia. I aspire to tell stories like this one.'

'It just reminded me that we never really know someone.' Melanie opened her Kindle. 'But I've read a few by this author and I've loved them all. She writes characters I get really invested in.'

The conversation flowed around the table and Rachael leaned back, sipping her wine. She loved the warmth of this group of women. Sharing books, wine and snacks was relaxing yet stimulating at the same time. Rachael still marvelled at how she'd never been *a reader* but now she couldn't imagine a day *without reading*, even if it was just one chapter before bed. She'd been thinking a lot about the bookshop idea. Before she'd become so invested in books herself, she may not have given it serious thought. But now. Well. Now that she'd discovered reading. Not just reading, but sharing and discussing books, she wanted everyone to.

'Earth to Rachael.' Meggie nudged her, laughing. 'Where did you go just then? We were talking about next month's book.'

'Oh. Actually, I was thinking about the bookshop idea.' As Rachael said the words she saw Hannelore spin in her seat, a look of total surprise on her face. *Hmm. What's with Hanna?* 'But tell me, what did we choose?'

'*Head for the Hills* by Tricia Stringer.' Harriet turned her phone around to show Rachael the cover. 'It's set in South Australia in a small town like this one. It's about sisters, I think and a proposed development in the town and how the community responds.' She chuckled then. 'Makes me think of Barrington. See what you think Rach. Perhaps you should get Steve to read it after you.'

'Yes. Maybe I should.' Rachael chuckled and then frowned. Steve was getting a lot of push and pull from parts of the community about the planning scheme and various developments. He said it was one of the hardest parts of his role as Mayor.

Millie and Kristen cleared the plates, saying they had something special for dessert. As they walked away, Hannelore turned to Rachael. 'Bookshop idea?'

'Yes. Greta isn't renewing her lease next door, and we were talking the other night about what Barrington *doesn't* have, to fill that little shop. Rose told us how hard it is for Indie authors to get their books into chain book stores and I've been running some numbers on whether a little book store could pay its way in a town this size.' Rachael included Rose in her answer, as she had moved to sit beside Hannelore.

'I've been thinking about it too, Rachael.' Rose laid her arm across the back of Hannelore's chair, who was keenly following the conversation. 'I'm wondering if a very niche bookstore would work.'

'Niche?' Rachael stopped then, as Millie and Kristen returned with a platter of simply gorgeous little individual pavlovas with cream and berries and a dusting of icing sugar on top. 'Oh gosh Millie, these look divine.'

'Too good to eat.' But Meggie reached for one as she said it, giggling and shrugging at the same time. 'Did you make these Millie?'

'No'. Millie was standing behind Hannelore's chair and patted her daughter on the shoulder. 'Hanna made them. They're very light and perfect in every way.' She leaned toward Rachael slightly. 'I had to taste test one earlier, but if you don't tell anyone, I'm going to have another.'

'I'm right here Mum.' Hannelore smiled. *So like her mum.* 'And you don't need permission to have a second one. No one does. I've made plenty, especially for book club. Leftovers can be sold in the café tomorrow.'

Only one mini pavlova remained on the platter. Kristen offered it to everyone but they all said they couldn't fit any more in. Rachael remembered Rose hadn't answered her question regarding the bookshop.

'You said niche Rose, about the bookshop. What did you mean?' Rachael tried not to look at the last dessert. She hoped someone would eat it, or that Millie would take it back to the kitchen. She itched to take it off the plate herself.

'It's something I've been thinking about, and I had a chat with a couple of Indie authors I know. Just to test the idea.' Rose cleared her throat.

'Yes?' They were all focussed on Rose, but none more than Hannelore.

'What if it *was* an Aussie-Indie-book-shop? Where Indie authors like me could display and sell their books. I'm not saying to exclude traditionally published books. But *specialise* in Indie books.' Rose sighed then. 'But I have no idea if it will work. It's just something I'd love to see here. Selfish, really.'

'Not at all!' Hannelore was glowing. 'I'd be its best customer. I love Indie books and I try to buy directly from the authors online. But postage can add quite a lot, which makes an Indie book more expensive than the others. If we could buy them at bookstore prices. Well. I think it's worth looking into.' She turned to Rachael. 'What do you think Rachael?'

'I'm no expert and I suspect book margins are low. So I still wonder if there's a business model that would make it work. Steve has doubts, but he's willing to give it a try for six months. But do we attract someone to do it? Someone with experience? Do I run it myself? I'm not even sure about buying stock.' Rachael hesitated. It would be too much for her and she knew it.

Meggie stood up. 'I have an idea.' She turned to Rachael. 'Is it possible for us to go upstairs and see your apartment? I know it's not ready yet, but I want to check something out.'

Rachael didn't hesitate. Meggie's movement seemed to bring them all to their feet, chatting and laughing at once. Rachael felt something in the air. An intensity that hadn't been there before. 'Follow me girls, I have the keys.' They left the last little pavlova sitting by itself in the centre of the table.

———

RACHAEL WALKED SMARTLY UP THE STAIRS, BARELY registering her feet on each step. The others clattered up behind her, laughing and chatting as they did. She unlocked and threw open the door and they fanned out in the main living area. There were no furnishings yet, but white shutters had been installed at the windows and the new kitchen counter was in. The bathroom and kitchen had been tiled and the walls painted.

They oohed and aahed over everything, but she noticed

Hannelore and Rose had walked straight into the smaller bedroom, where Robbie had already installed the window seat and bookshelves. 'Rachael, this is fabulous!' Hannelore called out. 'It's just like I imagined!'

Meggie almost ran into the room, with Rachael behind her and then the others crowded into the small room after them. 'The soft furnishings have been ordered, and we're putting a big old armchair just there, facing the window, and a wee desk and chair against that wall.' Rachael pointed, moving in a half circle. Hannelore and Rose were perched together on the bare window seat.

Meggie walked across and sat between them. 'Did you know there's a town in Scotland, and another in Wales, that are tiny, but achieve great tourist numbers? Day tourists and overnight visitors.'

'Um. I've never been. But where are you going with this Meggie?' Rachael leaned against the door.

'They're famous for their bookstores. The little town in Wales has about twenty-seven, I think. Some are second-hand, some antiquarian, and others are almost thrift shops. But masses of tourists visit and spend the day browsing these shops.' Meggie's voice had risen in her excitement.

'We're only doing *one* bookshop, Meggie.' Rachael was confused.

Meggie continued as if she hadn't heard. 'The one in Scotland, called Wigtown also has a reader festival. Or writer festival. Maybe both, I'm not sure. But they have something else that's unique.' Meggie was on a roll, Rose was beaming and nodding and Hannelore clapped her hands.

'There's one particular little bookshop. It's tiny. It has an apartment upstairs. You can stay in the apartment and work in the bookstore, for a few days or a week.' She raised her eyebrows. 'Would you believe it's booked out more than a year in advance? People *pay* to work in the bookstore and live upstairs.' As the words tumbled from Meggie, Rose and Hannelore shared a look of utter delight. Rachael felt herself swept up in their excitement.

'Are you suggesting we market the apartment and bookstore together? Like a specialty thing?' Rachael had never heard of such a thing. *People pay to work in a bookstore while on holiday.*

'It needs more thought, Rach.' Harriet spoke up and moved closer to Meggie. 'But my head is going at a million miles an hour and I have a whole heap of ideas I want to explore. Marketing ideas.' She hugged Rose. 'And we need your input and connections too, Rose.' Turning back to Rachael, she added, 'If you're keen Rachael, I propose we have a brainstorming session and come up with a business plan. I think it's viable. More than viable. We may have something that can be another unique attraction for Barrington.'

Hannelore raised her hand. 'May I please be involved in the brainstorming? I adore this concept.' Rachael smiled warmly at her and said 'yes' with gusto.

The biggest surprise was Kristen, from the back of the room. 'I'd like to be involved, too, in the brainstorming session. Um, I have an accounting degree. I'd be happy to do the business modelling for you Rachael.'

Rachael felt her eyes fill with tears. She had no idea if the concept was viable, but the support in the room for her and her project made her want to try. She smiled and nodded, afraid that if she spoke, her tears would fall.

Millie materialised beside her and placed an arm around her

shoulders. 'Let's pick a night, shall we? We can do it in the café after hours. I'll supply snacks.'

'We'll bring a whiteboard. And butchers paper for the planning session.' Meggie and Harriet were standing together now.

Rose walked to Rachael. 'When do you want to do this Rach? Before Christmas? Or in the new year?'

Stunned, and moved, Rachael gulped, then wiped a stray tear from her cheek. 'Thank you. All of you. The apartment will be ready early in January if the plumbing fixtures arrive this week. So I'd like to do it sooner, rather than later, if possible.'

'All right. Thursday night? Does that suit everyone?' Millie had taken charge and Rachael was pleased. They all agreed although Melanie asked if Ben could come in her place. She thought he'd have more to offer.

'I'll see if Steve can join us too.' Rachael looked around. 'Anyone else?' They all began talking at once.

Kristen spoke quietly, but Rachael held up her hands for the others to stop. 'Yes, Kristen?'

'My Aunt Judith. Mum's older sister. She's retired here now. She's, um, an ex-librarian and worked part-time in a little bookstore in Brisbane. She might have some useful information.'

'Bring her along then Kristen, if she's happy to join us.' Rachael clapped her Hands. 'I'm excited. I can't tell you how much.'

Later, walking home, Rachael thought about how much her life had changed since they'd lost Debbie. It was bittersweet because somehow Rachael felt she'd been granted a second chance at happiness. After months of believing she'd never be happy again.

26

HARRY

AFTER SUPERVISING THE NEW KITCHEN AND LAUNDRY appliances, Harry couldn't shake the feeling that he was somehow in the wrong. He was annoyed at Freddie for compromising him on Friday night in front of Melanie and Ben. *Compromising. What am I? A regency-era damsel-in-distress.* He snorted at his thought. But he prided himself on his integrity, like his father. *He wasn't raised to sneak around.* And he certainly wouldn't do it with his friend's little sister.

'Something up mate?' Robbie was shuffling the washing machine into place. Harry grabbed one side of it, and together, they lifted it onto the tiled area. They stood back, looking at it for a moment, before Harry began removing the wrapping from the matching dryer.

'No Dad.' Harry kept his face down, concentrating on the job at hand. His father could read him like a book. 'Just thinking about the cupboard doors for the laundry. I'm going to stain them before we hang them.' He *had* been thinking about that. Before he was thinking about his current dilemma.

'Alright. Good. The drop sheets are down in the living area, we can put them on trestles and do the first coat.' Robbie turned and grinned at Nicole as she bustled in, carrying several swatches of fabric. 'Hello love.'

'Hello.' She smiled at them as she looked around, poking her head into the kitchen before returning. 'This is looking fabulous.' She waved the swatches. 'Rachael is dropping by shortly, we're choosing the cover for the window seat mattress. But it's morning tea time, and if you're ready for a break, I thought we could pop downstairs to the café before she arrives.'

Robbie grinned. 'Yes. I'm in. I'll just wash my hands.' He strode to the bathroom, saying over his shoulder, 'Are you coming, Harry?'

Harry straightened and stretched, then called out to Robbie, 'I'll stay here and get that first coat on the doors. But you can bring me back a muffin or caramel slice.' He didn't want to see Hannelore. He'd been keeping a low profile all week.

Robbie returned to Nicole, putting an arm around her waist. 'Are you sure, Harry? The doors can wait thirty minutes.'

'Too hot for coffee. I've got water in the esky.' To demonstrate, Harry lifted the lid of his lunch esky and took out a flask of cold water.

'Okay, mate. We won't be long.' Robbie and Nicole clattered down the stairs and Harry took a swig of water before lifting the laundry cupboard doors onto the trestles in the main living area. He quickly gave them a first coat of timber stain. They were old cedar doors Nicole had found at a second-hand shop in Taree. Standing back, he admired them for a moment.

It only took him fifteen minutes, so he moved into the small room he called *the reading room* in his head and perched on the window seat with his phone in his hand. He lost track of time until a voice in the doorway startled him so much that he dropped the phone.

'Damn!' he picked it up and looked at Hannelore, leaning in the doorway wearing an amused expression. 'I didn't hear you come in.'

'The door was open.' She stepped closer. 'I've brought you a muffin. Chocolate chip. ' She held out a brown paper bag that emitted a delicious aroma.

Harry shoved the phone in his back pocket and reached for the bag. 'Thank you.' He looked at his watch. 'I thought Dad would be back by now.'

Hannelore perched beside him on the window seat. 'Rachael and Steve came into the café. They're talking colours for the window seat cushion with Robbie and Nik. Robbie sent me up here with your muffin. He said you'd be hungry.' She giggled. 'Actually, he said you're *always* hungry.'

Harry chuckled. 'Yeah. That's true.' He opened the bag and took the muffin out before placing it on the now-empty bag between them. 'But not so hungry that I don't share.' He deftly broke the muffin in two and handed half to Hannelore.

Waving it away she laughed. 'You eat it, Harry. I snack all day in the kitchen.' She patted her flat tummy. 'I don't need it.'

'I beg to differ. And who turns down a shared chocolate chip muffin?' He held the treat out to her again and she laughed and took it.

'You win. Lucy made these, they're delicious.' Hannelore took a large bite. Harry watched her as she ate.

CHAPTER 26

He didn't think the Freddie-story had reached her ears. She wouldn't be so friendly if it had. Harry thought he'd try his luck. 'Want to go to the pub for dinner tomorrow night? It's schnitty night. We can see if Cal and Kristen want to join us.'

'Oh, that would be nice but I can't tomorrow. Although I do love a schnitty.' She repositioned herself to face him directly, and he watched her face light up as she added, 'There's a brainstorming session at the café tomorrow night, for the bookshop.'

'Bookshop?' Harry had no idea what she was talking about.

'Oh, Nik wasn't at book club this week, so you may not have heard. Rachael is exploring the idea of turning Greta's little store into a bookshop. There's a few of us getting together to work through some ideas, as Harriet and Meggie say a town this size wouldn't support a regular bookshop.' She turned her attention to the muffin, but Harry could see how excited she was. *The girl loves a bookshop! Who knew?*

'No, I didn't know that.' Harry's mind was whirring with this new information. *And she hadn't said no to a date, just that she wasn't free on Thursday.*

'Yeah, Rachael's filling her in now, downstairs. Nik likes the idea.' Hannelore smiled then and nudged Harry with her shoulder. 'How about tonight at the pub? What's the Wednesday night special?'

Harry hesitated. He'd planned to drive out to the Campbells and catch up with the lads. He was hoping he could get a few minutes with Freddie while he was there, to put her straight. He didn't want her telling anyone else they were an item. And he wanted to let Melanie and Ben know it wasn't true. But he needed to speak to Freddie first. And he wanted to find out who the young bloke is and why she can't see him openly.

Hannelore's face closed up and she got off the window seat. 'I saw you on your phone when I walked in Harry Stewart. You've already got a date for tonight, I suspect. Or maybe a booty-call. Well, good luck with that.' She stalked out and Harry had no idea what to say, so he said nothing.

27

—————

HANNELORE

Damn Harry Stewart. Hannelore had thought she could trust him. That he just might be one of the good ones. Like Robbie. And Finn. But he had been so engrossed with his phone when she walked in, she wondered if he was checking out the profile of tonight's date.

For a moment she considered slipping into the pub after work just to see who he was with. What she's like. Then she chastised herself. *Don't put any more energy into Harry. He doesn't deserve it.*

Robbie, Nicole and Rachael met her at the door of the café on their way upstairs. Back in the kitchen, she began working with Kristen. Lucy and Millie were serving at the counter as the town seemed to be swarming with tourists.

'So how's Harry?' Kristen passed pot holders to Hannelore. 'The apple turnovers are ready.'

Hannelore lifted the tray of turnovers out and slid in another tray, this one with dozens of tiny Choux pastries on it. They were for a croquembouche wedding cake she was making for a small

138

event Meggie had organised, out at Finn's winery on Friday afternoon. Millie and Lucy were going just after lunch to serve the finger food, and Hannelore and Kristen were heading out to help after the café closed. 'Oh, you know Harry.'

'I don't really. We went to school together and he was always nice to me, but we didn't socialise. He spent most of his weekends and holidays going to camp draft events with his dad. He won a lot of buckles, I think.' Kristen passed a platter of sandwiches and fruit to Hannelore. 'The big table in the front please.'

Hannelore delivered the platter and returned, peering through the oven window to check the pastries. 'These are nearly ready.' She made room on a cooling rack, then withdrew the tray from the oven. They were perfect, uniformly round and firm, and golden brown on the outside.

Kristen reached out and touched one. 'These are gorgeous Hanna! I've never tried to make Choux pastry. Too tricky. And I can't wait to see you assemble the croquembouche. Do you fill the profiteroles first?'

'Yes. I'll make a vanilla cream and pipe it into the centre of each pastry shell, then make a caramel mixture with the consistency of warm toffee. I dip the top of each filled pastry into the caramel and build a tower, with the caramel holding it all together. But I won't do that until Friday morning.' Hannelore picked up one of the tiny pastry casings. 'These are just right.'

Hannelore busied herself putting them away, while Kristen prepared the meal orders Lucy or Millie brought in. The rush seemed to last hours but finally began to slow.

Millie popped her head in the door. 'Would you two like to have lunch? It's almost two and I think Lucy and I can manage for half an hour.'

'Sure.' Kristen turned to Hannelore. 'Chicken salad wrap?'

'Yum. Yes please. Want a drink?' Hannelore passed the container of green salad to Kristen.

'Chai latte on skim for me.' Kristen shredded the chicken, looking at Hannelore quickly as she spoke. 'A bit of caramelised balsamic for dressing?'

'Perfect. I'll have a chai latte too.' Hannelore made their drinks, chatting for a moment with Millie about the Choux pastries. She blushed when Millie told her they looked perfect. Better even than the ones her father used to make.

At the back table, Hannelore stretched her legs out, pointing her toes back and forward. 'Busy today.' She sighed.

'I don't mind. Makes the day fly by.' Kristen bit into her wrap, closing her eyes for a moment.

'It really does.' Hannelore laid hers back on the plate. She'd already consumed half.

'Back to Harry. You delivered the muffin to him earlier.' Kristen's tone was light but questioning. 'You were up there for a while.'

'Harry shared with me.' Hannelore giggled.

'What? Harry shared what?' Kristen was laughing too.

'His muffin. He broke it in half.' Hannelore sipped her chai. 'Then he asked me out to the pub. For Thursday night.'

'Thursday night? We've got the brainstorming thing here.' Kristen paused. 'But he asked you out, hey?'

'So I played it light and said I was free tonight ... and ... get this ... he just clammed up for about a minute. *He just left my invitation hanging.*' Hannelore tried, but failed, to keep the annoyance from her tone.

'Really? That's odd.' Kristen frowned.

'Not really. He was on his phone when I went up there. He was like, *glued* to it. He didn't see me for about a minute. I think he was on app. You know, a dating app.' She picked up her wrap and bit into it aggressively. After chewing and swallowing Hannelore continued as Kristen said nothing but looked surprised. 'Honestly, he was doing it the other day in the café too. Glued to his phone. I think Harry Stewart is a player. I think he likes a booty-call.' Which reminded Hannelore again of Anthony-the-lying-cheater, her old boyfriend from the West.

'I don't know Hanna. It just doesn't ring true for me. Harry doing that. He's a good-looking bloke, he'd have no trouble getting a date.' Kristen looked thoughtful. 'I can ask Callum. He might know.'

'Please don't.' Hannelore finished her drink and checked her watch. They still had ten minutes of break time, but she needed to change the subject. 'What was it you wanted to talk to me about? You said on Friday night that you wanted to ask me something on Monday, but you never did.'

'I did. I will. Things have changed a bit in the last few days, so I decided to wait.'

Kristen packed their plate and cups onto the tray she'd left on the side of the table. 'I've been wanting to ask how it's working out for you, living with your mum?'

'Oh. On one hand, it's been great. We had some stuff to resolve and being together at night has given us a chance to talk about a lot of issues.' Hannelore swallowed but waved her hand indicating it was of no importance now. 'And we're in a good place.' *We really are.* 'But moving in was meant to be temporary until I was sure I wanted to stay. But now I think I do want to stay, here in Barrington.'

'That's great! So happy you're staying.' Kristen's gaze was serious. 'Do you think Millie will move in with Finn at some point, out at his place?'

Hannelore thought about it for a moment. 'I'm not saying she *never* will. But I think Mum likes her independence. She loves having her own place. Sure, she stays at Finn's a couple of times a week, and I think he used to stay with her sometimes, too, before I came.' She looked at Kristen. 'Is that why you're asking? Do you think I'm cramping Mum's style?'

'No. Not at all that I can see.' She giggled. 'It's more about me, really. I'd like to move out of home. I've decided to stay in Barrington too.' She blushed. 'And now that I'm dating Callum, who also lives with his parents out at their farm, I've been thinking it's time I found a place of my own.' She nibbled her lip. 'I thought if Millie was spending a lot of time at Finn's, maybe I could share the post office flat with you? Then I thought about the apartment over the café, but Rachael will want too much rent and frankly, I love the bookshop idea.'

'Of course. I totally get it. And I would like to move out and give Mum back her privacy. The post office apartment would have suited the two of us, especially as I still haven't got a car. But I don't think Mum wants to move out.' Hannelore reached across to Kristen, touching her hand. 'But I like the idea. We could share a house. I'm happy to look at options.'

'Good, because there's been a development this week.' Kristen stood up, the tray in her hands. 'We better keep moving.' She continued once they returned to the kitchen. 'You know I mentioned my Aunt Judith? She's coming to the brainstorm tomorrow night?' When Hannelore nodded she added, 'She's been staying with us, but she's found a big old house on

Gloucester Street that she loves and has put in an offer to buy. But it will take most of her reserves and she asked me this week if I'd like to rent a room from her.'

'Really? Hannelore was intrigued. 'Is it walking distance to the café?'

'Yep. Only two blocks.' Kristen's eyes sparkled. 'She hasn't settled yet, it will be later in January. But she says it has a section with a bedroom, bathroom and lounge with a separate entrance that the current owners use for short-term accommodation. And the main house has three bedrooms and two bathrooms.'

'Would she be, you know, okay for you to have Callum, um, visit?' Hannelore didn't think Kristen and Callum were sleeping together. But perhaps that was mainly due to their living situations.

'Well, that's just it. She's older than mum. Quite a bit older actually. But she's always been the *cool aunt*. I can tell her anything. And I told her about Callum on the weekend. She's been great and you'll meet her tomorrow night. And yes, she'd be okay with Callum staying. When I'm ready to take that step.' Kristen blushed.

'Okay. Good. Thanks. I'm keen to meet her. But no promises regarding moving in. Not yet anyway.' Just then Kristen's phone buzzed and she dug it out of her pocket.

'Callum.' Kristen waved the phone in the air, then read the text. Hannelore began unpacking the dishwasher. 'Oh. He's busy tonight. Family thing. We'd planned to catch up.' She looked across at Hannelore. 'Want to have dinner at the pub tonight? Just us.'

'Sure. Mum's going out to Finn's anyway.' Hannelore wondered if she'd see Harry. And she wondered who he'd be with.

28

FREDDIE

THE UNIVERSITY YEAR ENDED WEEKS AGO, BUT FREDDIE had stayed on to do an advanced course in equine health. But now she was home for three months, back in Barrington.

Angus Hamilton had asked her to help in the clinic in the lead-up to Christmas, then full-time in January while Max was on holiday with his family. Working at Barrington Vet Clinic was a great experience. It was for her third-year clinical placement, and then in February and March, she had work lined up in Tamworth at a horse stud, which met her practical requirements.

Freddie was enjoying life. She adored her family, but being the only girl, after six boys, had its downside. When she was little, she adored having big brothers to defend her, teach her stuff and fuss over her. As she grew, she'd become a tomboy, wanting to keep up with them on the farm and at sports. She could drive a tractor, ride a motorbike and drench cattle.

It wasn't until her senior year at high school that she realised she was only noticed for her good grades and sporting ability. The one or two boys who made moves to ask her out were shut down by Callum or Douggie, the two brothers closest to her in age.

Arriving at university was almost like starting over for her. None of her brothers had been to university, although they all had a trade, which helped on the farm. Callum was a diesel mechanic, Douggie had his own hay-making business and the older boys, all married now, had various qualifications in agricultural fields. But that made university Freddie's domain. She decided, from the very first day that she'd reinvent herself. And she did.

Freddie continued to get good grades, but she spent many nights out clubbing with other students. She drank a little, smoked some weed which she hadn't enjoyed and experimented with sex. She dated a few boys but didn't get invested. She even spent one night, after too much wine, in bed with a girl. The sex was great, but she enjoyed the mind games more, the power she felt when dating a man. She'd spent a week with a lecturer. Not one of hers, but he was putty in her hands. He adored her, but she treated him badly and callously told him she'd report their affair, just to see how far she could push him.

Meeting someone in her hometown hadn't been on her radar. But he was a bit different to the men she'd grown up with and their romance had lasted months. Longer than any other. Freddie knew some of the attraction, for her, was the sneaking around. They could be caught at any moment, and her parents would be devastated, and her brothers would be angry. And that made it more exciting than anything else. But now, having been caught by Harry-bloody-Stewart, then Ben and Melanie Evans, she wondered if she'd gone too far.

She needed to consider whether they came clean and admitted their romance. *That's what he wants. What he'd wanted for the longest time.* It was cute that he cared so much he'd risk the ire of her brothers. *But what did she want?* Harry Stewart? He was sexy as hell, but Freddie was sure he'd never touch her. He was friends with her brothers. *But it could be fun pushing him.*

Freddie was helping her mum prepare dinner. Not her favourite job, but she knew her mum did most of the *inside* work by herself. And by working with her mum in the kitchen over the years she'd learned how to cook a lot of basic meals. It had helped her survive at university. While the others were eating take-out every night, Freddie cooked something she could get three meals out of.

It was roast lamb tonight. Just Callum, Douggie, Freddie and their parents. Freddie was laying the table and chatting with Douggie, when Callum came into the room, showered and clean. 'You clean up all right brother.' Freddie teased. Callum had been covered in grime an hour earlier, after repairing the hay baler.

Callum shot forward, chasing Freddie around the huge timber dinner table. They were both laughing when their mother said sternly. 'Stop it. Honestly. How old are you two?' They stopped, but she was laughing too.

'Set another place, Freddie. There's six of us tonight.' Callum nudged her with his shoulder. Freddie back-handed him, but not hard.

'Who's coming? Kristen?' Douggie handed Callum a beer, his tone teasing. Freddie shot a glance at her mum, she wasn't sure if she was up to date on Callum's romance.

But her mum only smiled, saying, 'You can invite Kristen anytime you want Cal.'

'Thanks Mum.' Callum blushed. 'I'll ask her out here for dinner one night over the Christmas break.' He turned to Douggie. 'Harry said he'd drop in. He won't be expecting a meal, but I'm sure he won't say no.'

Freddie felt excitement, then fear, rush through her. Harry? Oh no! *Was he going to tell her parents? Or her brothers?* She knew he wouldn't want it to get out that she was sneaking around with *him.*

'Doncha like old Harry?' Douggie looked through the window. 'He's just driven in, I'll go get him. Turning back to Freddie, he added, 'You better tell Dad it's dinner time. He was working on the books in the study.'

Harry seemed eager to join them at dinner and with little encouragement, regaled them with stories of his time up north on one of the largest cattle stations in the country.

Freddie studied him during the meal but said little. He directed an occasional comment to her but mostly spoke to the rest of her family. Harry Stewart was a cut above, and she knew it.

She'd become quite good at reading people, and in her heart, she knew he wasn't a player, and as much as she could flirt and make him uncomfortable, his manly-code-of-honour would keep him from reaching out to her. *He could be a challenge though.* She wondered if pursuing him would be worth it.

Freddie joined the conversation when they had dessert. Good old-fashioned peaches and ice cream. Her father's favourite. 'Why did you really come out here Harry?' Freddie smiled sweetly. 'Was it to see me?'

Harry hadn't expected that and she delighted in his discomfort. He stuttered, 'What? No.' Then he glanced at her father and seemed to recover quickly. 'Of course I like to see you Freddie. How are you going with your studies?'

Freddie chatted about the advanced course she'd just

completed, and about the opportunity to work at the horse stud in Tamworth next year. 'I'd be happy to check your horses over, Harry. No charge. It's all good experience for me.'

He was ready for her this time. 'That would be great Freddie. Let me know when you're free. Dad and I will get the horses into the yards.'

'Sure. I'll do that.' Freddie answered chirpily, but her mind was racing. *Smooth Harry. Very smooth.* And now she knew that *he knew* she was messing with him. He wanted her to stop, but gosh, he doesn't know how much she enjoys a challenge. As the night wore on, her fear that he'd tell her parents or brothers about the other night receded. And if he left it too long, he'd *never* be able to tell them. *He was compromised now. Big time.*

29

MILLIE

The Brainstorm for the Bookshop
Present: Millie, Hannelore, Kristen, Judith, Harriet, Meggie, Rachael, Steve, Rose, Nicole, Ben

HARRIET AND MEGGIE ARRIVED AT FIVE AND BEGAN TO set up as Millie and her team finished up for the day. Robbie took Lucy home, but Nicole arrived and helped Hannelore move the tables into a U-shape, with a whiteboard at the front. Kristen had ducked off to pick up her Aunt Judith. Harriet set up a laptop and projector and as Millie wondered what that was for, Steve and Rachael arrived, followed closely by Rose and Ben.

Kristen rushed in, with her aunt right behind her. 'Hi every-one, this is my Auntie Judith.' Kristen linked her arm through Judith's and introduced everyone around the table as they all found seats.

Millie smiled at Judith. She was very like Cathy, Kristen's mum, but a bit older. Short silver hair and a friendly face. And maybe a twinkle in her eye. Millie immediately liked her and wondered if she could invite her for coffee sometime.

Meggie kicked off the meeting, with a brief overview of the problem, explaining that Rachael was interested in exploring if the empty shop next door could be a viable bookstore. She also mentioned the apartment upstairs that was almost ready to let for short-term accommodation.

'I know we've all been talking about it, but I want to touch on the bookstore with apartment concepts in the United Kingdom that are working spectacularly well over there.' Meggie nodded to Harriet who projected an image of a cute bookstore onto the screen laid over the whiteboard. Millie hadn't noticed that. *Clever.*

'This is Hay-On-Wye in Wales that boasts more than twenty bookshops.' Images of the street filled with bookstores and visitors flashed up. Meggie continued, 'And here is an apartment above one of the bookstores. You can see it's cosy and has clever reading spaces, like the reading room Rachael has created upstairs.'

'There's a similar village in Scotland called Wigtown. Wikipedia says it is Scotland's National Book Town. It has a lot of second-hand book stores and an annual book festival.'

The images were pretty. Millie had never been to Scotland, but she wondered now if she could plan for an overseas trip with Finn. Maybe in a year or two.

Meggie spoke again about the apartment in Wigtown that was booked out three years in advance with a six-night minimum, and visitors could run the bookstore below for the week. Millie was fascinated, and when she looked around the tables, she saw they all were, but none more than Hannelore.

Harriet turned the laptop off at that point and Meggie lifted the screen to provide access to the whiteboard. 'I suggest we do a quick SWOT, together, then have a break. SWOT stands for Strengths, Weaknesses, Opportunities and Threats, for anyone not in the know.'

She turned to Millie. 'Millie and the team have generously made some snacks for us. Then we'll look at an action plan, which will include Kristen doing some business modelling in the next week or so.'

Meggie facilitated proceedings, with Harriet scribing on the whiteboard. It seemed the whole room was invested, and at times, Meggie had to slow their suggestions down to let Harriet keep up.

STRENGTHS
HIGH TRAFFIC MAIN STREET POSITION.
SMALL, WON'T NEED ENORMOUS FIT-OUT OR STOCK.
ADDS A FURTHER SHOPPING OUTLET FOR LOCALS AND VISITORS.
FILLS AN EMPTY SHOP ON THE MAIN STREET.
WEAKNESSES
VERY SMALL AND WON'T HOLD MUCH STOCK.
VISITORS DON'T COME TO BARRINGTON FOR BOOKS.
IT'S JUST ONE LITTLE BOOKSTORE.
BOOKS MAY BE PRICED HIGHER THAN CHAIN STORES.
MAY NOT ACHIEVE THE PROFITS NEEDED TO SUPPORT A MANAGER AND STAFF.

Judith had said very little but was making notes on an iPad. *Interesting.* Millie loved the idea. That it was right next door to the café was a bonus. And she thought a portion of tourists would enjoy browsing a little bookstore at the end of a busy day outdoors as much as she knew *she* would.

OPPORTUNITIES
MAKE IT A NICHE INDIE ONLY STORE.
OR AUSSIE ONLY, INDIE AND TRAD (ROSE EXPLAINED
INDIE IS SELF-PUBLISHING AND TRAD IS TRADITIONAL
PUBLISHING).
LINK IT TO THE ACCOMMODATION UPSTAIRS.
USE THE ACCOMMODATION UPSTAIRS FOR A WRITERS-IN-
RESIDENCE PROGRAM.
RUN A SMALL READER/WRITER FESTIVAL EACH YEAR.
A ROBUST CHILDREN'S BOOK SECTION.
THREATS
IT WON'T GET THE TURNOVER TO MAKE IT VIABLE.
THE APARTMENT BOOKINGS MAY SUFFER IF THE
BOOKSHOP DOESN'T SURVIVE.
ATTRACTING A MANAGER WITH EXPERIENCE COULD BE
PROBLEMATIC.
OPENING HOURS MAY REQUIRE MORE STAFF THAN IS
FINANCIALLY VIABLE.
MIDWEEK VISITATION IS MUCH LOWER THAN WEEKENDS.
BARRINGTON'S TOURISM OFFERING IS ABOUT OUTDOOR
ACTIVITIES SUCH AS KAYAKING AND BUSHWALKING. IT'S
A SPORTY TOWN WITH A CROSS-COUNTRY MARATHON
EACH YEAR – MARKETING IT FOR BOOK LOVERS SEEMS
COUNTER-INTUITIVE.

And then it got interesting. Millie saw Judith smile at Meggie, then raise her hand. 'Yes Judith, we'd love to hear your thoughts.' Meggie's tone was warm and inviting.

Judith cleared her throat, then began. 'You all know I'm Cathy's sister and I've just moved here. I'm a retired librarian and I worked part-time in an independent bookstore for many years. If you move forward, I can assist with selecting and buying stock, and I understand the overheads and costs, too.' She turned to Kristen. 'I can share those industry standards with you, Kristen, to help with the modelling.'

Judith turned to Rachael. 'I think you have a really interesting opportunity here. I gather from the conversation that you don't necessarily want to run the bookshop yourself. But it needs to pay its rent. Is that a fair assessment?'

Steve answered. 'Yes, Judith. We've discussed this a lot in the last week or two and Rachael doesn't want to be tied to running the bookshop. But she will run the apartment bookings and business. And yes, the rent isn't high, but we'd like to see a return on our investment, especially if we do some of the fit-out.'

Judith nodded, her smile broad. *She's got something up her sleeve* Millie thought. 'It's about marketing and enthusiasm.' Judith looked at Hannelore and Kristen, then turned her gaze to Rose, before sweeping around the entire group. 'Barrington is in the unique position of having our very own best-selling Indie author living here. And she has connections. Can you add these points to the opportunities please Meggie?'

Aussie and Indie book store (mainly).
It may be the only Indie bookstore with apartment offering in the State.
Offer the apartment mid-week for writing retreats and residencies.
Create a community NFP (Not For Profit) – volunteers (local and visitors) man the bookstore with one paid manager.

CREATE A DESTINATION-LED MARKETING CAMPAIGN –
COME TO BARRINGTON TO MEET THE AUTHORS – SAY 48
WEEKS OF THE YEAR. ROSE MAY HAVE TO DO AN EXTRA
WEEK HERE OR THERE IF NECESSARY.
READING/WRITING RETREATS.
SMALL FAN FESTIVALS IN TRADITIONALLY QUIET TIMES.

'Oh gosh, Judith! A community not-for-profit to run the store! With volunteers.' Rachael clapped her hands. 'I just love it.'

Ben had participated eagerly, and now he turned to Rose. 'What do you think Rose? Will some of your author friends be interested? Selling their books here, but also staying for a writing retreat-slash-residency?'

Rose's face said it all. 'Yes! They will love it, I know they will. I have at least a dozen that I could start with, to kick it off. But getting our books into a brick-and-mortar storefront is brilliant – and you'd be amazed just how many readers want to buy a signed paperback. And meet the author.'

Millie stood, intending to get the snacks ready. An hour had gone by in the blink of an eye. Judith seemed unfazed by the proceedings. She moved across to Steve and Rachael and was soon joined by Ben and Rose. Hannelore and Kristen were deep in conversation with Meggie and Harriet.

Nicole followed Millie to the kitchen. 'The girls are excited. I've been sceptical about making it financially viable but Judith's not-for-profit concept and clever marketing may just make it one of Barrington's most unique selling points.'

'It's only recently that Hannelore told me how much she loves reading and books.' Millie stopped, her hand poised over a platter of cheese, dip and crackers. She gazed at Nicole, then said in almost a whisper, 'I wonder if she wants to change career? Her father talked her into this one, but she originally wanted to be a librarian.'

'I can't answer that Millie, but I can tell you she's the best pastry chef I've ever known. It's unlikely she'd give that up.' Nicole picked up the second platter. 'But if you're worried, you should talk to her.' Millie smiled and they returned to the group. *But what if she wants to run the bookshop?*

Meggie kept them working while they snacked. 'We've got an action plan now, and some of you have homework.' Millie chuckled at that.

ACTION PLAN

LOOK INTO THE NOT-FOR-PROFIT STRUCTURE.

BEN/STEVE

IT MUST BE COMMUNITY BASED.

ARM'S LENGTH FROM STEVE AND RACHAEL – WHO WOULD BE THE LANDLORDS OF THE SHOP.

DESIGN THE INTERNAL FIT-OUT – UNDERSTAND THE FOOTPRINT FOR SHELVING AND STORAGE TO DETERMINE STOCK QUANTITIES. **ROBBIE/JUDITH**

BUILD A LIST OF POTENTIAL AUTHORS TO SUPPLY BOOKS. **ROSE/JUDITH**

CONSIDER SUPPLIERS OF TRAD PUBLISHED BOOKS.

DISCUSS WRITER RETREAT OPPORTUNITIES – GATHER INTEL ON WANTS/NEEDS.

CONDUCT SOME READER/BUYER RESEARCH. VIA SOCIAL MEDIA READER GROUPS EXTERNAL TO THE AREA. VIA AUTHOR INTEL (FROM THEIR READER GROUPS). **JUDITH/HANNELORE/ROSE**

LOOK AT POTENTIAL OPENING TIMES AND ROSTERS. HOW MANY VOLUNTEERS MAY BE NEEDED. OPERATIONAL BUDGET. **JUDITH/KRISTEN**

CONSIDER THE OVERALL MARKETING. **MEGGIE/HARRIET** PAID ADVERTISING. SMALL EVENTS. SOCIAL MEDIA MARKETING. CONTENT DEVELOPMENT FOR SOCIAL MEDIA.

At one point, Millie saw Judith, Kristen and Hannelore speaking quietly together, and she wondered if Hannelore really was interested in managing the bookshop. Although she didn't have the experience. Millie sighed. *Just when they were getting their relationship on track.*

30

HARRY

Harry woke and stretched and a small smile
played around his lips. He'd dreamed of Hannelore and wondered
again if he should ask her out. The brainstorming session for the
bookshop on Thursday night had been a success, Nik said. She'd
also mentioned how invested Hannelore seemed to be. *Maybe
she'd be receptive to another invitation to dinner?*

It was early, and while the morning was still cool, the day was
expected to become quite hot. It was Sunday, and Robbie and
Nicole were driving to the coast with Millie and Finn for a seafood
lunch by the water. Lucy was working at the café until noon when
Harry would pick her up. This morning he planned to get the
horses in to trim their feet. Then, if Lucy had time, he'd take her
for a ride to the river. They could swim the horses and have an
afternoon picnic.

Another thought occurred to him then, and he swung his legs
out of bed and stood in one fluid movement. *He could ask
Hannelore if she'd like to come for the ride and picnic too. Lucy*

mentioned earlier in the week that Hannelore had asked about their horses, if they were quiet, and where Lucy went riding.

Padding to the kitchen, he found Robbie making coffee. 'Morning Dad.' Harry pulled his favourite mug from the cupboard and passed it to his father.

'Hey Harry. We're leaving early, Lucy is getting ready now, she needs to be at the café by seven.' He handed the mug back to Harry, steam rising from it. 'We're going to have breakfast at the café with Finn. Millie will get her team sorted, then we should head to the coast around half eight.' He grinned then. 'So you're on your own for breakfast today.'

'Ha, all good. As much as I love the big breakfasts Lucy whips up on weekends, toast and vegemite will do the trick today.' Harry grinned and nudged his father. 'Remember when that was all we ever had Dad? Except when you had a rush of blood and barbecued bacon and eggs for us?'

'I did that for *you*, mate. After you turned eighteen and started having a few beers with the Campbell lads, you'd be a bit worse-for-wear some Sunday mornings. And we often had Callum stay, and sometimes Douggie too. The greasy fry-up was for your benefit. Good for a hangover.'

'Aw, thanks Dad.' Harry waggled his eyebrows. 'I remember you sitting up with us some nights, drinking around the fire. You needed the fry-up as much as we did.'

Robbie snorted, then grinned. 'You'll never really know for sure, son.'

Lucy bounced in as they finished their coffee. 'What's so funny?' She grabbed a tub of yoghurt from the fridge and a handful of strawberries. She plonked herself on a bar chair at the kitchen counter, her eyebrows raised as she waited for a response.

'We were joking around about the crap breakfasts we used to make before we moved here with you and Nik.' Harry walked around the kitchen and sat beside his step-sister. 'We're so lucky to have you.' He placed an arm around her shoulders and squeezed them.

Lucy grinned and nodded. 'You *are* lucky Harry Stewart.' She giggled then and Harry looked over her head to Robbie, who gave him a pleased nod.

Standing, Harry leaned over and kissed the top of Lucy's head. 'We really are lucky, Luce.'

Nicole bustled in and Lucy quickly finished her breakfast then turned to Harry. 'You'll pick me up at twelve, Harry?'

'Of course.' Harry hesitated. 'What are your plans this afternoon Lucy? Do you have homework?'

'Nah! Finished that on Friday night.' She looked at him hopefully. 'I wondered if we could go for a ride. Banjo looks a bit fat.'

'He's not fat, Lucy!' Harry laughed out loud. 'But yes, I was thinking we could ride out to the river, perhaps take a picnic with us, and have a swim.' He loved seeing the happy grin she flashed him. Good.

After the others left, Harry brought all the horses into the small paddock beside the house, where he'd spread some hay. He dealt with Robbie's stock horse first, a large gelding called Blackjack. Tying him to the hitching rail, Harry filed his feet and checked his teeth. He caught Honey then, and Diana followed her to the rail.

Nicole generally rode Honey, and Lucy rode the smaller mare, Diana. But since he'd been home, Harry had been working with a couple of younger stock horses and had started Lucy on Banjo, a chestnut gelding. His own mount, Lawson, was a quarter horse he'd bought from a breeder in the Darling Downs. He hoped to enter him in the camp draft event at the Barrington rodeo in the new year.

Keeping Lawson and Banjo in the smaller paddock, he released the others and glanced at his watch. He'd need to drive into town in half an hour. He checked there was water in the horse troughs, then strode back to the house. He'd just wash his hands and face. There was no point having a shower if he was planning a swim at the river.

Cattle dog Scout and her offspring Minnie were lying in the shade of the overgrown lemon tree near the back of the house. Harry knelt to pat them both and checked they had water too. He glanced up at the tree. *He really should trim that back, it was out of control. A job for another day.*

Whistling quietly to himself, he washed up in the laundry trough and ran his damp hands through his hair. Thick and dark, it was standing up a bit on one side. He slapped his hat on and strode to his car.

The main street was quiet as he parked outside the café. He was a few minutes early but he walked inside. He'd pick up something for lunch and their afternoon picnic. Lucy had been working all morning, she'd be hungry. And he wanted this to be a treat for her.

Kristen greeted him at the counter. 'Hi Harry, Lucy's just about ready to go.'

'Good. While I wait, can I have a couple of ham salad wraps please?' Harry scanned the cakes and slices on display, wondering what Lucy would enjoy.

'Lucy said you're going riding this afternoon, Harry.' Hannelore's voice broke his concentration and he spun around.

She was standing at the counter, untying her apron, smiling broadly. Before he could respond, she continued, 'Thank you for inviting me, I'm keen to meet your horses.'

'Um, er, yes. Um, good.' Harry was confused. Lucy appeared behind Hannelore, who was now wearing a slight frown. Lucy nodded her head, pointing silently to Hannelore.

Harry straightened, speaking with more confidence. 'Yes. Lucy mentioned earlier this week that you were keen to see the horses and maybe take a ride.' Lucy, still standing behind Hannelore, nodded vigorously and gave Harry a thumbs up.

Hannelore looked at Lucy as she stepped up to the counter, where she placed three salad wraps. 'Lucy?' Hannelore sounded uncertain. She looked at Harry. 'You didn't know, did you Harry?'

'I knew you were keen and that Lucy planned to invite you.' Harry improvised. 'But I wasn't certain you would be free today.' He gestured towards the kitchen. 'Able to get away.'

Kristen popped her head out of the kitchen. 'Go Hanna. I've got Mum here. We'll be fine.'

Harry nodded a silent thank you to Kristen, then turned back to Hannelore. 'We're planning to have a quick lunch before we ride.' He pointed to the sandwiches. 'Then have an afternoon snack by the river.' Looking again at the display, he pointed to a very rich-looking chocolate cake. 'And three pieces of that please.'

Hannelore seemed to relax slightly. She lifted a cake container onto the counter, opening the lid to reveal an assortment of tiny sweets. With just a glance Harry identified tartlets with a strawberry on top, mini muffins and several pieces of chocolate slice. 'My contribution. As a thank you.' He loved the way her eyes widened when he peeked inside the container.

'Oh, you can ride with me anytime Hanna Tucker, if you're

providing dessert.' Harry laughed loudly and Lucy and Hannelore followed him out, calling their goodbyes to Kristen and Cathy as they went.

It was crowded in the Ute, but Lucy slid into the middle seat without complaint, and Harry turned towards Copeland and home. 'Have you ridden much Hanna?' He was wondering which horse to give her. Maybe Honey, the one Nik rode most often. She was quiet and steady yet had a smooth action.

'A few times.' Hannelore sounded a bit nervous. 'Only at horse-riding places, you know, where they just follow the horse in front. I don't know much.' She paused then, and glancing at her, he saw she was smiling as if remembering something fun. 'There was this one time, in Margaret River. I stayed at a friend's farm and we rode their stockhorses. We rounded up some cattle and brought them into the yards. I had the best time!' Her eyes were shining and Harry saw a glimmer of something. *Happiness? Interest for sure.*

'That's great Hanna.' He nudged Lucy. 'Which horse for Hanna do you think?'

'Honey.' Lucy sounded sure. She turned to Hannelore. 'She's the mare Mum rides most of the time. She's very steady.'

'Okay. I'll do whatever you tell me, Lucy. You're the boss.' Hannelore sounded more relaxed and Harry smiled internally. This could be an interesting afternoon.

Harry slowed the car, then turned into the driveway which was framed on both sides by poplar trees. He continued slowly, knowing that the first glimpse of their home, the old Courthouse that Nik and Lucy had renovated, would make a spectacular impression. He was right.

'Ohh.' Hannelore breathed the words quietly and leaned

forward. He slowed the vehicle slightly. 'What year was it built?' She stared straight ahead as the two-storey sandstone building came into full view.

'In the eighteen-eighties. It was the original police station and jail downstairs and the courthouse upstairs.' Lucy answered, her pride in her home evident.

'It's magnificent.' Hannelore turned to Lucy. 'Will we have time to have a look inside?' She swivelled in her seat, her face aglow with interest.

Just as Harry said 'yes' and pulled in beside the house, Hannelore spoke again, her voice louder this time. 'The horses! I can see the horses!' He'd barely stopped the vehicle and she was out of the car, all thoughts of a house-tour seemingly forgotten as she walked briskly to the side paddock where Banjo and Lawson were tied.

'Go with her Lucy. Don't let her get in the paddock with them.' Harry spoke quietly, pleased to see Lucy catch up with Hannelore before she reached the horses, slowing her down.

Harry bustled over to the tack room hidden partly behind the house and carried more hay across, calling to the mares in the larger paddock as he walked towards the girls. 'C'mon, c'mon.' He was pleased to see the other three horses arrive at a trot. He threw the hay to them, noting Hannelore had her hand through the fence, stroking Lawson's neck. He walked up to Honey, clipped a lead rope to her halter and in two paces had her tied beside Banjo and Lawson.

They stood for a few minutes, Harry between the girls, leaning on the fence. Lucy introduced Hannelore to all the horses and told her about their different personalities. Hannelore was entranced.

'Right. The afternoon will go quickly.' Harry was all business now. 'Let's nip upstairs and have our lunch first. We'll take water with us, and the desserts you made will fit in my saddle bag.' Looking from Lucy to Hannelore, he added, 'I don't suppose you mentioned we might swim at the river, Lucy?'

'I did Harry, and Hanna nipped home after the morning rush and got her swimsuit.' Lucy folded her arms and gave Harry a cheeky I-told-you-so look.

'And jeans, socks and boots. They're in my backpack, in the car.' Hannelore stood beside Lucy and crossed her arms too, and he laughed.

'Okay. You're sorted. Lunch, then change and we'll head off.' Harry was pumped. Hannelore and Lucy were vibrating with excitement.

They ate quickly and the girls changed, putting their swim-suits on under jeans and tee shirts. He threw a pair of board shorts into the saddlebag with their container of snacks. Lucy would carry another flask of water in her backpack.

Out at the hitching rail, he passed a tube of sunscreen to Hannelore. 'A bit on your face and arms. It won't get much hotter, but there's a kick in it today.'

Lucy helped Hannelore with Nik's helmet and then put her own on. Harry just crammed his cowboy hat on a little harder. 'Alright, Lucy, you mount Banjo, and I'll let you out into the houseyard.'

Harry turned to Hannelore, who was standing beside Honey, murmuring softly as she stroked her neck. *Good. She has a gentle touch.* 'Are you ready Hanna?' He saw her gulp, then nod. 'Alright, I'll hold her head while you mount up.' He watched as Hanna placed her left foot in the step, then bounced on her right foot once, twice, then swung up into the saddle as if she'd done it a thousand times. He walked around the horse and checked her feet were firmly in the stirrups. He noted she held the reins correctly, and not too tight.

Looking up at her, sitting high in the saddle, he couldn't see beyond her happy grin. *The girl loves horses. Who knew?* 'Are you able to take Honey through the gate and wait beside Lucy?' He'd put her on a lead rope if he had to, but she nodded confidently. Tapping Honey gently with her heels she turned her without tugging at her mouth. She walked her through the gate and stopped right beside Lucy. *Hmm. Good control.*

As he led Lawson through and closed the gate, he looked at Hannelore from behind. *Sits well. And a good seat.* He had another quick, appreciative look at her backside sitting neatly in the stock saddle. *Lovely seat.* He chuckled.

'What's so funny Harry?' Lucy squinted at him as he threw himself up into Lawson's saddle and drew in beside them. He improvised. 'I'm not used to seeing you on Banjo. He's much bigger than Diana. I was just chuckling at how you looked when you first started riding.' He winked at her. 'You're an accomplished stockwoman now.' Lucy blushed and leaned forward, patting Banjo on the neck.

'Alright ladies. We'll ride on the verge until we get to Barrington East Road. It's wide all the way along, and the horses are used to cars going by. Lucy, you can lead and we'll put Hanna between us. We'll just walk until we get to the turn-off.'

Then to Hannelore, he said, 'We'll walk for the first bit so you and Honey can get used to each other. I'm right behind you, and if you feel uncomfortable at all, I'll be beside you in seconds.' He smiled then. 'But Hanna, I think you're okay. You sit well, hold the reins lightly and seem comfortable.'

'Thank you Harry.' Her eyes were shining, her face flushed. She was just so darn happy that he felt himself grinning back at her.

They walked the horses briskly for about fifteen minutes, then turned off to the smaller road, still riding on the wide verge, away from any traffic. Lucy tapped Banjo into a trot, and Hannelore followed suit on Honey. She rose to the trot perfectly and Harry congratulated himself for staying at the back. *Safety purposes of course.* But the sight of her firm bottom rising up and down on the saddle did something to him. *Settle Harry.*

Further along, they crossed the road and rode in a wide grassed area beside the river, following its meandering path. They were riding together now and Lucy asked Hannelore if she wanted to canter. She nodded yes while gathering the reins in more firmly.

He let the two of them canter ahead, following behind on Lawson in a slow canter. Lucy slowed Banjo as they approached the place they often stopped at, where the bank was not steep, and they could walk the horses into the river. Hannelore seemed to take a moment to slow Honey, and Harry was just about to catch up to her and grab the bridle when she slowed to a trot, then a walk, and turned back to join Lucy.

Harry dismounted quickly. Looping Lawson's reins over his arm he reached out, holding the other horses as the girls got off. He noticed Hannelore rub her backside and inwardly chuckled. *She'd be sore tomorrow.* 'Lucy, can you unsaddle Banjo? We can walk them into this shallow part here, riding them bareback. Or you can lead them in if you prefer.'

'Sure.' Lucy began unsaddling Banjo and Hannelore immediately did the same with Honey. He hadn't expected that. They sat the saddles under the nearby tree. 'We'll take off our jeans and boots Harry, then it won't matter if we go in up to our waist.' Lucy looked to Hannelore, who nodded in confirmation. 'I think we'll walk them in, rather than ride.'

'Good idea.' He waited until the girls were ready. They left their tee shirts on over their swimsuits. He handed them the reins but asked them to wait for him. He unsaddled Lawson quickly, then standing on the other side of the horse he removed his boots, jeans and shirt and pulled his board shorts on.

Leading Lawson towards the girls, he thought he saw Hannelore give him a quick look up and down. But she turned to speak to Lucy before he could be sure. Harry interrupted their quiet chat. 'Alright. I'll take Lawson in and you follow. It's best to keep near the edge so they're walking, rather than swimming. Once they've cooled we'll tie them to the tree and we can swim.'

They went in with the horses, and the girls played around, splashing water over the horses' backs and each other. Lawson snorted and moved away, but the other horses enjoyed it. Twenty minutes later, they had let the horses drink, then tied them up by the tree, away from the saddles. Lucy kept her tee shirt on and ran back to the riverbank, diving out over the river. Harry had a moment's worry until he reminded himself that Lucy swam here all the time. Hannelore removed her tee shirt and hung it from a branch to dry.

All the moisture seemed to leave Harry's mouth. He swallowed as she walked towards him wearing a hot pink bikini. It wasn't skimpy or revealing. It was a bit like the ones they wore in the fifties. Fuller briefs and wide shoulder straps. He met her eyes and looked away, gulping. She was perfectly proportioned with what his father would call an *hourglass figure*. Her large breasts were held firm and high in the bikini top, and lovely rounded hips were accentuated by the slightly old-fashioned bottom piece. A string bikini wouldn't have affected him more. He needed to get in the river. Quickly.

He turned, ran two steps and dived over the water, entering it where the current ran swiftly. The water took him downstream, past Lucy. He began swimming to the side, then slowly worked his way back to where both girls were splashing around near the riverbank.

They waved to him, then pointed to the other side of the river. There were a few boulders there, half submerged, that provided a relaxing place to sit away from the current. They seemed to race each other across and he had a moment of pride when Lucy reached the rocks first. She had no confidence just a few years ago when she first arrived, and he had brought her here many times, improving her water skills.

Harry joined them but remained submerged to his chest. Hannelore was animated, talking about the ride, Honey, and how much she loved it. It was music to his ears. He already liked this woman. That she loved horses was a bonus. Later they dried off in the sun, then Hannelore pulled her tee shirt on, saying she didn't want to burn. They ate most of the treats she had supplied. *And the woman can cook.* Harry grinned as he lay back momentarily, pulling his cowboy hat over his face.

HANNELORE

Acknowledging internally that Harry was unaware of Lucy's invitation to ride-and-picnic, Hannelore was too excited to push the point. And to his credit, he appeared delighted.

Lucy was quiet when Hannelore first met her, but the evenings they'd spent baking together had broken through her reserve. Now she was open and chatty, especially when Hannelore asked about her animals and home.

One night, while they waited for a tray of individual apple strudels to cook, Lucy quietly told Hannelore the reason her mother had moved them to Barrington.

They had escaped an abusive partner and stepfather and Nicole had been physically hurt. Lucy confessed she had been traumatised and had withdrawn, speaking only to her mother, who had home-schooled her for almost a year.

But they met Robbie and Harry the day they moved to Barrington, intending to renovate the old courthouse into their home and short-term accommodation. Robbie, assisted by cattle dog Scout and his horses, helped Lucy find her voice again.

Lucy's story moved Hannelore, and her version of Harry – as a caring big brother – seemed quite a contrast to her own version of him *as a player*.

Despite her doubts about Harry, the lure of a horse ride was too strong to turn down. And she'd have Lucy there. What could go wrong?

Hannelore listened attentively to Lucy's description of her home and the renovations they'd undertaken. Her first glimpse of the stately building had taken her breath away.

Although older than the bank and the post office building where she lived in the apartment above, it had the same graceful lines and stately charm. She'd had a quick peek inside while they had lunch, but there wasn't time for a full tour. There were other buildings, too, that Lucy referred to as The Stables and The Garage – that had been renovated into accommodation sympathetic to the style of The Courthouse. Hannelore hoped she'd have a chance to see them properly, perhaps with Nicole one day.

But no sooner had she marvelled at The Courthouse (it would always require capitals when she thought of it), than she spotted the horses in the paddock to one side. She had scrambled out of Harry's Ute and almost jogged towards them, but Lucy had caught her up and quietly said, 'Slow down Hanna, you'll startle them.'

And then the magic began. She rode a pretty grey mare called Honey, who responded to her touch beautifully, and once they started, her nerves vanished in the pure joy of being on horseback. Lucy was in front and Hannelore knew Harry was behind her, but she focussed only on the horse beneath her, the view of the mountains, then the river, confident that Harry would alert her to anything else.

And that's when she met him. *The Harry Stewart Lucy talked about.* The caring-big-brother-capable-cowboy. Yes, she saw the way he looked at her in the swimsuit and if she admitted it, she liked that *he liked* what he saw. But it was much more than that. His gentleness with the horses. The way he instructed her patiently, without judgement. The way he joked with Lucy yet watched her as she swam and cavorted in the water, ensuring she was safe.

And that was another thing. Hannelore had felt safe and cared for the whole day. From her first moment with the horses until the last when they returned them to the paddock after brushing them down.

She knew he was watching, without criticism or male-chauvinist-bossiness, and she also knew he would help if she needed it. But he was happy to let her do everything herself without making her feel *small*, or unskilled. *Those* feelings she was familiar with. She admitted to herself that the way her father had treated her mother much of the time, and even Hannelore when she was his apprentice, was not acceptable.

Seeing Millie with Finn now, how they were with each other, had raised her expectations. She had friend-zoned Harry as a player. But maybe there *was* more to him? *Something to think about.*

———

They were sitting under the big plum tree in the front yard, playing a ball-throwing game with Minnie while Scout slept beside them, her head on Harry's leg, when Robbie and Nicole returned.

Lucy ran over to the car as her mum got out, telling her about Hannelore riding Honey and their picnic at the river. Robbie and Nik joined them under the tree, chatting about the seafood lunch in Forster and their time with Finn and Millie.

'Has mum gone out to Finn's tonight?' Hannelore stood, wondering if Harry would drive her back to town or if she should call Millie.

'No Hanna.' Nicole grinned. 'She picked up some fresh prawns and she's planning to make you a garlic prawn pasta dish. Something she said you love.'

'Oh!' Hannelore's mouth watered. She knew that dish and her tummy gurgled just thinking about it.

'I heard that Hanna!' Lucy laughed and Hannelore blushed.

'I'd better get you back to town Hanna.' Harry spoke quietly. 'We were going to ask you to stay for dinner, but you've got a date with some prawns. Garlic prawns.' He grinned and nudged her with his shoulder.

'Uh huh.' She laughed with him. 'And I'm keen. Mum hasn't cooked this for me since I left home.'

Nicole looked at her watch, then at Lucy. 'Shower, Luce, and I'll start dinner.' She turned to Hannelore, giving her a quick hug. 'You can drop out here and ride Honey anytime. I don't ride much myself.' Hannelore saw the quick glance she gave Robbie. 'Except for the occasional river picnic.'

Lucy said goodbye and hurried into the house, followed by Robbie and Nicole. Harry picked up Hannelore's backpack. 'Is there anything else Hanna? Oh, your container is in the fridge ...'

She reached out, touching his hand. 'Leave it, Harry. Lucy can return it next time she comes to work.' Somehow touching his hand turned into holding it. Or maybe he was holding hers. She didn't pull away, and they walked to his vehicle. 'Um, there's a few treats left. Enough for dessert for the four of you.' She heard the pride in her voice. She didn't know how to thank Harry and Lucy for the afternoon they'd given her. *But she could feed them.*

'Excellent. I hope Dad doesn't find them first. He's got a sweet tooth.' His grin was disconcertingly lop-sided as he opened the door for her. She wanted to say something, but he passed her the backpack and closed the door. Hannelore watched him walk around the front of the car to the driver's side. She could have sworn he was whistling, but he stopped when he opened the door.

They drove to the main road in silence. Hannelore was trying to form the right words to thank Harry, and she was hoping she'd be invited again. He surprised her when he spoke first. 'Tell me more about the book shop project Hanna.'

'Oh. Yes! The bookshop!' She paused to mentally shift gear, but once she started, Hannelore couldn't keep her enthusiasm at bay. 'It began as a possibility to fill the shop downstairs once Greta moves the last of her stock out before Christmas. Rose suggested it. A bookshop for Indie authors like her.' She sat up straighter and laughed while clapping her hands quickly. 'The whole concept is because of us, actually.'

'Us?' He looked puzzled.

'Yes! That day you showed me the apartment upstairs, and I said that small room would make the perfect reading room.'

'Really? That wasn't *us*, Hanna. That was *you*. Your concept. But as soon as you said it I could totally see that room as you described.' He took one hand off the steering wheel and patted her leg quickly, then just as quickly removed it. 'Go on.'

'Oh okay. Thank you.' Hannelore paused as Harry drove across the bridge. 'Um, so Rachael was keen on the idea but concerned it wouldn't be viable. You know, the population of Barrington not being big enough to support it. And that's when Meggie told us about small towns in Wales and Scotland that have dozens of bookshops and they're actually a tourist attraction.' She'd thought about that many times. A trip to the United Kingdom to see those small towns was now on her bucket list.

'A tourist attraction?' Harry shook his head in seeming disbelief.

'I know! Right?' Hannelore leaned forward as Harry turned up the main street. It was close to dusk and not busy at all. 'But wait! That's not the best part!' She heard him chuckle as he pulled into a spot in front of the post office but kept speaking. This was a subject close to her heart. 'There are a few bookshops over there.' She waved one hand around. 'In the UK. They have an apartment upstairs that tourists can stay in AND *actually work in the book-shop*. Or *run the bookshop*. For like, a week!' The concept still boggled her mind.

'Oh.' Harry's tone had a touch of disbelief in it.

'Oh indeed!' Hannelore turned in her seat, eyebrows raised. 'I'm amazed too, but it's true. And they're booked out months, even years, in advance!' She leaned towards him as she spoke and somehow one of her hands was in his again. 'You may not believe this Harry Stewart, but *readers* are enthusiasts. It's more than a hobby, or a pastime. It's a lifestyle.'

'So Rachael wants to package the apartment and bookshop?' He had a small crinkle on his forehead, but rather than sounding sceptical, she sensed he was trying to grapple with the concept and bed it down in his mind.

'Yes! Exactly. And the brainstorm brought up more ideas and Kristen's Auntie Judith is going to help and Meggie and Harriet are looking at the marketing.' She heard herself and knew her words were running together, but she was pumped. 'We're investigating running it as a not-for-profit and using volunteers.'

Hannelore stopped then. She badly wanted to be involved with the book shop but she hadn't thought through what that might look like for her. She needed to talk to Millie.

Pausing, her hand still in his, she looked into his eyes. She wanted to thank him for the day, and now she was home and needed to go inside. She wished the moment would slow down for her. Hannelore retracted her hand, then raised it and touched the side of his face.

Harry blinked and his features seemed to soften. In almost a whisper, she spoke, hoping he would recognise the sincerity of her words. 'Thank you Harry. Really. For today. I had the best time.' His face was closer now, his gaze intense. *Was he going to kiss her?* She frowned. She'd hoped he would take her words seriously.

Turning properly in her seat, she opened the car door, reached for her backpack and stepped out. Holding the door open she looked in at him. 'I'm serious Harry. Thank you.' As she closed the door she thought she heard him say, quietly, 'I know that.'

32

RACHAEL

Barrington Book Club – Rachael, Rose, Millie, Hannelore, Kristen, Melanie, Harriet, Meggie, Laura, Nicole, Judith
Apologies – none
Book – ***Head for the Hills*** by Tricia Stringer

RACHAEL PAUSED AT GRETA'S GIFT SHOP AND PEERED through the window. It was empty of stock, the garden centre had picked it all up this week. There were still some shelves along one wall and a small counter, but it was otherwise bare. Greta's mum had taken a turn for the worse and she wasn't returning. She'd paid rent to the end of December when the lease finished. The timing was good.

'It's not large, but with clever shelving and fittings it can be fit for purpose.' Judith had materialised beside her, a large tote bag over one arm.

'Hello Judith.' Rachael smiled warmly at her new friend. She had been buoyed by Judith's participation at the brainstorming for the bookshop and she was hoping she might take on the management, if only for the first year or so. 'So pleased you're joining our book club.'

Judith laughed then, joyous and loud. She leaned in, saying in a stage whisper, 'It's not the only reason I've moved to Barrington, but it could be one of them.' Rachael laughed with her, then linked her arm through Judith's. They walked into the café side-by-side.

'Hi Rachael, hello Auntie!' Kristen waved from behind the counter. 'Coffee? Or straight to the wine?'

Rachael laughed again when Judith answered, withdrawing a bottle of white wine from her tote. 'Straight to the wine dear. Open this one first, it's cold.' Kristen took the bottle of wine, handed several wine glasses to them and pointed to the table in the back where the others were already gathering, chatting and finding their seats.

A chorus of hello's greeted them, and Judith was made welcome, sitting next to Laura. They knew each other, Laura had negotiated the purchase contract on Judith's house.

Rachael gestured to the long board down the centre of the table, with an assortment of cheese, cold meats, dips and crackers taking up almost the entire length. 'This is new Millie.'

'Another Hanna-idea. Robbie made the boards up, it's good for groups. We've got a few share platters on the menu here, but we've been using them more for Barrington Elopements. They're easy to set up, even on trestle tables in a paddock.' Millie chuckled. 'We did one of those mid-week. Only twelve people, with a long table set up between rows of grape vines out at Finn's.'

'His wine and our food and the photos taken by a local lass, Trudy. Stunning pics, some in black and white. It was a cloudy afternoon, and it's all a bit moody in the background, but the couple and their guests were playful and happy.' Millie shook her head. 'So much talent in this area.'

'Yes.' Rachael glanced at Hannelore, chatting with Harriet and Rose at the other end of the table. 'So much talent. I saw photos on social media of the croquembouche Hanna made recently for another wedding. To be honest, I'd never seen one before. It looked amazing!'

Millie sighed. 'My girl. So clever. And with a great work ethic.' She shook her head and Rachael heard an unexpected wistfulness in Millie's tone. 'But she's still working herself out.' More quietly she added, 'The relationship between her father and me didn't set a good example.'

Just as quietly Rachael replied, with one hand lightly touching Millie's shoulder. 'You're an independent businesswoman, Millie, in a healthy relationship, surrounded by friends in a community that respects you. That's the example you're setting.'

Millie nodded and took a deep breath. 'Thank you Rachael. I needed to hear that.'

The wine bottles were passed along the table. Laura had brought a red and Judith's bottle of white was almost empty. Rachael had dropped two bottles of champagne in earlier in the day and asked Millie to keep it cold until the end of their book club gathering.

'So. *Head for the Hills* by Tricia Stringer.' Rose held up a copy of the book. 'Who loved it?' She turned to Rachael. 'The Council election, Rach? Did that trigger anything for you? Were you hoping she'd win?'

'Funny, but I really didn't. Yes, it made me think of the election here. And you, Steve and Jill are doing a great job with your colleagues on Council. But I did want Margot to find her passion. Objecting to the development though,' Rachael laughed then, 'was definitely a trigger. All small towns must go through similar things. And the community was fabulous. And very real.'

'It was the family connections for me.' Judith spoke confidently. 'You all know my younger sister Cathy. Kristen's mum. But I also have sisters Bernadette, Diane, Teresa and Jeanette. I know.' She rolled her eyes. 'Big Catholic family. We've had our moments over the years. Our family tiffs.' She grinned at Kristen who nodded and giggled, almost dropping the olive she was adding to an already-laden biscuit.

'The family dinners, and the menus. Catering for various dietary requirements. So real. And it made me think of them so much that while reading this book, I contacted each of my siblings, some by phone, facetime and messenger.' Judith smiled wistfully for a moment. 'But I've always been a Tricia Stringer fan. I've read every one of her books. Loved them all.'

Hannelore nodded enthusiastically, then chimed in, 'I loved the social media conversations in the book. Hilarious! The one who always responded in capital letters, like she was shouting. Funny and clever. But the story, so small town, reminded me a bit of Barrington.' She bit her lip then and glanced at Rose. 'Not in a bad way and I know I've only been here five minutes, but the community. You know.'

Rose laughed and nudged Hannelore with her shoulder. 'So funny. And yes, I found myself thinking of Barrington too. And some of its characters.' She leaned in. 'The one that shouted on social media.' Rachael held her breath, wondering what Rose would say next. 'Joyce Wilson. The mail contractor. Just saying.'

'Ba ha ha. Too funny Rose. But yes, you're right!' Laura guffawed, and Melanie snort-laughed. 'Stop it, Rose! Joyce is a bit ... er ... opinionated. And hard of hearing.'

The conversation continued, and at one point, Hannelore brought two jugs of water to the table while Kristen tidied away the remnants of their snacks.

The chat petered out when Millie placed a small plate, dessert fork and spoon in front of everyone.

Rachael cleared her throat. 'I ... er ... have an announcement.' She looked at Kristen. 'Could you bring some champagne glasses please, and the two bottles of champagne I dropped in earlier?' Kristen and Hannelore hurried to the kitchen, returning with the items.

'Ooh, champagne. Lovely.' Melanie held her glass out, and then passed it to Harriet when it was full. Within minutes they all had a glass in front of them.

Rachael lifted her glass. 'Thanks to you, all of you, we're going to open a bookshop in Barrington.' They all began chatting and laughing and saying congratulations, and how exciting, but Rachael held up her hand until she had their attention again. 'Raise your glasses ladies. To Hanna, for the fabulous reading room idea upstairs. To Nik for pulling the renovation design together. To darling Rose for the idea of the bookshop. To you Harriet, and Meggie, for running the brainstorm.' She turned to Judith then. 'And to Judith, our newest friend. Your not-for-profit concept is a winner. Our accountant has already begun the paperwork to set it up so that Steve and I remain at arm's length.'

Rachael brought the glass to her lips, taking a large sip. The champagne fizzed as she held it for a second in her mouth, then swallowed. In her mind, she saw Debbie's face, happy and smiling and part of this group. She'd be pleased, Rachael knew that. And her heart swelled.

'I'm so excited Rachael.' Hannelore almost wriggled with enthusiasm. 'Do you have any idea who will manage it yet, and how the volunteer roles may be sorted?' Turning to Rose, she continued. 'And Rose, can you tell me which authors will be coming? Are we doing the author-in-residence thing?' Turning back to Rachael quickly, a small amount of champagne spilled from her glass. 'When will the apartment be ready? Is Robbie fitting out the shop? When will the books arrive?'

'Stop! Hanna!' This was Millie, laughing and shaking her head. 'Take a breath, Hanna. And can you please bring out your dessert for tonight?'

'Oh. Yes ... sorry.' She pushed her chair back and stood, taking another sip from her glass before placing it gently on the table. Then she grinned. 'But I'm excited!' They all laughed as they watched her almost run back to the kitchen.

Harriet asked Rachael a question and she turned her attention away from Hannelore's hasty retreat. 'Sorry Harri, I didn't catch that.'

'Hannelore's questions are good. Excellent. Would you like to convene another catch-up to sort out the volunteer system, discuss the author program and bookings for the apartment, and so on?'

Harriet stopped speaking, bringing her hand to her mouth in shock. Rachael spun around, and there was Hannelore, almost to the table, carrying the most gorgeous confection Rachael had ever seen. She knew it was a croquembouche from pictures she'd seen. But it was so beautiful up close, with delicate strands of toffee laced around it and what looked like caramel, or maybe butterscotch, sauce dripping in lazy rivulets in and around the profiteroles.

'Ohh. That's stunning!' Rachael moved back in her seat, as Hannelore placed it gently on the board in the centre of the table, right in front of her. 'Gosh. Hannelore. So much work must go into this.'

They all marvelled at it and Hannelore blushed and looked flustered until Millie said she'd serve it up.

'It seems such a shame to cut into it.'

'Wait, I'm taking a photo of it.'

'Hang on, let's get a photo of all of us with it.'

They all moved to one side of the table, and Hannelore stood on the other, her back to them, taking a selfie that included the side of her face, the gorgeous dessert, and everyone laughing. *How perfect. Debbie would love this.*

Returning to their seats, Millie served them all a couple of profiteroles covered in toffee strands, and Kristen passed around a small jug of extra caramel sauce. Rachael had never tasted anything quite like it. It melted on her tongue. She looked at Hannelore in awe. 'You, my young friend, are a rare talent. This is perfection. I've never...' She couldn't find any more words.

'Uh huh!' Rose clapped her hands, then stopped, her face suddenly solemn. *What?* But she continued. 'What happens at book club, stays at book club. I vote we don't tell the men how spoilt we've been tonight. Champagne, and then this.' She waved towards what was left of the cake. 'This absolute wonder.'

Laughing and talking at once, all of them complimenting Hannelore, Rachael sat back again, just letting the happy energy envelop her.

Judith lay her empty plate on the table in front of her. 'I've scraped the plate clean. Any cleaner and you'll think I licked it. Which I almost did.' Rachael laughed then, her whole body shaking. Judith thumped her on the back a couple of times.

'We need another get-together for the bookshop. To sort out and answer all those questions you asked, Hanna. And we need a name. For the bookshop.' Harriet had her phone out. 'When can we get together? Before Christmas? Or in the new year?'

'Soon? Before Christmas?' Hannelore's tone was pleading, but her face was flushed with excitement.

'Yes. If everyone can make it, let's do it soon. Next week?' Rachael looked at Millie. 'Can we meet here Millie? But let me pay for snacks for the group. You do so much, with book club every month.'

'Next week is fine. The food doesn't cost much and the girls prepare it. We experiment on book club members with new items and serving ideas. It's all good. And I never pay for wine.' Millie chuckled and waved Rachael's offer away.

'Wednesday night? At six? I'll let Meggie know.' Harriet was tapping away on her phone, and in moments, she'd sent an invitation to all of them.

Nicole spoke up then. 'Um, would it be okay if Harry comes?'

Rachael saw Hannelore spin around in her seat towards Nicole, her eyes wide with shock. 'Harry?' she squeaked.

'Yes. If it's alright. He'll be doing the interior fit-out of the shop with Robbie. He said he has some questions.' Nicole looked across the table to Judith. 'For you, I think Judith.'

The evening seemed to break up then, with some drifting outside to their vehicles, and others carting plates and glasses back to the kitchen. Rachael walked outside with Judith, stopping again in front of the little shop. Judith looked through the window, then stood back and peered at the top floor of the building, where the apartment was. 'I'd love to see upstairs when it's ready Rachael.'

'Of course.' Rachael was quietly thrilled with it. The soft furnishings had arrived and it was almost ready for the photographer, Trudy, to take photos for the website and social media pages. 'I'll speak to Harriet. Perhaps anyone keen can meet here at five-thirty, before next week's meeting. She can amend the invitation and re-send.'

'Perfect, thank you.' Judith turned then. 'Here's Kristen, she's running me home.' As Kristen approached, Judith added, 'It's a good thing, Rachael, this bookshop. A really good thing.'

Rachael waved them off and strolled home, as she did after every book club meeting. During the short walk, she carried Debbie in her heart, even letting a few tears slide down her cheeks. But more and more, her walk home was happy rather than sad. Joining book club, reading, had begun as a way of holding Debbie's memory close. But lately, it was more than that. It had become a walk of purpose. She, Rachael Webb, was doing something for herself. She knew Debbie would be pleased if she were alive, and Steve told her often how proud of her he was. But it was her own approval, her confidence in her decisions, that she enjoyed the most. 'Better late than never, Rachael Webb,' she whispered as she opened the front gate.

33

MILLIE

Walking home from book club together, Millie pondered how to broach the subject of Hannelore's career with her. She seemed pensive as they walked and Millie sighed quietly. Best to have the conversation sooner, rather than later.

Once upstairs Hannelore headed straight for the kitchen, calling over her shoulder. 'I'm putting the jug on Mum. Fancy a chamomile tea?'

'Tea. Yes. Lovely.' Millie paused in the living area. 'I'm just going to slip into my yoga pants while you get it made.'

Alone in her room, Millie removed her tailored work pants, replacing them with a pair of comfy, stretchy yoga pants and slipped an old tee shirt over the top. Back in the living room she saw a pot of tea on the coffee table near the window, and two cups. Millie chuckled. Hannelore had the same habit, always changing out of her work gear as soon as she arrived home. *Like mother, like daughter.*

Reappearing in boxer shorts and a tee shirt just as Millie

poured two cups of tea, Hannelore flopped into the other chair. 'Big day today.' Picking up the teacup nearest to her she blew on it, then peered over the rim at Millie, grinning, 'But the book shop project is so exciting and I can't believe it's come together this quickly!' She hesitated then. 'Is it always like this here? Everyone working together on a project?'

Sipping from her own cup Millie smiled at her daughter, loving her enthusiasm. 'In my limited experience, it has been. It may not be everyone in the community, but this group has welcomed me from the start.'

Millie watched as Hannelore placed her cup back on the table and peered through the window, her expression thoughtful. The café sign was visible and Millie looked at it too. *Darling Debbie. Losing her had been terrible. Worse than terrible. But would the opportunity to stay have arisen without her loss?* Millie shook her head, sadly contemplating how such a tragedy could also bring transformational change. For herself, and Rachael too, she suspected. And Hannelore.

'Hanna, love. Can we talk for a moment?' Millie was tentative. She loved how easy living and working with Hannelore was after years of conflict and arguments.

'Yes. Mum, there's something I want to talk to *you* about. About my career, actually.' Hannelore sat up straighter, her tone serious. But Millie detected nerves too. *So this was it. She wants to leave the café to run the bookshop.*

'I'm listening. And Hanna, I'll support your decision, no matter what.' Millie set her cup down and waited.

'Will you Mum?' Hannelore nibbled on her bottom lip for a moment. Something Millie hadn't seen her do in years. She looked young and vulnerable. But she seemed to gather her thoughts and courage and drew her shoulders back. 'I want to stay here. In Barrington.'

Raising her eyebrows, Millie nodded happily. 'Good. And?'

'I've been thinking about my future. And I know I haven't been here long, not even four months.' She looked around the apartment for a moment, and when her gaze settled back on Millie, her eyes were filled with tears. 'I have no right to ask you this after what I put you through, Mum. And I'm so grateful for the opportunity to work with you and share this gorgeous apartment.' She shook her head, tears falling. Millie passed her a tissue and Hannelore murmured, 'I don't deserve it.'

Millie moved to embrace her daughter, comfort her, but she hadn't finished. She lifted her head, wiped her eyes and looked directly at Millie. 'Would you consider letting me buy into the business? The café business? Not a full partnership, but a share?'

Shocked, Millie sat back. *Wow! She did not see that coming!* Before she could gather her thoughts to respond, Hannelore was already on her feet, speaking quickly. 'I know. It's too much. You don't trust me. I don't blame you, Mum. But if you let me stay on, I'll prove to you that I deserve a chance.'

'Wait! Wow! Sit down honey. You threw me. Let me process this.' Millie held her hand out, taking Hannelore's and gently tugged her back to her chair. 'You want to stay in hospitality?'

Hannelore frowned then. 'Of course!'

'Hanna, I thought you were going to tell me that you want to run the bookshop.' Millie chuckled and Hannelore gave her a watery smile. 'I honestly thought you were going to tell me you want a career change. I've been thinking it for the last few weeks, since the bookshop idea came up, and, well, you've completely thrown me now.' Millie started laughing and Hannelore giggled too.

'I love the bookshop idea. Adore it. And I'd love to volunteer to do a shift, you know, once a week or so. I'm passionate about it, actually, but Mum, I love my trade.' More quietly she added, 'and I think I'm good at it. The pastry chef stuff, anyway.'

'You are Hanna. You're amazing. Not just creative with food, but your ideas for new menu items and the way we do food for events. You've been an absolute godsend.' Taking a deep breath, Millie continued. 'And you'd like to be in the business with me? The café? As a partner?' She couldn't believe it and the idea of Hannelore here permanently, and part of the business, fizzed away nicely somewhere deep inside her.

'Yes. I do. But I have some long-term ideas too.' Pausing, Hannelore took another sip of her tea, then screwed her nose up. 'Not so nice when it gets cold.'

'Okay. Long-term then. What are you thinking?' Millie was keen to hear more. She was already impressed with the small changes Hannelore had implemented, so she shouldn't be surprised she had long-term plans.

'Well. Before the bookshop took on a life of its own, I considered asking Steve and Rachael if I could rent the little shop and turn it into a specialist bakery. Wedding cakes, events. And make food for the café there too.' Hannelore waved her hand, as if waving the idea away. 'But the bookshop came to life before I could do more than investigate a few things, like set-up costs.'

Millie wanted to say she'd thought the same thing, about the little shop. But she raised her eyebrows. *She'd investigated costs?*

'And I spoke to Kristen briefly.' She waggled her eyebrows at Millie. 'She's almost an accountant, you know. She could be doing your business accounts, Mum.' Millie nodded, indicating she should continue. 'But then I realised that setting up next door was just duplicating what you have in the café. And that's when it came to me.' Her eyes were shining as she waited for Millie's response.

'When it came to you? You'll have to elaborate Hanna.' Millie's tone was encouraging. *Her daughter was an entrepreneur in the making.*

'It came to me that I could work with you, as a partner of sorts, and invest in the few pieces of equipment you don't have that I'd need, and run my own little business from within the café. Still work in the café over busy periods but build up a specialty 'patisserie' for want of a better term.' She waggled her eyebrows then. 'Kristen said it could be a separate profit centre. I buy the additional equipment and the ingredients for my orders. We could keep part of the pantry and a fridge aside for my stuff. You know, so I'm not cooking with ingredients you've paid for. And the café closes in the evenings, so I could work then or before opening hours when I have events. And if you like the idea, I'd make items for the café too, things you currently buy in.'

'Wow!' Millie was blown away. Hannelore had put quite a lot of thought into it. She was impressed. 'I like it.' Millie stood up and pulled Hannelore to her feet, drawing her into a tight, squeezy hug. 'I love it Hanna, I really love it.'

Stepping back, her hands still on Hanna's shoulders, she pursed her lips. 'My girl. My strong, independent girl. I am so proud of you. But what makes me the happiest is that you want to stay. Here. Work with me.' Suddenly overwhelmed, Millie wiped her own eyes with the back of her hand.

'Really? Really Mum? Have you honestly forgiven me? I

treated you so badly.' Hannelore shook her head. 'I can't believe it. I love you, Mum.'

'One thing you'll learn, one day when you have your own family, is that I'll always be on *Team Hanna*. No matter what. Yes, your words hurt me at the time, but they were said in anger and confusion. There wasn't anything to forgive Hanna. It was brave of you to come here and face me, thinking I was angry with you. Having you here, working with me, has been the happiest few months of my life.' Millie hugged her again, quickly.

Laughing, Hannelore said, 'I'm not sure I believe *that*. I see how you are when Finn is around. I don't think you light up for me in quite the same way.' She ducked as Millie playfully slapped at her, laughing too.

'Maybe not. But that's all I'm saying about that.' She drew her lips into a firm line and Hannelore laughed harder.

'And Mum, there's no rush to move ahead with this idea, but I love that you're okay with it in principle. Now that I'm staying, I think I'll move into Judith's big old house with Kristen. It will give you back your privacy.' Hannelore picked up the cups and empty teapot and walked to the kitchen.

Following her, Millie said quietly, 'I love having you here Hanna. And Finn has offered me a home with him and I've thought about it, wondering if you and Kristen could live here together.'

'Mum. I can see you're not ready for that. After what you went through with Dad. And I know Finn is different, he's lovely. But stay here. Keep your independence. We'll see each other every day at work and we can have dinner together too, some nights. I'd like to come to Finn's again, and maybe I can cook for the both of you at Judith's. She's already said we can do that anytime, have friends over.' Hannelore looked more relaxed now. And happy. Millie felt light and happy, too, but also tired. And she wanted to go to her room and call Finn quietly.

'It's getting late, love, and we have that group in first thing tomorrow. We need to work out the next steps with your business idea, though. Let's talk more over the next few days.' Millie patted Hannelore on the shoulder. 'Good night.'

'Thanks Mum, I'm so pumped I'm not sure I'll sleep.' Hannelore began walking toward her room. She turned then. 'I have some notes, and a business plan framework. I also thought we should probably check with Steve and Rachael that they are okay for us to use the premises for a second business.'

Shaking her head, Millie said, 'You're a marvel, Hanna. Yes to all of that. Perhaps we can ask Meggie and Harriet to help with the business planning, and a marketing strategy when we're ready.' She chuckled then. 'Have you thought of a name for this little business of yours?

'Ha ha. Yes. Kind of. Um. *Nothing but the cake. Bite Size. Small Slice. Tiny Tarts.*' Giggling she left the room, calling back, 'It needs a brainstorm!'

Still chuckling, Millie stepped into her room, closed the door and dialled Finn's number.

She leaned back against her pillows as he answered. 'Millie.' His tone was warm, deep and sexy. She shivered for a second. His voice *got* her every time.

'Finn. I have news.'

34

FREDDIE

Working at the Vet clinic with Angus Hamilton was the best! With his partner Max away, Angus let Freddie assist with surgery and took her on all the big animal calls too.

Yesterday they had pregnancy tested a yard of heifers out at Fraser's place, then spent time with their horses. They bred polo horses, the finest Freddie had ever worked with. She'd been in her element and Angus had commented that maybe she should specialise in equine health. Freddie wondered that too, but being an all-round Vet was better if she wanted to secure a job in a country town that would lead to a partnership, or associate option later on.

Tired and grubby, she was driving home to the farm when she received a text.

Can I see you tonight?

Pulling into the spot by the tractor shed where she usually parked her jeep, Freddie stopped and sent a message back.

> Sorry. Big day. Too tired.

> Ok. Let me know when you're free. We need to talk.

> Ok.

Freddie frowned. He usually ended his messages with kisses. *Was he getting over her?* Surely not! But he had been badgering her for ages to go public about their relationship. She wrinkled her nose. *That would take all the fun out of it.* She tried to picture herself without him in her life. Just to see what it might feel like. But was honestly unable to believe he'd dump her. Smirking to herself, she walked to the house.

35

HARRY

Dressing carefully in a plain navy polo shirt, dark jeans and boots, Harry waited in the kitchen for Nicole. They were going to the bookshop meeting tonight and he wanted to be early, if he could. He knew Hannelore would be there and was hoping he could ask her to dinner at the pub, or even just a drink, after the meeting.

Breezing in with her tote bag in one hand and what looked like a book of paint colours in the other, Nicole stopped when she saw Harry. 'Good. You're ready then.' Turning to Robbie, she asked, 'Are you sure you don't want to come?'

'No. I'll stay here and have dinner with Lucy. Harry has the plans we sketched, and most of the ideas are his, so I'd only be taking up space.' Robbie grinned at Harry, and he was chuffed he was going to present their ideas for the bookshop fit out on his own.

Nicole laughed and kissed Robbie on the cheek. 'Alright then Robbie. But I suspect it's more about you and Lucy watching a show together.' She quirked an eyebrow and Harry glanced at his father. He looked sheepish. *Nik knows him so well.*

'What's the show Dad?' Harry took the bag from Nicole. He had their plans rolled up with an elastic around them in his other hand.

'The Horse Whisperer. Robert Redford.' Robbie chuckled. 'Lucy's read the book, but the movie has only just come on the streaming channel. I haven't seen it since it was first shown at the cinema.' He blinked, and Harry realised that would have been before he was born, when his parents were dating, or engaged.

Nicole didn't miss a beat. 'Excellent. She'll love that. There's cold roast beef and salad for your dinner and I think Lucy brought something home from the café for dessert. Enjoy.'

Clattering down the stairs, Harry leaned forward to open the front door for his step-mum.

'Thank you Harry.' She touched his cheek with her free hand fleetingly and Harry felt himself grow warm. Nicole's easy, generous affection always moved him. They were lucky, he and his father, to have Nik and Lucy in their lives.

Harry opened the door of his Ute for her, and after she slid in he handed her the tote bag and the roll of plans. Sketches really, but if Rachael liked them, he'd draw up plans.

Driving slowly to the main road, he glanced at Nicole when she spoke again. 'Your idea to create more space in the bookshop is brilliant Harry. They'll love it. It's good you'll be there to explain the concept.'

Harry grinned then. Couldn't help himself. And he hoped she was right. 'Thanks Nik.' He hoped she knew just how much her words meant to him. How much *she* meant to him.

36

JUDITH

Eager to tour the apartment upstairs, Judith arrived early and dropped her bag off to Kristen in the café. 'Are you coming up Kristen?' Judith glanced outside. Rachael was at the door with a few of the others.

'I am. We're going to lock the café up.' Kristen chuckled. 'I'm keen to hear what you think Auntie.'

Rachael led the way with Hannelore and Kristen right behind her. Judith waited until last to walk up the stairs as she needed to take her time after the knee replacement earlier in the year. She wondered for a moment if the other knee should be done too.

A tall good-looking young man was just in front of her, but he waited and offered his arm, which she took gratefully. 'You must be Judith. I'm Harry Stewart.'

'Ahh. Hello Harry. I wondered who you were. You've done the renovation up here, I understand.' Judith smiled up at him. He was matching his pace with hers, and having his arm to lean on

196

made it much easier for her. The rest of the group were milling around by the front door and Judith stepped inside confidently but smiled her thanks to Harry as she approached Kristen and Hannelore.

Rachael was in the centre of the room, explaining some of the changes they'd made with infrastructure and furnishings. It was a pretty apartment and had it not been for the stairs, Judith could picture herself living here.

Rachael moved closer. 'Hanna, would you like to lead the way into the reading room? It's your brilliant idea, after all.' Hannelore nodded, but Rachael hadn't finished. 'You go in with Hanna, Judith. It's not a large room.'

Judith followed Hannelore in, with Kristen beside her. 'Oh.' She turned around full circle, taking in the window seat, which her niece was now perched on with Hannelore.

The bookshelves on either side even had books in them. Judith stepped closer. Australian authors. Bryce Courteney, Colleen McCullough, Di Morrisey.

Moving to the side, she ran her hand lightly over the top of the little writing desk. If it wasn't an antique, it was an excellent reproduction and the chair in front of it worked beautifully. A place to write. Letters, books, poetry. Lyrics for a song.

Something about the room just oozed creativity. The armchair on the other side had a small side table where you could lay your book and a cup of tea. *Or a glass of wine.* She chuckled at her own thought. It was only then she realised the room was silent. They were all watching her. *Really? Was her opinion so important?*

Judith made a decision. She strode to the window seat and wriggled her bottom in between the two girls. It was a tight fit and made them all giggle. Looking first at Rachael, then Harry and Nicole, she sighed.

'What Judith?' Rachael looked anxious. 'Have we forgotten something?'

'Not at all.' Judith smiled, and waved a hand in the air, gesturing to the elements in the room. 'Your only problem will be that once readers or writers stay here, they won't want to leave.'

Millie was standing by the armchair, looking at her daughter with pride. Well-deserved pride, Judith thought to herself. But she turned her gaze to Rachael. 'What a fabulous project Rachael. The apartment is a winner, even without the tie-in to the bookshop. I don't think I've ever been in a more inviting reading room.' Glancing around again she noted Rose wasn't with them. 'Has Rose seen this room?' She chuckled. 'Once she does, she might move in permanently.'

Nicole stepped closer to Rachael. 'We brought her up here before we bought the little desk. We found it at an estate auction in Tuncurry. Rose said then, we'd have no trouble getting authors to book in for a writing retreat. But she messaged she'd be late tonight, I think she has the baby with her, so she's probably waiting downstairs for us now.'

Millie instantly moved toward the door, saying over her shoulder, 'I'll nip down and unlock the café.' But Hannelore moved just as quickly. 'I'll do that Mum.' And she was gone, Kristen close behind her.

Harry strode in and held out his hand. Judith took it gratefully and allowed him to pull her to her feet. She patted his arm. 'Thank you Harry.' She thought he mumbled 'my pleasure' as he tucked her hand into the crook of his elbow and walked her slowly back down the stairs. The others walked down in front, with only

Rachael bringing up the rear, as she locked the doors behind them.

Judith smiled to herself. She wished someone would take a picture of her being escorted to the café by the very handsome Harry Stewart. *Wait until I tell my sisters about this.* They would tease her endlessly, a thought she delighted in.

37

MILLIE

Hannelore left the café before Millie, wanting to shower and change before her date with Harry. Although Hanna said it was 'just dinner at the pub', Millie suspected she was trying to play down her interest.

Millie thought again about Ben's words as she walked across the road to the apartment. He said he'd known Harry since he was a boy and believed him to be hard-working and respectful. But a recent event, which he didn't elaborate on, had given him cause to wonder if Harry may have picked up some other habits while working up north. His words had been meant, not to slander Harry's character, but as a word of caution for Hannelore's bene-fit. But Melanie had already told Millie about the night they found Freddie and Harry together, so she had context for the conversation.

In recent weeks, Hannelore had told Millie more about her relationship with Anthony-the-untrustworthy. Her words, not Millie's. She discovered he was using a phone app to hook up with girls when Hannelore worked late. Or early. He'd said the other women meant nothing, but Millie was happy Hannelore had seen through this and left him. Hannelore had exclaimed in horror, 'If one woman can *mean nothing*, then they all can. That was his attitude, Mum. *Women mean nothing.*' Millie agreed.

Just inside the apartment, Millie had barely put her bag down when her phone rang.

'Hi Finn.'

'Millie. How was your day?' His tone was warm and interested.

'Busy, but it's so much easier with Hanna here now. I might be getting lazy.' Millie chuckled at her own words.

'You! Never!' But his tone was light. It was so *easy* with Finn. He continued. 'Luke and I are coming into town for dinner. We're sick of our cooking. Would you and Hanna like to join us at the pub?'

Millie hesitated. Dinner with Finn and Luke would be lovely. But Hannelore was going to the pub with Harry. On a date. 'Hanna has other plans. Um, a date. At the pub. I better check with her first, if she's okay with me being there.'

'Sure.' She loved the way nothing phased Finn. 'If she's not keen that we're there, how about Chinese at the RSL?'

'Give me a few minutes, I'll call you back.' Millie put her phone down. As she did, Hannelore appeared wearing white jeans and a soft pink sleeveless shirt. Her hair was tied back in a loose ponytail and Millie could see she wore no make-up, just a touch of pale pink lip gloss and mascara. She was secretly pleased Hannelore wasn't overdoing it for her date. She looked happy, natural and gorgeous.

'Was that Finn?' Hannelore fiddled with her necklace, then

turned around. 'Can you do this up please Mum? I seem to be all thumbs.'

'It was Finn.' The clasp slipped from Millie's fingers. She picked it up and tried again, peering at it. 'I don't think it's you, Hanna. This clasp isn't closing properly.'

'Oh. Darn. I wondered.' Hannelore turned around, taking the necklace back and glaring at the clasp for a moment. 'I'll take it to a jeweller in Forster next time I go over.'

'Would you like to borrow something of mine?' Millie had a simple rose gold chain that had belonged to her mother that would look lovely with Hannelore's outfit.

Hannelore looked down at herself, touching the neckline of her shirt. 'No. It doesn't need anything. I'm keeping it simple.' She spun around then. 'What do you think? I don't want to be a try-hard.'

'If that means overdressing, then no, you're not a try-hard. You look fresh and pretty and just perfect for a pub date.' Millie smiled. 'But yes, that was Finn. He and Luke are coming into town. They asked if we'd like to join them at the pub for dinner. I, um, said you had dinner plans there yourself. I also said I don't want to, um, cramp your style. So we can go to the Chinese if you'd rather dine in privacy.'

Unsure of Hannelore's reaction, she was surprised when Hannelore laughed. 'Small towns Mum. Sometimes the dining options are limited. There's no reason you can't have dinner at the pub with Finn and Luke. And if I was more confident with Harry I'd say we'd join you. Eat together. But Mum, I want to talk to him and work out where we are tonight. Whether he should be in my friend zone. Or if he's boyfriend material.' She held her hand up when Millie was about to speak. 'And I heard what you said, what Ben told you. But I can work this out for myself.'

'Alright.' Millie was pleased. 'I'll let Finn know. We won't sit too close, but maybe you can join us for a drink or chat at the end of your date?'

'That would be lovely. I'll go over now, I'm meeting him at six. What time will you be there?' Hannelore picked up a small clutch.

'I'll call Finn back, but I expect we'll arrive in about half an hour.' Millie stepped closer and gave Hannelore a quick hug. 'Enjoy your night.' She cocked her head to one side. 'You know what Hanna? I like Harry Stewart, despite Ben's words. You make your own mind up.'

'I like him too Mum. There's something I want to ask him, and once I know the answer, I'll make my mind up.' Hannelore kissed her on the cheek and left.

Millie picked up her phone. 'Finn. The pub is fine. Say six-thirty?' She rushed to her room, to shower and change.

38

HANNELORE

The Second Bookshop Brainstorm
Present: Rachael, Rose (and Harper), Judith, Kristen, Nicole, Harriet, Ben, Millie, Hannelore and Harry
Apologies: Meggie, Laura

'Angus has been called to a foaling, and he's taken wee Charlie with him.' Rose rocked gently from side to side with little Harper on her hip. 'Harper should be alright, she's had supper and may just go to sleep on my lap.'

Hannelore smiled at Harper and pointed to the soft toy she was holding. It was a cute little black and white cattle dog. 'What's your puppy's name?'

'Woof.' The little girl held the toy out and Hannelore took it. She was surprised such a small child could articulate the name.

'Thank you. Woof is lovely, is he a good dog?' She was rewarded by the little sprite nodding vigorously, and a soft chuckle from Rose. Hannelore handed the toy back, then raised her eyebrows to Rose.

'Before you say anything Hanna, watch this.' Rose pointed to herself and asked the child, 'What's my name?'

'Woof.'

Hannelore giggled.

Rose pointed at Ben, who'd just arrived. 'Who's that Harper?'

'Woof.'

'What's your name?'

'Woof.'

Rose sighed then and winked at Hannelore. 'We occasionally get a Mum-mum or Dada, but basically every living thing she meets is called Woof. Even her brother. We have a young cattle dog called Woof because Charlie couldn't say Ruff when he was small, and Harper adores him.'

Harry appeared then and he tickled Harper's cheek with one finger. 'How's Woof?' The little girl held the soft toy out for Harry, who took it, then pretended it was trying to jump out of his hand back to Harper, who laughed and clapped her hands. *This is a side of Harry Stewart I haven't seen. He's good with babies.* Hannelore wanted to say something, but Harriet clapped her hands from the top end of the table, and they all moved to find chairs.

Somehow she was sitting between Harry and Judith, with Rose on the other side of Harry.

'I'm going to throw to you Rachael, just to fill us in on where you're up to with the structure of the business.' Harriet sat down and Rachael began to speak.

'The not-for-profit structure is in place, so we're good to begin ordering stock and sorting out rosters and management.' Rachael smiled across the table at Judith. 'Judith has agreed to be the store manager for the first six to twelve months while we become established, but after that, she wants to be a regular volunteer, like most of us. She will help us find the right manager and train them, once we are certain the business model can sustain that.'

They all clapped and Hannelore was pleased. Kristen had already mentioned Judith would do it, at a reduced rate of pay to help the project get off the ground. So many good people around the table. Rachael continued. 'And the apartment is ready. I want to thank Nik for her styling help and Robbie and Harry for achieving the vision.' Then she turned to Hannelore. 'But it was you, Hanna, who suggested the reading room and without that, I don't think this project would exist. Thank you.'

Hannelore blushed and mumbled away their thanks, but she was secretly pleased. She was totally invested in the project and wanted it to succeed, so badly.

Judith took a sip of wine and looked at Harry. 'And Harry has sketched up an interior fit-out for the shop, which I'm dying to see. Thank you Harry.'

Now Hannelore was curious. She knew he was a builder, with his dad, but she didn't know he had design skills.

'Um.' Harry cleared his throat. 'The shop is quite small, and we want to maximise shelf space, while not compromising the aesthetics of the space.' He began unrolling the plans in his hand. 'The building is old and originally had high ceilings. Fourteen feet high, to be exact. But at some point, a false ceiling was installed in the gift shop area. We've removed a few pieces of it and discovered that the ceiling cavity is, in fact, closer to sixteen feet high, before it meets the bearers of the floor above.'

Harry pointed to the plans and Hannelore leaned forward,

although she tried not to block Judith's view. 'I have a few copies.' Harry passed more sheets around, but Hannelore wanted to focus on the original in front of her. 'I propose that in the entrance of the shop, and above the counter, we leave the high ceiling. We can have bookshelves that go all the way up, with sliding ladders.'

Hannelore drew in a breath. 'Ooh.' *Sliding ladders. How gorgeous.*

The others were smiling and pointing to the plans, then, and there was an atmosphere of excitement around the table. Harry continued. 'Over the majority of the shop and over the bathroom, office and kitchenette at the back, we can install a mezzanine level. It will make a really cosy area, and almost double the footprint of the shop.'

'I love it!' Rose's eyes were glowing. 'Gorgeous. Maybe we can have some chairs, or bean bags up there so that people can browse and even sit down and read.'

'Yes.' He grinned at Rose. 'There's room. The front section of the shop will be airy and open, with room for an author signing desk to one side.' Harry pointed. 'Here, near the window.'

'Oh gosh, Harry.' Judith touched his arm briefly, but her gaze was on Rachael as she spoke. 'This is a whole new ball game. More shelf space, more titles and an area for readers and browsers.'

Hannelore could see Harry glowing with pride. He'd put a lot of thought into the design and she could picture it. *Harry Stewart is clever.* 'We could have a spiral staircase to the mezzanine, which won't be accessible for all.' Hannelore saw Judith frown. But then Harry added, 'But we can put a sort of dumb-waiter style lift arrangement here, behind the stairs, to lift books up and down.' Hannelore saw Judith nod then. She wondered if the spiral staircase would be difficult for her. She hoped not.

Ben leaned forward. He hadn't said much. 'I have two questions. For you Harry, and you Rachael.' Everyone looked at him in expectation.

'Love the stairs and the book-lift idea. How much additional space and cost would be needed to make it a single-person lift to the mezzanine?' Ben glanced around the table. 'Accessibility for all.'

'Let me talk to Robbie about that. But I think you're right. It wouldn't require a lot more space to run a simple lift to the next level.' Harry tapped some notes into his phone.

'And my next question is for you Rachael. But Harry I'd like your opinion too.' Ben smiled at Millie. 'You too Millie. The pantry and walk-in cool rooms for the café run behind the gift shop. That's why it's so much smaller. But if I'm correct in my thinking, none of those reaches more than seven feet from the floor, so there is empty space above them.'

Hannelore caught his meaning straight away and jumped in excitement. 'Yes! You're right Ben. The mezzanine could extend above the back area of the café, over the office, pantry and cool rooms.' She half stood. 'I can run and measure that up now.'

Ben laughed. 'Wait Hanna.' He turned to Millie. 'Is there any use for the space above those areas that you can use in your business Millie, if you were able to access it?'

Millie shook her head. 'Honestly Ben, the café is well designed and even with some additional kitchen equipment,' she glanced at Hannelore, 'we have enough room. Kitchen design is about time and motion and having to nip up to another level for pantry items, for example, is not productive. Our storage area is large, and on some rare occasions, I use Finn's cool rooms for overflow, but that's mostly when we're planning an event at the winery.'

'Rachael?' Ben turned to Rachael, but Hannelore could already see she had thought about it.

'My only hesitation is about the success of the bookshop as a business. What if it doesn't work? Could another business, a different business, utilise the mezzanine area?' Rachael shook her head then. 'I can visualise it for a bookshop. But for something else? I'm not sure.'

Nodding to Ben, Harry took the floor again. 'I'll speak to Robbie. But I agree with Rachael. Until the shop is proven, as a business, pushing into the space above the café may be an unwarranted expense.' He spoke directly to Rachael then. 'Or do you think the mezzanine area in principle is something to save for later? Once you're confident the bookshop is working?'

Hannelore was sure he'd be disappointed if Rachael canned upstairs altogether, but she was impressed that he was slowing down to let her speak to it.

'No Harry. The plans you've drawn up are perfect and very clever. I think the additional space gives the business a head start to be successful. But the extra space above the café can wait.' Rachael laughed. 'It will still be there in a year if we need to consider it then.' To Ben she said, 'but good thinking Ben. If it's a roaring success, we can expand, rather than move to other premises.'

There was general agreement to this, and Hannelore sat back as lots of conversations began around the table. Kristen and Millie walked towards the kitchen and Hannelore jumped up to follow them. They had platters of sandwiches and petite sweets for the group to enjoy. They still had to work through timing and opening hours. Judith was going to present next on stock and

Rose had a plan drawn up with interested independent authors, including their wholesale prices.

Returning with the platter of desserts, she looked from Rachael to Harry. 'One more question. How long will it take you to do the fit-out?' Harry reached for a strawberry tart and Hannelore moved the platter out of reach, giggling. 'I need an answer Harry Stewart.'

'Well if that's the only way I can have one of those sweet bites, I can tell you we need six weeks to complete it. If we start before Christmas, we can have it ready to open in early February.' Harry looked at Judith. 'Provided stock will be here by then.'

'You betcha Harry.' Judith clapped her hands. 'How about Valentine's Day? For the opening?' We'll have Rose as our first signing-author, and she's all about small-town romance.'

'Valentine's Day. Yes.' Rachael smiled happily.

'Good for marketing too.' Harriet sipped her wine, looking thoughtful. 'Romancing the Region.' Turning to the group, she raised her glass, 'to the Barrington bookstore.'

Most raised their glasses, but Hannelore hesitated, and so did Rose.

'Is that the name, Rachael?' Rose turned, which woke Harper, who had been fast asleep against her chest. Harper began to fidget, then cry, and Rose held her close, rubbing her back. But she cried harder. Harry put his glass down and played a silly game of peek-a-boo with Harper, whose sobs gradually subsided.

The others were speaking quietly together, but Hannelore was fascinated by Harry and Harper. After a few moments, the little girl stood in Rose's lap on wobbly legs, then leaned towards Harry with her arms out.

Without hesitation, Harry scooped her up and nestled her on

his lap, facing the table. He cut tiny pieces from the chocolate cake on his plate. He'd already demolished two strawberry tarts, and after receiving a nod from Rose, allowed Harper to pick them up one at a time and pop them into her mouth. Her hands and mouth were covered in chocolate in moments, and she left cute little fingerprints on the front of Harry's shirt, but he didn't seem to mind. *Harry Stewart is a baby whisperer.*

'Back to Rose's question.' Rachael leaned forward. 'I've been calling it *the little Barrington bookstore* in my head, but really, is that the best name?'

'Let's throw some ideas around, I'll note them down.' Harriet picked up her iPad. 'Go.'

'Book Nook.'

'The little Indie Bookshop.'

'Book Haven.'

'Story Nest.'

'Little Barrington book store.'

'Author Attic.'

'Any others?' Harriet looked up from her screen. 'At the end of the day, Rachael, it's your call.'

'I love them all. So creative. Can you read them out again please Harri?' Rachael sat back as Harriet read the names again, more slowly.

'I thought it needed Barrington in it, but it really doesn't. When people are already here, they don't need the name of the town.' Rachael sighed. 'I'm torn.'

'And whichever name you choose, we will always add 'in Barrington' in the messaging and call-to-action.' Harriet added.

'*Book Nook* and *Story Nest* are cute names, but there's something about *the little Indie bookshop* that has a ring to it, for me.' Rachael turned to Rose. 'Which one do you like Rose?'

'Um, *the little Indie bookshop* was the one I threw in, actually.' Rose looked sheepish.

'Will we need to explain what 'Indie' means?' Ben looked concerned. 'I didn't know, before this project.'

'Most *readers* know the term. But it is a unique selling point. We're working with Indie authors too, for the signings.' Judith turned to Rose. 'I think your suggestion works well Rose. And if Rachael is happy with it, I move we lock it in.'

'You're nothing if not definite, Judith.' Millie laughed. 'I'm loving this about you.'

'Me too!' Hannelore took a deep breath. '*The little Indie book-shop*. I can see it now.' She sneaked a look at Harry, who had Harper leaning back against his chest, her eyes drooping with tiredness. Rose drew a wet wipe from the bag slung over the back of her chair and gently wiped the little girl's hands and face. She squirmed but remained snuggled against Harry's chest. *Harry's broad chest.* Harry met her gaze, and while she was tempted to slide her eyes away from his, she didn't.

Rose made moves to leave, and Harry said quietly, 'I'll carry her to your car, Rose. Are you parked in front?'

'Yes. Thank you.' Rose murmured goodbyes to all and Harry followed her to the car, the little girl asleep in his arms.

Hannelore helped clear up as Kristen and Judith left after Rose. When Harry returned, Nicole, Harriet, Millie, and Ben were chatting near the entrance. He walked to the table in the back just as Hannelore finished wiping it down. When she straightened, he was right there.

'Hannelore.'

'Harry.' She glanced at the small chocolate stains on his shirt front.

Harry looked down and laughed. 'It'll wash out. She's a sweet one, little Harper Hamilton.' He shook his head, a half-smile on his face. 'I'm not sure if you've met her big brother. Wee Charlie they call him. He's a wee devil, that one.'

Laughing, she nodded. 'I've met him. Once or twice. A handful to be sure. And cute as a button.'

'Um. I wondered if you'd like to have a bite to eat with me at the pub. Not tonight, I've got to drive Nik home. But tomorrow, if you're free? Now that we've finished the apartment, I'm going to start gutting the gift shop tomorrow. We need to order materials now, in case some suppliers close over the holidays.'

'The little Indie Bookshop.' Hannelore corrected him.

'Yes. Good name.' He waited, looking at her quizzically.

'Yes. I'll have dinner with you. After work tomorrow.' She stepped closer, saying more quietly, and Harry?'

'Yes?' He whispered it, their heads close together.

'I'm impressed with your ideas. The plans for the mezzanine. And the staircase.' Eyes shining, she added. 'Love the staircase.'

Harry seemed to bask in her praise for a brief moment before he turned as Nicole called him from the other end of the café. 'Are you almost ready Harry?'

'Yes. Coming Nik.' Then to Hannelore, he murmured, 'Tomorrow. After work. Just the two of us.' She watched him stride to Nicole. He shook Ben's hand, kissed Millie on the cheek and walked outside, opening the door for Nicole as he did.

Hannelore gave the table another quick wipe to hide her response to Harry. He was way more layered than she'd expected. In a good way. What else would she discover if she spent more time with him? Walking towards her mother and Ben, she noted they were in deep conversation. She couldn't hear the conversation, and they stopped when she drew near.

'Alright Millie. Hanna. I'll be off then.' Ben smiled, but it didn't quite reach his eyes. *What?* 'Good outcomes here tonight. This project will be great for the town.'

'Goodnight Ben.' Hannelore glanced at Millie, but she'd turned to pick up her keys from the counter.

Walking home, Millie seemed quieter than normal. 'Mum? Is there something wrong?' After their recent conversations, Hannelore didn't want any secrets between them.

Millie sighed. 'Harry Stewart, Hannelore? Are you, um, seeing him?'

'Not really.' Hannelore was uncomfortable, but she wanted to be open. 'But I do like him. And we're going to the pub after work tomorrow. I guess it's a date. So um, maybe.'

Another sigh. 'I like him too. Harry. But Hannelore, Melanie told me something recently and Ben mentioned it again tonight. I won't repeat it. But I want you to be careful.'

'You can't say that and then not tell me. And why is Ben even saying anything, I thought he was friends with Robbie and Harry?' Hannelore could hear the rise in her voice. She was irritated. Not with her mother. Maybe with herself, because she had reservations that all was not what it seemed with Harry-bloody-Stewart.

'Ben saw you talking. He said he thought Harry might be seeing someone else. He wasn't sure. He was a bit uncomfortable saying it, I think.' Millie took a deep breath. 'I know your last relationship didn't go the way you wanted. My gut feeling is that

Harry is okay. Better than okay. And Hanna, I trust your judgement. My only advice is, don't rush in.'

'Thanks Mum. I do have reservations about Harry. I won't rush in. I've been getting mixed signals. I appreciate Ben caring enough to speak up.' Hannelore breathed out, smiling inwardly. She wasn't used to people, almost strangers, caring about her. One of the good things about small town life.

Later that night, lying in bed, Hannelore thought about Harry. He was good with children, which she found disarmingly attractive, and he was smart and had great ideas for the shop. He opened doors for women and carried a small child to the car for her mother. But he also seemed to be on his phone a lot, and she was sure he was using dating apps for hook-ups. But if he was single, maybe that was okay? Would he stop if she dated him? Could she ask him about it? She fell into a restless sleep.

39

———

FREDDIE

Beer in hand, Freddie walked from the bar to the bistro door for the third time. He wasn't there and he hadn't answered her text. *He never ignored her texts.* She was annoyed.

About to turn back to the bar, movement in the bistro caught her eye. *Hot Harry Stewart.* Was he here alone? She knew her brothers weren't in town today, they'd gone to a clearing sale in Wingham. He turned from the bistro bar, looking all-kinds-of-delicious in dark jeans and a pale blue shirt. He had a beer in one hand and a glass of wine in the other. She wrinkled her brow. Was he on a date? She watched him walk to a booth on the other side of the room. Aaah. The new girl. Hanna. Freddie had wondered if they were seeing each other.

Tapping her foot impatiently on the floor, Freddie checked her phone again. Nothing. Placing it in the back pocket of her tight skinny-leg jeans, she pushed the door to the bistro open and sauntered in. Harry was deep in conversation with his date.

Freddie went to the bar, leaning against it for a moment. Decision made, she strode to their booth.

'Harry.' Freddie drawled his name, her tone low. He turned his head so quickly to look up at her, she almost laughed out loud. He looked extremely uncomfortable.

'Hello Freddie.' But his voice was even.

'Hanna, isn't it? Nice to see you again.' Freddie slid into the booth beside Harry.

Hannelore's smile was warm and friendly. 'Hello again Freddie. How are you? Is Angus Hamilton keeping you busy?'

Freddie paused. She liked this girl. She was nice. Friendly. She sighed to herself but spoke in warm tones to Hannelore. 'Yes. The clinic has been busy. Not a lot of large animal work this week.' She let her thigh touch Harry's and he moved his leg away.

'Are you by yourself tonight Freddie?' Hannelore was still smiling. If she was on a date with Harry, she was very relaxed.

Shaking her head, Freddie checked her phone. 'I'm waiting for a message. From a ... er ... friend.' She felt Harry's stare and stood up. 'I'll go back to the main bar, where I said I'll be.'

Hannelore smiled again. 'If your friend can't make it, come back and eat with us.'

Freddie just nodded, suddenly feeling close to tears. She couldn't look at Harry. 'Thank you Hanna.' She almost ran from the room, pushing through the door to the main bar.

40

HARRY

'Does Freddie have a thing for you Harry? Or is she on your booty-call rotation?' Hannelore looked him in the eye as she spoke. Her tone was even, not even a hint of accusation. But he could tell she wanted the truth.

Sighing, he shook his head. 'There is no booty-call rotation, as you call it. And I suspect Freddie is trying to mess with me to get a reaction.' He leaned back. 'She is the younger sister of some of my best mates. I wouldn't go there under any circumstances, but frankly, I think she's playing games and I'm worried about her.'

Hannelore took a sip of wine. 'Okay. I'll take that at face value. I can see she tries to get your attention. I can also see that you didn't show interest tonight and the last time we were here with her. So why does she do it?'

'Hanna, we're on a date, having dinner together. I'd rather not talk about little Freddie Campbell. I want to get to know you.' Harry hoped he could change the subject. While Hanna didn't seem upset, she did seem to be considering her options. *Please don't friend-zone me.*

'And you don't mind that Mum and Finn and his son are coming here for dinner too?' Hannelore picked up the menu.

Truth be told he *did* mind. He wanted Hannelore to himself tonight. And he was more than a little irritated by Freddie too. But if he wanted to get to know Hannelore, then getting to know Millie was important. And Finn. And he didn't know Finn's son. He'd moved to Barrington while Harry was away up north.

'Honestly?' Harry grinned. 'I'd like to have you all to myself Hanna Tucker. But I also want to get to know your Mum, and Finn and his son. What's his name?'

Her smile was his reward. *Note to self, be honest with her. Always be honest with her.* 'Lucas. But we call him Luke. He's a bit younger than me and maybe not as *country* as you and your friends. But he's been good to Mum. And me. I think he'll turn out a lot like Finn. And *he's* one of the good ones.'

'Good. I look forward to meeting him.' He paused. 'What would you like for dinner? I'll order when you're ready.' Harry peered at the menu in her hand. Even upside down, he could see she was looking at the wood-fired pizza selections.

'Fancy a pizza to share? I couldn't eat a whole one. But we could share a dessert after if you need something more.' Hannelore turned the menu around. 'There's a gourmet chicken one, where they use pesto for the base sauce that I'd like to try.'

'Sure.' Harry didn't care what they ate. And sharing seemed more intimate than separate meals. He liked the idea. 'Gourmet chicken pizza it is.'

Harry ordered at the bar and returned with a bottle of wine and a second glass. He placed them down and noted her raised eyebrows. 'Bruce at the bar said the Sav Blanc you're drinking goes well with the pesto chicken pizza. I thought I'd try it.' He opened the bottle and topped up her glass before half-filling his own. 'I know you think I'm not usually a wine drinker. And you're right. But I'm not usually out with anyone who drinks wine.' He shrugged as she nodded.

'So the women you *usually* go out with don't drink wine?' Hannelore leaned back, exuding disbelief from her tone, her gestures, her expression.

'What? No...' Harry wanted to correct her then and there, but her face changed from sceptical to welcoming. She waved and half stood, and Harry turned around. Millie and Finn were walking over to them. Harry stood up too.

'Mum. Hi. Hello Finn.' Hannelore, now fully upright, kissed Finn on the cheek.

Harry greeted Millie warmly and shook hands with Finn. He'd only met him a couple of times but Robbie said he was a 'good bloke'.

'We're going to find a spot in the beer garden.' Millie spoke brightly, but Harry thought she looked uncertain.

'You can join us Mum, there's room.' Hannelore spoke louder than was necessary and Harry saw Millie glance at Finn. Without words, something passed between them. Harry had seen it many times with his father and Nik. It was a couple-thing.

Millie patted Hannelore on the shoulder. 'Luke is just parking the car around the back. He'll be looking for us in the beer garden.' Finn nodded, took Millie's hand, and they walked away, after murmuring, 'Enjoy your night.'

Hannelore remained standing, and Harry could sense her indecisiveness. He stepped closer and took her hand in his.

'Hanna? Our conversation before your Mum walked in was going somewhere. You have questions, and if I'm not mistaken, you've formed some assumptions about me that make you wary.' She gave him her full attention but withdrew her hand.

'That's true Harry.' She glanced toward the back of the room, where her Mum had just disappeared from view. Turning back to him, she looked him in the eye, her gaze unblinking. 'Will you tell me the truth, Harry? Answer any questions I ask?'

Returning her gaze, he spoke from the heart. 'Yes.'

The simplicity of his answer seemed to satisfy her, and she relaxed. 'Alright Harry Stewart. And I will do the same.' He wasn't sure what she meant, but she continued. 'Ask me anything too. No games. I don't want to play games.'

'No games Hanna.' He slid back into the booth, but she remained standing.

'The meals will take a few minutes. Harry, do you mind if I just pop out the back, and say a quick hello to Luke?'

Harry grinned. 'Of course not. And maybe we can all eat dessert together later if you want.'

He watched her walk quickly from the room while he thought about her words. He felt certain she'd been with someone before who played games. He got it. So no romance tonight, but maybe they could reach a point of mutual trust. And respect. He could build from there. It was a good place to start.

Returning in just a couple of minutes she seemed more relaxed. Sliding into the seat across from him, she smiled. 'Thank you. I said a quick hello to Luke and.' She stopped.

'And?' Harry prompted.

'And told Mum I'm okay. We're okay.' Her smile faltered slightly and she looked vulnerable but determined. 'Mum could see I was second guessing, um, you. Just at that moment. I want her to enjoy her night too, so I let her know we're just talking, clearing the air.'

Her words moved him, and without thinking he reached across the table, covering her hand with his. 'You're a lovely person Hanna. Making sure your mum is okay is very generous. And now I'm going to tell you that I like you even more and I can't wait to clear up your misgivings.'

'Alright Harry Stewart. Maybe I like you too. But I still have questions.'

41

FREDDIE

Freddie saw him at the bar in the bistro. She was furious. He had ignored her texts but was here anyway. She pushed open the door and stalked towards him.

'Luke!' Her tone was loud and aggressive. She tried to mentally relax, but everything they said about redheads was true for her. Once her temper was up, there was no easy way to pack it away.

The way he turned, looked at her and said quietly, 'Freddie,' inflamed her more.

He turned back to the bar to make payment for the tray of drinks in front of him.

'Don't turn your back on me!' She half growled, half shouted and she knew everyone seated nearby was looking. She didn't care. Her focus was on him.

Lucas turned around and sighed. She saw the look of resignation on his face. And that's when she knew. *He was over her.* If she wasn't so angry, she'd cry.

CHAPTER 41

And then Harry Stewart was there, glaring at Luke. 'What's going on? Freddie, are you alright?'

Luke took a step back. Harry was older and bigger and seemed tense. Ready for trouble.

The dam burst. Without realising how invested she was in Lucas, in him always being there for her, she sobbed. Big, gulping, unladylike sobs. She threw herself into Harry's arms.

'Take your drinks mate. Go now!' Harry growled.

Another voice chimed in. Freddie lifted her head from Harry's shoulder. Hanna was there, hands on hips. 'Luke? Are you okay?' She turned to Harry. 'What the hell is this about Harry?' More softly, she said, 'Freddie? Are you alright?'

It was the gentleness in her voice that undid Freddie. She knew Harry was only protecting her because he had big-brother feelings for her. Nothing else. And he liked this woman. Hanna. Freddie liked her too. Freddie stepped out of Harry's embrace, turned and strode from the room. She almost ran back through the bar and outside to her car.

42

HANNELORE

Lucas hadn't moved, but Hannelore was shocked at Harry's attitude to him. After Freddie ran out she hesitated. Go after her? Or make sure Luke was okay? She decided to sort Harry and Luke out first.

'Luke?' Hannelore was confused. 'What's going on with you and Freddie?' Before he could answer she glared at Harry. 'And what has it got to do with you? Unless Freddie is more to you than you admit?'

Harry looked startled. 'You're Luke? Finn's son?' He relaxed slightly.

Lucas sighed but raised his chin and glanced from her to Harry and back to her. 'Yes. Freddie and I, we've been seeing each other. For months. But she wanted to keep it a secret from her brothers.' Looking at Harry, he raised his chin. 'You're not her brother, why are you stepping in? Or are you keen on her yourself? I know you've seen her naked.'

Luke's last words fizzed away in Hannelore's mind. *Stay calm, stay calm.* 'Yes, Harry. Why?'

Harry frowned again at Lucas but gave Hannelore a watery smile. 'Not here at the bar Hanna.' To Lucas he said, 'Have you ended it mate? Is that why she's so upset?'

'Like you said. Mate. Now is not the place. And it's none of your business. Tell her brothers if you like.' Luke straightened his shoulders and picked up the tray of drinks. 'I'm taking these out to Dad and Millie, then I'll call Freddie.'

Hannelore nodded. 'Good idea. She's angry and probably shouldn't be driving.' A thought occurred to her. What would she do if this had been her? She took the tray from Luke's hands. 'If it was me, I'd be in my car, trying to calm down before I drive home. I'm happy to go outside and check on her. But Luke?'

'Yes.'

'If you care about her and want to sort this out, then *you* should go out there. Check on her. Don't call. Go and find her. I'll take the drinks out to Mum and Finn.' Hannelore had barely finished the words when Lucas took off, striding purposely from the room in the direction Freddie had gone.

Hannelore turned to Harry. 'I'm going to take these out to Mum. And our pizza has just been delivered to our table. I'll be right back.'

<hr>

AFTER SIPPING HER WINE, HANNELORE MOVED A LARGE slice of pizza to her plate. Harry's gaze was wary, but he didn't speak. He took a piece of pizza too, then washed the first bite down with a gulp of wine.

'Steady Harry.' Hannelore felt in control. They would talk and she would understand Harry better. In her heart, she didn't think he'd been sleeping with Freddie. She hoped for Luke's sake he hadn't. He placed his glass back on the table.

'Question. Are you, or have you ever been, in a relationship with Freddie?' Hannelore kept her voice even, but the answer could change the direction of her life.

'No. Not ever. She *is* like a little sister to me. But I've been worried about her. And her brothers *don't* know she's been seeing anyone.' Harry looked like he wanted to ask a question of his own, but Hannelore held her hand up.

'Wait please Harry, there's more. *Have* you seen Freddie naked? What is that about?' She really wanted the answer to this one.

'Yes. Unintentionally. After the night she flirted with me at the pub, in front of you, I wanted to talk to her and set her straight. You wouldn't let me walk you home and I was disappointed. Driving away from the pub, I went down the back lane, the one that runs behind the shops on the main street. Freddie had left earlier. She'd told Callum she was going home, but her car was parked at the back of the Vet Clinic.' He took another bite of pizza.

Hannelore waited until he swallowed, then said, more gently. 'Go on.'

'I wasn't sure if she was checking on an animal, you know, at the clinic. But I wanted to speak to her, so I went in. The door was unlocked. There's a flat in the back. The Vets use it if they have a sick animal needing intensive care. And Freddie stays there sometimes when she's working for them.'

He leaned back and closed his eyes briefly as if remembering. 'I don't know what I expected, but seeing Freddie lying naked in the bed wasn't it. Her back was to me, but then Luke stepped out of the bathroom, doing up his jeans. I was shocked, to say the least. It was obvious they'd had sex. I was angry. I felt protective of her, but also realised she was a lot more grown-up than I realised. Than her brothers realise. I ordered her to get dressed, and she yelled at Luke to leave. Screamed at him. He left.'

'And then?' Hannelore's tummy did a backflip. She had no idea what he was going to say next.

'Luke had barely left and Freddie was dressing.' Harry looked her in the eye. 'I turned my back, but I still wanted to get to the bottom of this. Why was she flirting with me if she was seeing someone?' He shook his head. 'And then Ben and Melanie Evans were there and it all changed in an instant.'

'Changed? How?' Hannelore took another sip of wine. She was curious but no longer upset.

'Freddie went from being pissed off with me, to crying and upset in an instant, throwing herself into Melanie's arms. It was an act. I knew it. But Ben was furious. Freddie told them she'd been sneaking around with me because she didn't want her brothers to hurt me.' Harry looked mildly outraged. 'And I have no idea why she did that. Said my name and not Luke's.' Shaking his head, he added. 'I still don't know. I've tried to catch her alone to talk to her, but with no luck.'

'Alright then.' Hannelore reached for a second pizza slice.

'Alright?' Harry's expression was hopeful.

'I believe you Harry. About Freddie. But Harry, I still need to know if you're seeing other women. If you're making booty-calls? No judgement. You're entitled to. But will you stop if you start seeing someone?' Hannelore's tummy did that little flip-flop thing again.

'I want to know *why* you think I'm making booty-calls? What have I done to give you that impression?' He looked confused, but his response had her almost sliding from her seat and leaving. She'd caught him on his phone *dozens* of times.

Hannelore raised her eyebrows. 'Just answer Harry.' She knew her words dripped with annoyance.

'No.'

'No you're not making booty-calls or no you won't stop making booty-calls.' Hannelore folded her arms across her chest.

Harry leaned forward. Now he looked annoyed. 'I don't. I wouldn't. So therefore I can't stop something I'm not doing.'

'Pfft.' Hannelore breathed in through her nose sharply. 'You said you'd answer honestly.'

'It's the truth Hanna.' His gaze was steady, but sad. 'I get that you've been hurt before and have trust issues. I understand. But if you can't trust me Hanna, there's no point.' He gestured around the table, at the food and drinks.

Not sure what to say next, she gave it one last try. 'Your phone Harry. You're always swiping on your phone. I've seen you. You're so engrossed that you don't even know I'm there, at times.' He blushed. Actually blushed. 'Caught, Harry Stewart.' She began to get up.

'Wait.' Harry, still looking uncomfortable, picked up his phone. 'I have a secret, um, obsession. It started when I went up north.' He fiddled with his phone.

Hannelore remained seated and raised her eyebrows. What? Was he playing games on his phone? Watching porn? What? He turned the phone around so she could see it. He didn't have many apps, and she couldn't see any dating ones. But maybe he just deleted it. Or them. She frowned. He pointed to one app and she leaned in, looking closer. It was the reading app that came with the phone.

'Yes?' She looked up at him.

Harry sighed. 'Open it Hanna.'

Hannelore took the phone and tapped the app. A book appeared. Opened at page 163. She read a few words. She knew this book. It was *The Grazier's Son* by Cathryn Hein. It had been a book club read. 'You read?'

'Yes. Don't judge me.' Harry was embarrassed.

'No judgement here Harry Stewart.' Hannelore's finger hovered over the phone and a smile hovered around her mouth. 'May I?'

'It can't get any worse. Go ahead.' Harry cocked an eyebrow at her. His expression had lightened.

Closing the book he was reading, she clicked on the library. Hannelore drew in a breath and grinned at him, before looking back at the screen. There were dozens of books. More than that. Most of them he'd read, but there were a few in his unread list. One of Rose Gordon's and three others Hannelore recognised. And their next book club title. While surprised he had a few romance titles there, although, to be fair most were rural romance, there were also some Aussie crime and mystery stories. And one historical.

Harry Stewart's reading list was very similar to her own. But she could see his reading on the app had begun a long time before she came to Barrington. Hannelore scrolled further back and then chuckled. She chanced a glance at him. He was fidgeting. She paused, handing the phone back, now giggling. She tried a sip of wine, but her giggles bested her and she set it down, laughing louder now.

Harry leaned in, placing his huge paw over her hand. 'Stop. Please Hanna.' She wiped her eyes. She'd laughed so much she was teary.

43

HARRY

'I'm sorry Harry. But this is ... um ... unexpected.'

Harry withdrew his hand, covering his face for a moment.

'You seemed to have started with ... er ... let me see ... the Bridgerton Series.' Her eyes were twinkling, but he groaned.

'Hanna. Stop. Please.' He held his hand out and Hannelore placed the phone in it.

'And now I have more questions Harry Stewart.' She looked at the pizza, there was one piece left. She cut it in half, took one piece and pushed the platter closer to him. 'I can't eat more than this Harry, please help me.' He'd already had one more piece than she had, but it was tasty. He took the piece she offered. It seemed more than just pizza. It felt like a peace offering.

'Okay, Hanna Tucker. But can you keep this,' he pointed to the phone lying by his plate, 'on the down-low?' Harry topped up her wine glass, he couldn't have any more himself, he was driving.

'Yes. If that's what you want. Of course.' He could see she was enjoying his embarrassment.

'I have to ask you, Hanna, if this,' he waved at the phone again, 'puts me in your friend zone? You know, a friend you can share books with?'

'Hmm. Let me think about that. Before I answer, can I ask you about your *secret* obsession? She whispered *secret*. 'How it started?' Hannelore giggled and covered her mouth with her hand. 'Sorry. But Bridgerton? Really?'

'Alright. But hear me out please, before judging.' The waitress cleared their plates and offered the dessert menu, which Hannelore took but didn't look at. She was focused on him. He hoped it was a good thing, as he cleared his throat. 'I've always read. Not a lot, but paperbacks. John Grisham. Lee Child. Blokey books.'

'Blokey books.' She nodded, repeating his words.

'Moving up north, there wasn't much to do in my free time. Others in the bunkhouse played cards and drank. Sometimes a lot. I've never been a big drinker and I was saving my money, so I only played cards occasionally. And the nearest bar was over a hundred kilometres away.

One of the jillaroos left a few books behind when she went back to her family property. The first Bridgerton book and two by Fiona McArthur. They were tossed in the bin, and I pulled them out. I loved the Aussie ones, it felt like she was writing about people and places I knew.'

'And Bridgerton?' Harry knew he was drawing it out, but he loved that he had her undivided attention.

'Bridgerton. Well, that was a surprise. I'd watched a few movies with Lucy. You know, Pride and Prejudice and the like. I expected the book to be like that. But it wasn't. It was something else altogether.' He waggled his eyebrows and she laughed, nodding vigorously in agreement. 'I liked it. The book. The dialogue. The characters.' He sighed. 'And yes. The romance.'

'And?' Hannelore finished her wine, then looked at her glass. He topped it up again.

'And that's when I began reading with the app on the phone. Downloading the eBooks. They're cheaper than paperbacks and always in your pocket if you have a moment to take a break.' Harry heard himself speaking. *I sound defensive.*

'And no one knows what you're reading. Or how many books you have.' Hannelore finished his thought out loud. He nodded and he watched her tap her fingers on the table, seemingly deep in thought. 'So in answer to your question.' Hannelore stopped, looking over his shoulder. He turned to see Millie and Finn approaching. Hannelore waved, then said quietly, 'We will finish this conversation Harry Stewart. But not right now.'

'Hi Mum, Finn. How was your dinner?' She slid over, making room but her Mum shook her head. Harry saw Finn was holding her hand. *Cute.*

'Lovely. It was just the two of us. Luke didn't come back in after you brought the drinks out to us.' Millie glanced at Finn. 'I don't suppose you two know anything about it, or about the girl he's been seeing. Who he's never mentioned?'

Harry was about to answer but Hannelore was quicker. 'Not much Mum. I'm sure Luke will tell us when he's worked it out himself. That he didn't come back may be a good thing. For him.'

'I suspected he's been seeing someone.' Finn spoke softly. 'He's a good lad and he'll tell us when he's ready.'

Harry wasn't so sure about Lucas. But he said nothing.

'Will you drive Finn home, Mum?' Harry saw Hannelore

nibble her bottom lip. She looked uncertain. 'Or are you staying in the apartment tonight?

'I'll drive him home and stay there tonight Hanna.' Millie answered quickly and Hannelore seemed relieved. 'So we'll say goodnight now. We'll just drop over to the apartment to get my car.'

'Goodnight Mum. Finn.' Hannelore smiled at them both and Harry stood, shaking Finn's hand and saying goodnight too.

Hannelore watched them walk through the door before she turned. 'Where was I? And do you fancy dessert Harry?'

'I always fancy dessert Hanna. I'm happy to share.' Harry was feeling lighter, he could sense a shift in Hannelore and he hoped it meant they were over any obstacles preventing them from moving forward. 'And I'm keen to hear your answer too.'

Hannelore stood suddenly, tugging on his hand. 'Come with me. I have a brilliant idea for dessert.' He raised his eyebrows, but she shook her head. 'Don't rush to the end-game Harry.'

Within moments they were out of the pub, on the main street. He followed her gaze to the apartment across the street. The light was on. Millie was probably throwing a few things into an overnight bag. But instead of walking across the road, Hannelore strode quickly down the street, her hand still in his. He had to lengthen his stride to keep up.

They were almost to the café before he realised where she was going. She unlocked the door and stepped back, letting him go through. 'Dessert Harry, come with me.' She locked the front door and using her phone as a torch, led him through to the kitchen, where she turned a light on. 'Sit.' She pointed to a bar chair near the counter as she tied an apron around her waist.

'Okay. Can I help?' Hannelore shook her head and he watched

as she moved quickly around the kitchen, placing a small number of little pastry balls on a plate before putting something in a tiny pot on the stove.

'Choux pastries.' She spoke aloud, describing what she was doing. The efficiency of her movements mesmerised him. She stirred the pot; it smelt like caramel or butterscotch.

'Cream.' She squeezed some into each little pastry from a funny bag in her hand, before turning to stir the sauce again. Harry's mouth was watering. 'And sauce.' He watched her place about ten little golden balls onto a plate in a pile, then tipped the hot, thick, liquid over them all. *Definitely butterscotch.*

Pulling up a chair beside Harry, she sat the platter in front of them and offered him a spoon and fork. 'Try one. Stick your fork in and roll it in the sauce.'

Harry did as she asked. Hannelore watched him intently as he chewed, although it almost melted in his mouth, then swallowed. 'Wow! That's probably the most delicious thing I've ever tasted.' He reached for another one as he noticed the flush of pleasure that warmed her face. He finished his second one just as Hannelore finished her first. He ran his tongue around his lips. The sauce was amazing. She watched him closely, her eyes now focused on his lips. She licked her own, her eyes still on his.

Without taking his eyes from her mouth, he placed his fork on the plate, reached over and dragged her chair close to his, until her whole body was almost between his legs. She gave no resistance and he leaned forward, one hand lightly touching the back of her head. His lips met hers. She closed her eyes. He gently kissed the corners of her mouth, then her bottom lip, tasting a little drop of sweet sauce lingering there. She leaned closer and he stood. Pulling her to her feet he held her tightly and kissed her again, more urgently.

She melted against him and made a tiny moaning sound as she wound her arms around his neck, pulling his head down. Now he was at her throat, nipping and tasting, then her collarbone. Her head lolled back and he bent further, one hand around her back, the other inside her blouse, touching her breast. With her hand now in his hair, she lifted his head and kissed his mouth again, murmuring, 'Harry.'

Sexy Hanna. Gorgeous Hanna. He wanted to go further, unbutton her shirt and he thought, in the moment, she'd let him. But with an internal sigh, he slowed, moving his hands to her back, although he did let one slide over her beautifully rounded bum first and kissed her gently on the mouth, then the tip of her nose.

Sighing, she nestled into his arms and a feeling of protectiveness enveloped him. 'Hanna?' He murmured her name. He waited. His heart rate dropped slightly as he held her gently.

'Harry.' She took half a step back but placed one hand on his chest. He held it with his own.

'Would you like to come home with me Harry? Mum's not there.'

His mind screamed *yes, yes I want to come home with you.* But his head, and perhaps his heart, said *slow down, treat her right.*

'I'd love to Hanna. I want to.' He drew her close again and just held her. She snuggled against his chest. 'Although you've tried to seduce me with pastries and some sort of wickedly sexy sauce, I need to tell you that I don't put out on a first date.' He felt her laugh against his chest. After a moment she looked up at him.

Trying to look shocked, he added in a not-very-convincing

English accent. 'A Bridgerton wouldn't, you know. Not straight away. There needs to be a build-up of sexual tension.'

Hannelore giggled and leaned against him, her whole body touching his. 'What's this then, Harry Stewart?' She wriggled her hips. 'Your phone?'

'But will you still respect me in the morning?' He was enjoying this game. The banter, the fun of it. Harry could wait. Wanted to wait. He wanted to take his time. He bent his head and whispered in her ear, 'This is just the start Hanna. We have time. Let's not rush.' She sighed and muttered something.

'Sorry Hanna. What was that?' He grinned.

'You better be worth the wait Harry Stewart.' He laughed at her words. 'And just so you know. In case you're not sure. You're NOT in my friend zone.' Standing on tiptoes she kissed him again and just for a moment he wondered if he *should* stay with her. But no, he'd stand by his decision.

'Let's finish these and clean up here and I'll walk you home.' Ten minutes later, standing at the downstairs door of her building, Hannelore kissed him with an intensity that almost undid his reserve. She placed her hand on his cheek and looked at him seriously. 'I think you're one of the good ones, Harry Stewart. And I love that you read.' She added in a stage whisper, 'But I'll keep your *dirty little secret*.' She blew him a kiss, unlocked the door and slipped inside.

44

MILLIE

Finn slipped out of bed quietly just after eleven, when Lucas came home. Millie half sat up. 'Is it Luke?' she whispered.

'Yes. I'll have a quick word with him.' Finn leaned over and kissed Millie quickly. 'Go back to sleep, I won't be long.'

Millie must have slept then because it was after twelve when Finn returned to their room. She turned the bedside lamp on and swung her legs out of bed. 'Bathroom,' she murmured. Returning a few minutes later Finn pulled back the covers for her. Millie lay on her side and ran a finger down the crease on his forehead. 'Is he alright, Finn?'

'Yes. He will be.' Finn sighed. 'He's young, but it's obvious he has strong feelings for Freddie. Freddie Campbell, that's who he's been seeing.'

Taking her hand, he brought it to his lips, kissed her palm, and then held it against his chest. 'He's only just realised that Freddie has been playing him. Or maybe just playing games. She's been telling him for months that her brothers will beat him up if they find out they've been sleeping together.'

Finn turned to face Millie. 'They're big men, the Campbell lads. But despite that, Luke has been asking her to tell them. He said they'd tell them together, go to her house. Even tell her parents. He hates all the sneaking around.' He stopped, his brow furrowed.

'Hmmm.' Millie had a theory of her own.

'Hmmm?' Finn gave her a half-hearted smile.

'I suspect the sneaking around and fear of being caught is part of the excitement for Freddie. I don't know much about her, but I've seen this sort of behaviour before.' Millie paused. 'I'm worried she will hurt him. Luke.'

'Me too.' Finn drew her close and kissed her gently, and Millie relaxed into him. 'But he's a grown man and needs to make his own mind up. He found her crying in her car after she stormed out of the pub, and they sat and talked for a while, but they got hungry.' He chuckled. 'Luke is always hungry. Then they drove out to the fuel stop on the main road and had burgers. My understanding is that she wanted to go somewhere to, um, hook up. But Luke told her that wouldn't be happening until she introduces him to her family. She drove home alone.'

Millie traced circles on Finn's chest as she murmured. 'That was brave. If what she says about her brothers is true.'

'Testament to his feelings. I hope she realises that.' Finn groaned softly as Millie's fingers circled lower. He captured her hand and turned over, throwing one leg across hers and beginning a little body drawing of his own. 'But let's talk about *my* feelings right now Millie.'

Millie giggled, wriggling beneath him. 'Enough talk Finn.'

AS SHE DROVE HOME AFTER AN EARLY BREAKFAST WITH Finn, Millie wondered how Hannelore's date had ended. Lucas wasn't up when she left, but she knew Finn was planning to have another chat with him when he woke, if he was receptive.

Millie had showered at Finn's. She chuckled to herself. She'd *needed* to, then she held a hand to her burning cheek as images of their midnight love-making came to mind. Running lightly up the back stairs to the apartment Millie checked her watch. She only had half an hour to get changed and open the café. Struggling to get her key in the back door, she was surprised when it opened and Hannelore, already dressed for work, said, 'Good morning Mum.'

'Good morning.' Millie came in and closed the door. She looked over Hannelore's shoulder, half expecting to see Harry there.

Hannelore leaned on the kitchen door jamb, feet crossed and eyebrows raised. 'I slept here alone Mum, if that's what you're wondering.' She stepped into the kitchen. 'Tea? Or coffee when we get to work?'

Millie could see the teapot steaming. 'Tea would be lovely, thank you. Can you pour me a cup while I get changed please?' Seeing Hannelore nod, Millie stepped out into the living area and then stopped. 'Does that mean your date didn't go well?' She cocked an eyebrow.

Hannelore laughed, then waved her hand at Millie. 'Go and get changed Mum, or we'll be late.' Millie wanted to ask more but turned and rushed to her room.

Fifteen minutes later she was ready for work, sipping from her teacup while Hannelore quickly tidied her breakfast dishes. Tea finished, Millie handed the cup to Hannelore, who rinsed it under the tap and wordlessly turned it upside down on the draining board beside the sink.

Hannelore waited while Millie locked the front door of the building. As they walked across the street together, Hannelore gave Millie a cheeky look. 'I would have.'

'Would have what, Hanna?' But Millie thought she knew where this was going.

'Invited Harry to stay.' They were across the street now and walking briskly toward the café. 'I asked him to come home with me. He said no.'

'What?' Millie stopped, suddenly worried for Hannelore. *Wasn't Harry keen?*

'Keep walking Mum, people are waiting.' Hannelore increased her pace but Millie snuck a look and saw she was grinning. 'Oh, hang on. Kristen has just opened up.' She slowed slightly and Millie matched her pace.

'We had fun.' She turned to Millie then, her eyes glowing. 'I know you won't mind, but we snuck into the café after the pub and I made dessert. Profiteroles and butterscotch sauce.' Her face took on a dreamy quality. 'We shared it. The dessert.'

Millie nudged her. 'And?'

'And. It was romantic and sexy and we kissed. A lot.' Hannelore turned to her, her eyes dancing. 'Oh Mum, Harry Stewart knows how to kiss. And for a minute there, I thought. Well, I asked him.' She giggled. 'He has a secret that I'm not allowed to tell anyone. A fabulous secret that just makes me like him more. And I could tell he wanted to.' She gave Millie a side-eye glance. 'But he said,' she laughed loudly then, 'that he doesn't put out on a first date! So funny! And Mum it was just perfect. So perfect.'

They were at the door and Millie felt herself basking in the happiness radiating from Hannelore. 'I'm pleased for you Hanna, really pleased.' They shared a look and stepped inside the café, calling out good morning to Kristen.

———

HARRY DROPPED INTO THE CAFÉ JUST AFTER THE breakfast rush. He and Robbie were working in the gift shop. 'The Little Indie Book Shop,' Millie murmured to herself. While they hadn't been overly noisy, a lot of dust was swirling out of the open door, so Millie had closed the café door.

'Good morning Millie.' Harry's words were warm, but his smile slightly uncertain. *How much had Hanna told Millie?*

'Harry.' Millie kept her voice neutral and thought she'd tease him a bit. 'Can I get you anything?' He was peering over her shoulder, and Millie moved in front of his line of sight to the kitchen. 'Coffee? cake? Dessert.'

His gaze promptly returned to Millie's face. 'Um, a latte and two pieces of carrot cake please Millie.' She was about to let him off the hook, but Hannelore heard his voice and bounced out from the kitchen to the front counter.

'I've got this Mum.' Millie was effectively dismissed and chuckled as she popped into the kitchen with Kristen. Kristen put a finger to her mouth and they craned their heads to catch the conversation.

Harry murmured something and Hannelore laughed loudly. 'Pretty sure she's messing with you, Harry.' Millie heard

Hannelore and snorted before trying to stop her giggles with a hand over her mouth.

Noise from the coffee machine drowned out their next words and Kristen pushed a platter of sandwiches towards Millie. 'These are for the table near the window.' Bustling past Hannelore, and Harry, Millie delivered the order and turned to see Harry ready to leave, the coffee in one hand and their cakes on a plate in the other.

Giving her a broad smile Harry jerked his head at the plate. 'I'll bring this back shortly Millie.'

In mock horror, Millie stopped, put a hand on one hip, and pointed to the two forks on the plate beside the cake slices. 'Oh really, Harry Stewart. Can I expect the silverware back too?'

Harry stopped, looked at the forks and opened his mouth to speak, but Millie couldn't hold her laughter back. 'Messing with you Harry. Off you go.'

'Good one Millie. You had me.' He strolled outside, laughing.

Millie slipped behind the counter, thinking to share a smile with Hannelore, but she threw herself into Millie's arms and hugged her tightly. 'You're the best Mum.' She let go then, undid her apron and handed it to Millie. 'Ten-minute break. I'm going to check on their progress next door.' Before Millie could speak Hannelore was out the door, one step behind Harry. Millie shook her head but the light, happy feeling in her chest remained for the rest of the day.

45

FREDDIE

Callum asked Freddie to help drench the weaners before it got too hot and she was up early. Peering in the bathroom mirror, she saw her eyes were red-rimmed from crying. She drew in a shuddering breath, thinking about Luke's words last night. He'd told her to grow up. *It was over.*

Freddie had lost her temper and screamed at him and when that didn't work, she'd cried. Yet even though he was upset too, he wouldn't change his mind. She calmed down eventually and he drove them out to the highway to get a burger. Freddie spoke more calmly then and even said she'd tell her family they were together.

Freddie leaned over the bathroom sink, shook her head and cried again. Deep, wracking sobs that took her breath away. She had added that they could be exclusive and that's when she lost him. She saw it happen, almost in slow motion. Luke had gone pale but his body had tensed. He was angry. Quietly angry. She'd never seen him like that. He was always calm and considered, even when she hurt him. But last night was something else.

Luke's tone was icy. 'Are we *not* exclusive Freddie? Is that what you're saying?'

'No. Yes. Of course.' But he saw through her lies and turned away. 'But I care about you, Luke. Only you.' She'd pleaded with him then and placed her hand on his leg.

Luke removed her hand as if it burnt him. They were parked beside her little jeep at the back of the pub. It was the only vehicle still in the car park. Luke looked at her, his eyes filled with sadness. 'Go home Freddie. Drive safely.'

'But Luke.' She moved closer, letting her tears fall again, but he held up his hand.

'Stop it, Freddie. Don't try to manipulate me, it won't work anymore. I don't trust you.' He looked away from her, then said through clenched teeth. 'You have to earn my trust.'

Freddie's temper had reared its head again at his words and she leapt from the car, slamming the door. The window was down and she shouted, 'Fuck you, Luke Anderson! I don't have to earn anything!'

Yet he remained in the car park until she started her jeep and drove off, way too fast. But now, in the light of day, she realised what she'd lost. He may have been *the one* and she blew it.

'Freddie!' Callum was outside the bathroom door. 'The weaners won't drench themselves. Come on Sis!'

Freddie threw open the door and rushed past Callum, tying her hair into a ponytail as she went. 'I'm ready!' She shouted back. There was work to do.

46

———

HANNELORE

When Harry asked if she wanted to go home with him after lunch and take the horses to the river, Hannelore jumped at the chance. Lucy was working in the café in the afternoon, so it would be just the two of them for the horse ride. A shiver of delight and anticipation ran through her body. She checked with Millie, who told her to 'just go and have fun.'

The dogs, Scout and Minnie, ran around her legs when she stepped out of Harry's Ute. She patted them both, then threw the tennis ball Minnie brought to her while Harry dashed inside to get his riding boots.

They were alone at The Courthouse. Nicole had brought lunch to her men in town and was still at the bookshop, helping Robbie measure up for the built-in bookshelves. Hannelore wondered if Harry would invite her inside and show her his room. But he was focused on the horses, and when he returned from the house, they walked across to the horse-paddock. She could see them grazing at the far end, but when Harry called them, Lawson picked his head up and began to trot their way. The mares followed and Hannelore caught her breath at the beauty of them, the way they moved so freely.

Speaking quietly to each other and the horses, they brushed Lawson and Honey and saddled them. Harry pointed out where Nicole's boundary met his Dad's, and stopped by the driveway of the house they used to live in, the one Robbie had built for Harry's mum. It had the same wide verandas and country-look as a lot of homes Hannelore had seen around town, yet it was barely twenty-five years old.

'Who lives there now Harry? Does your Dad still own it?' Hannelore touched her heels to Honey's side and she walked on beside Harry's taller mount.

Harry paused. 'Not exactly. He owns the land but not the house. It's empty just now; the school board was renting it, the principal was there for a couple of years, and for the last two years, a couple of teachers have been sharing it.'

Hannelore frowned and looked at it again as they rode by. She wanted to ask more questions, but they turned onto the road to the river, and Harry let his horse canter. Hannelore loosened her reins, and Honey gamely kept up with the larger horse. She grinned at Harry.

Near the river, they slowed, then walked the horses to the very edge. 'Want to ride them in or lead them?' Harry dismounted and held Honey's bridle while Hannelore scrambled off.

'Lead them in.' She unsaddled Honey then kicked her boots off and shimmied out of her jeans, leaving her tee shirt on over her bathing suit—the one he'd admired on her last time.

Harry gave her an appreciative whistle while he leaned both saddles against the massive wild lemon tree. Stripped down to board shorts, he led Lawson into the water, looking over his shoulder to check on Hannelore and Honey who were right behind them.

After ten minutes splashing in the shallows, they let the horse drink, then walked them up the bank and tethered them in the shade. Hannelore hung her wet tee shirt from a tree branch, then Harry took her hand, and they stepped to the edge of the river together.

'Race you to the rocks over there.' Hannelore dove in while her words hung in the air behind her. She struck out strongly for the rocks, but the river was high and flowing strongly.

The current swept her downstream, the strength of it surprising her. But she remembered how Harry had returned to the side they entered from and swam back where the current wasn't as strong last time.

After only two strokes, Harry had his arm around her waist, pulling her close. He let the water carry them downstream for a few moments, and she wrapped her arms around him.

At a bend in the river, Harry released her. 'Swim to the side Hanna, it's slower there.'

Reaching the side, she found the bottom of the river and stood up with the water lapping around her shoulders. Harry was beside her. 'Are you alright Hanna? I should have told you it would be stronger than last time. There's been a lot of rain in the Tops.'

'It took me by surprise, but honestly, I didn't feel in any danger.' She nudged him with her shoulder. 'I was with you.'

Laughing, he nodded upstream. 'Best we get back to where we can see the horses.' He swam in strong, smooth strokes, and she followed in his wake, both staying close to the bank. Back where they started

Harry nodded toward the rocks on the far side. 'Want to try again? Or we can relax on the river bank.'

'River bank.' Hannelore had cooled down and she liked the idea of a quiet chat, lying in the soft grass together.

They climbed out, and Harry pointed to a grassy knoll, partly shaded by the lemon tree. 'I'll check the horses. I've got a water bottle and a snack in my saddle bag.'

Laying back with one arm behind her head, Hannelore watched him with lazy, half-closed eyes. She admired the efficiency of his movements and the way the muscles in his shoulders seemed to ripple in the sunlight when he reached for his saddle bag. Harry flopped down beside her, then shook the water from his hair, making her gasp as cold droplets hit her face and chest.

Passing her the water bottle, he cocked an eyebrow. 'Water? Or did you drink in the river, like the horses?'

'Water please.' Raising herself on one elbow, Hannelore took the water bottle, gulping down a few mouthfuls while he studied her. 'What?' She handed him the bottle and wiped her mouth with the back of her hand.

'You missed a drop.' Harry leaned in, lowered his mouth over hers and let the tip of his tongue touch her bottom lip. She shivered, and her heart rate sped up. *One kiss from Harry Stewart could raise her temperature. Who knew?*

But he stopped at one kiss. 'I'd like to kiss you a whole lot more, Hanna. You know that. But this is a public place, and anyone could drive by or pull in for a swim.'

Chuckling, she brought one hand to his chest. 'Small towns, huh?'

'Small towns.' Harry sat up, gazed across to the horses, then brought his eyes back to her. 'Do you like small towns Hanna? I don't think you've really told me what you think of Barrington.'

'I do actually. Like small towns. My brother Matty is a city boy.' She grinned. 'He's coming for Christmas for a couple of nights so you'll meet him. But yes, I like small towns. I especially like this one.'

'So you think you'll stay?' His tone was light, but she could see he drew in a breath as he asked. The air around them seemed suddenly charged with electricity.

'Yes. I'll stay.' She watched him let his breath out, then relax, stretching his legs out in front of him. Then she remembered that she had something else to tell him. She sat up and crossed her legs, suddenly brimming with excitement.

47

HARRY

Could this girl be any cuter? She moved quickly, her face bright with excitement. 'Is there something else? You look like you have news. Or a secret to tell.' Harry drawled the words, enjoying the play of emotion across her features. Her blue eyes darkened. He could swim in them, or get lost in them.

'Harry! I'm starting a business of my own. I can't believe I didn't tell you this already. But the Freddie thing sort of pushed it from my mind.' After she spoke, she seemed nervous for a moment, pulling a piece of grass out and studying it.

'Awesome Hanna. A business, wow. I'm intrigued.' He took the grass from her hand, which brought her focus back to him. 'And impressed.'

The words tumbled from her as she explained the conversation with Millie about buying into the business, and how she'd had the idea for a little patisserie in the gift shop before the bookshop idea.

'But the bookshop is brilliant, I love it so much.' She grinned. 'I bet you do too!'

Harry nodded. 'So the little patisserie idea has morphed into something else?' He thought he knew, but was enjoying her telling of it.

'Yes, back to buying in with Mum and running a specialist patisserie from *inside* the café. You know, have my own branding. Maybe even a sign outside with a logo.' She closed her eyes for a moment. 'Gosh Harry. A logo. For my own business.' She leaned back on her hands, and it was all Harry could do not to stare at her body in that hot-as-hell bikini.

'A specialist patisserie? Like the dessert we had last night? That was amazing!' He was impressed. She was a year or so younger than him and starting a business.

'Wedding cakes and event catering. Desserts mainly. And making items for Mum that she generally buys in. Oh, and I'm going to get Kristen to do my accounts and help with the business modelling like she is for the bookshop. And a lot of orders would come through Meggie and Harriet, from their Barrington Elopements business. And I'd still work for the café a few hours each week.'

Hannelore took a breath and made a face. 'Actually, there's a lot I need to do. A lot of planning. And we want to speak to Steve and Rachael and make sure they're okay with it. Mum is effectively sub-letting some of her space. And there's some equipment I need to buy.' He could see her mentally list-making as she blurted everything out.

Harry stood up and held out his hand. She gave him her right hand and he pulled her to her feet, then put his arms around her and drew her against his chest. 'If I can help with anything Hanna, let me know. If you want more shelves in the café or another bench. Anything.' He kissed her gently, then leaned back. 'I know!'

'What do you know Harry?'

'I can be your official taster. You know, to make sure you get all those little Frenchie bits and pieces right.' She laughed and hit him lightly on the arm. 'We better get these horses home Hanna.'

Back at his place, after they brushed and fed the horses, they walked across to his car together, holding hands. Robbie and Nicole's cars were there, but they didn't make an appearance. Harry was pleased, they were giving him some time with Hannelore.

'You said something earlier Harry, when we rode past the house you grew up in, that I meant to come back to.' Hannelore gave Scout a pat when she pushed against her legs. 'You said Robbie owns the land but not the house. Did the Education Department buy it for the school? How do you feel about that?'

'Um. Dad doesn't own it. I do.' Harry gazed across the paddock towards the house. They could just see the roof line in the distance. 'It was always going to be mine one day, and when we moved in here Dad gave it to me. The rental income has been coming to me.' He hesitated. 'I've thought about moving in there myself from time to time.'

'That was my next question, but I think I know the answer.' Hannelore leaned into him and he put his arm around her shoulders. He loved the way she felt, snuggled into him like that.

'You like living here, don't you? With Robbie and Nik and Lucy. They're your family and you love them. I get that. I like living with Mum too, at the moment.'

Harry sighed. 'Yes. For a long time, it was just Dad and me. I'd almost forgotten what it was like to have Mum in the house. Nik, well, she's not my mum, but she's *something*. Something Special. And Lucy. She *is* my little sister.' He almost choked on the last words and Hannelore reached up and stroked his cheek, her face full of compassion. 'I missed them when I was away up north.'

'I know how you feel Harry. I know exactly how you feel.' Hannelore's words, the way she said it, touched him deeply. *She's the one. I've found her.*

'Come in for a moment, then I'll drive you home.' As he spoke, Lucy stepped through the front door and called out. 'Are you ever going to come in, you two? I've been waiting!'

Harry took Hannelore's hand and they walked across to Lucy. 'And Mum said you have to stay for dinner, Hanna; it's all sorted.' Harry watched Lucy grab Hanna's free hand, tugging her inside, laughing.

48

MILLIE

Matthias arrived just before dusk on Christmas Eve. He could only stay two nights but Millie was delighted to have her children with her for Christmas. Finn had invited them to share Christmas lunch at the vineyard and Hannelore had created several beautiful desserts to take out there. There'd been some initial confusion, as Harry had also asked Hannelore to be with him on Christmas Day. She told him she could come for dinner, but not lunch.

When Finn realised this, he opened his doors and invited them all for lunch and dinner. They moved the festivities from his apartment to the cellar door and issued very casual invitations to their friends to join them for the day or just drop by for a drink and snack.

Millie was excited. Finn hadn't met her son, who was the same age as Lucas. Matthias said he was pleased she was seeing Finn, and Millie hoped they'd get on. Neither of her children mentioned their father or what he was doing for Christmas, and she didn't ask.

'Matty will be here around six, Mum. The traffic is heavy getting out of Sydney.' Hannelore glanced up from her phone. 'He says he's hungry and happy to meet us at the pub. I've booked a table, and it's us, Finn and Luke. And Harry. That's six.'

Millie glanced at her watch. It was only five-thirty but she could see Hannelore was eager to get across the road. 'Tell him to come here first Hanna, he can bring his bag up. I'll wait for him.' She paused, Hannelore had dialled her excitement down slightly. 'You should go over soon, make sure no one takes the table.' Now her grin was back to full radiance. Millie chuckled.

It was after six when he arrived, but Matthias hugged her tightly and followed her upstairs. He had an overnight bag and what looked like a pillowslip with a Christmas stocking on it. It was bulging with wrapped packages. It was the first time he'd bought gifts on his own, as in the past Millie had just added the kids' names to any gifts she purchased. His enthusiasm was contagious and he took a moment to carefully place his gifts under their small tree.

'Okay Mum. Lead me to the pub. I want to check out this Harry-bloke to make sure he's good enough for my big sister.' Matthias wrapped an arm around her. 'Not to mention the Finn-bloke dating my Mum.'

Millie giggled. 'You'll like them. I know you will. So come on then, let's go, they'll all be there now.'

The pub was packed and it took Millie a moment to spot their group. She thought they may have been bumped out to the beer garden area. It was a hot night and she hoped they'd be inside, in air-conditioned comfort.

Hannelore waved, then extricated herself from the booth, almost climbing over Harry in her haste. She flew across the room into her brother's arms. 'Matty! I thought you'd never get here!'

'Hello Sissi.' Their greeting was warm and they hugged for what seemed like minutes. Millie remembered how much they'd fought in their teens and had always hoped they'd be friends when they grew up. She wiped a small tear from the corner of her eye. Finn, Lucas and Harry were all standing, waiting to meet him.

Hannelore put her arm through Matty's and led him across. Millie followed and sidled close to Finn. 'Matty, this is Harry. Finn. And Luke.' They all shook hands and murmured greetings, then Millie slid into the booth with Finn beside her and Luke on the end. Hannelore quickly sat opposite, with Harry beside her and Matty on the end.

'Beer Matthias? Or wine?' Finn handed a drinks menu across. Millie saw the other men already had a beer and Hannelore had something clear in a tall glass. Vodka lime and soda perhaps. Harry's glass was almost empty.

'Call me Matty.' He grinned at Finn. 'I'll get the drinks. What would you like Mum? Wine?

'Yes please, Matty. There's a Tyrrells Semillon I like.' Millie looked at Hannelore. 'Want to share some wine?' She cocked an eyebrow.

'Sure. Get me a glass, I'll have some when I finish this.' Hannelore took a sip of her drink, her glass now half empty.

'What about you Finn? Luke? Another beer? Harry?' Matty stood as he asked, and Millie was pleased to see Lucas rise to his feet too.

'I'll have a wine. Dad will too, I think.' Lucas grinned. 'And Harry?'

'Better get two bottles, Luke. I'll come over with you.' Now Harry was on his feet. He was taller and broader than the other young men but they seemed relaxed with each other already. Millie watched the three of them navigate their way through the crowded room to the bar.

'Matty looks good, Mum. Happy.' Hannelore's eyes were shining.

'He does.' Millie chuckled, glancing from Finn to Hannelore. 'He arrived with his bag. And something else.'

'What?' Hannelore was giggling too. 'Tell me, Mum.'

'A Santa sack of Christmas presents.' Millie glanced across to the bar. The boys hadn't been served yet. 'Well, not a sack exactly. A pillowslip with a Santa stocking picture on it.'

'Nooo!' Hannelore stifled more giggles. 'Matty shopped?' Millie nodded. She knew Hannelore would be just as surprised as she was.

'So whatever is in those parcels, act excited or he may never do it again.' Millie leaned into Finn, who chuckled too.

'May never do what again?' Matty was back, carrying a bottle of wine and two glasses. Harry held more glasses and Luke carried two wine buckets.

'Have us all over for Christmas Day, isn't that right Finn?' Millie raised her eyebrows at Finn.

'No comment Millie Tucker.' He reached for a wine bottle and deftly opened it.

———

It was late when they finished and Millie was tired. She spent the last half hour leaning back in the booth, her hand in Finn's, delighting in the way the four young people chatted together, telling funny stories and sharing some of their childhood antics. Finn was relaxed too and she saw him watching Lucas surreptitiously. He'd been worried about him after the break-up with Freddie. But Millie agreed with Finn that Lucas had done the right thing. Freddie hadn't been honest and he'd lost all trust.

Matthias talked a little bit about his job. He'd been an intern with a city Council in their town planning department while studying, but he had finished university last month and would be applying for roles in the public and private sectors. Millie and Hannelore had already said they'd go to Sydney for his graduation in the new year. Lucas asked him a lot of questions about his degree and the work he would do.

'I need to get you home, Millie; you're having trouble keeping your eyes open.' Finn remained standing after returning from paying the bill with Harry.

'Yes. You're right.' Hannelore yawned. They all stood and moved towards the door.

'Where are you sleeping Matty?' Lucas frowned. 'Millie's place has only two bedrooms.'

'Oh.' Millie had thought at one point that she might go home to Finn's, but she was far too tired for that now. 'The couch is comfortable.'

'Come home with us mate. We have plenty of room. And you can give us a hand in the morning to set up for lunch.' Lucas nudged Matthias. 'I think we're going to get a lot more drop-ins than Dad's counted on.'

Matthias looked uncertain; his gaze fell on Millie, and she looked at Hannelore. 'What do you think Hanna?'

'Do it. You'll get a better sleep.' Hanna looked like she wanted to say more but she hesitated. 'If you want to, that is.'

'To be honest, I'm still a bit wired. I was hoping we could sit up and listen to some music, and have another drink.' Matty looked more closely at Millie, then held his hands up in mock surrender. 'The women are tired, Luke. Fancy a nightcap at your place?'

'Sure.' They were out of the pub now and Millie walked across the road, hand in hand with Finn. The boys were behind them, but Harry and Hannelore were still on the pavement saying goodnight to each other.

'I'll nip up and get my bag.' Matthias paused. 'I've had too much to drink to drive out myself.'

'All good Matty. Me too. Dad's the designated driver.' Luke laughed loudly. Millie unlocked the door and gave Matty the key to upstairs. He was back down in moments.

'Can you bring the presents out in the morning Mum?' He kissed her on the cheek but didn't wait for an answer, already chatting to Lucas as they walked up the street to Finn's car.

'Goodnight sweet Millie.' Finn leaned in and kissed her lips lightly. 'I like Matty. He's smart and independent and doesn't mind showing affection to his mum and sister.'

Millie shook her head. 'I wondered, during the worst of it, when the marriage fell apart, if the kids would be alright. And Matty doesn't call very often, but he's always happy to take my calls. But you're right. He's independent.' She sighed. 'He's not *needy*. I wouldn't have it any other way, but having him here for a couple of days. It means a lot.'

'I know.' Finn looked up and waved at the boys standing by his car. 'I have to go. But tonight's been good for Luke too. He's been moping around this week, and not very excited about Christmas, but he's enjoyed this.' Waving goodnight to Harry as he drove off, and Hannelore now hurrying across the street, Finn left. His last glance at Millie was so full of love that she almost followed him.

Instead, she held the door open for Hannelore and followed her up the stairs. Inside, they giggled, then poked, lifted and shook the presents Matthias had placed under their tree until Millie said, 'Stop it, we'll tear the paper, and he'll know.'

'Alright. But now that Matty is staying at Finn's, let's go out there early. We can have breakfast there and do Christmas morning with them.' She threw her arms around Millie, adding, 'It'll be the best Christmas we've had in years!'

49

JUDITH

Christmas seemed to have crept up on Judith. She'd been so focused on the bookshop project and preparing to move into her new home that she hadn't done much. But Cathy had, and Kristen. What she loved most, now she lived in the same town as Cathy, was that the rest of their siblings could come for Christmas next year and birthdays and other events and they had enough room for all of them. That thought alone kept Judith whistling happily to herself as she created stock lists and an inventory system for the shop.

The three of them had a quiet Christmas morning, and Judith laughed aloud when Cathy made mimosas for them. 'Champagne for breakfast. Well, I never!'

Their gifts to each other were small but thoughtful. They each gave and received books. Cathy had a new one about ancient herbal remedies. Judith loved the historical books she'd received and Kristen was trying to choose which romantasy book to read first. 'What is romantasy, exactly?' Cathy asked with her glasses on the end of her nose.

'Ha ha, they're not for you, Mum. But I do think you'll like the Maple Gardens Series by Phillipa Clark I gave you.' Kristen seemed joyous. Judith expected it had more to do with Callum picking her up later in the morning to take her to his home for lunch with his family.

'What did you get Callum for Christmas, Kristen?' Cathy picked up the large present and shook it.

'Stop it, Mum. It's a new Akubra hat. He was complaining that his farm hat had fallen to pieces and he was using his going-into-town hat for work. So I've bought him a new one.' She looked thoughtful. 'He's very fair. The red hair, you know. He needs to wear a hat.'

'Of course.' Cathy nodded. Judith hoped Callum had put as much thought into his gift for Kristen. She had offered the self-contained flat at her new home to Kristen. But Judith had run it by Cathy first.

'Honestly, Jude, since Graham died, Kristen has barely left my side. I'm worried I've been holding her back. I like Callum and she needs space of her own to build a relationship. Living with you will give her that.' Cathy sighed sadly. 'I'll never re-partner. Graham was it for me. But with you here now, I know I'll never be lonely. And I think Di, Bernie, Jeannie and Teresa will visit more now they're all on the verge of retirement.'

'You know Kristen is going to handle the accounting for the bookshop?' Judith had asked. 'She has an accounting degree that she's not using at the café.'

'I know. I'm excited for her. She's smart and grounded.' Cathy leaned forward. 'I'm not keen to volunteer at the bookshop myself, it's way out of my comfort zone. But I've asked Millie if I can come back to the café as a casual. You know, over busy periods.' Her eyes twinkled. 'I've been dying to work with Hanna, her skills are way beyond mine. I think she can teach me some new tricks.' Cathy laughed and Judith was pleased she was happy for Kristen and Callum.

By mid-morning Kristen was dressed and ready for Callum to pick her up. She'd made a batch of sticky date puddings for dessert and had a bottle of Hannelore's delicious butterscotch sauce to take too.

After Kristen left, Cathy asked if she fancied watching a Christmas movie and having their lunch after that. In the end, they only got halfway through the movie, as they'd had phone calls from all of their siblings. After they enjoyed lunch Judith looked at Cathy as she put the leftover salad into the fridge. 'I'm going to have a nap, Cath. All this food has made me sleepy.'

'Oh good.' Cathy roared with laughter. 'Me too!'

Judith had trouble sleeping, so she thought about how settled she felt. Moving to Barrington had been the right decision for her, although it had started as a retirement plan to stop Cathy from getting lonely and give Kristen a chance to spread her wings. The bookshop had been a surprise, and Judith felt her involvement in the project had created a whole new life for her, just when she thought her days would feel slow and hard to fill in.

50

HANNELORE

Christmas Day! It's Christmas Day! Excitement coursed through her veins from the moment she opened her eyes. She thought about last year when she was living in Margaret River.

Anthony-the-untrustworthy had gone out without her on Christmas Eve, and he'd arrived at her place late the next morning with a hangover and no present. It wasn't that he didn't give her a present that annoyed her, it was that he didn't care enough to make any effort. A card or a bottle of wine would have been something. She'd bought him several gifts, but when he arrived empty-handed and unapologetic, she hadn't given them to him.

They'd argued, and she would have spent Christmas alone, except her boss from the bakery had called to say Merry Christmas and then invited her over for lunch. There'd been others there, backpackers who worked casually at the bakery too, and she'd had a good day.

But her first Christmas with her Mum and Matty in Barrington was the best ever. And Finn, Lucas and Harry. They'd loved Matty's presents. He'd bought books for Hannelore, perfume for Millie, and a gift card for the cinema at Tuncurry. Millie had bought him two business shirts for his job interviews, and Hannelore had given him a bottle of cologne and a Barrington baseball cap, which he wore all day.

Finn's gift to Millie was beautiful. It was a rose gold knot ring, which she instantly adored. Hannelore wondered for a moment if he was proposing, but he made no move to go down on one knee, and Millie seemed happy to slip it on the middle finger of her right hand.

Millie gave Finn a coffee machine, and he said she'd have to teach him how to use it. They'd bought a Wi-Fi speaker for Luke, which he immediately hooked up, playing old Bing Crosby Christmas tunes all morning.

Luke and Matty said they'd stayed up until after midnight, drinking and chatting, but they seemed fine this morning. By mid-morning they were all over at the cellar door. Finn had three types of roast in the smoker, and all the traditional vegetables, and Millie and Hannelore made a variety of fresh salads.

'Do you know who is coming, Finn, apart from Harry and his family?' Hannelore bumped into him as she stepped out of the cool room.

'Not really, but I put it out there, and I think a few will drop by between lunch and dinner.' Finn seemed unperturbed, and Hannelore crinkled her brow.

'You're not worried about food levels? I can make some canapes.' She stopped speaking when he shook his head.

'We can have fifty turn up Hanna, and it won't matter. It's Barrington. They'll bring something. There will be plenty.'

Finn was right. The Stewarts stayed all day, but others came and went. Harry held her close and gave her a small gift. Too thin to be a book, Hannelore unwrapped the latest eBook reader, already loaded with several books. It was perfect and she hugged him tightly. She'd given him a leather case for his phone with his initials on the front.

During the day, Ben and Melanie and the girls dropped in, as did Laura and Big Ben. Rachael and Steve came on their way out to Jamie's place, and Harriet, Drum, Billie and little Hamish dropped by for a couple of hours too, as did Rose and Angus with their little ones. Meggie and Max were still away, but Callum arrived after lunch with Kristen and Freddie. Finn was right, everyone brought something, and the food supplies remained strong all afternoon.

'I'll help you back there Hanna.' Kristen called out when she arrived. Callum shot over to speak to Harry and Ben, and Freddie headed across to the hay bale Lucas and Matthias were perched on, beers in hand.

Hannelore dragged Kristen into the back room and hugged her quickly. 'How was it for you? At Callum's?'

'Lovely. I helped his Mum with lunch, and they adored my dessert.' Kristen sniggered. 'Your butterscotch sauce Hanna, it went down a treat.' She giggled again. 'Callum gave me a pair of riding boots and said he'd love it if I spent some time on the farm. His brothers teased him, but there was no meanness in it.' Kristen looked over her shoulder. 'Freddie has been a bit morose. She made a show of joking with her brothers while we ate lunch, but I think she's miserable. It's about Luke, isn't it?'

Hannelore nodded. 'It is. But I'm not sure if her family knows. And I think Luke ended it the other night.'

'She's over there now.' Kristen peered out into the area they'd set up with chairs and hay bales. 'Talking to Luke. And someone else.' Kristen turned back to her. 'Is that Matty, your brother? He looks a bit like you.'

Hannelore looked out, then frowned. 'Yes, that's Matty.' Freddie had her back to her, but she could see Luke's expression. He wasn't happy. 'I better go over there.' But before she moved, Harry strolled across, Callum with him, sitting next to Luke, who immediately relaxed. *You're a class act Harry Stewart.*

'So Hanna, tell me about *your* morning with Harry.' Kristen put her hand to her chest. 'Isn't it divine that our men are already friends?'

'It really is.' Hannelore would have said more, but Matty was walking towards her.

'Matty, this is Kristen. We work together.' Hannelore watched him shake Kristen's hand with a charming grin.

'I've heard a lot about you, Kristen, and I've just met Callum.' Matty smiled but gave Hannelore a look. An I-need-to-speak-to-you-alone look. Kristen saw it too and picked up a tray of mini quiches, murmuring as she left, 'I'll just take these out, shall I?'

'What is it Matty? Has something happened?' Hannelore was concerned.

'Freddie, Callum's sister. She's had a few drinks, I think. More than a few. She's flirting with me, Hanna. In a really obvious way. And I'm pretty sure she's the girl Luke was telling me about late last night. He was upset. He didn't give me her name, but his description matches Freddie.' He breathed out through his nose. 'She's hot. Sexy. But she's a piece of trouble if ever I've seen it.'

'You won't do anything, will you Matty?' Hannelore could see Luke was still uncomfortable, but he was talking with Harry and

Callum now, and Melanie Evans had led Freddie over to a table full of snacks.

Matty snorted. 'Of course not. Luke is family now.' He grinned then. 'Or I expect he will be in the fullness of time.'

'Good. Thank you. Luke is lovely, but Freddie has been, um, playing games. He's broken it off, but seeing her today will be hard.' She grabbed Matty's arm. 'Let's go over.'

As they approached, she saw Freddie, still with Melanie, double over and rush from the building. She raised an eyebrow at Harry and would have gone to check on the girl, but Melanie followed her out. Callum frowned and made to follow, but Harry touched his arm and spoke quietly.

Not long after, Ben Evans came to say goodbye. He had little Bronte in his arms and Tiffany by his side. 'Thank you Luke, Hanna. We're off now.' He turned to Callum. 'Um, Melanie is out in the car with Freddie. We're going to take her back to your place, it's on our way.'

Callum seemed relieved. 'Thanks Ben. I don't know what's gotten into her today. She was drinking beer faster than Douggie was.'

'She's young, mate. We've all been there.' Ben said goodbye to Finn and hugged Millie. Hannelore could see how well her mother had been accepted into the community. It made *her* feel part of it too.

They ate leftovers for dinner, and Hannelore was surprised when a few more people dropped by and joined them. It felt like a community event or a really big extended family. Hannelore loved it. The nicest part for her was when Robbie, Nicole and Lucy left. Harry was staying a bit longer; he'd brought his own car. It wasn't that they left, it was what they did beforehand. Nicole kissed her on the cheek, and Lucy hugged her quickly, but it was Robbie who moved her. He wrapped his big arms around her, so much like Harry, and held her tightly. 'We can't tell you, Hanna, how happy we are that you're here. And you're staying.' And he was gone, but Hannelore, her heart filled with love, walked over to Harry and waved as they drove out.

'Robbie.' She couldn't speak, she was too close to tears. Harry wrapped his arms around her and rocked her against his chest. 'I know. I saw. Dad loves you already.' She sniffled. That his Dad loved her brought on more tears. 'But.' Harry paused, and she chanced a look at him. He kissed her lightly, then pulled her against him again. 'But not as much as I do Hanna. Not as much as I do.'

On tiptoes, she kissed him back, lingering for a moment, her teeth nibbling his bottom lip. He drew in a sharp breath. 'I think you need to show me Harry. And soon.'

51

HARRY

WHEN MILLIE SAID SHE'D STAY AT FINN'S TO HELP clean up in the morning, then bring Matty back to get his car, Harry knew this was the opportunity he'd been waiting for. He whispered in Hannelore's ear, 'May I drive you home tonight?'

Hannelore nodded and wrapped her arms around his waist. 'Yes. I was hoping you would. I'll tell Mum, and say goodnight to Finn and the boys.'

Hannelore approached Millie, and they stepped to one side, had a brief conversation and hugged each other. Harry said goodnight to Finn and the boys, thanking them for a great day. He waited patiently while Hannelore hugged and kissed them all goodnight, before taking his hand and walking to his Ute.

Starting the vehicle, Harry took her hand and spoke quietly. 'I'd like to stay with you tonight Hanna, if that's what you want too.'

Squeezing his hand, she murmured 'Yes'. That was enough for

Harry and he drove slowly away. 'Music?' He let the question hang for a moment.

'No. Thank you. I just want to enjoy the drive. With you.' She gazed through the windscreen. The sky was clear and filled with stars. 'This has been the best Christmas Day for me. Ever.'

Chancing a glance at her as he turned onto the main road into town, he saw she was still looking straight ahead. 'Really?'

Nodding, she sighed and half turned towards him in her seat. 'I'm sure I had some lovely Christmas Days when I was little. But I don't remember any. Most of my memories are of Mum and Dad working, sometimes even on Christmas Day, and arguing with each other. There was so much tension, that Matty and I just kept our heads down and helped when asked. So different to today.'

'You worked today too, Hanna. You and your Mum and I saw Matty helping Luke at the bar and with the barbecue. Finn didn't stop all day.' Harry knew where she was heading with the conversation, but he sensed she needed to say it.

'But it wasn't work. Not really. It was different to any Christmas I've ever had.' She seemed to be searching for the right words. 'It was just like an enormous *family* Christmas Day. Everyone helped, and even the guests brought plates of food to share.' Hannelore paused and Harry slowed as he drove down the main street towards her place. 'In fact. There weren't any guests, were there?' The question asked, she answered it herself. 'Everyone who came, everyone who stayed or just dropped in for an hour, they *are* family aren't they? That's how it is here.'

Harry parked in the space behind the building and stopped the car. He undid his seatbelt and turned towards Hannelore. Her cheeks were wet with tears but her face was alight with happiness. He grinned, nodded and thumbed the tears from her cheeks. 'And now you understand. It's one of the reasons I came home myself. Even when Dad and I were on our own, before Nik and Lucy arrived, there were places to go for Christmas. Sometimes it would be lunch with the Campbells and dinner with Ben Evans senior. We'd call in on old Fred Saunders, although we lost him last year. One year there were more than fifty people at Ben's place. A bit like today really.'

Hannelore nodded happily and he released her hand, stepped out of the car and met her as she opened her door. Hand in hand, they walked up the back stairs to the apartment and Hannelore let them in.

Once inside Hannelore threw the lights on in the living area, then looked uncertain. 'Would you like another drink, Harry? Or a cup of tea?'

Harry wrapped his arms around her and nuzzled her neck. 'Take me to your room Hanna.'

Leading him by the hand, she opened her bedroom door. 'I'll um, just freshen up. Make yourself comfortable.' She kissed him lightly, then dashed across the hall to the bathroom. Harry took his shirt off and waited for her return. He contemplated having a quick shower. The day had been warm. As if she could read his thoughts, Hannelore opened the bathroom door. She stood there in nothing but a towel, and steam from the shower billowed out.

'I need a quick shower.' It was more a question than a statement. Harry walked to her wearing just his jeans. He reached for her, but she let the towel drop and turned, stepping into the foggy shower. Harry hesitated, but she threw a sexy look over her shoulder and raised an eyebrow. Harry knew an invitation when he saw one and he had his jeans and jocks off in seconds.

52

HANNELORE

When Hannelore spoke to Millie, to let her know Harry was taking her home, she hinted he'd stay the night. In her heart, she knew Millie would be okay with it, but hearing her say it meant a lot. They even shared a little joke, and Millie nudged her with an elbow and whispered, 'I'll text in the morning before we head home.'

The ride home was almost as special as the day had been. Hannelore needed to express her thoughts about the day, and Harry was patient. Knowing he *got it, got her,* cemented her feelings for him. And that left just one thing.

As she undressed in the bathroom, she chanted to herself, 'Christmas day, consummation day.' For a moment she wondered how it would start. The sex. What would Harry do first? And then it hit her. She didn't have to let *him* lead. Feeling brave and sexy and naughty all at once, she turned on the shower and opened the bathroom door, a towel barely covering her nakedness. He was standing there, dressed only in jeans, looking delicious as his hot eyes roved from her face to her toes and back.

All she did was raise an eyebrow and turn. Harry was naked and holding her before her towel hit the floor. *Sexy Harry Stewart.*

Harry walked her backwards until she was under the water. Then Hannelore turned them until he was under the water. She reached up to kiss him, but he held up a soap bar, shaking his head. 'Turn around Hanna.' His voice was gravelly, his tone deeper than usual. Trembling, she turned her back to him with her arms over her head. He soaped her body, from her shoulders, down her back, to her legs. He returned to the small of her back and her bottom, standing so close she could feel his erection bumping against the top of her bottom cleavage. Desire fanned through her, and she bent over slightly.

Harry groaned. Taking her in his arms, all soapy and slippery, he kissed her deeply, then nibbled his way down her neck to her collarbone. She wanted him. Now. But he passed her the soap and turned away. Hannelore giggled. *Okay, Harry Stewart.* She soaped his back, bum and legs, and when he tried to face her she held him in place, her naked body hard against his back, and reached around him with the soap. She did his chest first, then his thighs.

'Hanna!' There it was again, that gravelly tone she loved. *His sex voice.* Then she reached his penis and wrapped one hand around it. Hannelore made an O with her mouth as she explored the girth and length of him, then spluttered when she swallowed some shower water. 'Enough!' *That tone really did something to her.* Harry turned around, wrapped one arm around her waist and carried her out of the shower, reaching back to turn the faucet off with his other hand. He picked up the towel she'd discarded earlier and half-dried her, before giving his own chest a token wipe. He tossed the towel to one side and holding her so close that her feet barely touched the floor, he walked her backwards across the hall to her room.

Throwing the covers open, he backed her onto the bed and covered her with his body. 'Are you sure Hanna?' He hesitated, and she nodded vigorously, murmuring 'Don't stop.' Kissing his way down her body he paused at the apex of her legs and looked up at her.

'No!' She tried to wriggle away, but he held her firmly.

He stopped. 'No?' He waited.

'I can't take any more Harry, make love to me. Now. Please.' Hannelore moaned. She was so close and she wanted to feel him inside her. She reached down and touched herself, feeling her slickness. *She'd never been more ready.*

Harry moved from the bed quickly. 'Don't move a muscle.' He almost growled the words and she moaned again. *That voice.* He was back, tearing a condom packet open with his teeth. She reached down to help him but he pushed her hand away. 'Don't Hanna.' His teeth were clenched, and she realised he was close, too. She opened her legs, nudging him into position and he sheathed himself inside her in one thrust. Hannelore rose to meet him, arching her back. He filled her completely, and began to move slowly, his hot eyes watching hers as he increased his rhythm. She couldn't hold on. Crying out, she let go and Harry thrust twice more, then cradled her in his arms, kissing her face gently, touching her hair with one hand as his breathing slowed.

Rolling onto his back, she rolled with him until she was snug against his side, his arm around her. Hannelore's breathing slowed and she ran her fingers lightly over his broad chest. Harry's body seemed to vibrate and she quickly looked back to his face. He was laughing, silently. 'A quickie Hanna. Not what I planned for our first time.' He rolled on his side, facing her. 'But the sexual tension.' He didn't finish, and she nodded. 'You're beautiful Hanna.'

'You're beautiful too, Harry Stewart.' She leaned in and kissed his lips, and let her teeth find his bottom lip. He groaned and the hand around her back found its way lower, rubbing her bottom, the backs of her thighs. 'Oh!' She thrust against him, heat pooling in her belly.

'I think we need to try again.' *That voice.* 'I know we can do better.' Harry pulled her on top of him, and she wriggled down until she felt him, hard again, touching her outer lips. She sat up and enveloped him, and he breathed in sharply through his nose. 'Cute move. But I've got this now.' He flipped them over, and she stopped thinking and allowed herself to simply feel, and respond.

———

HANNELORE WOKE AS TENDRILS OF DAWN LIGHT slithered through the shutters. Not yet five, she stretched. Harry was asleep, the sheet pulled up to his waist. *Beautiful man.* She crept from the bed to use the bathroom and brush her teeth. Her nether region was tender. She giggled. They'd made love three times before giving in to fatigue. It was so good, better than she could have imagined. Returning to the bed, she placed her hand on his chest and Harry opened his eyes.

'Good morning Hanna.' He stretched. She snuggled in and kissed him gently. 'You've brushed your teeth.' She nodded and he breathed in deeply before sliding out of bed. 'I'll do the same.'

Hannelore must have dozed off because he returned with a

towel around his waist and two cups of tea. She sat up, holding the sheet to her chest and took the cup he passed her. 'Thank you. I could get used to this.'

'That's what I'm hoping.' He perched on her side of the bed and they chatted generally while they sipped. Twenty minutes later he took their empty cups to the kitchen and Hannelore wondered if they'd make love again. She wanted to, but she was a bit tender. Standing at the bedroom door, Harry removed his towel with a flourish. 'Another shower, my lady? And then breakfast. I'm starving.'

In the end, they didn't have breakfast at the apartment, because Millie called and asked if they'd like to come to Finn's. Both of them.

53

———

MILLIE

'Hannelore and Harry will be here by eight.' Millie passed Finn a cappuccino. He still had to learn how to use the coffee machine. She didn't mind. It was as much for her, when she stayed here.

Finn sipped, then gave her a surprised look. 'It tastes like the ones you make at the café!'

Millie laughed. 'It should. I've used the same coffee beans.'

'I've messaged Luke to tell him Hanna and Harry are returning for breakfast.' Finn took another sip and gave her a delighted look. Millie felt a bit smug. 'There's not much to clean up, but the boys can help me put all the chairs away and I'll clean the barbecue after breakfast.'

'Alright. The café opens tomorrow, but I've given Hanna and Kristen the rest of the week off. Cathy is coming in, and young Lucy.' Millie looked outside. 'Oh, Luke just walked across to the cellar door. Shall we go down?'

Downing the rest of his coffee, Finn gave Millie a quick kiss on the lips. 'Take your time Millie.'

After making the bed and brushing her hair, Millie walked outside as Harry arrived, with Hannelore perched up beside him. Hannelore was radiating happiness and looked all loved up. So much so that Millie was afraid she'd laugh if she met her eye. The men didn't seem to notice, or if they did, they said nothing. Hannelore followed Millie into the kitchen area and Millie had to ask. 'Did you have a, er, good night?'

Hannelore set down the packet of eggs she was holding and threw herself into Millie's arms. 'So good Mum. Best Christmas Day. Ever.' She stepped away and Millie knew her own face reflected Hannelore's happiness. 'And not because of, um, you know.' Her daughter leaned in and whispered, 'Although *that* was amazing.'

'Not because of *that*?' Millie repeated, trying not to laugh out loud.

Hannelore threw her arms out wide and turned in a half circle. 'The whole day. Was. Just the best!'

Millie had to agree. It had been her best Christmas Day too. Harry seemed a bit sheepish when he said good morning to Millie, but he quickly jumped in to help the others pack the chairs and trestle tables away.

When they finished, Finn had bacon and eggs ready on the barbecue and they sat down together. Hannelore found an unopened bottle of champagne and made mimosas, and it really did feel like a family meal, although she noticed Luke wasn't saying much.

'Luke?' Millie looked at him, speaking gently. 'Can I get you anything else?'

'Oh no. Thank you Millie.' Luke and Mathias shared a look and Millie wondered what *that* was about. 'Actually, if you can spare me for a couple of weeks Dad, I might ride back to Sydney with Matty.'

Finn indicated he'd heard but kept eating his breakfast. Hannelore jumped in. 'That's a good idea, Luke. Matty rents a nice place in North Sydney. It's central to everything.'

'Just for a couple of weeks. I'll stay with Matty and have a look around Sydney. A bit of a holiday.' Luke sounded defensive and Millie hoped Finn would say something to put him at ease.

Millie wasn't disappointed when Finn finally gave voice to his thoughts. 'That's a good plan, Luke. Take more than a couple of weeks. You must have at least four weeks' vacation owing to you.' He turned to Matthias. 'Are you sure it's okay? You have room?'

Matthias laughed and clapped his hand on Luke's back. 'I've got two weeks off myself. I've already applied to the Council to make my internship a full-time position, but I won't know until mid-January. I've applied for several other roles and have three interviews after New Year. But in the meantime, Luke and I can hang out. Friends have invited me to share a holiday house up on the northern beaches over the new year, and Luke will be welcome there.'

'Thanks Dad.' It was said quietly, but sincerely. Millie breathed a silent sigh of relief.

———

LATER, AFTER ALL THE YOUNG PEOPLE HAD LEFT, MILLIE curled up next to Finn on his sofa. 'Will you be okay for a couple of weeks out here? Without Luke?'

'We've got a small function on New Year's Day, but you're doing the food for that. If you can bring Hanna and maybe Kristen or Lucy, we'll be fine.' Finn sighed. 'I know it's about Freddie. How she was yesterday. Drinking too much and flirting with Matty right in front of Luke. It hurts him to see her like that. But he's right about Freddie. She needs to grow up.' Finn put his arm around Millie. 'I just hope he doesn't get a taste for Sydney and decide to move there. I wouldn't try to stop him, but I love having him here.'

'I know Finn. But a couple of weeks away will give him some perspective.' Millie frowned, trying to remember a conversation from their last book club. 'Actually, Freddie's only in town until Meggie and Max return from their holiday. That's about the third week in January. Then she's going to a horse stud in Tamworth for two months. Her university placement, I think.'

'Oh. Good. Maybe Luke should stay away until she leaves.' Finn smiled wryly. 'But if he's anything like me, the heart wants what the heart wants.'

'But Luke isn't the problem. It's Freddie.' Millie moved slightly and wriggled until her legs were across Finn's lap. He obligingly rubbed her feet as they chatted. 'A few weeks here, then to a job where she knows no one. It might give her time to think about what is important to her.'

'We can hope.' Finn sighed. 'Or Luke meets a girl while he's away.' Millie doubted that but didn't voice her thoughts.

'Did I tell you, Finn, that I'm staying here tonight?' Millie smiled sweetly. 'And there's no one about at all. No Luke downstairs.'

'Hmm. I picked up on that when you told Hannelore, quite loudly I might add, that you were planning to stay here.' Finn removed Millie's legs and somehow she was on her back on the couch and he had his body over hers. He bent down, kissed her, then sucked her bottom lip into his mouth. Millie wriggled. *Clever Finn.* 'But I thought the comment was for Harry to hear, to know he could stay with Hannelore a second night.' He teased her mouth again, then repositioned himself until he was almost fully on top of her. 'I didn't realise it was because you were planning a little, er, seduction of your own Millie Tucker.'

'Shut up and kiss me Finn.'

54

RACHAEL

Barrington Book Club – Rachael, Rose, Millie, Hannelore,
Kristen, Melanie, Harriet, Laura, Nicole, Judith
Apologies – Meggie
Book – ***Back to Birdsville*** by Fiona McArthur

CHRISTMAS WAS BITTER-SWEET FOR RACHAEL. IT WAS the first without Debbie and every task she undertook triggered a memory: the ornaments on the Christmas tree she'd made at school, the smell of ham baking, how she loved to wrap the presents in a different theme each year.

On Christmas Eve Rachael and Steve declined all invitations and stayed home. They shared a bottle of wine and spent hours looking at photos of Debbie over the years, at times crying so hard that neither could speak. But their grief was shared and somehow cathartic, and they woke the next morning determined to do their best for Jamie and little Woz. They spent Christmas Day at the Tait homestead and Warwick delighted in everything, bringing smiles to all their faces. Even Jamie's. Ben and Melanie came with their girls for lunch, then went to Finn's later in the afternoon. Rachael and Steve thought about going too, but in the end, they went home to a quiet dinner after Woz fell asleep on Jamie's lap late in the afternoon.

So a new year. A new project for Rachael. Steve was immersed in his role as Mayor. Rachael drew in a deep breath, happy to be attending the book club meeting tonight. She'd missed her friends over the last couple of weeks and knew book club would provide laughter and inspiration and part-fill the Debbie-sized hole in her heart. Rachael's shared grief with Rose had deepened their connection, and she looked forward to seeing her.

Millie and the younger women were setting up the table in the back when Rachael arrived. Melanie, Harriet and Laura greeted her with smiles and hugs and suddenly she had a glass of wine in her hand. Judith arrived next and Rose rushed in last. She walked quickly to Rachael, her face flushed, and hugged her tightly. 'Wee Charlie,' was all she said by way of explanation, and Rachael laughed out loud. *Wee Charlie.* She wondered if they would still call him that when he started school or played football in his teen years. Angus was a strapping man. Charlie would likely be a tall, strong lad before too long.

Laughing out loud, right from the start, lightened Rachael's heart and she was warmed by the quick look of acknowledgement Rose gave her. Rachael squeezed Rose's hand. But they joined in the general chat about Christmas, their short breaks, holidays, the weather and even the rain damage out on the Barrington West road.

Millie, Kristen and Hannelore brought charcuterie platters to the table, and they settled into their usual seats.

Harriet smiled warmly at Rachael. 'I know we're here to chat about *Back to Birdsville*, which I adored. But Rachael, how is the bookshop renovation going? Are we on schedule for a Valentine's Day opening?' She wrinkled her nose. 'I peeked in the windows, but they're covered in brown paper.'

'Well. I'm not sure how much to tell you.' Rachael drew her words out and saw she had everyone's attention. Glancing at Judith, she grinned. 'Only Judith and I have been inside and I think I'd like to keep it under wraps for now, hence the papered-up windows. But I can tell you that a Valentine's Day opening is still the plan.' From the corner of her eye, she saw Hannelore blush. 'Well, perhaps Hanna has been inside too. She seems to have some *influence* over one of our builders.' Rachael giggled. Millie had mentioned only yesterday that Hannelore and Harry were now an item.

The focus of the group moved quickly to Hannelore, although Rachael thought most of them would know about her new romantic attachment. Harriet nudged Hannelore. 'That's news to me Hanna Tucker. Although it was pretty obvious at our last meeting that Harry had hot eyes for you.'

'Hot eyes?' Laura snorted. 'Is that what you call it? Oh yes, it was obvious.' A few of the others teased Hannelore for a moment, but Rachael saw her discomfort lessen and she lifted her chin.

'Yes ladies, it's a *thing*. Except I may have competition.' Hannelore looked straight at Judith. 'It was you he held hands with, Judith, when we inspected the apartment last time. Should I be worried?' She waggled her eyebrows and Judith roared with laughter.

'Oh, I wish Hanna.' She wiped a tear from her eye, still grinning broadly. 'In my head, I call him *Handsome Harry Stewart*.' She wagged a finger at Hannelore. 'But don't you tell him that.'

Millie chimed in drily. 'What happens at book club, stays at book club. Right Hanna?' Giggles, laughter and general chat followed this remark and Rachael sipped her wine, basking in the friendship and warmth of these women.

'Okay. No sneak peek at the bookshop allowed, so let's chat about this fabulous book.' Harriet waved a paperback copy around. 'This was a first for me, with this author. Now I want more.'

'I've already told Ben we must schedule a Birdsville trip.' Laura sighed. 'So many great places to visit in Australia, but this one is firmly on my radar now. And Ben's. We listened to the audiobook while driving to Sydney and back last month. The narrator was brilliant.'

'The author knows her stuff. The descriptions of the town and terrain, not to mention the medical information, rang true for me. No question about it.' Melanie sighed.

Rose nodded across to Laura. 'And it has all the small town feels I love and understand, you know, from living here. Same feels, different town.'

'Oh yes! And it was funny too in places. And the local cop, *Atticus*. Perfectly named. And cousin Scarlet, the horse, the wedding! I could go on.' A dreamy expression came over Hannelore's face as she spoke, and Rachael chuckled to herself. *Hanna Tucker has it just as bad as Harry. She's all loved up.*

Judith topped up Rachael's wine glass. 'I've loved this author for years. She has dozens of books out, at least fifty, maybe more. Her early stuff was focused on medical romance. I'm fairly sure she was a midwife early in her career, so that's why it rings true. I'd recommend her backlist, they're all best sellers.' She popped a cracker laden with dip onto her plate. 'Actually, Fiona McArthur is one of the authors I've contacted about doing a writer's residency and book signing. She has some books traditionally published, like this one, but she also indie-publishes. And she's a great presenter.'

'You've contacted Fiona McArthur? Really?' Rose almost bounced with excitement. 'And? Will she come?'

They all looked at Judith. 'Yes! She's keen. I have others lined up too. No one has turned me down.'

'Wow!' The book discussion was abandoned as the group segued to several conversations at once about Judith's list of attending authors. Judith opened her iPad and read the list aloud and even Rachael knew some of the names. Hannelore and Rose were particularly excited and suddenly it hit Rachael that *The Little Indie Bookshop* was destined for success. How could it not work with all the enthusiasm, and experience, driving the project?

A wave of emotion rushed from her chest to her face. Rachael tried to stifle it. Tried to speak. But her words came out as a sob. 'The bookshop. (sniff). The project. It's going to work, isn't it? (sob).' Judith patted Rachael's back and Rose leapt from her chair and rushed around the table, placing her cheek against Rachael's. Their tears mingled. But they were happy tears.

'Yes!' Hannelore shouted the words and punched the air. 'Yes, it's going to work! Of *course* it will work.' And then they were laughing. Rachael with them. And congratulating her and each other and all speaking at once.

'Dessert girls. This calls for dessert.' Millie must have retreated to the kitchen during the commotion and now slid a timber board onto the table. Rachael was intrigued.

'Another Hannelore idea. It's a deconstructed pavlova board.' Millie pointed to the items. 'Mini pavlovas, fresh cream, chocolate sauce and a raspberry coulis plus Kiwi fruit, strawberries, raspberries and blueberries. Construct your own with your favourite toppings.'

'Ooh. Fancy.' Judith popped a pavlova shell onto her plate. 'I'm in, thank you Hanna.'

'Hanna has news too. That *doesn't* concern Harry Stewart.' Millie giggled, then looked proudly at her daughter. Rachael knew about this, Millie and Hannelore had invited her and Steve for coffee a couple of days ago.

'Ooh. News. What Hanna?' Harriet was slathering cream onto her pavlova shell. 'Pass the raspberries please Nik.'

Hannelore looked equal parts nervous and excited. 'I'm starting my own little business, inside the café.' She turned to Rachael and grinned broadly. 'Thanks to Rachael and Steve for allowing it.' Rachael nodded back. She was thrilled for Hannelore. In many ways, she was like Debbie at that age.

'Okay. And now I need more information.' Harriet picked up her cream and berry-laden mini pavlova to take a bite, but a raspberry fell off, rolling down the front of her blouse leaving a trail of chocolate sauce in its wake. Harriet didn't hesitate. She picked up the berry and popped it into her mouth before ineffectively wiping her blouse with a napkin which only served to spread the smear of sauce. Licking the sauce from the tip of one finger, Harriet waved her other hand around her plate. 'What happens at book club... Remember?'

'You're hilarious Harri.' Rose nudged her friend. 'But tell us more Hanna, I'm intrigued.'

'A little patisserie. Tiny. But specialising in wedding and event cakes and gourmet items like eclairs and profiteroles.' Hannelore sounded more confident now and Rachael nodded encouragingly for her to continue. She had everyone's attention. 'I'll still work with Mum, but I'm buying in some equipment she doesn't have, and Kristen has done the business modelling, so it can be a cost centre of its own.'

'Profit centre, Hanna.' Kristen chimed in. 'This is a great way to start. Minimum overheads. And it will help Hanna keep her pricing very competitive.'

'Thank you, Kristen. I wouldn't be this far without your help.' Back to Harriet, Hannelore added, 'When Meggie returns from holidays I'd like to talk to you about what I can offer your elopements and events business.' Rachael almost held her breath, waiting for Harriet's response. She was an experienced businesswoman, and Rachael hoped she would be on board.

'Fantastic idea! We've been getting cakes made out of town. This is awesome news.' Harriet looked from Millie to Hannelore. 'And Finn will place orders too, I expect, for his wine-tasting days. And Millie, it means Hanna is staying!' Harriet clapped her hands and instantly they were all congratulating Hannelore and talking over each other again.

'Wait!' Laura held up her hand and they quietened. 'What are you calling your business, Hanna?'

'Yes! Do you have a name?' Nicole asked the question, but they were all eager to hear the answer.

'I don't. I have some ideas.' Hannelore swivelled to face

Harriet again. 'I was going to ask you and Meggie to help me brainstorm.'

'No need to wait.' Harriet picked up her notebook. 'Names for Hanna's business, everyone? Hanna, you start with the ones you've already thought of.'

'Tiny Delights, Patisserie Delights, um, Tiny Tarts.' Hannelore blushed when she uttered the last one.

'The Wee Bakery.' Rose chuckled.

'Sweet Haven.'

'Cakes are my Calling.' Rachael threw that in, thinking it might work with the café name.

'Praise the Pastry.'

'Praise the Patisserie.'

'Eat cake.'

'You can have the cake.'

'Say yes to the cake.' Millie giggled as she spoke, but Rachael pricked up her ears. Harriet did too.

'*Say yes to the cake.* Oh Hanna, if your main product line will be wedding cakes, this is one to consider. It's got a wedding vibe.' Harriet underlined it on her notepad.

'Actually, it's bigger than a wedding vibe Harri.' Rachael pointed to the café logo behind the front counter. 'If you design the logo in a similar style to the café logo, you could read it as *coffee is my calling* and *say yes to the cake.*' To me, it's giving the customer permission to have cake with their coffee but also suggesting that it's so good you *must* have cake with your coffee. And the wedding cake, birthday cake, event cake meaning too.'

'Oh. You're right Rachael. That's clever. And wedding cakes will be my premium line.' Hannelore looked around the table, her eyes lingering on Millie. 'What do you all think? Mum, it was your idea. I know it was spontaneous, but do you like it? Should we explore this one? It's my favourite.'

'It's a yes from me.' Millie seemed as thrilled with it as Hannelore.

Harriet tore the page of suggestions out of her notebook. 'Take them all home Hanna and roll them around in your head for a day or two. Maybe test the idea on a few people. Finn. Harry. And message Meggie too, she's great at this stuff.'

'I will. Yes, I'll do that.' Hannelore folded the piece of paper up and slipped it inside her Kindle.

'Now book clubbers. What will we read for next month?' Harriet gazed around the table. 'Next meeting is the week before the bookshop opens.'

'*The Summerfield Saddler* by Penelope Janu. It's small-town, with an environmental angle.' Hannelore held up her Kindle to show the cover. 'I've read it, but I think you will all enjoy it.'

'Done!' Laura clapped her hands. 'Pass that second bottle down Nik, I think I can squeeze a few drops of wine out, if no one else wants it.'

Later, as Rachael walked home alone, she wondered at the changes that had taken place since she joined the book club. The apartment, the bookshop, Hannelore's little business. In the past, she'd been averse to change, had even fought it. But the biggest change of all was within her. New projects, closer friends, *more* friends, more confidence. *Rachael Webb, through the unimaginable pain of losing Debbie, you've found yourself.* She looked skyward for a moment, letting a solitary tear slide down her cheek. She wiped it away, smiled, and walked lightly up the path to her house.

55

—————

FREDDIE

WITH A FLICK OF HER HAND, FREDDIE PUSHED HER phone from the seat beside her to the car's floor. Luke was in Sydney, with Hannelore's brother Matthias. He'd messaged to let her know, and she called several times, but he didn't answer. Luke simply messaged back to wish her Happy New Year and good luck with her work in Barrington. He said he wouldn't be back before she went to Tamworth.

Freddie fumed and hit the steering wheel with the palm of her hand as she parked at the back of the Vet clinic. Her plans for the summer with Luke were over. *They* were over. *How dare he?* She scrabbled around to get her phone from the floor, then stepped out of her jeep and slammed the door. But as she walked into the building, a wave of sadness hit her, and it was all she could do not to cry. Again.

Melanie greeted her warmly and Freddie tried to relax her face into some sort of smile. 'Happy New Year Melanie. Do we have any patients today?' She'd keep it professional.

'We do. Two puppies and Mrs Tubb's cat, Ginge, need vaccinating.' Melanie handed a file to Freddie and she called Mrs Tubbs in first.

'And how is Ginge, Mrs Tubbs?' Freddie had known the old lady all her life and spoke kindly.

'He's a wonder. Such a good boy. And so like old Ginger.' Mrs Tubbs looked fondly at her pet. 'He's not a mouse catcher though. There was one in the laundry last week and Ginge completely ignored it. I had to chase it out with a broom.'

Freddie laughed. 'I suspect he ignored it because he's not hungry, Mrs Tubbs.' She took the cat gently from her client's arms and weighed him. 'He's a bit heavier than he should be, are you giving him treats?'

Freddie prepared the vaccinations while Mrs Tubbs stoked the cat gently. He purred like a steam train. 'Well no. Not a lot of treats.' Mrs Tubbs hesitated. 'Just the special cat food he likes, and sometimes a wee bit of chicken in the evenings. And a small piece of my shortbread when I have my cup of tea in the morning.' Freddie turned her back, lifting a bottle of vaccine from the fridge, before answering. She needed to be gentle, but firm.

'Ginge doesn't need shortbread Mrs Tubbs. It's not good for him. And perhaps reduce the amount of, er, chicken, in the evenings.' Freddie injected the cat, who stopped purring briefly, then recommenced, louder than before. 'But he is one of the best-looking cats I've seen in a while Mrs Tubbs.'

This seemed to appease the owner and she smiled happily. 'You're a handsome boy then, aren't you Ginge? The Vet says you are.'

'Alright Mrs Tubbs. You're good to go. Just see Melanie on the way out, we'd like to check Ginge in six months.' Freddie opened the door and followed Mrs Tubbs to the front desk, handing the file to Melanie.

'You've got time to see the puppies Freddie, but we've had a call from Drum Murray. Their dog was bitten by a snake and they're on their way in. Angus is on his way too. Twenty minutes.' Melanie handed Freddie the file for the puppies and ushered the two little boys and their father into the surgery after her.

Freddie worked quickly, focusing on the puppies for their eight-week shots. She was still cleaning up when Angus arrived through the rear entrance carrying a young kelpie, with Drum and his daughter Billie right behind him.

Standing back, Freddie watched carefully as Angus administered Tiger Snake antivenom. She shaved and swabbed Bluey's foreleg in preparation for a catheter to administer intravenous fluids, and wondered if Billie, Drum's little girl, should be in the room.

As if in answer, Angus spoke quietly to Billie. 'Alright, stay with him Billie and keep Rusty calm, while I check something with Melanie.' Angus moved to the door and indicated Freddie should come too. She hooked the bag of fluids up to the stand and followed him out.

'It's touch and go, Freddie. Drum said it was a big snake.' Angus shook his head, his concern evident. 'You've got to love a kelpie. Billie almost stepped on the snake by the side of the stables and Rusty jumped on it. Billie ran to get Drum and when they came back, the snake was dead. But Rusty was bitten twice, at least. Can you set up a bed in the hospital? If he gets through the next hour, we'll move him in there. I may need to give him another vial of antivenom.' Freddie nodded and walked through to the hospital while Angus updated Melanie.

They sent all the non-urgent patients home. Rusty wasn't responding and Angus administered more antivenom. They moved him to the hospital and provided a chair for Drum. Billie sat on the floor by Rusty's bed and coaxed his head into her lap.

Back in the surgery, Freddie assisted Angus in stitching a pet rabbit with a torn ear and removed plaster from the foreleg of an old dog.

Melanie poked her head into the surgery. 'I've put the closed sign on the door and I'm going to pick up the sandwiches and coffee I ordered from the café.'

'Enough for Drum and Billie too?' Angus sounded gruff, but Freddie knew he was worried for Rusty.

'Of course Angus. And you and Freddie.' Melanie sounded mildly exasperated.

'Would you like me to run down and get it all Mel?' Freddie had her hands in the sink, scrubbing them clean after surgery.

'Would you?' Melanie looked to Angus for confirmation. 'Thank you, I've still got to make a few calls to reschedule patients.' Angus nodded and walked through to the hospital.

It was after the lunch rush, and the café was quiet when Freddie walked in. 'Hi Millie. I'm here to pick up an order for Melanie. At the Vets.' Freddie didn't want to meet Millie's gaze. She'd been there on Christmas Day. *Don't get all judgy with me Millie Tucker.*

'It's done Freddie, I've got the sandwiches in a bag and a tray for your drinks. It's quite a lot.' Millie's tone was warm.

Freddie looked at her in surprise. 'Thank you. Um, yes, thank you, Millie.' She took the tray of drinks, but it wobbled and she had to use both hands.

'Hold on Freddie.' Millie began to undo her apron. 'I'll walk down with you.'

'I've got it, Mum. Hello Freddie.' Hannelore appeared from the kitchen and took the tray of drinks from Freddie's hands. 'I'll take these if you can bring the sandwiches.' Hannelore looked at Millie. 'I've put some caramel slice in too. For Billie. Melanie told us about her dog, when she ordered.'

'Thank you.' Freddie looked at Millie, hoping her words sounded genuine. She followed Hannelore out of the café but fell in beside her as they walked along the street. She desperately wanted to ask about Luke. If they'd heard from him, but she was embarrassed.

Hannelore asked about Rusty, and Freddie told her he'd been bitten more than once by the snake.

'Oh no! Billie will be devastated. Harriet told me how much she adores Rusty.' Her eyes were wet with tears and Freddie was surprised, but it made her like her more. Anyone who cared for animals was alright.

Melanie unlocked the front door to let them in, and Hannelore handed the drinks over to her and turned to leave.

'Thank you Hanna. For helping.' The words sounded lame in her head, but Freddie suddenly wanted to make an effort with Hannelore. 'Um, would you like me to let you know? About Rusty?'

Hannelore stopped. 'Yes, if you don't mind Freddie. Do you want my number?' She looked eager.

Freddie pulled her phone from her back pocket and handed it to Hannelore. 'Just put it straight in my phone Hanna. We might not know for a couple of days, but I'll call or message you.'

'Thank you, Freddie.' Hannelore's gaze was friendly. 'You do great work. Caring for animals.'

She waved as she walked away and Freddie felt happy and ashamed. Happy to receive Hannelore's praise, but ashamed of her behaviour. Not just on Christmas Day, but every time she'd been in Hannelore's company. *Maybe I do need to grow up.*

56

HANNELORE

Walking home with Millie, Hannelore felt her phone vibrate in her pocket. She knew it was Harry, she'd seen him several times during the day, as he and Robbie were building the shelving in the bookshop. They had the bearers and joists installed for the mezzanine and were waiting for materials to arrive for the staircase. Harry asked her to have dinner with him, but she wasn't sure what Millie's plans were. She had stayed at Finn's more often than usual since Christmas, and Hannelore knew it was to give her some privacy with Harry.

As Millie opened the downstairs door, Hannelore cleared her throat. 'Mum?'

'Yes.' Millie closed the door and walked upstairs beside Hannelore.

'What are your plans this week? Um, I'd like to have Harry over for dinner. He always invites me to the pub, but I'd like to cook for him.' Hannelore unlocked the apartment door and stepped in after Millie.

Millie seemed to hesitate, and Hannelore could see she was weary. 'It's alright Mum, it doesn't have to be tonight.'

'I'd say I'll go to Finn's, but he has to go to the Hunter region early tomorrow.' Millie trailed off.

Hannelore gave her a quick hug. 'I was only thinking of dinner, Mum. Harry doesn't have to stay over. Not every time. And we're catching up with Kristen and Callum on Saturday. We're helping Kristen move in with Judith, then ordering in some pizza.' She moved to the kitchen. 'Would you like a drink? Or a cup of tea?'

'Do we have any berries left? Fruit. I'd love something cold.' Millie strolled towards the hallway. 'I'll get changed. But honestly Hanna, I'm tired and I'd love a quiet night. Do you mind going out with him tonight, instead of cooking?' She hesitated, as if she was going to add something, but decided against it and retreated to her room.

Hannelore threw fruit and ice into the blender with a splash of water and made a frappe for them both. At the last minute, she added two nips of vodka. She poured it into tall glasses and added a strawberry to the rim of each glass, then set them on the coffee table between the two comfortable chairs by the front window.

Millie returned in yoga pants and a tee shirt, her feet bare. She clapped her hands. 'Oh, this looks good, thank you.' She plonked herself in one of the chairs and drank several mouthfuls.

'Hold on Mum!' Hannelore laughed. 'There's vodka in it. Take it easy.' She moved to the other chair and tucked her legs under herself, tentatively sipping the beverage. 'You can't taste the vodka, but I put two nips in.'

'Did you call Harry? What have you decided?' Millie took another sip and sighed contentedly.

'I haven't. But I am going to cook tonight. For us Mum. You and me. There's leftover cold meat in the fridge and lots of vegetables. How about a home-made fried rice?' She giggled. 'Now that I've sat down, I can't be bothered going out. Actually, I'd like to cook for all of us next week. You and Finn and me and Harry. It will be a double date.' She laughed and Millie's expression lightened.

'If you're sure.' Millie still seemed tentative, but added, laughter now in her voice. 'And a double date would be a riot! We'd love that.'

'I'll go to my room and call him now, then get changed.'

'What can I do to start dinner?' Millie set her glass down and looked ready to stand.

'Absolutely nothing Mum. Don't move a muscle. I've got this.' Hannelore walked to her room, but Millie's bedroom door was open and she saw her copy of *The Summerfield Saddler* on the side table. She quickly grabbed it and returned to the living area, handing the book to Millie, who looked surprised. 'Why don't you read while I sort out Harry, then dinner? Just relax Mum.'

Back in her room, Hannelore called Harry.

'Hey you.' His tone was warm.

Smiling, she said quietly. 'Hey. Are you still at the bookshop?'

'No. I'm at home. Needed a shower. It was dusty work today.' Harry's voice sounded muffled. 'Sorry, just getting dressed. Are you okay for dinner tonight?'

'That's why I called, instead of messaging. No. Sorry. Mum's tired. I'm going to stay in and cook for her. I've just made us both a fruit frappe, with vodka.' Hannelore giggled.

'Refreshing.' If he was disappointed he didn't say, and

Hannelore was grateful there was no pressure to catch up. 'Actually, Lucy will be pleased if I stay home. I haven't been spending much time with her lately. I'll see if there's a movie she'd like to watch with me.' He paused. 'Any suggestions?'

'You do know they've made a series out of Bridgerton, don't you?' Hannelore tried to sound innocent, and not laugh, but Harry was having none of it.

'You promised, Hanna.' But he chuckled as he spoke. 'You said you'd keep my dirty little secret.' In a stage whisper, he added, 'But if Lucy suggests Bridgerton, I'll act like I'm doing her a favour and know nothing about the storylines.'

'Ha ha Harry Stewart. You'll get caught one day.' Then she lowered her voice. 'I'll miss you tonight.'

'I'll miss you too.' Harry was muffled again, and she heard him speak to someone. 'I'm staying in Luce. Tell Nik I'll come and help in a moment.'

'Alright Hannelore Tucker. See you tomorrow. I'll be in early for coffee.'

'Alright Harry Stewart. I'll make your coffee.' Hannelore ended the call and roamed out to the living area.

Millie looked up from the book, her face alight with interest. 'The dog's called Keith Urban. So funny.'

'I know. It's cute, right? There's another dog mentioned later on. I won't spoil it for you, but it made me laugh out loud.' Hannelore headed for the kitchen.

'Was Harry okay?' Millie called out.

'Of course. Took it in his stride and now he's going to have dinner with the family and watch a movie with Lucy. She'll love that.' Hannelore called back. Millie murmured words of agreement and Hannelore began dinner preparations.

Later, while they ate with their bowls on their laps, they chatted about Hannelore's business. She had registered the business name *Yes To The Cake* and snapped up the domain name as well. She'd ordered some equipment. Not everything she needed, but enough to start. Hannelore wanted to make some profit before investing more and had said no to Millie's offer of a loan.

Millie segued back to their current living arrangements. 'Hanna, I know Judith offered you accommodation in her house too. Are you going to take that up?'

Hannelore shook her head. 'If Kristen and I weren't seeing people, it would be fun to be there together, you know, doing girl stuff. But we're both in relationships and it wouldn't be much different to us sharing this place, Mum. You and Finn, Harry and me. I'm happy to just stay here. If it doesn't bother you? You stay a couple of nights a week at Finn's and Harry can stay here then. We don't have to see each other every night. It's early days and it's probably better we don't.' She frowned. 'As long as the arrangement works for you, Mum. And Finn.'

Millie looked pleased. 'Stay here Hanna. I was hoping you would. I might go to Finn's a little bit more. Sorry. But that's for me and Finn as much as for you and Harry.' She laughed, then covered her mouth with her hand. 'If it's not horrible for your mother to say that to you.'

'Ha, ha. I'm getting used to it Mum.'

'You'll save more here. You're close to the café. And you're right, you don't have to be together every night. We'll make it work. And back to your double-date-dinner idea. I'm in. I'm sure Finn will be too.'

Later that night Hannelore received a message from Harry.

> Three episodes of Bridgerton. Lucy
> kept pausing the show to explain the
> plot. Hope you had a good night
> too. XX

Hannelore laughed out loud.

> Thank goodness for Lucy. You read
> them, but did you really understand
> the complexities? Had a lovely night
> with Mum, thank you. XX

HARRY

Keen to spend more time with Hannelore, Harry pondered the situation overnight. She'd already said she was staying in the apartment and not moving in with Judith and Kristen. He understood, there wasn't much difference. He already knew Millie stayed at Finn's a couple of times a week. And while they were renovating the bookshop he saw Hannelore every day and they tried to take their breaks together. He acknowledged to himself, however, that he wanted more.

It was early, but he heard Robbie moving around in the kitchen. Harry padded out in his socks. 'Morning Dad.'

'Son.' Robbie poured hot water over the teabags in two cups. Harry added milk, and they leaned back on the counter, dunking their teabags in time with each other before tossing them into the sink. 'What on earth were you watching with Lucy last night?' Robbie raised an eyebrow, but Harry could see he was trying not to laugh.

'Girly stuff. Romance. Um, Bridgerton.' Harry shrugged.

'Lucy explained the plot lines to me. Based on romance novels, I understand.'

Robbie patted Harry on the shoulder. 'Better you than me son. But good on you. You made her night.'

Harry tried to keep his tone nonchalant. 'Lucy's great. I need to spend more time with her.'

'And Hanna?' Robbie sounded tentative now. 'Earlier in the day you were going to have dinner with her. Is everything alright?'

Laughing, Harry took a swig of tea. 'Yes. Better than alright. But Millie was tired and Hanna wanted to cook dinner for her and stay in, just the two of them.'

Robbie looked impressed. 'Hanna's a good girl. Millie works hard.'

'They both do Dad. Hanna has a great work ethic and she's focused on kicking off her micro-business.' Harry chuckled. 'Did Nik mention it? Has she told you her business name?'

'She did. Um,' Robbie looked towards the ceiling, searching for the answer. 'Say Yes?'

'*Say Yes to the Cake*. It's clever. She's clever.' Harry paused. He wondered if her new business would mean she would have less time to spend with him. He sighed.

'It is and she is.' Robbie turned to rinse his cup under the hot tap. 'Can I give you a word of advice, Harry?'

Harry was surprised but nodded. 'Sure.'

'Back her one hundred per cent. Listen to her when she's worried, or excited. Starting a business is a big step and she'll sometimes have doubts. Let her know she can share her wins, and worries, with you.' Robbie sounded a bit uncomfortable, but Harry listened to every word.

'I will Dad. I do. I'm proud of her.' Harry rinsed his cup out, then turned back to Robbie. 'I appreciate the advice.' Harry wondered at Robbie's motivation.

Somewhat gruffly, Robbie answered the unspoken question. 'You've got a good one there, Harry. Look after her.'

Noise at the other end of the house caught their attention. 'Lucy's up.' Robbie lifted his chin. Harry heard the bathroom door close.

'There's something else Dad. While we're on this subject.' Harry stopped, trying to think of the best phrasing for his question.

'Yes, mate.' Robbie refilled the jug and set it to boil.

'I um, only stay at Hanna's when Millie is at Finn's. I know she can't afford a place of her own, with the new business, but I'm wondering if I should move out. You know. So we have somewhere together.'

'Of course you want to be with her all the time. It's new.' Robbie seemed to think for a moment. 'But if you do that, too quickly, you're taking something away from her.'

'Taking something away? What?' Harry was confused.

'This is way out of my comfort zone, son, but I'll try to explain what I mean.' Robbie took a deep breath. 'If you move in together straight away, you take away the romance and excitement of the *courtship*. That's an old-fashioned term, I know, but hear me out. The anticipation of seeing each other, or not knowing when you can, er, have some privacy. Picking her up to take her out. Going to her place for a meal or a movie. It's romantic. Women love that. You don't want to rush her to the finals when you haven't experienced all the heats have to offer.' As Robbie finished, Lucy rushed in, dressed for work at the cafe.

'Are you talking about the rodeo Robbie?' She turned to Harry. 'Are you camp-drafting this year Harry?'

Harry looked at Robbie and they laughed loudly. 'I'm not competing Lucy, I haven't done enough work with Lawson. But I'm riding pick-up.'

'Pick-up?' Lucy screwed up her nose. 'Explain to me what that is again.'

'I'll be on Lawson in the arena for the bull and bronco riding, and when a cowboy reaches time or comes off, I'll pick him up on Lawson and keep him safe. There are two of us riding pick-up at all times.' The rodeo was only two weeks away and Harry had asked Hannelore to go. Robbie, Jamie Tait and Drum Murray were riding pick-up too, and Callum Campbell, but he was also competing in the camp draft. 'Hannelore is coming to watch, with Kristen. And maybe Harriet and Billie and some of the others. Would you like to come too and sit with the girls Lucy?'

'Oh yes! I'll ask Hanna and Kristen at work today.' Lucy hugged Harry quickly, then pulled a skillet from the cupboard. 'Scrambled eggs?'

'Yes please.' Harry and Robbie answered in unison and Harry plugged the toaster in and placed plates and cutlery on the counter.

'I'll just go and tell Nik we're making breakfast.' Robbie strolled from the room and Lucy chatted about the rodeo and the café.

Harry thought about Robbie's words. He didn't want to take the romance out of his relationship with Hannelore. He was enjoying the way it was, too.

'Harry! Earth to Harry!' Lucy was standing in front of him, hands on hips and egg flipper in her hand.

'Sorry Luce. What did you say?' Harry placed his arm around her shoulders, laughing.

'Parsley Harry. I need parsley. Can you please nip downstairs and cut some?' She handed him the kitchen scissors and pushed him away, but her face was suffused with happiness.

Harry obeyed, whistling loudly as he hurried down the stairs, two at a time.

58

FREDDIE

There was someone with Rusty for the next twenty-four hours and Angus administered a third anti-venom overnight. Drum let Billie stay up late, nursing her pet, but when she fell asleep sitting up he carried her to the bed in the flat at the clinic. Freddie offered to stay there too, but Drum said he'd watch over the dog. Angus sent Freddie home and went home himself, for a few hours.

Freddie woke early and hurried back to work. Billie was sitting with Rusty, her little face tired and worried. Drum appeared from the flat, his clothes rumpled.

'Morning Freddie.' Drum ran his hand through his hair, then turned as Angus emerged from the surgery.

'Hi Freddie, you're in early.' Angus sounded tired too, but he gave her an appreciative nod.

'How's Rusty?' Freddie followed Angus into the surgery. Drum partly closed the door to the hospital room and joined them.

Angus sighed. 'He's going to pull through, I think we're past the worst of it. The puncture wound on his ear is already healing but the one on his hind leg is swollen and painful.' He lowered his voice. 'I'm worried there may be too much tissue damage to save the leg.'

Freddie glanced at Drum, who'd drawn in a breath at Angus's words. Freddie nodded. 'When do you need to make that decision Angus?

'By tonight. Another twelve hours of intravenous fluids and antibiotics and we'll assess his progress.' Angus shared a look with Drum and Freddie knew he didn't hold much hope that the leg could be saved. *Poor Rusty. And little Billie.*

'What can I do?' Freddie saw movement from the corner of her eye and saw Billie standing at the door of the hospital room, tears coursing down her cheeks. *Billie heard. Oh no!*

Drum walked to his daughter and scooped her up in his arms. Angus turned to Freddie. 'Go in with Billie, Freddie. Keep her company. Drum is worried she hasn't eaten much since it happened. Try to coax her to eat, she might listen to you. We can ask Millie to send something along to us, they'll be open now.'

Freddie sat with Billie and Rusty. She changed the bag of fluids and Angus administered more antibiotics. Drum asked Billie if she'd like a milkshake, he was going to get coffee. She refused until Freddie said she'd like a milkshake, but only if Billie had one too, and it had to be chocolate. Billie nodded and Drum left.

'I know what you're doing Freddie.' Billie's voice was soft.

'What am I doing Billie?' Freddie patted Rusty, who opened his eyes. The brave little dog gazed adoringly at Billie.

'You're trying to get me to have something. The milkshake.'

Billie shook her head and wiped her eyes with the back of her hand. 'I just don't feel like eating or drinking. Not when Rusty can't.'

'You're right. Your dad is worried about you. But Billie, Rusty needs you to be strong. If you don't eat anything, you won't have the strength to help him.' Freddie decided the truth might be better. Billie was too smart to fall for lies. 'If his leg doesn't get better, where the bite wound is, Angus will have to operate. You'll need to help Rusty to learn to walk without the leg, if that happens. You might have to carry him to start with.'

Billie listened carefully and asked more questions. No one had explained the prognosis to her, so Freddie did, as simply and honestly as she could.

When Drum returned with drinks and toasted sandwiches, Billie took the milkshake he offered and drank, then ate half a toasted sandwich. Freddie drank her milkshake too, and demolished a toasted ham and cheese sandwich. Angus came and went during the day, he had other patients in the surgery, but Freddie monitored Rusty and stayed with Billie.

Harriet dropped in at lunch time and Drum walked to the café with her. Billie didn't want to go and they didn't force her.

Freddie left Rusty and Billie for a short period to work at reception when Melanie had a break. Twenty minutes later, Billie opened the door to the hospital, crying, and beckoned Freddie to come in. Angus had a patient in the surgery, and there were none in the waiting room, so she strode into where Rusty lay on a soft bed on the floor.

The game little dog raised his head, and when Billie sat down beside him, he licked her hand. Rusty looked brighter than he had earlier. 'What is it, Billie?'

'His leg. The sore one. Rusty was trying to lick it.' Her blue eyes were filled with tears again, but Freddie shook her head.

'That might be a good sign, Billie. Let me check the swelling and heat level. Then we'll call Angus in when he's free.' Freddie moved her hands gently over Rusty but didn't touch the leg. She just let her hand hover over it, the hairs tickling her palm. 'I'm not a Vet yet Billie, but I think the swelling has gone down slightly. And it's not as hot. The antibiotics are doing their job.'

Drum and Melanie returned just as Angus became free. He knelt beside Rusty and gently touched the leg. Rusty turned his head and licked Angus's hand. Angus grinned. 'One more shot of antibiotics and another bag of fluid please Freddie.' He stood up, looking down at Billie. 'We're not out of the woods yet Billie, he's a sick little dog. But I think we can save his leg.'

Billie flew into Freddie's arms, hugging her tightly, then to Drum who picked her up and held her close, his cheek against hers.

'Freddie, you need to take a lunch break. How about I treat you and Billie to lunch?' Angus passed his card to Freddie. Billie began to shake her head, but Angus continued. 'Your dad and I will watch Rusty.'

'Alright, Angus.' Billie patted Rusty and stood up.

'Wash your hands, Billie.' Drum jerked his head towards the sink. Freddie joined her at the sink and they soaped up and rinsed off together.

Walking down to the café, Freddie asked Billie what she'd like for lunch.

'I'm not very hungry, Freddie. One of Hanna's chocolate brownies would be nice, and just some water. I've still got all that milkshake in me from this morning.' Billie patted her tummy.

At the café, Freddie ordered brownies for both of them, water for Billie and a coffee for herself. Hannelore brought their order over.

Freddie smiled at her. 'You've saved me a text message, Hanna. Rusty has turned the corner.'

'Oh, I was hoping you'd say that.' She looked fondly at Billie.

'Angus was worried, but he said Rusty is a brave little dog and he's beginning to feel better.' Billie took a huge bite from her brownie.

'That's good news Billie. And I know you stayed with him all night, and that would have helped him, I'm sure.' Hannelore patted Billie's shoulder.

'He'll need to be monitored for a few more days.' Freddie grinned at Billie. 'But Billie can sleep in her own bed tonight and come back in the morning.'

Billie shook her head. 'No Freddie, he'll be frightened by himself.'

'He won't be by himself, Billie. I'll stay with him tonight.' Freddie spoke firmly, confident Drum would want to take Billie home if their pet was out of danger. 'And I'm hoping you'll come back in the morning and bring me a coffee.'

Billie nodded her head this time. 'I can do that Freddie. You'll really stay with Rusty? All night long?'

'I really will.' At her words, Hannelore gave Freddie a warm smile.

MILLIE

'Matty got the permanent job at Council, he's over the moon!' Millie put her phone down and turned to Finn. 'He's had a great time hanging out with Luke, but he starts work next Monday. Have you heard from Luke this week?'

Finn shook his head. 'I've thought to call him so many times this week, but I don't want to pressure him to come home if that's not what he wants.'

'Oh, Finn. Matty hasn't mentioned anything about him staying, so I am sure he'll come home.' Millie hoped so, it was obvious Finn missed him. She did too.

The words were barely spoken when Finn's phone pinged. 'Luke.' He murmured. Clicking the phone he spoke more loudly. 'Luke! Hello, Millie just had a call from Matty.'

Millie strolled to the kitchen to give Finn some space. She unpacked the dishwasher and wiped the sink down. She was staying the night, and they'd eaten dinner. She wandered into the living area, wondering if she should find a movie they could watch.

'That was Luke.' Finn wrapped his arms around her from behind.

'You seem chirpy, is he coming home?' Millie turned and laced her arms around Finn's neck.

'He is.' Finn kissed her mouth, lingering for a moment. Millie play-hit him.

'Tell me. What's been going on?'

'He's had a lot of fun with Matty and enjoyed Sydney. But he doesn't want to live there. Too busy for his taste.' Finn straightened. 'Did you know he's been messaging with Hannelore?'

'Not really. I know she speaks with Matty quite a lot.' Millie chuckled. 'When I say speaks, I mean messages. They don't really speak. But I wasn't aware she's been talking to Luke too.'

'She has. He knows about how great Freddie was when Billie Murray's dog was bitten by the snake.' Finn frowned. 'Luke seems to think Freddie has matured.' He sighed. 'I don't know Millie. In just three or four weeks? She can't have changed that much.' He shook his head. 'It worries me.'

'He's a grown man Finn. And he set the boundaries with Freddie. Give him some credit.' Millie moved to the sofa and patted the seat beside her. 'I don't think Hanna would just blurt that out. He must have asked.'

'You're right. He's a quiet achiever.' Finn stretched. 'A movie Millie? Or maybe something for an hour and then we can go to bed.'

'Are you tired Finn?' Millie saw the stirrings of passion in his eyes. *Sexy Finn.*

CHAPTER 59

'Not really. You?'

I'm not tired at all. But bed sounds good.' Millie stood and stepped away from the couch. Finn hadn't moved. 'That's an invitation, Finn.' She giggled.

60

HANNELORE

IT WAS BOOK CLUB NIGHT AND HANNELORE WAS excited. They were getting their first sneak peek at *The Little Indie Bookshop* first. Although she'd been in and out for the first couple of weeks, Harry had banned her, on Rachael's orders he said, for the last few. She had imagined it many times but was excited to see it finished.

They met at the front door half an hour before book club and Rachael was jiggling with nervous energy. The windows were still papered over, but Hannelore was sure that would be removed in the next few days. They were less than two weeks from Valentine's Day and the grand opening.

Meggie was back from holidays, arriving with Rose and Harriet. Laura and Nicole were right behind them. 'Where's Judith?' Hannelore whispered to Kristen.

'She's inside. I only found out today that she's been in there for a week, unpacking stock with Rachael. Sneaky thing, she hasn't said a word.' Kristen shook her head in mock annoyance.

'Oh!' Hannelore was surprised. Harry hadn't said a word. *Harry Stewart can keep a secret.*

Rachael held her hand up and they all quietened. 'I'm not one for speeches. But before I open the door, I want to thank you, all of you, for your encouragement and support for this project.' Rachael knocked twice on the door and Harry threw it open from the inside.

Hannelore stood back to let the others through first, stepping in last with Kristen and Millie.

She gazed around in wonder, then spun on the spot. There were so many things to look at she didn't know where to start. Judith took Kristen by the hand and led her over to the floor-to-ceiling shelving in the main space.

The shelves were timber, with a dark stain. *Like a teeny Harry Potter library.* Hannelore was entranced and jumped when Harry took her hand. She grinned at him, then walked towards Judith. 'It has a rolling ladder!' She knew it would, but seeing it took her breath away. The bookshelves weren't full yet but she saw a sign saying Australian Indie Authors – Romance, Mystery, Crime, Non-Fiction. There was an old-fashioned front counter. She pointed to it and turned to Harry. 'Wherever did that come from?'

Harry looked over her head and when she turned she saw Robbie standing beside Laura and Melanie, pointing to the same counter. 'It's part of the original bank teller counter, from this very building. Douglas had it upstairs as a reception counter. We'd kept it in storage when we renovated and then moved it down here. We had to shorten it, but it works well, don't you think?'

'It's perfect! The whole shop is perfect.' Hannelore spied a lovely old writing desk in a similar style to the counter. 'Is that for author signings?'

Judith and Kristen joined them. 'Yes, when we have an author here. But the rest of the time it can be for customers to relax and read. Or write.' Judith pointed to another clever space at the front window. Two grandmother armchairs sat on either side of a small round table. 'Rachael said she doesn't mind if someone wants to bring their coffee in from the café and sit and chat here, or read.'

'It's so inviting.' Hannelore spun around. The spiral staircase was towards the back, but she heard a noise. As she watched, an elevator, big enough for one person, moved slowly up to the mezzanine level. Laura was in it and she waved.

'The mezzanine.' Hannelore called out to Rachael. 'Can we go upstairs Rachael?' She was at the staircase before Rachael had laughed and said yes.

Laura was at the top now and Hannelore quickly took the stairs, with Kristen and Harry behind her. At the top she paused, looking into the main room from above. 'Oh! I could live here. I never want to leave!' She saw Judith in the lift now, on her way up, and made room for the rest as they filed up the stairs.

Lower shelving on this level, mostly filled with children's books. The floor was covered with rugs and several small bean bags. Rose flopped into a bean bag. 'The children will adore it up here!'

Judith sat in a grandfather chair. 'This is intended as a reading chair. So adults can read aloud to children. We thought we might have volunteer readers twice a day, on weekdays, for a half hour or so. Books for pre-school age children at morning tea time, and for school age kids after school finishes. We'll trial it, and see what works.'

'Help me up, Harry.' Rose held out her hand and Harry obligingly pulled her to her feet from the bean bag. 'I could do it, but it wouldn't be pretty.' She laughed loudly.

Meggie turned to Judith. 'Do you think, perhaps on Saturday mornings, we could roster a 'reader' up here for a couple of hours so parents can browse downstairs?'

'Definitely.' Judith spoke but gestured for Rachael to move closer. 'But we don't want to become a drop-in centre. It happened at the library sometimes. Parents would drop their children, then disappear for an hour.'

'Yes. But I agree Judith, it will need to be monitored.' Rachael leaned in. 'So Meggie, Hanna, what do you think?'

'It's just beautiful!' Meggie looked down to the lower level. 'So perfect!' Oh, and Rachael, I have the photographer booked for the day after tomorrow. Will the signage be up?'

Rachael giggled and looked at Harry. 'It's up now Meggie.'

'What?' Meggie frowned. 'I didn't see it.' She looked doubtful.

'I didn't see any signage either. Or a logo.' Hannelore put her hands on her hips. 'Harry?'

Rachael laughed in delight, then clapped her hands. 'Downstairs everyone please.'

Judith stepped into the lift, but the rest trooped downstairs behind Rachael. Robbie was standing by the open front door.

'Step outside ladies.' He held the door open and Harry began removing the brown paper covering on the front window from the inside.

Hannelore stepped outside, close to Millie. It was dusk, and the main streetlights were on now. As they watched, a light came on over the front door and Hannelore saw an old-fashioned sign - an ornate piece of timber hanging from wrought iron brackets.

The Little Indie Bookshop was painted in an oval shape, in a rich russet on a cream background.

They turned to the front window and saw the same logo, except this one was a neon light version. 'I love it!' Hannelore turned to Rachael. 'The logo is perfect. Who did this for you?' She glanced at Laura. She was a graphic artist, but she shook her head.

'It's Harry's concept. We had the sign people draw it up for us, but he designed it.' Rachael turned to Laura. 'We're hoping you can manipulate it to be suitable for advertising and social media.'

Hannelore didn't hear Laura's response, she was focused on Harry. *Clever Harry Stewart.* And she knew she loved him, as he stood there, grinning sheepishly at her.

61

RACHAEL

Barrington Book Club – Rachael, Rose, Millie, Hannelore, Kristen, Melanie, Harriet, Laura, Nicole, Judith, Meggie
Apologies – none
Book – ***The Summerfield Saddler*** by Penelope Janu

RACHAEL WAS ECSTATIC. THE BOOKSHOP REVEAL HAD gone better than she expected and she delighted in their responses but paid particular attention to Rose and Hannelore. Rose had been meeting regularly with Judith for the opening and they had more than a dozen authors attending. Steve was in Sydney at a Mayors' meeting for two days, so he would get his first real look when he got back. He was coming to the photoshoot.

Valentine's Day was a Friday, so they had planned a weekend of celebration. With the logo only just designed, and photographs to be taken in two days, Rachael wasn't sure how many would attend. But she had faith in Meggie for the marketing, Judith for the business side and Rose for the authors and readers.

Millie had opened the café and they trooped inside, after thanking Robbie and Harry for orchestrating the 'reveal'. Rachael chuckled to herself again. The men had been keen. Robbie was justifiably proud of Harry's concept, but the execution had been even better than she expected. She had noticed Harry peering at some of the book titles and wondered if his involvement would turn him into a reader. Probably not, but it was a cute thought.

Rachael ensured the bookshop door was locked and entered the café, closing the door behind her. She could see her friends at their usual table, some sitting, others standing around, chatting. As she walked to them, they all stood and cheered and clapped. Rachael cried. She didn't think she would but she was jostled to her chair, hugged and kissed on her cheek and had a glass of champagne in her hand before she could wipe her tears.

Millie handed her a napkin to wipe her eyes and they remained standing and raised their glasses. 'To Rachael,' Millie shouted and they all took a sip.

'To The Little Indie Bookshop!' Hannelore called out and they drank again.

Rachael was bemused, and her face flushed with pleasure. She took a big gulp of champagne. 'Thank you. Thank you all.' She sipped again. 'If the launch weekend goes half as well, I'll be happy.'

Kristen and Hannelore dashed to the kitchen, returning with platters of finger food. Rachael settled back in her chair. They passed food around, topped up champagne glasses and chatted about the bookshop. They covered everything from the design and layout to the signage and logo and even the way

Judith had arranged the shelves. Those with children commented on how much their children would love the staircase and mezzanine.

Rachael glanced at Rose, who suddenly looked sombre. 'What Rose? Have we missed something important?' Rachael couldn't keep the concern from her voice.

'The mezzanine.' Rose shook her head sadly. 'Wee Charlie. He'll never be able to go up there without supervision.'

Meggie laughed and continued the train of thought, and that's when Rachael knew they were joking. *Mostly joking.* 'Rose. We just won't let Charlie in.' Meggie looked around the table, her face full of mischief. 'Maybe you'll need to steer clear yourself.' Meggie was laughing loudly now, and everyone was enjoying the banter. Rachael had some Charlie experience herself. She'd looked after Charlie with Woz from time to time. He was a handful. But also adorable.

'Charlie is just lively, that's all Rose.' Rachael spoke firmly. 'I volunteer to take him upstairs myself.'

Rose's expression cleared. Then became smug. She took a sip of champagne and gazed over the rim at Rachael, her expression innocent. 'Oh, will you Rach?' She sipped again. 'I was hoping you'd say that.' Then she laughed, long and loud, and Rachael joined in. *Funny Rose. Darling Rose.*

The conversation turned to the book they'd read that month. *The Summerfield Saddler* by Penelope Janu. Rachael had enjoyed it. The relationship between Mackenzie and Kit warmed her heart and the environmental aspect rang true, she thought.

'Did anyone else think about the rehabilitation of the coal mine down near Stratford? I asked Steve if he wanted to read it, but he was reading Council papers and said no.' Rachael sighed.

'I mentioned it to Steve too.' Rose laughed. 'He gave me a look and told me to summarise it.'

'I'm loving the small-town stories we've read lately.' Laura reached for a mini quiche. 'There's always something that makes me think of Barrington.'

Kristen was usually one of the quieter members of the group, but she directed her question to Rose. 'The dog. Keith Urban. I adored that. But Rose, is there a problem using a real person's name in a book like that?'

'Honestly, I don't know. I'd worry about it, being an Indie author. But Harper Collins published this book and I'm sure they know their legal stuff.' Rose added drily.

'Of course,' Kristen murmured.

Hannelore brought a tray of mini chocolate berry trifles in small glasses to the table. Rachael was almost reluctant to put her spoon in and disturb the gorgeous symmetry of the layers. 'This desert was caused by an accident,' Hannelore giggled. 'I broke a pavlova shell as I was taking it out of the oven.' She shook her head, still smiling. 'Sadly, it couldn't be saved.'

'It didn't say yes to the cake, and was punished.' Kristen nudged Hannelore and they laughed together.

Meggie seemed to prick up her ears. 'Did I hear right Hanna? That's the name of your new business. *Say Yes to the Cake?*'

'It is.' Hannelore suddenly seemed nervous. 'I want to make an appointment with you, to help set up a marketing strategy.' She nibbled her bottom lip. 'What do you think Meggie?'

'Love it! Harri told me about it a couple of weeks ago and I've been meaning to catch up with you. But we'd only just got back from holidays when we realised we needed all new school uniforms for Tommy, he's grown so much over the summer. And then we had to rush back to the city to move Indie from dorm accommodation at Uni to a share-house.' She shook her head. 'I'm not sure we'll ever take such a long break again. I've missed so much here!'

'Come and see me tomorrow Hanna, if you have time. Or we can meet here in the afternoon. I'm keen to understand where you're at.' Meggie raised her glass. 'Say yes to the cake!'

'Now that's all well and good Miss Hanna.' Judith held her glass of delicious-looking dessert up, turning it around, then peering into the top. 'But I'm dying to eat this and still want to know how the death of the pavlova shell led to its birth!'

Millie laughed out loud, and Hannelore went pink. 'Funny Judith. Okay, I'll tell you.' Hannelore pointed around the table at them all, looking stern. 'But don't try this at home, my business will be over before it's even started.'

Hannelore held her little glass of dessert up. 'So it's a trifle because of its layers. Broken pavlova bits in the bottom, then a layer of berries. I've used raspberries and blueberries for this one.' She looked at Judith again. 'The berries marinated in port in the fridge for a couple of hours first.'

Rachael put her nose close to the top of the glass. *Port. Ah, that was the fragrance.*

'And then a dollop of cream and a drizzle of chocolate sauce. Then another layer of each, with cream, a whole raspberry and a drizzle of sauce on top to finish.' Hannelore picked up the berry from the top of hers and popped it into her mouth.

Rachael dipped her spoon inside the glass and brought out a section, with all the layers. It almost melted in her mouth and the flavour was delicious. Very sweet and she could see why the desserts were petite, she wouldn't be able to eat a lot of it. So clever.

No one spoke as they all tried their dessert, and almost in unison a chorus of 'hmmm' and 'delicious' flew around the table.

'We do get spoilt at book club, that's all I can say.' Laura patted her tummy. 'Just as well its only once a month.'

'Before we finalise our book for next month, I've created a spreadsheet of jobs we'll need volunteers for at the bookshop opening. All three days, Friday to Sunday lunchtime. What's the best way to share this? I'd like you to add your name to a task and time slot if you have capacity. Wendy and her crew from the information centre have offered their services too, and some of the tennis ladies. My sisters Bernie and Diane will be here, but Cathy's rostered on here with Millie and her team.' Judith was suddenly all business and Rachael was grateful.

Harriet chimed in. 'Send me your spreadsheet Judith and I'll set it up as a shared Google document and can email it to everyone.'

'Thanks Harriet. Does that work?' Judith gauged the response and Rachael could see everyone was on board.

'Excellent. Do we have a book recommendation for next month?' Judith asked the question but barely paused before answering it. 'Can I recommend one of our attending authors at the launch? Annie Seaton has a new one out. It's called *Bowen River* - the first in a new mystery series. It's the book she'll discuss with Rose at the launch.'

'Done.'

'Oh', Judith laughed. 'And I have copies already. At the bookshop. Message me if you'd like a paperback.' Judith waggled her eyebrows. 'Even if you do read on a device, Annie will be here signing.'

Rachael clapped her hands. 'Our first sales! I'll buy one Judith.'

Judith immediately nipped back to the shop and returned with the iPad to process card payments. 'I'll have to order another box from Annie – you've almost taken all of my stock!'

Later, after everyone left, Rachael waited while Judith returned the device to the store and locked it up. Millie had said goodnight and Hannelore and Kristen walked to the pub together. 'Another meeting about Hanna's business, I think. She's employed Kristen to do her books, and Millie is moving hers to Kristen too.' Judith nodded at the retreating figures of the girls.

'Young women. So clever. We didn't have the same opportunities when we were their age.' Rachael stopped. 'Maybe we did, but it wasn't as common.' She glanced at Judith. 'Did you drive down tonight?'

'I walked. I'm trying to get my steps up.' She chuckled and patted her middle. 'Not that it helps but I wonder what I'd be like if I didn't.' She laughed loudly and Rachael chuckled in sympathy.

'We can walk together Judith, I'm only in the next block from your house.' They crossed the street and Rachael thought of a funny conversation she'd had with Debbie one time. 'You never met my daughter, Debbie,' she began and Judith placed a hand on her arm.

'I did, actually, Rachael. Beautiful girl. When I visited Cathy, Debbie would let me sit in the café reading. She never let me pay for coffee. I was so sorry to hear of her accident.'

Judith nodded to Rachael, 'but tell me about your funny conversation.'

Normally talking about Debbie made Rachael sad. But tonight she wanted to share a funny moment with this gracious woman beside her, who had become a friend. 'It was a weight discussion. Debbie was struggling to get her post-baby figure back straight after Woz. Although honestly, a few weeks after we talked she'd run it all off at the café.' Rachael patted her own midriff, which had expanded slightly in recent years. 'She asked me what I did to lose *my* baby weight. I looked her in the eye, patted my tummy, and said *this is my baby weight, and it's all your fault.*' Rachael laughed at the memory and Judith chuckled with her. 'Then Debbie. Get this. She looked me right back in the eye and said with a perfectly straight face. "I'm twenty-eight Mum, you're going to have to let that go".' Rachael laughed again and Judith held her arm and laughed with her.

'Funny girl and a lovely memory.' Was all Judith said and they walked on in companionable silence.

At Judith's front gate, they stopped. 'Thank you for all your help, Judith. I don't think I'd be doing this without you.' Rachael leaned down to hug the slightly older woman.

'You've done me a favour, Rachael. I thought I was ready for retirement, but this project has given me something meaningful to do, in my new community. My sister Diane always says that joining something is the secret to a happy integration into a new community. Be involved. Volunteer.' Judith shook her head with a smile. 'She's so right. I've joined book club and now I'm involved in your project. I have new friends.' She touched Rachael's arm. 'Good friends. And a purpose. Honestly, I feel ten years younger!'

Rachael thought about Judith's words as she strolled home.

Even before the loss of Debbie, she'd been feeling her age. She'd slipped into retired-grandma-mode and had even begun dressing 'older'. Like *her* mother had done. But when she joined book club she'd tried with her appearance, not wanting to be the odd one out with all the young ones there. She'd updated her hairstyle and refreshed her wardrobe and now, here she was, nearing sixty with an accommodation business and a not-for-profit bookshop. *Debbie would be proud of me.* With her head high, she unlocked the front door.

62

HARRY - VALENTINE'S DAY

HARRY WAS PUMPED FOR THE OPENING OF THE BOOK shop this afternoon, but it was Valentine's Day and he didn't know what he could do for Hannelore to show her how much he loved her. He'd suggested dinner after the opening, but she said they were keeping the café open late and serving supper there, as the bookshop was small.

Everyone had been flat out in the lead-up to the opening. He and Robbie had finished the Carriage Shed for Nicole, and she had three authors staying there for the weekend. Hannelore had been working longer hours, doing a lot of food preparation. They'd spent two nights together when Millie was at Finn's. Harry knew their time would come to be together more permanently, Robbie's advice had hit home. But what to do for Valentine's Day?

Finn was running a bar for the opening night and had asked Harry if he would be there anyway, if he'd help him and Luke serve drinks. Harry had agreed, and also told Hannelore he was there if she needed anything.

She'd hugged him tightly and kissed him sweetly. 'Thank you, Harry. I'll be fine, I have Lucy and Kristen helping. And mum of course. But just knowing you're there if I need you means a lot.'

He popped into the café just after breakfast and ordered a coffee. Hannelore served him and perched on a chair beside him for a moment. 'Hanna, its Valentine's Day and, well, it's not going to be possible to do anything special today or tonight. But I want to.' He thought it was best to be honest, and maybe she had an idea, an option.

'I know that Harry. It will be frantic here all weekend. But it will settle by Sunday afternoon and I'm taking Monday off. Do you have to work on Monday?' Hannelore looked at him hopefully.

'I've been working weekends too, getting the shop ready. I'll let Dad know I'll have Monday off.' Harry nodded decisively and took her hand. 'Is there something you want to do? Would you like to have a night away?'

'You'll think I'm nuts. And unromantic.' Hannelore gave him a tentative smile. 'But with Mum at Finn's on Sunday night, I'd like to have you to myself. Come and stay with me, we can pick up a pizza from the pub and watch old movies together. That's my idea of romance.' She stood. 'I need to get back to work, but there is something I'd like to do on Monday if it's okay with you?'

'Anything.' Harry stood too, his curiosity aroused.

'Can we make a picnic and go for a horse ride? Somewhere I haven't been? Up in the Barrington Tops?' She kissed his cheek and walked briskly back to the counter, then disappeared into the kitchen.

'A picnic and a horse ride.' Harry murmured to himself. 'Hanna Tucker, you're easy to please.' But he was satisfied they had a plan.

———

HARRY SPENT MOST OF THE DAY IN THE BOOKSHOP, carrying boxes of books for Judith, running errands and making minor repairs. A wobbly table leg, move a chair upstairs to make more room in the main area. He met the author who was staying in the apartment for the weekend and helped her set up a table of books beside Rose and two other authors. He knew who she was. He wanted to say he'd read some of her books. But he wasn't ready to let *that* secret out of the bag. Wendy from the tourism office said the whole town was booked out, most of it for the bookshop opening.

By late afternoon a crowd had gathered. Mayor Steve Webb MC'd the opening while champagne and finger food was served. He introduced Rachael, Judith and the team and explained the not-for-profit structure, before welcoming Rose and her fellow authors. Harry was run off his feet with trays of champagne-filled glasses, and he marvelled at the number of visitors, and the general enthusiasm of the crowd. *So many avid readers and indie author fans.*

Harry knew they were going to move the crowd to the café for the author talks, where there was more room and seating. As he returned his empty tray to the temporary bar Finn had set up inside the café, Hannelore walked from the kitchen, carrying a large box. A heavy box on a tray. He hurried to her. 'Let me take that Hanna. What is it?'

He reached for it but she shook her head, grinning. 'Can you make way for me to come through the crowd, Harry? All the way to Steve?'

Harry stepped in front of her, saying 'Excuse me' and 'Can you let us through please,' creating a path behind him for Hannelore. He spotted Meggie on the mezzanine level with a camera and tripod. She'd been filming since it started, but not from that vantage point. He was in front of Steve now, but stepped aside and Hannelore placed the huge item on the reception counter. She tried to move away, but Steve reached for her arm.

'Stay here Hanna.' He murmured. 'Rachael.' Steve spoke into the microphone. 'Can you join us at the front please?'

Harry wanted to hustle to the front of the crowd to see, but realised he was blocking others with his height and bulk. He glanced up at Meggie and she beckoned him. He raced up the staircase and joined her at the balcony.

'This is for Rachael.' Steve put his arm around her shoulders. 'Hannelore, owner of *say yes to the cake*, has made something special for the opening. Hannelore?'

Steve handed the microphone to Hannelore, who just looked at it for a moment. As if she sensed him watching, she looked up, and Harry nodded to her encouragingly. She took the microphone. 'Thank you Steve.'

She reached for Rachael's hand and held it as she spoke. 'The little indie bookshop has been made possible by the dedication and generosity of Rachael Webb. I've been excited from the get-go.' Hannelore grinned and Harry saw a lot of people in the crowd nodding their heads.

'Rose Gordon Hamilton sparked the idea at book club, and

Rachael ran with it. There's a beautiful apartment upstairs that ties into the bookshop and you'll hear more about that from Rose and her author pals when we move into the café. You'll meet Judith and her team of volunteers there, too. But now, if you can help me, Steve, I'll reveal what I've baked for Rachael.'

Hannelore handed the microphone to Rachael, and with Steve's help, carefully lifted the box, which was really a lid, up and out of the way. Harry saw it from above, but even from there, he could tell it was a cake. 'Quick Harry, get me downstairs, we need a better angle.' Meggie lifted the camera from the tripod as Harry walked downstairs in front of her, cutting a path through the crowd to stand before the cake.

That's incredible! It was the front façade of the bookshop, with the sign in the window iced to perfection, and the sign over the front door rocking on little brackets. For a moment he wondered if it was really a cake. Even the café door to one side was there, and the café logo above the window on that side of the building. There were even tiny books on bookshelves. He heard lots of oohs and ahhs from the crowd, and Millie appeared with a large cake knife.

'Say a few words Rachael.' Millie whispered as she handed her the knife.

'Thank you Hannelore. And Millie. Thank you Harry and Robbie for the amazing work you've done here, and in the apartment upstairs.' She looked around the faces in the crowd, pointed to Harry, and added, 'Our builders. And Harry designed the interior with the mezzanine to give us more shelf space.'

Everyone looked at Harry and he was about to shrink back into the crowd. But Hannelore held her hand out and he strode to her, standing with her hand in his, beside Steve.

Rachael continued. 'Thank you, readers and book lovers, for coming tonight. I know you're all keen to move into the café and hear our fabulous indie authors. So I will cut this cake and declare the little indie book shop open!' Rachael pushed the knife through a spot to one side of the front door, then made another cut beside it and slid out a multi-layered slice, as if to prove it was a cake. With a flourish of the knife, Rachael added. 'The cake will be served after the author talks, so make sure you hang around.'

Busy behind the bar, Harry missed some of the author conversations at the front of the room. Rose ran a panel brilliantly with Phillipa Clark, Heather Reyburn and Michelle Montebello, all indie authors. Harry had read a few of their books. Not that he'd admit it to anyone other than Hannelore. And he was excited that more authors were arriving the next day, including Annie Seaton and Rhonda Forrest. He planned to hang around the bookshop, offering to help in any way he could. But his real intention was to hear and meet the authors.

63

HANNELORE

Rolling over, Hannelore gazed at Harry. It was early Monday morning and they'd had an early night, not even finishing the movie. The weekend had been exhausting. *But fabulous!* Harry was on his back, eyes closed. But there was something about the way he was breathing that made her think he was awake. Giggling, she poked him gently with her finger.

With lightning speed, he grabbed her hand and rolled onto his side facing her, eyes wide open, eyebrows raised. 'Yes? What are you going to do now Hanna?'

She tried to pull her hand from his grasp but somehow ended up hard against him. With her hand now captured between their bodies, he snaked his other arm around her back. 'You'll have to be up earlier than that Hanna. I've been awake for hours.' He kissed her gently.

'Hours? Really? I went to the bathroom an hour ago and you were snoring, Harry Stewart!'

'Impossible. I don't snore.' He kissed her again, taking his time.

Hannelore wriggled closer. 'I'm not going to argue with you now, am I?'

'Why argue at all?' Harry gave her the lop-sided smile she loved so much.

'Less talking more kissing, Harry Stewart. That's an order.' Hannelore attempted to look stern but he laughed and rolled over, hovering above her, his weight on his elbows.

'Your wish is my command, my lady.'

Hannelore wanted to say, 'You've been reading regency romances again', but all the kissing got in the way. *Love you Harry Stewart.* Another thought she wanted to articulate. But not right now. Right now she was busy. Very busy.

———

LATER, THEY SADDLED THE HORSES AND RODE WEST, wending their way ever higher as they rode past the Rawden Vale turnoff to the trail that led into the State Forest. Beyond that was the Barrington Tops National Park.

'How high are we, do you think Harry?' They were riding along a ridge, with stunning valleys on either side.

'Around one thousand metres above sea level here. But at the highest point, Pol Blue, it's just over fifteen hundred metres. That's where they get the snowfalls in winter.' Harry pointed to the west, where the mountainous terrain climbed higher. 'We don't have time to get right up there today. But if you look down there,' he waved his arm to one side of the ridge, 'that's the Dilgry River. We'll ride down to enjoy our picnic and have a swim.'

'Gorgeous.' Hannelore gazed around in wonder as they made their way down a cow track, or maybe a kangaroo path, to the river. She was having the best day, riding with Harry. She hoped they'd have many more like it.

Harry seemed to know exactly where he was going. They stopped at a bend in the river on a grassy bank, sheltered by gum trees and a riot of overgrown bottlebrush. After cooling the horses off in the water, they tethered them and spread out their picnic. Hannelore had expected to prepare the picnic, but Harry already had it sorted. He'd stocked the fridge at his house with everything they'd need and he made crusty ham rolls before they saddled the horses, and added crackers and pesto dip and some of Lucy's home-made caramel slice to their saddlebags. *You're all class Harry Stewart.*

They lay back on the grass after eating, chatting about the ride, horses, the area and sharing stories from their childhood. Hannelore was almost falling asleep, when Harry nudged her. 'Sorry Hanna, you look so relaxed, but we should make a move if we want to get back before dusk.'

'Of course.' Hannelore sat up quickly and rubbed her eyes. Harry was already on his feet and reached out a hand to help her up, pulling her close, his arms around her waist. She snuggled against him for a moment, her hands on his chest. A bubble of joy crept through her body and she looked up at him. 'This has been one of my best days. Ever. Thank you Harry.'

Harry pulled her closer until she was squashed against his chest. She couldn't see his face, but she heard his words clearly. 'Happy Valentine's, Hanna. I love you.'

Hannelore wriggled and he relaxed his hold. Placing her hands on either side of his face, she gazed into his eyes, hoping all the emotion she felt was reflected in hers. 'I love you too, Harry Stewart.'

Harry blinked a couple of times. Then turned, taking her hand. He murmured something as they strolled to the horses.

'Sorry Harry, I didn't catch that?' Hannelore reached for Honey's bridle. She must have fallen asleep because the horses were saddled again.

Harry drew in a deep breath. 'I said.' He paused. 'It's my best day. Ever.'

Hannelore threw herself into his arms, kissed him quickly, then rushed to mount Honey. If they lingered, she'd cry. Big fat, joyful tears.

THEY RODE HOME SIDE BY SIDE. HANNELORE TALKED about the weekend, and meeting the authors. And the fabulous response she'd had to the cake, and her business generally. She'd taken several cake orders and had appointments with three future brides. And that was on top of the enquiries already coming through from Meggie and Harriet.

As they drew near his home, Harry grew quiet. Hannelore glanced at him a couple of times, but he didn't comment. At the gate to his original house, the one they rented to the education department, he stopped. She drew in beside him and gazed at the homestead. She could see a car parked in front of the house.

'The new Principal has moved in.' Harry patted Lawson as he stomped a restless hoof. The horses knew they were almost home.

'I see.' Hannelore nodded, keeping a firm hand on Honey's reins.

'But I've only granted them a lease until the end of this year. The end of the school year.' Harry turned his horse and Hannelore tried to keep Honey in check beside him. She was pulling at the bit, eager to get home. 'Hold her steady Hanna. That's the way.'

Hannelore had to concentrate then, as they made their way home, and once the horses were tied to the hitching rail, she dismounted and rubbed her backside. 'That was a big day in the saddle for me.'

'You did well. We should do this more often.' Harry moved to unsaddle Honey, but Hannelore jumped in.

'I'll do it.' She laughed. 'I don't want anything to prevent us from doing this more often.'

They brushed the horses down, fed them and released them into the paddock with the others. Leaning on the hitching rail, looking back the way they'd come, Harry spoke quietly. 'There's a reason I've only offered the house to the school for a year.'

'Oh?' Hannelore glanced at him. Harry had segued back to an earlier conversation. *This must be important.*

Turning, he took her hands in his. 'I'm hoping, that by the end of this year, you might like to move in there. With me.' His gaze was steady, but she could feel the tension in his arms.

Smiling up at him, she barely got the words out before those big, fat, joyful tears fell. 'That's a good plan, Harry Stewart. At the end of this year, I *will* make a home with you.' She jerked her head towards his home across the paddocks. 'Over there. Nothing surer.'

Harry wiped her tears with his thumbs and kissed her gently. 'And until then, we'll continue this.' He waved a hand vaguely in the air over their heads. 'This courtship.'

Hannelore giggled. *So old-fashioned.* 'Courtship? Okay. I'll go with that.' *Harry Stewart. The Secret Reader.*

THE END

BOOK CLUB READING LIST

1. ***The Grazier's Son*** by Cathryn Hein
2. ***Lest We Forgive*** by Phillipa Nefri Clark
3. ***The Accident*** by Fiona Lowe
4. ***Head for the Hills*** by Tricia Stringer
5. ***Back to Birdsville*** by Fiona McArthur
6. ***The Summerfield Saddler*** by Penelope Janu
7. ***Bowen River*** by Annie Seaton

I hope you enjoy this story and take a moment to check out the books read by the Barrington girl-posse.

Please consider leaving a review. It really helps Indie authors build their following and to keep writing. A simple star rating and a couple of words—(loved it!)—are all that's needed. If you choose to write a longer review, thank you very much.

Susan Mackie

ACKNOWLEDGEMENTS

This book is dedicated to Diane M, who read the first book, Charlie's Will, on the day of release and wrote the first review. Diane has read every book since and is now on my ARC team. When Diane told me late in 2024 that she'd sadly lost her dear sister Judith to illness, I decided to write a character named Judith into this book. But Diane has a big family and lots of sisters – so (sneakily) they all get a mention.

A huge shout-out to my girls Emily and Jasmine for always being on Team Susan. Your absolute belief that I can do this lifts me when I'm low. And to Bloke for your unwavering support. Despite telling people (randomly) that *'Susan makes stuff up'*, you are always willing to post books out, carry boxes, set me up at markets, drive hundreds of kilometres for author talks and cook many, many meals. So grateful.

Thank you to my writing group: Phillipa, Michelle and Heather. Your support, guidance, and friendship are a blessing (and often a source of hilarity!). Without you, I would not have had the courage to give up my day job and do this writing-editing thing full-time.

The generosity of the authors I've met warms my heart. I've had fabulous author gigs with Julie, a debating gig with Stella and Cathryn, attended an outstanding event with Rachel (thank you for the invite) and create the RWAus magazine with Helen and Jan every month.

Thank you to the Book Club Authors mentioned in this book: Cathryn Hein, Phillipa Nefri Clark, Fiona Lowe, Tricia Stringer, Fiona McArthur, Penelope Janu and Annie Seaton – my characters loved reading your stories (as did I). And authors Michelle Montebello, Heather Reyburn and Rhonda Forrest – my characters were super excited to meet you!

Thank you to my ARC team and Diane M for the first read-through. A huge shout-out to Tanya M for proof-reading the final manuscript.

To Fiona Hayes for the stunning watercolour painting you created for this book cover (and earlier books) and all the movie dates we go on. You are a talent.

To Trudy Schultz and Angie White for your photography, and to Lorna for your friendship, free accommodation and help at the markets when I'm in your area. And to Debbie, for your fifty years of friendship.

Lastly – thank you book lovers – for reading my words, writing reviews and recommending my books. Without you, there'd be no words.

SUSAN MACKIE

A voracious reader, Susan dreamed of becoming a writer from the age of eight. Career advisors told her it wasn't a real thing and suggested journalism. So she became a journalist, then took a zig-zag path to publish her first book in 2020, via a varied career in publishing, marketing, tourism and small business. Susan even worked in State Government for a few years (but she doesn't talk about that much).

Nervous about the release of Charlie's Will, she told Bloke while sitting on the sofa one night, that she'd be happy if she sold fifty. Charlie's Will quickly reached Number One in its genre on Amazon - motivating Susan to crack on with more stories and take her writing seriously. Finally. Now Susan is a happy Indie Publisher and offers services to other writers (editing, formatting). She is also the publisher of the Love in a Sunburnt Land Anthology series, co-authored with four (quite brilliant) Aussie women.

Susan loves engaging with fellow authors and readers, and she discovered something she thought was kinda funny. A lot of authors tell her they're introverted. It's a writerly thing, apparently. But (and here's the funny bit), Susan isn't. Introverted. Not one bit. Not at all. Speaking and presenting at writers festivals, conferences and libraries is totally her thing.

So it's okay to send Susan a message, ask a question and chat on social media. She thrives on it and will always respond. Send her a photo of one of her books 'in the wild' and she'll share it. Everywhere.

If you enjoyed this book, join our Facebook group - The Barrington Book Club - and visit Susan's website on the link below.

www.susanmackie.com

ALSO BY SUSAN MACKIE

Charlie's Will

A Place to Start Over

The Bee Whisperer

Ragged Mountain Ranges

Meggie & Max

Something in the Water

Coffee is my Calling

The Barrington Book Club